PRAISE FOR

Eggs in Purgatory

"With a plot that holds interest and characters who are well-envisioned and well-executed, Childs will have readers planning another trip to the Cackleberry Club and its treats."
—*Richmond Times-Dispatch*

"Childs excels at creating comforting settings in which to put her characters, and the Cackleberry Club is a place you'd like to visit." —*St. Paul Pioneer Press*

"*Eggs in Purgatory* has plenty of humor, emotion, good food (with recipes), and fantastic plotlines to make it another success story." —*Fresh Fiction*

PRAISE FOR
THE SCRAPBOOKING MYSTERIES
BY LAURA CHILDS

"Childs rounds out the story with several scrapbooking and crafting tips plus a passel of mouthwatering Louisiana recipes." —*Publishers Weekly*

"The heroine is a plucky, strong, and independent woman who takes charge when necessary as she is the original steel magnolia." —*The Best Reviews*

"If you are a scrapbooker and like to read, then Laura Childs's Scrapbooking Mystery series is for you! These books are so great that I just couldn't put them down! I just can't wait for the next one to be released." —*BellaOnline*

"Scrapbook aficionados rejoice! Ms. Childs creates a charming mystery series with lively, quirky characters and plenty of how-to . . . Serving up some hors d'oeuvres of murder and mystery, creativity and fashion, she has a winning formula to get even the laziest of us in a scrapbooking mood."
—*Fresh Fiction*

continued . . .

"An entertaining who-done-it."   *—Midwest Book Review*

"Perfect reading."   *—Romantic Times* (four stars)

"Childs does an excellent job of weaving suspense with great tips for scrapbooking and crafting aficionados."

—I Love A Mystery

PRAISE FOR
THE TEA SHOP MYSTERIES BY LAURA CHILDS

Featured Selection of the Mystery Book Club
"Highly recommended" by The Ladies' Tea Guild

"A delightful read . . . Childs has an eye for great local color."   *—Publishers Weekly*

"A paean to Charleston, the genteel enjoyment of tea, and the tasty treats that accompany it."   *—Kirkus Reviews*

"Murder suits Laura Childs to a Tea."*—St. Paul Pioneer Press*

"Tea lovers, mystery lovers, [this] is for you. Just the right blend of cozy fun and clever plotting."

—Susan Wittig Albert, bestselling author of Wormwood

"It's a delightful book!"   *—Tea: A Magazine*

"Will warm readers the way a good cup of tea does . . . A delightful series that will leave readers feeling as if they have shared a warm cup of tea on Church Street in Charleston."

—The Mystery Reader

"This mystery series could single-handedly propel the tea shop business in this country to the status of wine bars and bustling coffee houses."   *—Buon Gusto*

"If you devoured Nancy Drew and Trixie Belden, this new series is right up your alley." *—The Goose Creek (SC) Gazette*

"Gives the reader a sense of traveling through the streets and environs of the beautiful, historic city of Charleston."

—Minnetonka (MN) Lakeshore Weekly News

Berkley Prime Crime titles by Laura Childs

Tea Shop Mysteries

DEATH BY DARJEELING
GUNPOWDER GREEN
SHADES OF EARL GREY
THE ENGLISH BREAKFAST MURDER
THE JASMINE MOON MURDER
CHAMOMILE MOURNING
BLOOD ORANGE BREWING
DRAGONWELL DEAD
THE SILVER NEEDLE MURDER
OOLONG DEAD

Scrapbooking Mysteries

KEEPSAKE CRIMES
PHOTO FINISHED
BOUND FOR MURDER
MOTIF FOR MURDER
FRILL KILL
DEATH SWATCH
TRAGIC MAGIC

Cackleberry Club Mysteries

EGGS IN PURGATORY
EGGS BENEDICT ARNOLD

Anthology

DEATH BY DESIGN

·LAURA CHILDS·

Eggs Benedict Arnold

BERKLEY PRIME CRIME, NEW YORK

THE BERKLEY PUBLISHING GROUP
Published by the Penguin Group
Penguin Group (USA) Inc.
375 Hudson Street, New York, New York 10014, USA
Penguin Group (Canada), 90 Eglinton Avenue East, Suite 700, Toronto, Ontario M4P 2Y3, Canada
(a division of Pearson Penguin Canada Inc.)
Penguin Books Ltd., 80 Strand, London WC2R 0RL, England
Penguin Group Ireland, 25 St. Stephen's Green, Dublin 2, Ireland (a division of Penguin Books Ltd.)
Penguin Group (Australia), 250 Camberwell Road, Camberwell, Victoria 3124, Australia
(a division of Pearson Australia Group Pty. Ltd.)
Penguin Books India Pvt. Ltd., 11 Community Centre, Panchsheel Park, New Delhi—110 017, India
Penguin Group (NZ), 67 Apollo Drive, Rosedale, North Shore 0632, New Zealand
(a division of Pearson New Zealand Ltd.)
Penguin Books (South Africa) (Pty.) Ltd., 24 Sturdee Avenue, Rosebank, Johannesburg 2196,
South Africa

Penguin Books Ltd., Registered Offices: 80 Strand, London WC2R 0RL, England

This is a work of fiction. Names, characters, places, and incidents either are the product of the author's imagination or are used fictitiously, and any resemblance to actual persons, living or dead, business establishments, events, or locales is entirely coincidental. The publisher does not have any control over and does not assume any responsibility for author or third-party websites or their content.

PUBLISHER'S NOTE: The recipes contained in this book are to be followed exactly as written. The publisher is not responsible for your specific health or allergy needs that may require medical supervision. The publisher is not responsible for any adverse reactions to the recipes contained in this book.

EGGS BENEDICT ARNOLD

A Berkley Prime Crime Book / published by arrangement with Gerry Schmitt & Associates, Inc.

PRINTING HISTORY
Berkley Prime Crime mass-market edition / December 2009

Copyright © 2009 by Gerry Schmitt & Associates, Inc.
Excerpt from *The Teaberry Strangler* by Laura Childs.
Interior text design by Kristin del Rosario.

ISBN: 978-0-425-23155-5

BERKLEY® PRIME CRIME
Berkley Prime Crime Books are published by The Berkley Publishing Group,
a division of Penguin Group (USA) Inc.,
375 Hudson Street, New York, New York 10014.
BERKLEY® PRIME CRIME and the PRIME CRIME logo are trademarks of Penguin Group (USA) Inc.

PRINTED IN THE UNITED STATES OF AMERICA

10 9 8 7 6 5 4 3 2 1

*For Dawn and the dogs
(With special affection for Honeybee,
Sam Henry, and Camille.)*

Acknowledgments

Thanks to Sam, Tom, Bob, Jennie, Dan, Asia, and Moosh. And thanks to all the readers who embraced *Eggs in Purgatory*, my first Cackleberry Club Mystery, with so much enthusiasm. You're the reason there's a second one.

CHAPTER 1

IT might have been Kindred Spirit Days in Elmwood Park, but Suzanne Dietz wasn't exactly feeling the spirit. Shifting from one moccasined foot to the other, stuck behind a table selling slices of soggy pineapple cake, hard-as-a-rock fudge, and gooped-up cherry pies for the Library Committee's fund-raiser, Suzanne would have much preferred to be back at her own place, the Cackleberry Club.

Closing her eyes against the intrusion of laughing clowns, frenetic jugglers, and accordion music, she imagined herself bustling about in her own cozy café this Sunday afternoon. If brunch ran late, as it often did, she'd be juggling plates of eggs Florentine, huevos rancheros, Slumbering Volcanoes, and towering omelets stuffed with gooey, molten Gruyère cheese.

Eggs, of course, were the morning specialty at the Cackleberry Club. But lunch was delectably creative, too, with menu items like drunken pecan chicken, brown sugar meatloaf, and frozen lemonade pie. And Suzanne also laid out a pretty snappy afternoon tea that could probably tempt even the most proper English lady.

"We ought to be selling our own cakes and muffins and scones," Petra murmured, as if reading Suzanne's mind. Petra was the second partner and principal baker and chef at the Cackleberry Club. "I don't know how we got roped into this. Trying to be do-gooders, I suppose. I thought we'd be selling books!"

"Me, too," said Suzanne as she brushed back shoulder-length silver blond hair and gazed with keen blue eyes at the morose selection of baked goods. "Ours would certainly be better quality. Unfortunately, this stuff is . . ." She glanced around to make sure one of the pie makers, a glum-looking little woman named Agnes, wasn't in earshot. ". . . beyond pathetic."

"I'm terrified folks will think these baked goods are from the Cackleberry Club," Petra murmured in hushed tones. Brown-eyed and square-jawed, Petra was big-boned and bighearted. She was known to show up at the front door of a new neighbor with casserole in hand, owned an overweight Russian Blue cat named Rasputin, and had mastered the art of trout fishing.

"Heaven forbid," said Suzanne, pushing up the sleeves of her denim shirt and letting loose a slight shudder. The Cackleberry Club was her baby and she considered herself a stickler for quality control.

"Just look at us," said Petra with a giggle. "We're two volunteers who are really curmudgeons at heart." In fact, they weren't curmudgeons at all. Suzanne, Petra, and their friend, Toni—the third partner in the troika that ran the Cackleberry Club—were just mature women who didn't give a rat's backside about what people thought or said about them. Now that they were on the high side of forty, careening toward fifty, they spoke their minds and lived their lives with grace and fortitude, without dwelling on past actions or feelings of remorse. For some reason, this somewhat pragmatic midlife philosophy led to better mental health and left them all feeling strangely liberated.

"We're on our own now," Suzanne had told Petra some

six months ago. "Free to blaze our own trail; free to make our own mistakes." Suzanne's husband had just passed away and, a few months earlier, Petra's husband, Donny, had gone into the Center City nursing home. But even as Alzheimer's had robbed Donny's mind, it had ignited Petra's spunk and determination.

As a final coup de grâce, Toni's slightly younger juvenile delinquent husband, Junior, had up and left her for a bar waitress with a head full of hot pink extensions.

That's when a merciful God had smiled down, taken pity, aligned the planets, and helped set gentle plans in motion for the Cackleberry Club to be—excuse the pun—hatched.

The Cackleberry Club, a whitewashed, rehabbed Spur station out on Highway 65 was a kitschy, quirky place. With a decent kitchen installed, battered wooden tables and chairs put in place, and legions of antique salt and pepper shakers and ceramic chickens arranged on shelves, a delightful little café with a tangle of wild roses out front had emerged.

Because there were a couple of extra rooms for sprawling, it became readily apparent that a Book Nook might bring in extra business. So cases of books, mostly mysteries, romances, and children's books, had been ordered and neatly arranged on shelves. Petra, who was a knitting and quilting freak, decreed there was also room for a Knitting Nest in an adjacent room. Colorful skeins of yarn and hundreds of knitting needles were carefully displayed, along with towering stacks of quilt squares. And once rump-sprung armchairs were liberated from attics, draped with woolly afghans, and arranged in a cozy semicircle, customers felt more than welcome to sit and stay awhile.

In a relatively short time, a few months to be exact, the

Cackleberry Club had emerged as the crazy quilt apex for food, books, knitting, quilting, and good old-fashioned female bonding that drew fans not just from Kindred but from all over the tri-county area.

Petra nudged Suzanne with an elbow. "Look. Mayor Mobley's squeezed in a little campaigning."

Suzanne gazed past the face-painting booth and the funnel-cake wagon to watch their pudgy mayor swagger along, glad-handing folks and slapping oversized campaign buttons into their palms. "What a slimeball," she muttered to herself. Though Kindred was a picture-postcard little town with historic brick buildings and well-kept homes skirted by towering bluffs and remnants of a hardwood forest, their mayor, as top elected official, left something to be desired. Suzanne always had the niggling feeling that Mayor Mobley was just this side of legitimate. And that various permits, licenses, and easements could be more easily obtained by greasing his sticky palms.

"Ozzie never came back for his pie," observed Petra, looking at the paltry few that had been reserved. Ozzie Driesden was the local funeral director as well as a civic booster. Of course, what funeral director wasn't a civic booster? They all wanted to win friends and influence people for that final trip to the great beyond.

"Hmm?" murmured Suzanne, still keeping a watchful eye on the swaggering Mayor Mobley.

"Ozzie bought a cherry pie earlier, but hasn't been back to pick it up."

"Tell you what," said Suzanne, frantic to ditch out. "I'll run the pie over to Ozzie, and you pull out your squishy black magic marker and slash prices on all this stuff. Hopefully, it'll magically fly off the table so we can boogie on out of here."

"Deal," said Petra, as Suzanne snatched up Ozzie's pie.

"But I think I'm going to slip a few ginger-spice cupcakes to that poor fellow sitting by the picnic tables. He looks like he hasn't had anything to eat in a week."

"Better taste them first," warned Suzanne. "You wouldn't want to kill him."

DELIGHTED to be done with the bake sale, Suzanne set off down Front Street, finally able to relax and enjoy the afternoon. What little was left of it, anyway.

An orange September sun hung low in the sky, but the faint rays were still warm and relaxing on her back. A lingering lazy-day feeling before the crispness of autumn took hold.

In fact, Suzanne was casting admiring glances at fire maples and daydreaming about riding her horse across a sunny hillside of blazing sumac when she pushed open the front door of the Driesden and Draper Funeral Home.

That's when the day's warmth and Suzanne's good humor suddenly came to a crashing halt.

The mingled aromas of overripe flowers, chill air, and . . . what else? . . . chemicals? . . . jarred her mind and assaulted her sensibilities.

Suzanne wrinkled her nose and set her jaw firmly. Well, of course it's going to smell funny, she told herself, taking a few tentative steps into the entryway. It's a funeral home. There's always going to be . . . chemicals.

She shook her head as a shiver oozed its way down her spine. When Walter had died, they'd held his visitation right here, in this very place.

Squaring her shoulders, Suzanne crossed the whisper-soft celadon green carpet and called out, "Ozzie?" in what she hoped was a confident and slightly authoritative voice.

She waited a few moments, keeping company with a grandfather clock, a wooden podium reserved for guest books, and a small brocade fainting couch that had a small table with a box of Kleenex snugged up next to it. Sighing, Suzanne decided it was time to be a little more proactive.

Gripping the pie tighter, Suzanne struck off to her left and peered through the open doorway into the smaller of the two chapels. The room was tastefully furnished in shades of dove gray and mauve. And it was empty, except for a nondescript sofa and a semicircle of black metal folding chairs that looked like a cluster of skinny crows.

"Ozzie?" Suzanne called out again. "I brought your pie." But there was no answer, save the ticking of the staid grandfather clock.

Suzanne re-crossed the entry hall. Maybe Ozzie was scurrying about in the other chapel. She touched fingertips to an ornate brass pull and slid open a heavy wooden pocket door. As she glanced in expectantly, a bronze coffin met her eyes. Lid propped up, resting on a wooden bier, the coffin was flanked by two pots of slightly drooping irises.

Oops, this room is ocupado.

Suzanne caught a quick glimpse of cream-colored satin brocade as well as the coffin's occupant lying in still repose. Letting out a quick breath, she quickly turned her gaze to a brass candle holder that held six white tapers. And couldn't shut the door fast enough.

Shifting uncomfortably, a little unnerved, Suzanne stared at the double doors that led to the back of the funeral home. The room where Ozzie did his sad business.

"Hey . . . Ozzie?" she called out again, drumming her fingers nervously on the underside of the tin pie plate.

No answer. Nada. And the insistent ticking of the grandfather clock was beginning to seriously grate on Suzanne's nerves. Glancing at the offending antique clock, she suddenly recalled fragments of a long-ago childhood story, whispered at night around a flickering campfire. Something about a grandfather clock that stopped dead the exact moment its creaky old owner drew his final, rattly breath.

"Silly," Suzanne murmured to herself. She wasn't a big believer in legends or signs or portents. Suzanne was a woman who believed in living fully and wholly in the present and not fretting unduly about what might be coming down the road. That didn't mean Suzanne hadn't noodled a five-year plan or even a ten-year plan, because she had. But that was for business. Mostly, in her personal life, she just tried to keep things on an even keel and obsess as little as possible. She found this approach helpful in retaining positive mental energy. It wasn't a bad way to keep crow's feet and wrinkles at bay, either.

Shifting the pie to her left hand, Suzanne smoothed the front of her blouse, then placed her palm flat against one of the double doors. They were swinging doors, of course, similar in design to the service doors restaurants installed between dining room and kitchen. Except, in this case, there was no eye-level window to peek through. Because who in their right mind wanted to see into the back of a funeral home, anyway?

Suzanne pushed lightly, felt the door move inward.

So not locked, she told herself. Which meant Ozzie was probably puttering around in back. And since there was a body out here, there probably wouldn't be one in back. At least she hoped there wasn't. Suzanne couldn't recall any recent obituaries in the *Bugle*. Could only think of the one last Thursday for Julius Carr.

And she'd just encountered *him*.

So . . . okay.

But as the door continued to swing inward, it clanked hard, hitting a rolling metal cart. Suzanne did a double take. The cart lay wheels up, half blocking the door. To either side of her, stacks of blue and white pharmaceutical boxes, no longer lined up nice and neat on their grid of shiny metal shelving, were tumbled haphazardly on gray linoleum. Suzanne could read the labels on the upended boxes--Hizone, Lynch, ESCO.

What just happened here? she wondered.

And suddenly heard a faint clink.

What was that? The snick of a metal door, the click of an instrument being set down?

Sure it was. So Ozzie was back here. Probably.

"Ozzie," Suzanne called, rounding a corner. "What the heck hap . . ."

Suzanne stopped dead in her tracks, her words segueing to a sputter, then a dying gasp. Her mouth opened reflexively, snapped shut, then opened again. But no sound issued forth.

Because Ozzie was back here, all right. Splayed out on an enormous metal table like some sort of medical experiment gone horribly wrong.

Suzanne's eyelids fluttered uncontrollably as she took in the ghastly scene. Plastic hoses kinked around Ozzie, his right arm stuck rigidly out to one side. And there, sticking into that arm, his very white, waxy arm, was a large needle attached to a length of tubing.

Suicide? The word exploded in Suzanne's brain like a thousand points of light. *Oh no, not Ozzie Driesden. He wouldn't do that, would he?*

Suzanne's stomach lurched unsteadily and the beginnings of bitter, hot bile rose in the back of her throat.

Struggling to force her mind to work, to reboot her

brain's frozen hard drive, she thought to herself, *Got to get help.*

As that thought popped into her head like a bubble above a cartoon drawing, there was a sudden, sharp snap, like a freshly laundered towel jerking on a clothesline. A soft shuffle sounded behind Suzanne, then a cold, wet, foul-smelling rag was clamped viciously across her nose and mouth.

Throwing up her hands in protest, the pie flipped end over end and crashed to the floor. Struggling blindly, not thinking clearly now, Suzanne inhaled sharply and involuntarily breathed in the prickly chemical that soaked the rag. Her heart lurched painfully in her chest and her lungs burned like hot coals. Staggering drunkenly, Suzanne's spinning mind spat out a single word: *Camphor?*

Then her head was filled with the drone of a thousand angry hornets and her knees began to buckle like a cheap card table.

No . . . chloroform, was Suzanne's last semi-lucid thought as blackness descended and she crumpled atop the ruined cherry pie.

CHAPTER 2

"BREATHE deeply," urged a voice from above her. Suzanne's eyes fluttered wildly for a few moments, then peeped open. And Suzanne found herself gazing up into the face of a kindly-looking EMT wearing a blue uniform with a red-and-white patch. He was young and good-looking, with an olive complexion and curly, dark hair.

When did EMTs get so young? Suzanne wondered to herself. *And when did I start thinking guys in their early thirties were young?*

That brought a semblance of a giggle mixed with a few hiccups.

"She's coming around," said Petra.

At hearing her friend's calming voice, Suzanne lifted her head. Not a great idea. Her brain was still spinning like a centrifuge even though her body was laid out flat on the floor, right where she'd fallen.

Cotton in my head, Suzanne thought, crazily. *And bright red cherry pie all over the floor.*

The EMT, whose name tag read J. Jellen, held a plastic mask to Suzanne's mouth and smiled encouragingly. "Breathe," he instructed.

Suzanne fought to bat the mask away.

"It's only oxygen," Jellen told her, calmly. "Help clear your head."

"Breathe the Os, honey," Petra pleaded, kneeling down next to her.

Suzanne breathed in deeply and, a few moments later, really did feel better. She relaxed, inhaled a few more Os, then raised a hand and pushed the mask aside. "What happened?" she asked Petra. "How did you get here?"

"When you didn't come back right away, I sent Sheriff Doogie over to check on you," explained Petra. "He'd been hanging around the park, snarfing down hot dogs and cookies. After he left, and when I saw the ambulance heading over there—Doogie must have found you and called for it right away—I came running. Like the proverbial cavalry." Petra put a hand to her ample chest. "Well, a cavalry that walks awful darn fast, anyway."

"Doogie's here?" asked Suzanne, struggling to sit up.

Petra nodded. "And a deputy." She peered anxiously at Suzanne. "How much do you remember, honey?"

It was starting to come back to her now. Suzanne touched a hand to her head and sighed deeply. "Oh man. Ozzie . . . ?"

Petra gave a solemn shake of her head.

"Dead?" asked Suzanne. Her mouth felt parched.

"Afraid so," Petra whispered.

Suzanne pushed herself into a sitting position, gritted her teeth as her head spun wildly, then struggled to get her legs under her. The paramedic, Jellen, curved an arm around her waist and asked, "You sure you want to do this?"

Suzanne nodded and suddenly found herself being lifted with ease by the helpful paramedic. She continued to stare down at the floor for a long moment, noting the sticky smear of cherry pie and a flattened hunk of golden crust that seemed to carry the partial imprint of a shoe. Then she raised her eyes.

Ozzie was still lying there, of course. That harsh reality hadn't changed one iota. But now Sheriff Roy Doogie and his young deputy, Wilbur Halpern, were circling the metal table like coyotes surveying roadkill. Another fellow, George Draper, the Draper of Driesden and Draper, was standing there with them, making nervous, futile hand gestures. Obviously, Draper had been summoned posthaste.

"Killed himself," said the deputy. He shook his head even as he hooked both fingers in his belt in a kind of postmortem show of disapproval.

Sheriff Doogie, a big bear of a man in rumpled khaki, turned toward George Draper, Ozzie's partner, now the sole owner of Driesden and Draper. "Had he been depressed?"

Draper, who was tall, gangly, slightly stooped, and looked like *he* might be suffering a mild bout of depression, gave a slightly furtive shrug. "Maybe. A little bit."

"What are you talking about?" Suzanne suddenly croaked as she staggered toward them. She was fighting mightily to get her feet and legs to coordinate with her brain. But walking a straight line wasn't easy.

Sheriff Roy Doogie shifted his bulk and bobbed his head at Suzanne. He was the duly elected sheriff of Logan county and had been in office for more than a dozen years. With his meaty face, cap of gray hair, and rattlesnake eyes, Doogie only looked slow-moving. Truth was, not much got past him.

"You feeling better now, Suzanne?" Doogie asked as she continued to wobble toward him. "You must've had quite a start, seeing poor Ozzie like this. No wonder you fainted dead away."

"I didn't faint," Suzanne protested. "I've never fainted in my life."

The young deputy let loose a slightly derisive snort. "Then how come you was sprawled on the floor?"

"If you give me a minute, instead of jumping to conclusions," snapped Suzanne, "I'll tell you."

"Tell us what?" asked Doogie. A frown and something else . . . curiosity? . . . had insinuated itself on his lined face.

"Someone attacked me!" Suzanne told him in a rush. "From behind. Clamped some kind of damp cloth over my mouth and . . . and . . . *drugged* me!" She touched the back of her hand to her head, trying to recall the exact sequence of events. But everything was still fuzzy, like a long-ago dream that could only be remembered in disjointed fragments.

"Huh?" said the deputy.

"What are you sayin'?" asked Doogie. His jowls sloshed vigorously as he stared at Suzanne, his eyes suddenly wide with surprise.

"I came back here to deliver Ozzie's pie," explained Suzanne, "and that's when I saw him. Just . . ." Suzanne grimaced as she glanced past Doogie. ". . . just lying there."

"Was he dead?" Sheriff Doogie asked.

"I don't know," said Suzanne. "Well, I *suppose* he was. I mean, he must have been. He was all white and waxy-looking, just like he is now." She felt hot tears prickle her eyes, but fought to keep them back. Men were funny about tears. Disdainful really. If she could keep the waterworks under control for the time being, her story would carry far more credibility. Suzanne tried to emphasize the chain of events with another hopefully cohesive statement: "Before

I had time to react and really get a decent look, someone grabbed me from behind and slapped a rag across my face. Drugged me," she added again, for emphasis.

Sheriff Doogie seemed to be having trouble comprehending all this. "You mean they chloroformed you?"

"I don't know if that's the technical term," said Suzanne, starting to feel a little frustrated, "but yes. Someone chloroformed me. Like a friggin' bug dropped inside a Mason jar for biology class."

Doogie snatched his modified Smokey Bear hat from his head and slapped it against his knee. "Heck you say!" Doogie still seemed reluctant to buy into Suzanne's story.

"Sheriff Roy Doogie!" said Petra, in her sternest, steeliest voice. "You listen to Suzanne. She doesn't make up stories!"

Sheriff Doogie ushered them all into the small parlor, the unoccupied parlor, where they sat on lumpy couches and love seats and Suzanne told her story again. Slowly, filling in the details.

Doogie went over a few parts with her. "So when you came in carrying the pie, the boxes were spilled all over." It was a statement, not a question.

"Yes," said Suzanne. "Like maybe there'd been a struggle."

"And then you saw Ozzie. With the . . ." Sheriff Doogie pointed an index finger at his own forearm. ". . . with the thing . . . the needle . . . stuck in his arm."

"Yes," Suzanne said again.

Doogie's lined face sagged. "Well, shit."

Suzanne glanced around the semicircle of somber faces. "He was murdered, wasn't he?" she said. But she really wasn't asking a question, either.

"We don't know that for sure," said Doogie, still hedging.

"Whoever attacked me had probably just murdered Ozzie," Suzanne said, forcefully this time.

Petra, who was perched next to Suzanne, gripped her forearm tightly.

"Wilbur," said Doogie, glancing at his deputy. "Go out to the truck and fetch my kit."

Wilbur rose hastily and left the room.

Petra stared directly at Doogie and said in an accusatory tone, "This could have easily been a double murder, Sheriff."

Doogie lifted both hands to belly level and made a calming gesture. "Now we don't know anything like that. But I'm going to go ahead and treat this as a crime scene . . . give it some serious investigation."

"You're going to call in the state crime lab?" asked George Draper. He hadn't said anything up to this point. Now he looked colossally unhappy.

"First things first," Doogie told Draper. "First thing I want to do is go back in there and take my own look-see. Is there anyone else besides you and Ozzie who worked back there?"

"Ozzie had a sort of lab assistant," said Draper. "A young man he'd taken an interest in. Helped him, really. Fellow by the name of Bo Becker. I think Ozzie was hoping Bo might study for a degree as a diener."

"Get him in here," said Doogie.

WHEN Sheriff Doogie, Deputy Halpern, and George Draper trooped back into the embalming room, Suzanne didn't hesitate to follow. Petra was a little more reluctant.

Doogie placed a black leather case on a rolling metal

cart that normally held hemostats, dissecting scissors, and rib cutters.

As Doogie dug around inside his case, Suzanne asked, "Are you doing *CSI* stuff now?" She was feeling better. Not chipper, but definitely curious. And angry, too. After all, someone had tried to do her serious harm.

"Don't call it that," huffed Doogie. "Ever since that TV show, people put too much stock in all the whiz-bang assays and tests and electron microscope stuff. They don't realize it's good old legwork and deductive reasoning that really solves crimes."

"So what's your deductive reasoning on this?" Suzanne asked him.

"Just hold on," grunted Doogie. "First thing I want to do is take a careful look. You can learn a lot just through simple observation." He pulled a light from his case and untangled a long black cord.

"What's that?" asked Suzanne.

"UV black light," said Doogie. "These days, a county sheriff's got to be prepared for anything."

Suzanne had to agree. Kindred had been a sleepy small town for more years than she could remember. Now, like a bolt from the blue, they had a ripped-from-the-headlines type of murder on their hands.

"Kill the lights, will you?" Doogie instructed his deputy. The deputy, stumbling over his size-fourteen feet, hurried to comply.

Doogie flicked the switch on his SPEX Mini-Crime-Scope 400, shone it on Ozzie's knees, then slowly ran it up the length of Ozzie's body. Everyone clustered behind Doogie, holding their breath. They weren't sure what Doogie was going to find, but they were watching his every motion with rapt attention.

"Anything?" asked the deputy. He sounded wistful, like he'd been purposely left out of the action.

Doogie continued to run the light across Ozzie's neck and up onto his face. Hesitating for a split second, Doogie ran the light in a circle, then his eyes widened and his jaw dropped onto his second chin. "Oh, horse pucky!" he exclaimed.

CHAPTER 3

"WHAT?" demanded Suzanne. She'd been standing behind Doogie at a somewhat respectable distance. Now she elbowed forward.

One side of Doogie's mouth was pulled up in a petulant snarl. "You see this?" he muttered to his deputy. But Suzanne and Petra had already moved in, essentially crowding out the deputy. Doogie switched the black light to his left hand and pointed a pudgy index finger at Ozzie's mouth.

Suzanne, Petra, and the deputy all peered forward and gave slow nods. Doogie's light had revealed a few tiny white specks. Suzanne wondered if they were faint remnants of food or toothpaste or some type of drug Ozzie might have ingested or been force-fed.

But Doogie quickly answered her question.

"Somebody put sticky tape over Ozzie's mouth," Doogie said slowly. It seemed to be dawning on him that this was the pivotal point where taking a look-see had suddenly turned into a full-fledged murder investigation.

Now Doogie was more aggressive with his study. He shone the light slowly across every part of Ozzie's body, returning again and again to certain areas. "Doggone," muttered Doogie. "Stuff's on his wrists and ankles, too."

Deputy Halpern's face had blanched white and he looked a little shaky.

"So what exactly are you saying?" pressed Suzanne. There was a nasty churn in the pit of her stomach. She wasn't sure if it was the residual effect of the chloroform or just the psychic shock of gazing at Ozzie's dead body and knowing he was for sure murdered. But Suzanne mustered her inner grit and forced herself to focus. She wanted to hear an explanation directly from the sheriff's own mouth.

Doogie snapped off the black light and gazed directly at Suzanne with tired, hooded eyes. "Some maniac tied Ozzie down before draining his blood."

You could have heard a pin drop.

"So murder, not suicide," murmured Suzanne. She glanced at Deputy Halpern and took a certain amount of grim satisfaction in the fact that he looked awfully green around the gills.

"Gotta call the state crime lab in on this," said Sheriff Doogie. "This is a bad situation. We're gonna need technical assistance." He clumped across the room, hit the light switch.

Everyone blinked when the overhead fluorescents buzzed on. Under the suddenly glaring lights, the stainless steel looked much harsher and Ozzie's body looked even more pathetic.

"I'm going to wait outside with Mr. Draper," Petra told Suzanne, slipping away.

Suzanne nodded, but resolutely remained in the embalming room. She watched as Halpern packed up Doogie's case, listened halfheartedly as Doogie made his phone call to alert the guys at the state crime lab.

But curiosity had also sunk its talons into Suzanne. It was the first time she'd ever been in an embalming room and she was finding it fascinating, if not a little grim and unnerving. Wandering about the room, she glanced at head blocks and bottles of arterial fluid, winced at the overhead Stryker saw.

Doogie hung up the phone, sneezed, pulled a hanky from his back pocket, and let loose a loud honk. "They'll be here in an hour."

"What's that?" asked Suzanne.

"State crime lab," said Doogie, sniffling slightly.

"No, I mean in the sink," said Suzanne. She pointed toward one of a pair of deep, stainless-steel sinks. There appeared to be a soggy mess of ashes in the bottom of one.

Doogie shook his head, muttered the words, "Doggone hay fever," then peered into the sink and grimaced. "What is that crap?" He sounded surprised.

"That's what I just asked you," said Suzanne.

"Something was burned in there, then got doused with water," Doogie mused.

Deputy Halpern looked over, eager to be more involved. "You want me to clean it up?"

"No!" snapped Doogie. "We gotta bag it." He sneezed and glanced around the room. "In fact, we better start bagging everything."

"Even what's left of the cherry pie?" asked Halpern.

"Wilbur," said Doogie, and this time he sounded both cranky and tired, "just use a little common sense, will you?"

A few minutes later George Draper appeared with the hastily summoned Bo Becker. Becker was young, maybe twenty or twenty-one, and good-looking in a blond surfer boy kind of way. He wore pegged jeans, a black T-shirt, and motorcycle boots. Suzanne almost expected to see a cigarette pack, maybe Lucky Strikes, rolled up in his shirt sleeve.

"Somebody killed Ozzie?" Becker sounded suitably shocked and his expression was wary.

"You know anything about that?" asked Sheriff Doogie.

Bo Becker glared in Doogie's direction. "You accusing me of something, Sheriff?"

"We have a wrongful death on our hands," said Doogie in a somewhat matter-of-fact tone. "And quite possibly a number of suspects. If someone in this room is privy to information concerning Ozzie Driesden's death, it might be best to get it out on the table now. Since it's only a matter of time before we start handing down indictments and making arrests." He stared forcefully at Becker. "So, young man, we can do this the easy way or we can do this the hard way. It's entirely up to you."

"Don't try to intimidate me," snorted Becker, "because I don't know squat about this." He shook his head like a swarm of gnats was attacking him. "Heck, I *liked* Ozzie. He gave me a job when not many folks around here would even talk to me. So why would I want to go and kill him? Spoil a good thing? What's my motive, smart guy?"

"You don't need a motive," said George Draper, finally speaking up. "You've been in trouble before. You have a record."

Doogie scratched the side of his face and cocked a keen eye toward Becker. "Izat so?"

"Give me a break," said Becker. "That was penny-ante shit. Reform school stuff."

"Statistics prove that petty criminals almost always graduate to committing felonies," said Doogie. He sounded like he was reading from a Criminal Justice 101 textbook.

"Shove your statistics where the sun don't shine," snarled Becker, radiating hostility.

Doogie responded with a thin, reptilian smile, then said, "I think we ought to finish our conversation in a more conducive environment. Say, down at the law enforcement center?" He glanced at Suzanne. "I'll be in touch with you later."

"Sure," said Suzanne, still feeling a little dazed. She walked past the tumbled boxes, the smeared cherry pie, through the door, and out into the entry hall.

Petra, who was sitting primly on the fainting couch, gave Suzanne a baleful look. "Somebody's going to have to tell Missy," she said in a quiet, gentle voice. Missy, Melissa Langston, was Ozzie Driesden's girlfriend. Although things seemed to have cooled between the two of them in the past few weeks, Missy would certainly have to be informed. Had the right to be informed.

"Oh man," said Suzanne, making a slight grimace. She knew Ozzie's death was going to come as a terrible blow to Missy.

"We could have Sheriff Doogie stop by," suggested Petra, who was standing now, more than ready to leave.

"Or I'd be happy to speak with Missy," volunteered George Draper, as he shepherded them toward the door.

Suzanne and Petra exchanged glances, then Suzanne nodded. "Thank you," she told Draper. "I think that might be best." Suzanne was grateful that Draper had so willingly stepped in. He was trained to deal with death and grief, while Sheriff Doogie, as messenger, might just drop the news on Missy like a hot potato. Or handle it like that old joke about the woman who received a telegram then begged the messenger to please sing it to her, because she'd always wanted a singing telegram. The punch line of the joke, of course, was, "Da, da, da, da, dum, Fred and the kids are dead."

"Maybe we could . . ." began Petra. She was positioned at the front door, about to turn the knob, when it suddenly flew open.

"Oh dear," Draper murmured from behind them, as he recognized the woman who'd suddenly appeared in the doorway.

A plump woman with tough, gray, Brillo-pad hair and wearing a bright purple dress stared silently at Petra and Suzanne. She cradled a large bouquet of pink and white Stargazer lilies in her arms.

George Draper rushed to greet her. "Mrs. Carr, we weren't expecting you today." Suzanne suddenly realized that Nadine Carr was the wife of the corpse in the next room.

Nadine Carr stared at Draper, then shifted her inquisitive glance to Suzanne and Petra, who had a nodding acquaintance with Nadine. She'd eaten at the Cackleberry Club a couple of times. Maybe purchased some skeins of yarn there, too.

"Hello," said Nadine. She hesitated, taking in everyone's stricken face. "Is . . . is something wrong? I saw a sheriff's car parked outside."

"Right this way, Mrs. Carr." George Draper took Nadine by the arm and gently guided her away. She walked, somewhat unsteadily on two-inch squash heels, toward the parlor where her wizened little husband, in his one good suit, was laid out in a bronze Eternalux casket.

"This place is suddenly Grand Central Station," remarked Suzanne.

"Poor Nadine," said Petra, staring at the not-quite-closed door. "What do you suppose he's going to tell her?"

"Whatever it is," said Suzanne, "it's going to come as a bombshell."

Suzanne and Petra fell silent and focused their attention on the mumbled conversation that was taking place in that little parlor. Most of the mumbling was being done by Draper and they caught a few words such as "frightful" and "shocking."

There were a few moments of silence, then a hoarse outburst of, "Oh no!" as Nadine's sad words floated back to them. "Dead? Ozzie? I can hardly believe it!"

"Believe it," muttered Suzanne, as she breathed a prayer of thanks to the Almighty that she'd been fortunate enough not to be summoned along with poor Ozzie.

CHAPTER 4

"WERE drugs stolen, too?" asked Toni. Reddish blond hair piled atop her head like a show pony, wearing tight 501 jeans and an equally tight Aerosmith T-shirt, Toni was juggling a Scramble Deluxe and a plate of Jumpin' Jack Spuds. She teetered on red high-heeled sandals that matched her enameled red toenails. Toni was a true believer in the concept of an endless summer and wore cork wedge sandals from March until the first snowfall. Except, of course, when she wore cowboy boots.

It was Monday morning at the Cackleberry Club and the breakfast rush was in full force. Eight hungry male bodies were perched on stools and hunched over breakfast plates that sat atop a vintage marble counter appropriated from a now-defunct pharmacy in neighboring Cornucopia. These men, mostly truckers and neighboring farmers, ate silently but with great gusto.

The rest of the tables, covered in blue–and–white oil-cloth, were also filled with customers. Happy, hungry customers who were chowing down on stacks of buttermilk pancakes dripping with maple syrup, blueberry muffins, eggs mornay, Eggs on a Cloud, and Slumbering Volcanoes, this last being a tasty concoction that featured an egg baked inside a scooped-out tomato with artichoke hearts, parmesan cheese, and loads of garlic.

Hunkered in the steamy kitchen, Petra sizzling thick-cut strips of bacon and links of sweet Italian sausage on a blackened expanse of grill, the three women were still puzzling over Ozzie's murder, like a well-oiled team of detectives.

"What do you think?" Petra asked Suzanne. "Was this about drugs?" Petra talked as she moved about efficiently in her white chef's jacket, comfy crop pants, and modified chef's hat that looked like an imploded mushroom.

"We don't really know about the drug aspect yet," Suzanne told Toni. "In fact, we're not sure if the pharmaceuticals were spilled during the struggle or if Ozzie stumbled in and caught drug thieves in the act. I'll have to check with Doogie about that."

"But would drug thieves go so far as to *kill* Ozzie?" mused Toni.

"Of course they would," said Petra, expertly flipping two sausages onto a waiting plate and sounding a little outraged. "Druggies hold up Seven-Elevens, break into clinics, and even mug old ladies for chump change."

"It's the duct-tape part that weirds me out," continued Toni.

"Taping Ozzie's mouth, hands, and feet is totally grisly," agreed Suzanne. "It's like something from one of those horror flicks, like *Saw* or *Hostel*. Like . . . torture."

"And that *machine*," said Toni. "You think Ozzie realized what was happening? That his blood was . . . ?"

Suzanne could only shake her head. "If Ozzie had been fully conscious, it must have been a nightmare for him."

"And nobody's spoken to Missy yet?" asked Petra. She spun around like a ballet dancer, dipped her ladle into a bowl of pancake mix, then dropped three little puddles of batter on the grill where they made a satisfying sizzle.

"It's not that I haven't tried," Suzanne told her.

"Call her again," urged Toni. "We've got to make sure she's okay. Do it now while I cover the café out front." Grabbing a large silver tray, Toni artfully arranged five plated breakfasts onto it, as though she were fitting together pieces of a Chinese puzzle.

Suzanne snatched the phone off the wall and punched in Missy's number. Because she'd tried calling so many times, she had it memorized. And since Missy was a good friend and constant customer at the Cackleberry Club, Suzanne was growing more and more concerned that she couldn't get ahold of her.

Missy had experienced her own share of bad luck over the past few months. She'd been the office manager for Bobby Waite, Suzanne's former lawyer, who'd suffered a very untimely death. Bobby's passing had pretty much rocked everyone's world. When the law office closed, Missy had accepted a job as general manager of Alchemy, a new fashion boutique that was slated to open this Friday in Kindred's picturesque downtown.

"Doggone," exclaimed Suzanne, frowning. "Number's still busy. And when I called last night, there was no answer at all."

"She's probably just too upset to talk to anyone," said Petra. "Just letting her phone ring into oblivion."

"I suppose," said Suzanne. She glanced out the back window and saw her dog, Baxter, lying in the sun. Most days, she brought Baxter to work with her and he enjoyed his day, alternately snoozing and terrorizing gophers that popped their ratty little heads up from the neighboring soybean field. He was getting older, his muzzle going white, but he hadn't lost his spunk for shagging rodents.

"Cheddar cheese strata's up," said Petra, quickly plating two more breakfasts. She blew a wisp of hair from her face, then muttered, "Now I gotta get my cookies in the oven."

"Chocolate chip?" asked Suzanne. Petra was renowned for her chocolate chip cookies. Suzanne was renowned for taking a half dozen home with her and polishing them off while watching *Sex and the City* reruns.

"Chocolate chunk walnut cookies," said Petra, giving a slow wink.

SUZANNE delivered more breakfasts, poured refills of coffee, joked with a few customers, delivered checks, and cleared tables. Toni was behind the counter, slicing a loaf of freshly baked wheat bread and making a ham, Gruyère cheese, and tomato sandwich for an early take-out lunch.

Suzanne smiled to herself, feeling content. This was the time of day she enjoyed most. When things were humming but not too crazy yet. When the aroma of cinnamon muffins, spicy kielbasa sausage, and fresh-brewed Kona coffee hung redolent in the air. And when she could stand behind the old brass cash register and accept both money and compliments from their customers.

The Cackleberry Club, in all its cozy, homespun glory, was a bit of a throwback. No frozen, prepackaged foods were heated in microwaves like chain restaurants were wont to do. In fact, the Cackleberry Club prided itself on serving made-from-scratch baked goods, using only cage-free eggs, and sourcing the freshest, local ingredients. Which, interestingly enough, was one of the hottest trends going in the fine dining industry today, whether it was

Jean-Georges in New York, Chez Panisse in Berkeley, or the French Laundry in Napa Valley.

Of course, none of those restaurants boasted a Book Nook and Knitting Nest. Or a fine collection of salt and pepper shakers, battered tin signs, and ceramic chickens crowded into a colorful flock on the café's high shelves. And Suzanne was pretty sure that none of those fancy restaurants had antique egg crates piled outside their front door or a tangle of wild roses crawling up a white trellis.

TEN minutes later, when Sheriff Roy Doogie swaggered into the Cackleberry Club, Suzanne really wasn't surprised. She figured he'd show up sooner or later. Doogie had a nose for questions and a craving for caramel rolls.

"Sheriff," said Suzanne, as Doogie slid onto the red vinyl stool at the far end of the counter. "How did it go with the crime scene boys?"

Doogie tilted his head back and peered down his nose at her. "They did their thing and I did mine."

"And your thing is . . . ?" asked Suzanne.

"Interviewing suspects."

Toni eased her way down the counter to join them. "You have suspects?" she asked. "So soon?" She sounded impressed.

Petra stuck her face through the pass-through and asked, "You want somethin' to eat, Sheriff? I got hot Italian sausage and a couple of cakes with your name on them. Oh, and a caramel roll, too."

"I ain't gonna say no," responded Doogie, as Suzanne laid out flatware and a white paper napkin and Toni poured coffee into an oversized ceramic mug with a chicken on the front.

"So," said Toni, sliding the coffee across the counter to Doogie, "who exactly are these suspects of yours?"

Doogie took a long slurp of coffee, set his cup down, and smiled a cat-who-swallowed-the-canary smile. "Sometimes they're right under your nose."

"What are you talking about?" asked Suzanne. "*Who* are you talking about?"

Doogie continued to be coy. "Let's just say a certain girlfriend has caught my attention."

Suzanne almost choked. "What?" she screeched, her voice rising a few octaves. "Please tell me you're not talking about Missy!"

Doogie waggled his head up and down in a sort of tacit nod.

"No way!" exclaimed Toni. "Missy and Ozzie were in love!"

"Not so much recently," said Doogie. He took another sip of coffee, then peered across the top of his cup at Suzanne. "You and Missy are friends, Suzanne. How much has she told you lately about her relationship with Ozzie?"

Suzanne thought carefully before she answered. "Not much," she had to admit. "But I don't think anything's changed. Of course, Missy's been up to her eyeballs with preparations for the launch of Alchemy Boutique."

"Huh?" said Doogie.

"Alchemy," said Suzanne. "I'm sure you read about it in the *Bugle*. It's the new boutique in the Chandler Building, next to Root 66 Hair Salon." When Doogie still looked puzzled, Suzanne added, "The shop that Carmen Copeland is opening." Carmen Copeland was a rather flamboyant romance author who lived in neighboring Jessup. Suzanne figured that by launching Alchemy, Carmen, in her somewhat snooty, superior manner, was attempting to instill a new level of style among the women of Kindred.

Suzanne felt pretty darned comfortable in her faded denim jeans, soft white cotton shirt tied at the waist, and turquoise jewelry, but she wasn't totally adverse to casually perusing Alchemy's offerings. But no way was she slipping on platform shoes or any kind of top or tunic that sported oversized shoulder pads. Been there, done that.

"I'm going to ask you a question and, however you answer it," said Doogie, "I want to make sure I have your complete confidence." He made a zipping motion across his mouth. "Okay?"

Toni nodded while Suzanne gave a reluctant, "Okay."

Doogie leaned forward across the counter. "How much do you know about Earl Stensrud?"

Now Suzanne was really confused. "Earl? You mean Missy's ex-husband? Why would you bring *him* up? That guy's ancient history."

Toni bobbed her head. "Last I heard Earl Stensrud was living in Kansas City."

"Not anymore he's not," said Doogie, with a slight air of superiority. "Earl moved back to Kindred a couple of months ago. He's selling insurance for Universal Allied Home and Life."

"Okay," said Suzanne, "that's an interesting little factoid. But why would you consider Earl a suspect? What made him pop up on your radar screen?"

Doogie looked pleased at Suzanne's question as he paused to scratch his ample stomach. "Because I have it on good authority that Ozzie and Earl were seen arguing in a bar this past Friday night."

Petra came steamrolling through the swinging door and plunked down sausages, pancakes, and a caramel roll in front of Doogie. "Which bar?" she asked.

"Schmitt's," said Doogie.

"That's no big deal," chimed in Toni, obviously eager to pooh-pooh Doogie's theory. "Everybody gets caught up in some kind of wacky argument when they hit a few bars." She went on to explain. "You have yourself a couple tequila sours, wolf down a few handfuls of stale popcorn, maybe buy a basket of pull tabs . . . next thing you know, you're snarling over some stupid little thing . . ." She grimaced, then her gaze slid to Suzanne and Petra, who looked slightly aghast. "At least that's what happens to me and Junior," Toni added in a small voice.

Junior was Junior Garrett, Toni's bad-boy estranged husband. He was a few years younger than Toni, a vo-tech dropout, self-proclaimed womanizer, and worked as a grinder and metal finisher over at Shelby's Body Shop. Toni's impromptu Vegas wedding to Junior had been a hideous mistake and now Toni was wrestling with the notion of getting out of it. Especially since Junior had a habit of disappearing with the local VFW's floozy bartender.

"It's doubtful," said Suzanne, "but I suppose Earl could be a long-shot possibility in this. But certainly not Missy, no way is Missy involved."

Toni looked thoughtful. "Did it ever occur to you guys that maybe Ozzie's partner bumped him off?"

Doogie lifted his shoulders in an indifferent shrug. "Maybe. I'm gonna talk to Draper later this morning." Doogie dug into his pancakes, took a couple of appreciative bites, then said, "It's a funny thing. Ozzie left a message on my answering machine yesterday. I was kind of working my way over to his place when Petra waylaid me in the park and asked me to check on Suzanne."

"It's a good thing you did," said Petra.

"Why do you think Ozzie called you yesterday?" asked Suzanne, her radar suddenly pinging. "Do you think that call was somehow connected to his murder? That he felt threatened by someone?"

"Don't know," said Doogie, as he continued to snarf his breakfast at an increasingly rapid pace.

"Maybe Earl Stensrud sold Ozzie an insurance policy and Ozzie wasn't happy," said Toni. "Maybe Ozzie tried to get his money back and Earl said no way."

"I ain't ruling anybody out at this point," said Doogie.

Toni rolled her eyes in a gesture of exasperation. "Then what about Suzanne? She was there. Is she a suspect, too?"

Doogie shifted his focus to Suzanne, who had grabbed a couple of tins of tea and was trying to decide between brewing a pot of jasmine or Earl Grey.

"Probably not," was Doogie's response. "She was awful loopy from that chloroform."

"Well, thank you, Dr. Doogie, for your expert diagnosis," said Suzanne. "And by the way, did you question that kid who was there yesterday? Ozzie's assistant?"

"Bo Becker," filled in Doogie.

"Holy buckets," exclaimed Toni, "I *know* that guy. Junior drove in an amateur stock car race against Bo Becker this past summer. Over at Speedway Park."

"Didn't I hear somewhere that Bo Becker was bad news?" asked Petra. "Wasn't he arrested for stealing cars?"

"Ayup," burped Doogie. "Did time in juvie hall."

"Then Becker's your guy," said Toni, pouncing like a hungry duck on a fat grasshopper. "Has to be."

"Talk like that leads to rumors," muttered Doogie. "And around Kindred, rumors spread like wildfire."

"Oh, stuff it," Toni told him.

Doogie squeezed his eyes shut and let loose an ear-splitting sneeze. "'Scuse me," he said, pulling out a hanky. "Must be pollen or dust in here." He wiped at his nose, glanced up at one of the shelves. "Probably dust. You got so darned many chickens up there."

"I'll have you know those are dusted religiously," said Toni, slightly indignant.

"Let's get back to the murder," said Suzanne. "What about the drugs? Did you determine if any drugs were missing?"

"Too soon to tell," Doogie responded. "Draper's gotta go through the inventory list and that's in some computer file."

"And the sticky tape remnants and stuff," said Suzanne. "The crime scene evidence. What have you found out about that?"

"Still at the state lab. Gonna take a while," said Doogie.

"Well, let me know, will you?" asked Suzanne.

"Maybe," said Sheriff Doogie, using the last chunk of his caramel roll to sop up the puddle of syrup on his plate, "as long as I get a little quid pro quo."

"What do you mean?" asked Toni. Her eyes shifted to Suzanne, then Petra. "What's he talking about?"

"I'd like you to keep your eyes and ears open, okay?" Doogie asked the three women. "I know you gals overhear all sorts of loose talk when folks sit down to eat."

"Addressing us as ladies is the correct and more polite term," said Petra. "Not *gals*. It serves no purpose to speak in tired, old, male chauvinisms."

"Whatever," muttered Doogie. He stood languidly, hitched his belt, and headed for the door. As was typical of Doogie, he never paid his bill because he never asked for a bill.

"Hey, Doogie-doo," Toni called after him, "don't let the screen door slap that wide load of yours on the way out." When Doogie turned his head and threw Toni a sour look, she added, "On the other hand, how could it not?"

CHAPTER 5

"CAN you believe it?" exclaimed Suzanne. "Doogie actually sees Missy as a suspect!" She was standing in the kitchen with Petra, helping frost cupcakes. Carrot cake with cream cheese icing.

"Doogie tried to project an air of confidence," said Petra, "like he was seriously large and in charge. But you could tell he was really in turmoil. I guess a county sheriff doesn't exactly have the experience and wherewithal that a big-city homicide detective might have."

"You have to admit," said Suzanne, "that Doogie does a dang fine job of rousting young lovers from Bluff Creek Park and shagging the occasional coyote that wanders into town. But for him to think Missy was involved . . . that's a horrible accusation. I can't quite get past such idiotic thinking!"

"Try to," advised Petra. "Otherwise it will just drive you nuts."

"Who's nuts?" asked Toni, pushing her way through the swinging door, cradling a plastic tub of dirty dishes on her hip.

"Suzanne's obsessing because Doogie said he was looking hard at Missy," explained Petra. "But, in the end, any suspicion he has won't amount to a hill of beans."

Still, Suzanne looked worried. "But if Missy had broken

up with Ozzie and was starting to see Earl again . . ." she began.

"Had she?" asked Toni. "Because that's not the impression you gave Doogie."

"I know that," said Suzanne. "I laughed at his suggestion of Missy being a suspect because . . ." She stopped suddenly.

"Because of what?" Petra asked quietly.

"I guess I was trying to protect my friend," said Suzanne.

"You were right to do so," said Toni, setting down her dishes and giving Suzanne a pat on the arm. In fact, we all need to stand together on this."

"Uh-oh," said Petra, licking a smear of frosting from the back of her hand. "Time for an affirmation?"

"Couldn't hurt," said Suzanne.

Whenever the ladies of the Cackleberry Club came across a quote, a saying, or a Bible verse they liked, they scribbled it on a piece of paper and tossed it into a Red Wing crock. Now they were in the habit of drawing a slip each day from their so-called affirmation jar and sharing it with each other.

Petra held out the crock to Toni. "You first."

Toni reached in, grabbed a pink Post-it note, and read, "Life's problems wouldn't be called hurdles if there wasn't a way to get over them."

"See?" said Petra, smiling at Suzanne. "Good one, huh?"

Suzanne smiled back. "You're right. Now you choose."

Petra grabbed a slip of paper, studied it, then read it. "The future belongs to those who live intensely in the present." She nodded to herself and murmured, "I sure *try* to live in the present."

Toni gripped Petra's arm, knowing she was thinking of Donny. "You do, dear," said Toni.

Petra blinked rapidly, then smiled at Suzanne. "Now you."

Suzanne grabbed a piece of paper and read it out loud. "Do or do not. There is no try."

"Sounds familiar," said Toni. "Is that attributed to anyone in particular? Maybe one of those really smart guys like Kierkegaard or Shakespeare?"

Suzanne held up the slip for Toni to see. "Yoda."

"From *Star Wars*!" shrieked Petra. "I love it!" And then she was bustling about the kitchen, washing her hands, ready to whip up a batch of corn muffins.

"We better hustle our buns and get today's luncheon offerings up on the blackboard," said Toni.

"Let's do it," said Suzanne, leading the way out to the café.

But there were more customers to be seated, coffee cups to be filled, and dishes to be cleared, so Suzanne ended up tackling the chalkboard herself. Using pink and orange chalk, she listed the four luncheon specials the Cackleberry Club was offering today: grilled chicken with avocado on sprouted wheat bread, asian chicken wrap, pita bread vegetarian pizza, and chicken citrus salad. Then Suzanne used a piece of yellow chalk to make a cartoon drawing of a wedge of pie and printed under it, *Frozen Lemonade Pie. $2.95 a slice.*

Suzanne didn't need to list the rest of their goodies, because most customers knew there was always a fresh assortment of cookies, bars, muffins, and scones. In fact, most were on display in the circular glass pastry case that sat atop the counter.

Because there was still a good thirty minutes before

the luncheon crowd began easing their way in, Suzanne went over to the sputtering old cooler in the corner and checked the shelves. On display were homemade banana and cranberry breads, jars of fat dill pickles, canned jellies and jams, cheeses, and boxes of string beans. These were items that local producers brought in to the Cackleberry Club to sell. It was really a win-win situation for everyone. Suzanne took a small percentage of retail sales and the growers and producers got the lion's share. She knew one woman who had helped finance her daughter's junior college education on what she'd made from selling her potato rolls and banana bread.

But as Suzanne's eyes scanned the shelves, she noticed they were very low on cheese. Ordinarily, they stocked several dozen wheels of organic blue cheese and cheddar cheese from Mike Mullen's Cloverdale Farm. He had a herd of doe-eyed Guernseys that were the sweetest, friendliest cows Suzanne had ever encountered. Whatever it was, the lack of antibiotics and hormones or the tender grass and organic grain they fed on, the milk from the Cloverdale cows yielded cheeses that were creamy and rich beyond belief. And very popular with customers, as the almost-empty shelf would attest to.

Suzanne made a mental note to call Mike and tell him they were perilously low on cheese, then she peeked into the Book Nook to check on things. This was book club night and Toni was leading a discussion on so-called chick lit books. For some reason Suzanne had yet to fathom, every one of those books seemed to have a hot pink cover with bouncy, funky type. Go figure.

Of course, the book club would also break halfway through the evening for a glass of wine. After quizzing Suzanne for suggestions, Toni had opted for a lovely, mellow Italian Pinot Grigio. A fine choice that would no doubt help the group segue from discussing sarcastic chick lit to bodice-busting romance novels.

Romance novels. Doggone it.

Scurrying across the well-worn Aubusson carpet to the romance section, Suzanne carefully checked the shelves. Carmen Copeland, their local romance author, was coming in Wednesday afternoon for a book signing and she wanted to be stocked and ready.

Well, okay. Phew.

They had at least twenty-five copies of Carmen's new book, *Ramona's Rhapsody*, on the shelf, along with at least two copies of each book in Carmen's backlist. So that ought to do it.

Carmen was one of a handful of authors who had jumped from mid-list mediocrity to the top of her genre. In leap-frogging thousands of other authors, Carmen had become rich, haughty, and imperious, not necessarily in that order. But Carmen's snippy attitude wasn't Suzanne's problem at the moment. Right now she was concerned about Missy Langston and was wondering how in heck she could get in touch with her.

Maybe drive over to her house after lunch? Stop by the boutique? Missy was probably there, unpacking boxes, frantically steaming garments and arranging them on racks.

Grabbing a couple of empty coffee mugs that had been left on the Book Nook's small counter, Suzanne scooted through the café and headed into the kitchen.

When Petra saw Suzanne burst through the door, she said, "Do you realize what a ferociously busy week this is going to be?"

Suzanne gave a knowing nod. She knew exactly what they had on the docket.

"We've got the Silver Leaf Tea Club coming in tomorrow afternoon," said Petra, ticking off the events on her fingers, "then the Knit-In for Charity on Thursday, and our Take the Cake Show on Saturday."

"I know," said Suzanne. "It's a lot."

"More than a full week," muttered Petra, as she dipped her frosting knife into a bowl of creamy vanilla frosting.

"That cake's for Saturday?" asked Suzanne. Petra was frosting a three-layer chocolate cake and had sketched out a Take the Cake logo and design. Her plan was to add mini fondant cakes and blue ribbons as decoration.

"It is in a way," said Petra. "Jenny Probst offered to display it in the front window of the bakery. Advertising made delicious."

Toni came slaloming in with a stack of clean dessert plates and slammed them down on the wooden butcher block table. "What's wrong?" she asked, at seeing Suzanne and Petra with such serious faces.

"We were just talking about how much we've got scheduled this week," said Petra. "What were we thinking?" She picked up a spatula and twirled it in the air. "We're going to run ourselves ragged!"

"We just got overenthusiastic," said Toni, matter-of-factly. "In case you two hadn't noticed, a lot of that goes on here. Somebody says something about knitting or cake decorating and the energy level ratchets up about a zillion degrees and suddenly we have a great big honkin' event on our hands!"

"You think we scheduled too much?" asked Petra. "In too short a time frame?" Now she and Toni both cast sideways glances at Suzanne.

"Of course we did," said Suzanne. "But I don't think

we'd want it any other way. All our events are great fun and help keep us on our toes."

Petra gazed down at the purple Crocs on her size-ten feet. "Such as they are."

"PETRA seems a little edgy, don't you think?" asked Toni, as they laid flatware and set water glasses on the tables.

"Mostly because of Saturday's Take the Cake event," said Suzanne. "She sort of spearheaded that whole idea, so I think she's feeling responsible."

"But we'll all pitch in," said Toni. "We always do. And we've got volunteers lined up like crazy."

"Thank goodness," said Suzanne, "because I'm pretty sure we're going to have tons of entries in the cake-decorating contest. And a whole lot of folks coming for the cake social."

"The cake judging is going to be my favorite part," said Toni. "I love watching *Ace of Cakes* on TV, and now we're gonna have our own mini competition."

Suzanne put the last water glass in place and surveyed the café. "We all set?"

"We better be," said Toni, slipping a long black Parisian waiter's apron over her jeans and T-shirt, "because here comes our first customer."

Both women stood there with smiles on their faces as the door slowly swung open.

Only it wasn't a customer at all. Standing in the doorway, staring at them with a stricken look on her face, was Missy Langston.

Suzanne took in Missy's sad expression, haggard look, and slumped shoulders, and murmured, "Oh no."

CHAPTER 6

MISSY Langston wasn't just upset, she was practically hysterical.

"My poor Ozzie is dead and now Sheriff Doogie says I'm at the top of his suspect list!" she wailed.

Suzanne led Missy to a table and got her seated. Toni quickly brought a glass of ice water.

"Take a sip," urged Toni.

"Why do people always bring you water when you're upset?" asked Missy, taking a tentative gulp. In her mid-thirties, Missy possessed fair, almost porcelain skin, hair the color of fine corn silk, and a full, ripe figure. She'd caught the eye of more than a few men in Kindred, but Ozzie Driesden had been her sweetie for more than two years. Except for lately.

Suzanne wanted to get right to the heart of Doogie's accusations. "Where were you yesterday afternoon?" Suzanne asked Missy. "Do you have an alibi?" She hadn't watched *Law & Order* all these years for nothing.

"I was at home," sniffed Missy. "I was planning to go to Kindred Spirit Days, maybe hang out a little, but I was just so tired from working twelve-hour days, trying to get Carmen's boutique ready. So I gave myself a break and took a nap."

"Poor dear," said Toni.

"Next thing I know," said Missy, "Sheriff Doogie is pounding on my door, telling me Ozzie is dead!"

Suzanne wrinkled her nose. George Draper had offered to break the news to Missy. Obviously, Doogie had engineered a serious change in plans.

"So Doogie just barged in?" asked Toni. "Just dropped the terrible news on you?"

Now Missy pulled a white hanky from her bag and dabbed at her eyes. "Yes." Her voice dropped to a hoarse whisper. "And it was shocking, just shocking! The news hit me like a ton of bricks." Missy took another sip of water.

"What did Sheriff Doogie say after he broke the bad news?" asked Suzanne.

Missy sniffled again. "Just rattled off a string of questions. Didn't display a speck of sympathy. Or decency," she added.

"And the questions were all concerning you and Ozzie?" asked Suzanne.

Missy bobbed her head. "Exactly. Sheriff Doogie asked me how long we'd been dating, how close we were . . ." She blushed slightly, then added, "really personal questions. Then he asked if Ozzie and I had cooled it over the past couple of months."

"What did you tell him?" asked Suzanne.

"I told him we'd cooled it a little bit," said Missy. "That I'd been so busy with the new boutique that I hadn't had a lot of free time."

"But your relationship had cooled off, hadn't it?" asked Suzanne. She felt so sad asking about Ozzie in the past tense.

"Yes." Missy's voice was a soft whisper again. "It had."

"What was the real reason?" Suzanne asked, although she wasn't sure she'd get a straight answer.

But Missy surprised her. Biting her lip, twisting her hanky around her thumb, Missy said, "A couple of months ago, I kind of pressured Ozzie for a commitment."

"Okay," said Suzanne. "I can certainly understand that."

Missy let loose a deep sigh. "But Ozzie said he wasn't ready for marriage. That he preferred the status quo, as he so inelegantly phrased it, and told me that maybe he wasn't even the marrying kind." Tears trickled down Missy's face. "Why do men do that?" she wailed. "Why do they get all cozy and buy you little gifts and lead you on like that? Then, when you dare to broach the subject of marriage, they turn completely squirrelly. What is it with this fear of commitment?"

"It's part of the male genetic code," said Toni. "Like being unable to put the toilet seat back down."

"Not all men are like that," said Suzanne. "But let me guess. Sheriff Doogie asked if you were hurt and angry about Ozzie being so noncommittal?"

"He did," said Missy. "In fact, he broached the subject a couple of different ways. Just kept coming at me."

"*Were* you angry?" asked Toni.

Missy frowned and studied her French manicure. "Yes." Seconds ticked by. "Maybe a lot angry. Furious, I suppose."

Suzanne pressed on. "And Doogie thought that Ozzie's cooldown might have put you over the edge? Might have served as an impetus to kill him?"

Missy's face turned harsh. "I think Sheriff Doogie's convinced I'm one of those scorned, revengeful, stalker-type women."

"You mean like in *Fatal Attraction*?" asked Suzanne.

"Except you'd never boil a rabbit in a pot," pointed out Toni.

Missy shivered. "No. Of course not."

"And what exactly did Doogie ask you about Earl?" said Suzanne.

"Um . . ." said Missy. "Earl?"

"He asked if you'd been seeing your ex-husband, right?" pressed Suzanne. "Dating him?"

"Yes," murmured Missy.

"And you *have* been seeing Earl, isn't that correct?" asked Suzanne.

"Really?" said Toni. "Earl?"

Missy looked slightly sheepish. "Yes. Some."

"Why would you do that?" asked Suzanne. "I thought you were through with him." After Missy's divorce was final, she referred to Earl Stensrud as a cretin not fit to sell watermelons by the side of the road.

"I was lonely . . . and felt rejected," said Missy. She seemed embarrassed by her own admission.

"I can see that," said Toni. "When Junior left me . . . the first time anyway . . . I thought I'd go berserk." She shrugged. "Now I'm getting used to it."

"The thing with Earl," said Missy, "is that absence really *did* make our hearts grow fonder. And once Earl moved back here, we kind of picked up where we left off and one thing led to another." She touched her hanky to her nose, sniffled, and continued. "A few phone calls, lunches out, a couple picnics, and suddenly, one night over a candlelit dinner, Earl was telling me how sorry he was that we ever got divorced in the first place."

"Let me guess," said Suzanne. "Earl proposed that the two of you consider making a go of it again?"

"We talked about that, yes," said Missy. "But please understand . . . after Ozzie sort of backed away from me, I was utterly devastated. Very vulnerable. And Earl can be quite charming."

Suzanne remembered Earl Stensrud as a man who picked his teeth with a matchbook cover, but made no comment.

"Anyway," said Missy, "once Sheriff Doogie got wind that I was seeing Earl again, he was delighted to add Earl's name to his suspect list. Oh, and the sheriff also had the audacity to call me a two-timer."

Suzanne raised her brows as she regarded Missy. "Doogie mentioned something about Ozzie and Earl getting into an argument last Friday night. What do you know about that?"

Missy waved a hand dismissively. "That was nothing. Just male turf war stuff."

Toni looked concerned. "Sheriff Doogie doesn't think the fight was just a minor incident. In fact, I wouldn't be surprised if he concocted a theory that you two were in this together."

Missy looked shocked. "Earl and I would never!" she sputtered.

"I wonder what Earl's alibi is," Suzanne wondered out loud.

"Hope he has a dandy one," said Toni, "because Doogie's on the warpath."

Sighing deeply, Missy said, "I'm just so heartsick and nervous over this entire situation. And of course it couldn't come at a worse time. Alchemy Boutique is slated to open Friday afternoon and Carmen is driving me insane. She nitpicks absolutely everything I do! The other day I mistakenly hung silk tank tops on the same rack as wool slacks and she threw an absolute hissy fit. Shrieked at me. Told me I'd committed a dreadful fashion faux pas."

"What a bee-atch," said Toni. She harbored no love for Carmen Copeland whatsoever, even if her books were constant best sellers in their Book Nook.

"Suzanne?" Missy turned needful baby blue eyes on Suzanne. "Do you think you could kind of look into things?"

"I don't think that's a good idea," Suzanne responded hastily.

"But you're so good at sleuthing around and unraveling things," said Missy. "Remember when Bobby Waite was murdered? You were the one who . . ."

Suzanne gave a reluctant nod. "Yes, I know. But this . . . this is completely different."

"No, it's not," said Toni, jumping in. "Missy's in trouble and she needs our help. *Your* help," Toni corrected.

Moments passed as both women stared at her, then Suzanne finally said, "Maybe I could just . . . I don't know . . . ask around."

Leaning forward, Missy threw her arms around Suzanne and gave her a big squeeze. "Thank you, thank you very much."

"I'm not promising anything," Suzanne cautioned.

"But you're tight with Sheriff Doogie," said Toni. "So maybe you'll have an inside track."

"I don't think Doogie ever gives anyone an inside track," replied Suzanne. "But I'll see what I can pry out of him."

Still looking shaky, Missy said, "I'd better get going before your luncheon crowd comes swarming in and sees me looking all red-eyed and awful."

"Here, honey," said Toni, handing Missy her handbag, "I'll walk you out to your car."

"Thank you," said Missy, "and thanks for being such good listeners." She started to stand, then sat down again, a look of pain on her face. "Oh. I almost forgot to tell you.

There's going to be a visitation for Ozzie tomorrow night at Driesden and Draper. And then the funeral will be Wednesday morning at Hope Church."

"So soon," murmured Suzanne.

"Isn't it?" said Missy. "But Ozzie only had the one brother, and I guess he just wants to move things along."

Now if only I could do that, too, thought Suzanne.

LUNCH was packed today and ran for a good two hours. At one point Suzanne had to run in and help Petra make a dozen more chicken wraps. Then Suzanne and Toni had to clean up quickly so they could set up for afternoon tea.

While Petra assembled small tea sandwiches of curried chicken salad and carrot, pecan, and cream cheese, Toni brewed pots of Yunnan black tea and rosehips tea.

That gave Suzanne a little free time to putter around in the Book Nook again. While customers came, browsed, and bought books, Suzanne worked at unpacking several new boxes of books that had arrived via FedEx that morning. By looking back at the last six months of sales, Suzanne had determined the reading trends of the local populace, and so had ordered mysteries as well as books about the stock market, quilting, knitting, and Mediterranean-style cooking.

Just as she was ringing up a children's book for a young mom and her five-year-old daughter, Suzanne caught a flash of jet black hair and the unmistakable sparkle of diamonds.

She glanced up to see Carmen Copeland, romance author and owner of Alchemy Boutique, gazing at her intently from across the room.

That was the wacko thing about Carmen. She never

smiled, never displayed any interest in anyone but herself. Carmen just appeared and projected the air of an entitled, wealthy duchess waiting for court buglers to announce her arrival and the red carpet to be rolled out.

"Carmen," said Suzanne, determined to be friendly even if it killed her, "wonderful to see you."

Carmen crossed the carpet and dumped her handbag, a gorgeous mahogany-colored alligator bag with a dangling charm, D for Dior, on the counter. "Did you hear about the murder?" she asked, a trifle breathless. With her dark hair, heart-shaped face, and drop-dead figure, Carmen was a truly gorgeous woman. Of course, the slinky emerald-green dress, strappy Gucci heels, diamond necklace, diamond ring, and twin diamond bracelets didn't hurt, either. Projected a certain air of luxe living.

Suzanne decided not to tell Carmen that she'd actually been at the scene of the crime. "I heard all about it," she told Carmen. "And then Missy dropped by a couple of hours ago, right before lunch. As you can imagine, she was extremely upset over Ozzie's death. Heartbroken, really." Peering closely at Carmen, Suzanne noticed that the tiny lines around her eyes seemed to have disappeared. Her lips were also much plumper, almost a trout pout, as one Hollywood gossip rag referred to collagen-enhanced lips. Yes, Carmen must have made a trip to a skillful cosmetic surgeon who specialized in injectables.

"Don't you find it weird . . . Ozzie being murdered on his own table like that?" Carmen's eyes sparkled, as though she was thinking about switching from writing romance novels to true crime.

"It's bizarre," agreed Suzanne, wondering just how much Carmen knew about the murder. How she'd picked up her facts.

Carmen gave a slight frown. "I just hope Missy is able to pull herself together. We've got our grand opening Friday and there are still a trillion details to take care of." Sighing, she said, "It's just so hard to find people you can count on."

Suzanne decided Carmen must have been born without a heart. Or else it had been surgically removed and replaced with a mechanism of stainless steel or some other hard metallic substance. And Carmen was a romance writer at that! Made her millions penning love stories!

"Missy's got a good head on her shoulders," said Suzanne, "but she's going to need time to grieve. It's only natural."

"As her employer, I'd prefer she do it on her own time," responded Carmen.

Suzanne wondered what would happen if she reached across the counter and gave Carmen a good smack upside of the head. Probably, she decided, Carmen would just smack her back. Carmen was like that. Mean. Fearless. Aggressive. Not unlike the timber rattlers that lived in the towering bluffs above Kindred. Even though the Midwest wasn't their natural environment, the rattlers were there, and they were dug in. It was as simple as that.

Something clunked against the counter, and then Carmen held up a large two-by-three-foot laminated poster that featured the colorful cover of her new book.

"I always have my publisher make posters and ship them to the more prestigious bookstores," said Carmen. "But we had one left over, so I thought I'd give it to you. See?" She pointed to a strip of paper that was striped across one corner. "It's even got the date and time of my book signing."

"Wonderful," said Suzanne. "We'll place it right by the romance section."

"Don't you think it would look better in the window?" asked Carmen.

Suzanne wanted to tell her it would be better still shoved down her gullet. But she didn't. Just held her tongue and accepted the poster.

ONCE Carmen had left, once Suzanne had dug out a copy of *Tragic Magic* for a customer, she poked her head into the café. Three tables each held groups of four women, all enjoying tea, triangle-shaped tea sandwiches, and gingerbread scones.

So . . . good. I can kick back in my office and place a few orders.

Because Petra was such a prolific baker, and business had been awfully good—knock on wood—they were forever ordering flour, sugar, butter, and spices from their local restaurant supply house. But the minute Suzanne sat down in her chair and snugged it up to the antique oak library table that served as a desk, the phone jangled.

"Suzanne," came a cheery voice, when she picked it up. "How do?"

She knew instantly it was Gene Gandle from the *Bugle*.

"It's Gene. From the *Bugle*."

"I know that, Gene."

"I'm just putting the finishing touches on a story here," said Gene, brightly. "And I wanted to make sure I included your perspective."

Oh crap. He's doing a story on Ozzie.

"Not sure what you're talking about, Gene," Suzanne told him.

There was a forced chuckle and then Gene said, "You're doing it again, Suzanne."

"What's that, Gene?"

"Playing dumb."

Suzanne snorted. "Thanks for your kind and generous observation."

"You know darn well I'm writing a story about Ozzie's murder," said Gene. "Gonna be front page. Above the fold," he bragged.

"And the headline will be forty-eight-point type?"

"I'm just trying to put together a credible story," Gene whined. "Before I have to turn it in to my editor."

"I'm sure Sheriff Doogie told you everything that he's able to release to the press," said Suzanne. "Or to the public, for that matter."

"And his information was pathetically scant," complained Gene. "Lacked detail. C'mon, Suzanne, you were there. You saw poor old Ozzie dead on the table."

Suzanne dropped the phone to her chest and stared at a small framed needlepoint that Petra had finished last week and set on the desk. She'd created a lovely montage of weeping willows, bubbling brook, and birch forest, along with a quote by Dante that read, *Nature is the art of God.*

"How did you know I was there?" Suzanne asked.

"It's my job to know things," said Gene.

"I don't think I can add anything, Gene."

"Then how about you share your suspicions?" he asked.

"No way," said Suzanne.

"C'mon," said Gene. "This is hot stuff. So far we've got a scorned girlfriend, a jealous ex-husband, and a young kid with a serious history of violence."

"Sounds like a made-for-TV movie," remarked Suzanne.

Gene's voice was upbeat. "Doesn't it? That's why I

wanted you to add your take on the matter. Help stir the pot, so to speak."

"That's the last thing I want to do, Gene."

"My editor's gonna want *something*," wheedled Gene.

"Put her on the phone, will you?" asked Suzanne. Laura Benchley was the managing editor of the *Bugle* and a terrifically smart businesswoman.

Laura came on the phone. "Hey, Suzanne. Things still humming along at the Cackleberry Club?"

"Can't complain," said Suzanne.

"Any chance I could get that recipe for oatmeal scones you guys served last week?" asked Laura. "They were fantastic."

"I'll e-mail it to you," said Suzanne.

"Okay if I publish it?" asked Laura.

"Sure," said Suzanne. "Why not?"

"How about you write another tea column for us? Could you get one done in about two weeks?"

"Can do," said Suzanne.

"We're gonna do a nice write-up in Thursday's paper on your Take the Cake Show," Laura told her. "Get even more buzz going."

"Appreciate that," said Suzanne.

"Okay then," said Laura. "I'll put Gene back on."

"Oh, but you're so much nicer than Gene," Suzanne said with a laugh.

"Don't pay any attention to him," said Laura. "He thinks he's Dan Rather." She laughed wickedly.

"Or Dan Rather-not," added Suzanne.

CHAPTER 7

MIDAFTERNOON found Toni and Suzanne hunched over the butcher-block table in the kitchen, munching leftover tea sandwiches and sipping fresh-squeezed lemonade. Afternoon tea service was winding down in the café, with just a few ladies lingering over a final cup.

"What did the nasty old dragon lady want?" asked Toni.

Suzanne giggled. She couldn't help herself. "You're referring to our dear Carmen Copeland?"

"Play nice, children," warned Petra, as she stacked leftover scones into a large wicker basket.

"Carmen brought in a poster to advertise her book signing on Wednesday," said Suzanne.

"Big whoop," said Toni. "I thought maybe she sashayed in to try to shanghai more workers for her snooty boutique."

"She already did that to Missy," Petra interjected. Then she gazed worriedly at Suzanne. "You think Missy will be okay?"

"Okay about Ozzie's death or okay working for Carmen?" asked Suzanne.

"Both, I suppose," said Petra.

"Missy will be fine," Suzanne assured her. "She's a survivor."

"Like us," said Toni. "Or more to the point, like you and Petra."

"Aren't you sweet," said Petra. She put her hands on her ample hips and smiled at them. "Now that things have settled down to a dull roar, I'm going to take a batch of scones, a jar of fig jam, and a big thermos of lemonade over to the fellows who are working on the Journey's End Church." Last month, the church, which was just down the frontage road from the Cackleberry Club, had been tragically torched by an arsonist. Now the site had been cleared, a foundation poured, and the church was slowly being rebuilt.

"Need any help?" asked Toni. They all felt terrible about what had happened to the church.

"I'm fine," said Toni, gathering everything up. "But my heart just goes out to Reverend Yoder. Do you know, he's been over there every day, wandering around nervously, trying to pitch in?"

"Traded in his reverend's collar for a chambray work shirt," said Suzanne.

"Reverend Yoder's just hoping the job will get done faster, I suppose," said Toni. "Wouldn't it be great if they could finish the church in time for Christmas? I just hate to think of those poor folks not being able to sing Christmas hymns in their own church."

"I know," said Petra. "But the unfortunate thing is, Reverend Yoder doesn't know the difference between a Phillips-head screwdriver and a flat-head screwdriver."

Toni popped a last bit of sandwich into her mouth and declared, "Neither do I."

"I suppose it's the thought that counts," continued Petra. "I love that he cares so passionately about getting his church rebuilt and bringing his congregation back together." On Suzanne's invitation, the congregation had met a few times at the Cackleberry Club. Now they were using St. Sebastian's Church at off hours. A nice ecumenical arrangement between two different religions.

Petra hadn't been gone more than two minutes when there was a loud, erratic banging on the swinging door that separated the kitchen from the café.

Uh-oh, thought Suzanne. *An unhappy customer?* She walked over, gave a tentative push on the door, and was startled to find a somber-looking Junior Garrett staring back at her. "Junior!" she exclaimed.

"Aw crap," muttered Toni. Only last week her estranged husband had displayed a wandering eye for curvy-bordering-on-chubby women who favored tight angora sweaters. In other words, not Toni.

"Toni back here?" Junior asked, shrugging back his dangling forelock, not even bothering with a polite hi-how-are-you. "Sure she is," he scowled, answering his own question. "She's always hangin' out at your little sorority house. You girls probably have your own secret handshake and decoder rings."

Toni lunged for Junior. "Don't be an ass, Junior," she said, swatting at his head.

"Hey, lay off!" Junior cried, ducking as her fingernails grazed him, then hastily retreating a few steps.

"What do you want?" asked Toni, lunging again and, this time, getting a firm grasp on the back of his shirt. She twisted sharply, gathering fabric while she shoved Junior back out into the café and steered him to a seat at the counter. "And keep your voice down," she hissed at him. "We still have customers."

"Jeez," said Junior, looking like a puppy who'd just been walloped with a rolled-up newspaper for making doo-doo on the floor. "I just dropped by to say hi."

"Hi," said Toni through gritted teeth.

"Now good-bye," Suzanne said, airily.

"No need to give me the bum's rush," complained Junior. "I just wanna get something to eat." He turned innocent eyes on both of them. "I been working since five this morning."

"A quick bite and then you'll leave?" asked Suzanne. She wasn't fond of Junior Garrett, and she knew he wasn't good for Toni. Treated her like a doormat. Cheated on her, too. Only problem was . . . Toni wavered between wanting a divorce and having second thoughts about getting back together with Junior. Lot of that going around these days.

"I suppose we could spare a sandwich or two," Toni told him, ripping Junior's trucker's cap from his head and plopping it on the counter in front of him, like she was lining up Exhibit A for the jury.

"You'll settle for leftovers?" asked Suzanne, relenting some.

"Sure," said Junior. "Whatever."

"You'll get whatever," breathed Toni.

But when they brought Junior a plate of tea sandwiches and a scone, he peeled the top slice off his sandwich and stared suspiciously at the chicken salad. "What's this?" he demanded. "Don't you girls got anything fresher?"

"When you're getting something for free," said Toni, "you take what's set in front of you and don't make a fuss."

"Hey," protested Junior, "I can *pay* for this. I just got myself a brand-new job."

"What do you mean, a new job?" asked Toni. "I thought you were still working at Shelby's Body Shop. Please don't tell me you got fired. Again."

"No, no, nothing like that," said Junior, suddenly looking a little smug. "I should've been more specific. What I meant to say was I've taken on *another* job. You girls think I want to fix fenders and do paint touch-ups all my life? No way. Not this *paisano*."

"You have a second job?" asked Suzanne. That Junior was able to hold down one job was remarkable. That he'd taken on a second job was an alert-the-media event.

"I'm double-dipping from the trough of commerce!" Junior chortled, as he greedily stuffed a cucumber and cream cheese sandwich into his mouth. He seemed delighted with his mini bombshell.

"Better not let Shelby's hear you talk like that or they'll bounce you on your skinny butt and send you packing," warned Toni. "You haven't even been there six months. Aren't you still on probation?"

"Probation's a way of life with Junior," muttered Petra, who had returned and was now banging pots and pans in the kitchen.

"What is this other job, anyway?" Suzanne asked him.

Junior hunched his shoulders and looked slightly evasive. "I got a kind of delivery service going."

"And what is it you deliver?" asked Suzanne, praying one of their suppliers hadn't hired Junior to schlep eggs and milk all over the county.

"Yeah," said Toni. "And where exactly are you delivering it to?" She'd noticed Suzanne's suspicion toward Junior. Now she was feeling that way, too.

Junior puffed out his chest, trying to look important. "Are you kidding? They got me running all over the dog-gone place. Supposed to drive up to Minneapolis tonight and then to Des Moines next Wednesday."

"And just what is it you're delivering?" Suzanne asked again.

"Auto parts," snapped Junior. The fact that he said it a little too quickly and the answer sounded a little too rehearsed made Suzanne doubly suspicious.

"That's interesting," said Suzanne. "Because I thought most parts supply places had their own fleet of delivery trucks and drivers."

"Yeah," said Toni. "You see those panel trucks with the little orange caps on top driving around all the time."

Junior's scowl was almost menacing. "Why can't you girls ever be happy for me? Why do you have to put me down all the time? Bash me like all I am is some stupid piñata."

"Maybe because you always seem to be just this side of the law?" Suzanne shot back. "Maybe because you were miserably remiss in giving your wife the love and devotion she deserved? And now you're dragging your clodhoppers when it comes to giving Toni a well-earned, well-deserved divorce."

"What if she don't want one?" asked Junior.

"Oh, she wants one," chimed in Petra.

"DON'T you just wonder what Junior's up to?" Suzanne asked Toni as they set the tables for tomorrow's breakfast.

"Huh?" asked Toni as she piled sugar cubes into antique china sugar bowls they'd picked up at area tag sales.

"What I'm saying," said Suzanne, "is I hope Junior's not involved in anything illegal."

Toni looked thoughtful. "Like what?"

"Oh," said Suzanne. "Maybe like . . . drugs?"

Toni looked startled. "He wouldn't do that. Junior's not *that* idiotic."

Suzanne gazed at Toni and lifted an eyebrow.

"Okay," hedged Toni, "Junior may be one taco short of a combo plate, but I doubt he's involved in drugs!"

"I don't know," said Suzanne, still not convinced. "You hear all these rumors about meth labs in rural areas. Just like in big cities, a lot of small towns have terrible problems with stuff like crystal meth and methamphetamines."

"Holy buckets," said Toni. "Sheriff Burney over in Deer County busted a meth lab just last month."

Suzanne finished folding a linen napkin into a tricky bishop's hat, then suddenly frowned and looked up, a question clouding her face.

"What?" asked Toni.

"What if Ozzie's murder was related to drugs?" said Suzanne. "What if he was killed by some amateur meth lab chemists who were desperate for chemicals?"

"That's quite a brainstorm," allowed Toni. "You oughta give Sheriff Doogie a jingle and share your theory with him."

"Last time I shared anything with Doogie it was a basket of onion rings," said Suzanne. "And that's just 'cause he sat down and started helping himself."

SATISFIED they were set up for tomorrow, Suzanne and Petra wandered into the Knitting Nest. This was clearly Petra's domain—she being a confirmed knitter and quilter. Now she was fussing about happily, arranging skeins of mohair yarn, alpaca, and even a few skeins of cashmere. She'd stocked up like mad and was obviously ecstatic about the big Knit-In this Thursday. At last count, she had almost thirty women coming.

"So how does this Knit-In work?" asked Toni. "Is everyone going to start a new project or will they bring stuff they've been working on?"

"A little of both," said Petra, dumping an assortment of knitting needles into a large, flat basket. "The important thing is, all our knitters have gotten pledges from friends and families. And all the finished garments will be put on sale and the money given to charity."

"You are such a sweetheart," said Suzanne. She fingered a cowl-collared shawl that was hanging on the wall. It was knitted with Noro yarn from Japan and done in subtle colors of rust, orange, blue, and yellow. "Did you knit this?"

Petra nodded.

"And it's for sale?" asked Suzanne.

"Oh sure," said Petra.

"Then put a red dot on it for me, will you?" said Suzanne. "Like those fancy art galleries do, to mark a piece sold."

"La-di-da," sang Toni. "Suzanne's been to an art gallery."

"It was more of a framing store," said Suzanne. "Over in Cornucopia."

Plopping down in one of their squishy chairs, Toni wiggled her butt and unfurled her latest issue of the *National Inquisitor*. Petra didn't approve of Toni's subscription to the Hollywood gossip rag, but it was one of Toni's guilty little pleasures. Like Suzanne's passion for chocolate. And fine Bordeaux wine. And Sarabeth's peach preserves from Dean & DeLuca. And a few other things she couldn't go into detail on.

"Lookie this," said Toni, holding up a page. "Here's a photo of Jessica Simpson wearing a checked shirt a lot like mine." She squinted at the grainy color photo. "Except she's got more in the cha-cha department."

"Give her another fifteen years," said Petra, "then she'll be well acquainted with the indisputable laws of gravity."

Toni grabbed a copy of the Kindred *Bugle*, turned to

the back page, and said, "Time to check out the personals column."

"Pass," replied Suzanne.

"No, really," said Toni. "There are some good guys here. Listen to this one. Outdoorsy guy . . ."

"That means he shoots baby animals and chews tobacco," said Suzanne.

Toni snorted, but continued, ". . . who's low-key but fun-loving and seeks a possible long-term relationship."

"Low-key probably means he's a slug," pointed out Petra.

"And fun-loving is code for likes to get drunk," said Suzanne.

"What about the part where he's seeking a long-term relationship?" asked Toni.

"Just means he wants somebody to cook for him, do laundry, and sandblast the scum off his bathroom walls," laughed Suzanne.

"You guys are so cynical," said Toni. "I think he sounds like a heck of a prospect."

"You mean better than Junior," said Petra.

"Anybody's better than Junior," agreed Toni.

Suzanne wandered over to Petra's newly done display of knitting needles. "Tell me about these bamboo needles."

Petra's face took on an almost beatific look. "Oh, they're simply *wonderful*," she cooed. "Bamboo knitting needles are exceedingly smooth and have a very soothing feel. The amazing thing is, the yarn won't slip off, but it will slide exactly the way you want it to. And the bamboo makes a soft, clicking sound. It's almost spiritual. Zenlike," she added.

"We could all use a little Zen in our lives." Suzanne sighed.

"Thinking about Saturday," said Toni, "I'm wishing I knew a little bit about Zen. Or Yoga. To help me chill out."

"Gonna be crazy," agreed Suzanne.

Toni put her feet up on a leather footstool. "It'll be a miracle if we get through it."

Petra glanced up from arranging her yarns and smiled serenely. "I don't believe in miracles. These days I *rely* on them."

CHAPTER 8

THE sun was just beginning to dip below the horizon when Suzanne stepped outside the back door of the Cackleberry Club. Everything, as far as she could see—fields, woods, faraway farmhouses—was bathed in a golden reddish light. It reminded her of a line from Shelley's poem "To a Skylark."

In the golden light'ning of the sunken sun
O'er which clouds are bright'ning, though dost float and
    run.

The broad, leafy field of soybeans rippled like waves as the breeze washed across it. Across Suzanne's field.

She and Walter had bought the land adjacent to the Cackleberry Club some five years ago, as a kind of investment. Now she leased the land and the farmhouse to a farmer named Ducovny.

Squinting across the field, Suzanne was just able to make out a shimmer of buildings. Ducovny and his wife lived in the farmhouse and took care of the horse she had bought for herself a month or so ago. A nice reddish brown quarter horse named Mocha Gent. Stocky and blocky, Mocha was just the kind of horse who could dodge and dance his way around a barrel racing course, or chug along on long trail rides. Lots of evenings, Suzanne and Baxter would down a quick dinner, then drive back to the farmhouse where Suzanne would throw an Indian blanket and worn leather saddle on Mocha's broad back, then take a leisurely canter around the perimeter of the field. Sometimes Baxter lazed in the barn on a bale of hay, sometimes he loped along beside them.

"Hey, Bax," Suzanne called to Baxter, whose tail gave a welcoming thump, then revved into a fast drumming motion. "Ready to pack it in for the day?"

"Roowr," he growled. Ready to go.

"Me, too," Suzanne told him. "I'm beat." She unclipped Baxter from his long lead and opened the passenger door of her Ford Taurus. Baxter jumped in and settled down on the front seat.

Suzanne had intended to go right home. Fix a quick supper, slip into a warm bath, then maybe catch an old black-and-white movie on Turner Classic Movies. Maybe *Sunset Boulevard* or *The Maltese Falcon* was playing tonight. Or something light and frothy, with Fred Astaire.

Suzanne was bone tired and still reeling a bit from Ozzie's murder. But the notion of meth lab assholes breaking into Driesden and Draper to steal drugs intrigued her. Kept whirling in her brain like a big thumpin' load of towels tossed in her old Kenmore washer.

"Change of plans," she told Baxter as they zoomed along. "Hope you can wait ten more minutes for din-din." When Baxter gazed at her with limpid brown eyes, she added, "I'll make it worth your while."

"Grrrr?" he growled.

"Yeah," she said, "I could probably manage gravy."

Hanging a quick left, Suzanne cruised slowly through Kindred's downtown. It was both peaceful and pretty. Lots of vintage yellow and red brick buildings standing shoulder to shoulder, like old World War I soldiers. Diagonal parking on the streets. Nice shops like Kuyper's Drug Store, the Kindred Bakery, the Ben Franklin, and Root 66, a hair salon run by Gregg and Brett, two gay guys who did a mean color and foil and whose styling techniques ran the gamut from sleek and posh to Hindenburg-sized beehives.

The largest, really the prettiest, building downtown was the Chandler Building, a three-story tower of red stone. This was where Bobby Waite's law offices had been located, and this was the building that his widow, Carmen Copeland, had recently purchased. Now the first floor had been turned into Alchemy Boutique. As Suzanne crept slowly toward it, she could see large, well-lit windows swagged with elegant mauve draperies. Quite a change from the garish video store that had inhabited the space earlier. And, as Suzanne coasted past the front, she saw black lacquered mannequins dressed in chic, red sheath dresses and short, thigh-skimming geometric shifts. Since all the lights blazed inside, Suzanne imagined that Missy Langston was working away, artfully arranging bangles and bags, hanging jackets and T-shirts, putting on the finishing touches for the big opening.

Then Suzanne swung out Valley View Road, past the OK Used Car Lot, the Lo Mein Palace, and Pizzaluna's, and pulled into the parking lot of Westvale Medical Clinic. Turning the engine off, Suzanne listened to the tick-tick-tick of her engine cooling. She touched her palms to her cheeks, blinked at herself in the rearview mirror, and thought about the many times she'd breezed over here when Walter was on staff.

But that was then and this was now, she told herself. Grief was still a part of her life, but she'd tucked it deep inside her heart where it would always remain a part of her, but hopefully mellow. Like a sand pebble in an oyster that, over time, acquires a shimmering luster.

Suzanne grabbed her hobo bag and said, "Hang tight, Bax. I'll only be a couple of minutes." Then she climbed out of her car and scurried through the front door.

A woman in blue scrubs glanced up from behind the front desk and exclaimed, "Suzanne! Is that really you?"

"Esther!" called Suzanne. "How are you? You look great!" Esther was the office manager at the clinic.

Like she'd been perched in an ejection seat, Esther popped up and flew around the front desk to greet Suzanne and exchange hugs. "Hey, sweetie!" she exclaimed, clearly delighted to see Suzanne.

"I mean it," said Suzanne. "You look terrific. What's your secret? Did you lose weight or something?" Esther was in her early fifties, but had been blessed with a clear complexion, hazel eyes, rich brown hair, and very few wrinkles.

Esther giggled. "I've been on the seafood diet. I see food, I eat it."

"Seriously," said Suzanne, studying her. "There's something different."

"Botox," whispered Esther. "There's a dermatologist over in Jessup who's an artist with the syringe. He made two tiny injections right in the lines between my eyes . . . you know, those nasty elevens . . . and they were suddenly gone. Vanished! I said, thank you kindly, Doctor, now please make short work of my crow's feet, too."

"Ah," said Suzanne. Might that deft dermatologist also be the secret behind Carmen's slightly plumped-up face? Could be.

Suzanne was about to pull out a pocket mirror and contemplate her own elevens when Esther asked, "What brings you in? We close in ten minutes, you know."

"Right," said Suzanne. "Sorry. I was wondering if Dr. Hazelet was still around. I have a quick question for him. Nothing concerning health," she added hastily. "Just . . . a question."

"Sure," smiled Esther. "Let me buzz his office. See if we can catch him."

Two minutes later Dr. Sam Hazelet was grinning at Suzanne as they stood outside the clinic's front door. He was tall, early forties, good-looking, with tousled brown hair and blue eyes. Of course he looked adorable in his white coat over a pale blue shirt and slightly loosened Ralph Lauren tie with its scatter of polo ponies.

"It's good to see you again," he told her. His words sounded more than genuine and Suzanne blushed slightly. This was a man she wouldn't mind getting to know better.

"Great to see you," she replied. *Okay, a good and a great,* she told herself. *Now how do I phrase my particular question?*

Sam Hazelet seemed be studying her. "You feeling okay?" he asked. "Because . . . ah . . . well, I heard about what happened yesterday. With Ozzie and with you." He looked extremely concerned. "In fact, why don't we go in and do a quick blood draw? Make sure you're all right."

"I'm fine, really," Suzanne told him. "I just stopped by to ask you a quick question."

He moved a step closer and Suzanne could smell what was either aftershave or a much better grade of hand soap than the clinic used to use. Something faintly peppery.

"Yes?" he said.

Suzanne didn't hesitate. "It concerns Ozzie Driesden's murder."

"Lot of theories going around about that," said Sam. He rolled his eyes. "Thank goodness I'm not the duly appointed county coroner. Although I think I might have to take a turn at it next year."

"All those theories?" said Suzanne. "I have one, too."

"You want to go somewhere for coffee?" Sam asked. "Talk this over?"

"No," said Suzanne. "I mean, no, thanks. This isn't a good night for me." She didn't have anything going, but she needed a little think time. Besides, if she and the good doctor were going to start something, she wanted it to be done at a careful, relaxed pace, not over a hurried cup of coffee.

"Okay," said Sam. "So give me the elevator test."

"Pardon?" said Suzanne.

"We're riding from the tenth floor down to the first floor. You've got approximately twelve seconds to make your pitch."

"Oh," said Suzanne. "Okay. It occurred to me that Ozzie's murder might have been peripheral. That some meth lab guys broke in to steal drugs and Ozzie just happened to be in their way."

"Interesting," said Sam.

"So what I wanted to know from you," said Suzanne, "was if drugs that are commonly used in funeral homes for . . . you know . . . embalming purposes . . . might also be used to cook up a batch of crystal meth?"

Sam stared at her, his eyes crinkling slightly at the corners. "And you came up with this on your own?"

"I think so," said Suzanne. "Although I could have seen a similar plot on TV. Maybe *CSI: Miami*?" She thought for a few moments and then asked, "Or did Sheriff Doogie already talk to you about this?"

"Haven't seen the good sheriff lately," said Sam. He crossed his arms and seemed to regard her with curiosity. Then he launched into a quick lesson on illegal drugs.

"Meth and ecstasy are the most common drugs produced in what's commonly referred to as mom-and-pop labs," he told her. "On the street, meth is often referred to as crank, zip, or cristy. The pure smokeable form, methamphetamine hydrochloride, which is the really bad stuff, also goes by a batch of names. Ice, quartz, blizzard, glass, sparkle, and white lady."

"Wow," said Suzanne. "You really know this stuff."

"I served on a community action board once," said Sam. "During my residency. Anyway, to answer your question, yes. Embalming fluid generally contains formaldehyde, methanol, ethanol, ether, and other solvents. The basic formula depends, of course, on which manufacturer you buy your embalming fluid from. They're all slightly different."

"But not by much," said Suzanne.

"That's right," said Sam. "So a crew of crank-head, meth-lab freaks would probably jump at the chance to get their hands on any kind of embalming fluid."

"Hmm," said Suzanne.

Sam Hazelet glanced over at her car. It was the only one left in the lot. "You've got a dog."

"Baxter," said Suzanne.

"Looks like a nice enough guy."

Suzanne smiled. "I could introduce you sometime."

Sam smiled back. "Soon, I think."

CHAPTER 9

ON the way to her house on Laurel Lane, on the north side, the oldest part of Kindred, Suzanne took a slightly circuitous route and cruised past the Driesden and Draper Funeral Home. It was a big old rambling place, American Gothic with a few touches of Victorian thrown in for good measure. Set back from the street, the wooden clapboard building had been painted a somber gray with white trim. Like a modestly dressed Quaker.

On a whim, Suzanne pulled over to the curb and gazed up at the roofline with its fanciful array of turrets, finials, and balustrades. And wondered why so many funeral homes had a certain creep factor about them, always looked like a place where the Addams Family could settle in nicely.

Then, for no reason at all, except pure curiosity, Suzanne crept around the corner and crunched down the back alley that ran directly behind the funeral home. A thick, tangled line of cedars formed a sort of natural barrier on the right side of the alley. Probably helping to screen the loading and unloading of caskets. On Suzanne's left was the rear wing of the funeral home, a stone block addition that had probably been added some twenty years ago.

Just ahead, the alley widened out slightly. And as Suzanne approached the rear, covered portico, she noticed a red car, an older model Mustang coupe, parked beneath it.

As she rolled to a stop, the assistant, Bo Becker, came bounding out the back door, his arms stretched wide around a half dozen containers of white lilies and one huge bouquet of purple and gold chrysanthemums.

Hastily unrolling her window, Suzanne called, "Bo? Hello there. I'm Suzanne Dietz, the lady who found Ozzie yesterday? Could I talk to you for a second?"

Bo never bothered to look up. He dumped the flowers onto the pavement, jerked open his car door, spread out a black plastic tarp on his backseat, then began piling in containers.

"Excuse me?" Suzanne called again. How rude was this?

Bo slammed the door shut, grabbed the big pot of mums, and flipped open his trunk. Dressed in jeans and a khaki green T-shirt, he looked just as casual as he had yesterday. Except that his hair was combed back flatter and probably held in place with a gob of gel.

"Please don't be rude," said Suzanne.

Bo loaded the final pot, then glanced over at her. "You here to jump on the bandwagon, too?" he asked. "Accuse me of murdering Ozzie?" His handsome face twisted with anger, his voice dripped poison. "Because that fat old sheriff sure got it in his head that I'm involved."

"I wasn't going to accuse you of anything," said Suzanne. "I just wanted to ask you a couple of questions."

"I'm busy," snarled Bo. He stared at a smudge on his car's rear fender, then used the bottom edge of his T-shirt to wipe it away.

"That's a pretty neat car you've got," said Suzanne. "I love that candy-apple red color." Maybe she could flatter him a little. Pretend to be a motor head. Although if he said anything about rims or carburetors, she'd be outed immediately.

"This here's a ninety-four Mustang with a custom Borla exhaust," Bo announced, a smidgen of pride in his voice. "Can't nobody touch her."

"I believe it," said Suzanne. She let a few moments slide by. "I was a friend of Ozzie's, too. I'm just as upset about his death."

Bo slammed the trunk. "Tough shit."

SUZANNE gazed into her refrigerator, then grabbed a plastic container of leftover chicken chili and a carton of sour cream. While she heated her chili on the stove, she measured out a cup of kibbles into Baxter's bowl. Then she opened a can of Newman's Own Chicken and Brown Rice Formula, scooped a third of the can into a small bowl, added a small amount of water, and warmed it in the microwave. When it was a nice, smooshy gravy consistency, Suzanne poured it over Baxter's food, added a Rimadyl tablet, and set the dish on a raised metal feeding stand, a new addition in her kitchen.

"There you go, pal. Kibbles *avec poulet*."

While her chili steamed and bubbled, Suzanne pulled a piece of cornbread from the freezer and popped it into the microwave. Then she gazed around her kitchen.

It was a cook's toy store, really. Renovated three years ago so she and Walter could indulge their secret little foodie passions. They'd installed a Wolf gas range with char broiler, Sub-Zero refrigerator, and granite countertops. It was all quite gorgeous and very Food Network, but not terribly practical now that she was alone. Now it felt a little like a restaurant kitchen, superbly equipped, but a trifle impersonal, too. Maybe, once she started entertaining again, her kitchen would magically transform into a warm, welcoming space where everyone would want to congregate. On the other hand, that might depend on who she entertained.

Her chili heated, Suzanne poured it into a handmade ceramic bowl that was one of a set she'd purchased at the Darlington College Art Fair and added a dollop of sour cream. She set it on a wicker tray along with the cornbread, paper napkin, and spoon and carried the whole shebang into the living room.

As she ate and halfheartedly watched the nightly news, Suzanne's thoughts wandered back to the murder. She wondered who could carry so much anger and malice in their heart that they would kill Ozzie Driesden? Someone right here in Kindred? Someone close to Ozzie? Someone so close that Ozzie never suspected until the final moments when he was held hostage, drugged, and then had his blood drained?

Suzanne shook her head, grabbed the remote control, and switched over to *Wheel of Fortune*.

Gotta watch something a little lighter, she told herself. *Stop these dark thoughts from rattling around inside my head.*

Vanna was rah-rahing and busily turning over letters. The clue was "thing."

Suzanne stared at the letters that had been revealed on the board. Two G's, a B, a T, and an R.

"Eggbeater," she said aloud, just as contestant number three piped up with, "I'd like to solve the puzzle."

Naturally it was eggbeater.

Okay, Suzanne told herself. *If I can look at those puny clues and pull eggbeater out of the sky, why can't I dredge up a suspect or two?*

Of course, Sheriff Doogie had already taken care of that.

* * *

TWENTY minutes later, Suzanne was in her suede jacket, blue jeans, and boots, standing in a sweet-smelling hay barn, saddling her horse. With the cinch snugged tight, she led Mocha outside, grabbed a handful of slightly oily mane to help pull herself into the saddle, and then was off in a slow canter around the perimeter of the field.

The sky had faded to a smoky purple, the final glory of the day manifesting itself in a wash of thin clouds and a handful of glittering stars, like a child's game of jacks tossed out onto a dark blue blanket. From onesies all the way up to tensies.

Across the field, Suzanne could see the lights of the Cackleberry Club. The little place glowed like a beacon and Suzanne figured that book night, *romance* book night, was probably a rousing success. At least it would be once Toni trotted out the cheddar cheese biscuits and Pinot Grigio.

Suzanne worked her horse for a good forty-five minutes, practicing from going from a fast walk right into a canter. Doing a little remedial work on neck reining while they were at it. Mocha had spent his summer grazing with a herd of cows, so he was lazy, obstinate, and a little out of practice. Then again, so was she.

Suzanne walked him slowly back to the barn, letting the big horse cool down gradually. Standing in his box stall, she pulled off the saddle and blanket, wiped him down with a chamois cloth, then grabbed a curry comb. The horse's wide back quivered and his front feet stomped as she ran the metal teeth over him. He liked the sensation, but was uncertain about all her fussing. Oh well, he'd get used to it.

Dust motes twirled in the low light as Suzanne groomed

her horse. And her thoughts drifted back to Sam Hazelet. Their earlier exchange bothered her a little. She liked him, could probably *seriously* like him, but she was a little nervous now that she'd maybe sent the wrong signals. Had she been too cool? Too indifferent? Or too pushy?

What should she do? she wondered. Hang a sign over her heart that said, Open for Business? Or just bag those worries and let things take a natural course? Yeah, probably that would be best.

Suzanne hung Mocha's bridle on a peg, then poured out a couple cups of oats into his feed box. As she turned to leave, Mocha lifted his large head and stared at her with luminous brown eyes as if to say, *Leaving so soon?*

"You need a buddy, don't you?" she said. "It's probably lonely out here when nobody's around. Tell you what, I'll try to find you some kind of buddy."

AT nine o'clock when Suzanne came barreling through the front door of her home, feeling relaxed, at peace, and a little wobbly in her knees and thighs, the phone was jangling. She snatched up the receiver on what was probably the final ring before it switched over to the answering machine.

"Hello?"

"Hello . . . again. This is Sam."

"Oh . . . hi." Balancing on one foot, she tried to slide off her left cowboy boot by scraping it against the right one. Her technique wasn't working very well.

"You sound out of breath," said Sam.

"I was just . . . outside," she told him. "Goofing around."

"Listen, when we spoke earlier, I forgot to ask you something."

"Shoot," said Suzanne, staring down at the inlaid turquoise leather on her half-off boot, fully expecting Sam's question to be either murder or drug-related.

"Would you have dinner with me Friday night?"

Suzanne's grin, as she accepted, was a mile wide.

CHAPTER 10

TUESDAY was Eggs in a Basket day at the Cackleberry Club. Suzanne and Toni crowded around the butcher-block table with Petra, arranging thin slices of ham in muffin tins, then watching as she poured a thick, foamy egg mixture on top. Once each "basket" was filled and topped with a generous spoonful of shredded cheddar cheese, they were slid into a hot oven.

"Look who's queen of the rodeo this morning," exclaimed Petra as she cracked more eggs, single-handed, into an antique speckled ceramic bowl. Toni was all duded up in a new hot pink western shirt with silver embroidery and matching silver buttons. On her feet were a brand-new pair of buckskin-colored Tony Llama boots.

"Gifts from Junior," she told them, trying to sound offhanded. "He says he's been inspired to share the wealth."

"You saw Junior last night?" asked Petra, slightly aghast. She paused, eggs in hand.

"I thought you declared a moratorium on seeing Junior," said Suzanne, jumping in. "I thought you'd pretty much decided you were going for the big D."

"Di-vorce," said Petra, enunciating the word in an exaggerated manner.

Toni looked pained. "But Junior brought gifts. What was I supposed to do? Act like an ingrate?"

"You could try saying no," said Petra. She turned toward her grill, grabbed a spatula, and flipped a half dozen blue-berry pancakes.

"You could have told him not to darken your doorway," said Suzanne.

"Junior's TV was on the blink and he wanted to watch reruns of *American Gladiators*," Toni explained, a little defensively.

"I think there's more to Junior's visit than meets the eye," said Petra. "Trust me, he's after something. The new duds were just to butter you up." She glanced at her pan-cakes. "These are ready."

"You think?" Toni's face fell. "I guess I hadn't consid-ered that particular angle."

Suzanne held out two plates for Petra's pancakes. "I think you better sniff out some details on Junior's so-called delivery job," she told Toni. Then she bumped the swinging door with her hip and sailed out into the café. The place was only half full, but it was still early. Pretty soon they'd have a packed house, folks coming from all over the county to enjoy their food and, Suzanne liked to believe, the homey ambiance of the Cackleberry Club.

Suzanne delivered her plates of cakes, brought pitchers of maple, blueberry, and boysenberry syrup, poured refills of coffee and English breakfast tea, then finally looked up and drew a deep breath. And noticed Earl Stensrud, Missy's ex and now, she supposed, Missy's boyfriend for a second term, occupying the far table near the window. Earl was digging into a fluffy omelet that Toni must have delivered. Funny she hadn't mentioned Earl being here.

Sidling over to his table, carrying a pot of coffee, Su-zanne said, "Morning, Earl. How's breakfast?"

Earl grinned up at her with his narrow face, receding

hairline, and a speck of spinach caught between his front teeth. "Tasty," he told her. "Best spinach and feta cheese omelet in town."

"Well, I coulda told you that," said Suzanne. Pouring out a slow stream of coffee into his cup, she added, "I understand you moved back here to sell insurance."

Earl's head bobbed like it was spring-loaded. "For Universal Allied Home and Life. Most people are unawares, but insurance is the most important financial instrument a person can have." He paused, then gave a questioning squint. "You got enough insurance, Suzanne? Business insurance, I mean. For the Cackleberry Club?"

"We're pretty well set," she told him, hoping to avoid the inevitable sales pitch.

"I could offer a free analysis," said Earl. "You might find a need to up your coverage." He glanced around. "Place looks fairly profitable, but if something were to happen . . ." Now Earl looked serious, like he'd peered into the not-so-distant future and seen an unhappy vision looming before him.

"I'm not losing any sleep, Earl," Suzanne told him.

"Got flood insurance?" he asked. "What if there's a flood?"

Catawba Creek, a babbling little trout stream that hadn't flooded its banks even once in the last century, was at least six miles away. Suzanne told him so.

Unfazed, Earl plowed on. "Hit by lightning?"

Suzanne sighed. "I'll take my chances."

"Fire?" Earl glanced sideways out the window where workers were hoisting beams and pounding away at two-by-fours, busily rebuilding the Journey's End Church.

"Don't even breathe that word in here!" warned Suzanne. "The Journey's End Church fire was a trauma for everyone."

"Suit yourself, Suzanne," said Earl, taking a slurp of coffee.

"I always do," she replied.

"I understand Missy's got you nosing around town concerning Ozzie's murder." Now Earl gave her a hard stare.

"Maybe," said Suzanne, being a little evasive.

"She thinks you're quite the little Nancy Drew." He let loose a mirthless chuckle.

"Missy's a friend," said Suzanne. "I'd do anything to help her, especially after the rude treatment she's received from Sheriff Doogie."

Earl cocked an index finger at Suzanne. "If you're such a hotshot investigator, maybe you oughta take a look at George Draper."

"Ozzie's partner?" Suzanne's brow furrowed. "I'd say you're out of your mind."

"The thing of it is," said Earl, glancing around and lowering his voice, "I sold Driesden and Draper an insurance policy a few months ago."

"So what?" replied Suzanne. "You've probably been offering free analyses to everyone and his brother-in-law. They just happened to take the bait."

"It was key person insurance," said Earl, enunciating each word carefully.

Suzanne stared at him, wondering where Earl was going with this. "Meaning?" She tapped her foot impatiently.

"Meaning," said Earl, "that if one partner died, the other would receive a rather tidy sum of money." He paused. "Enough to buy out the other's interest and then some."

"How tidy is that sum?" asked Suzanne. "Can you give me a number?"

Now Earl looked aghast. "That would be unethical."

"But it's okay to point fingers," Suzanne chided. "To toss out innuendos about your client."

Earl threw up both hands in a gesture of frustration. "I'm just saying, Suzanne."

Back in the kitchen, Suzanne said, "Earl Stensrud is a real slimeball."

Petra ducked down and peered out through the pass-through. "He's out there?"

"Yes," said Suzanne. "And, interestingly enough, he's trying to deflect any scrutiny that might be directed at him onto George Draper. Call it the old pinball technique."

"Scrutiny on Draper for Ozzie's murder?" Petra couldn't quite believe it.

"Earl assured me that George Draper was going to benefit greatly from an insurance policy he sold to Driesden and Draper," said Suzanne.

"Huh," said Petra, pulling a tin of bubbling, golden brown Eggs in a Basket from the oven. "I didn't think anyone ever benefited. Insurance companies are tighter'n razor clams." She sprinkled on some additional shredded cheddar for good measure. "They just *hate* opening their pockets and paying out claims."

Toni came bustling in with a stack of dirty dishes. "I just caught the tail end of your conversation and you're right about insurance companies and insurance *salesmen* being tightwads. Guess how much of a tip that moron Earl left me?"

"How much?" asked Suzanne. Earl Stensrud did strike her as a parsimonious ass.

"Fifty cents!" shrilled Toni. "Can you believe it? That comes to something like . . . six percent!"

"Makes Junior look like Rockefeller," mumbled Petra.

"Doesn't it?" answered Toni.

* * *

JUST before lunch there was a run on the Book Nook. Suzanne wasn't sure if it was because of the Knit-In Thursday or Saturday's Take the Cake event, but customers were grabbing books on knitting, needlecraft, quilting, baking, and cake decorating like crazy. One book, written by two women who called themselves the Knit Wits, was a humorous take on knitting. It illustrated simple stitches and fun projects as told through their own trial and error.

Suzanne was about to run across to the café to help set up for lunch when a yellow Post-it note stuck to the back wall caught her eye. It said *CHEESE* in block letters.

Slipping into the office, Suzanne thumbed through her Rolodex and dialed the number for Cloverdale Farm.

"Mike," she said, when she finally got him on the line. "We're down to our last two wheels of cheese. Are you planning a delivery anytime soon?"

"Sure am," he told her, "but it ain't the kind you're thinking of. I got two prime Guernseys ready to calve any time now. And, wouldn't you know it, this is the week Ruth Ann picked to visit her sister in Sioux Falls."

"What if I drove over to your place?" asked Suzanne. She could hear a barnyard symphony of mooing, chewing, and clip-clopping in the background.

"That'd be fine, Suzanne," replied Mike. "I got a cooler full of cheese, so . . . you know where to find me."

"I'm guessing in the barn?" said Suzanne. But he'd already hung up.

Then, just as Suzanne was scratching a note to herself, the phone rang. She snatched it up. "Hello?"

"Suzanne? It's Missy."

"Hi, honey, how are you?" Suzanne hated to ask if Missy

had been burning the midnight oil last night. Because she was pretty sure she had been, judging by the stress and tiredness in her voice.

"Hanging in there," said Missy, sounding slightly bereft. "I was just wondering if you'd heard anything. Or done a little . . . I don't know what you'd call it . . . sleuthing?"

"Lots of rumors flying around," said Suzanne, "but nothing concrete." She sure as heck wasn't going to tell Missy that Earl, her ex-husband and beau du jour, was casting aspersion on her former beau's business partner. Suzanne shook her head. It was all very confusing. "I'll keep my ears open though," Suzanne promised.

"Well . . . okay." Missy sounded disappointed. "Are you coming to the visitation tonight?"

"Of course," said Suzanne, thinking it might shake out as a rather strange gathering.

"If you come up with anything . . ." said Missy.

"Absolutely," said Suzanne. "You'll be the first to know. Hey, maybe Sheriff Doogie will drop by and I can pump him for information."

"I think he'd sooner have his stomach pumped," Missy replied in a sour tone.

BUT Missy was wrong about that. Because Sheriff Doogie did drop by right before lunch, just as Suzanne was jotting the specials on the board. And, for some reason, Doogie seemed far less reticent in discussing Ozzie's murder.

"How goes the investigation?" Suzanne asked, as Doogie slid his khaki bulk onto a nearby stool. She continued to scratch away with her colored chalk, writing down *Corn Chowder, Egg Salad Sandwich, Turkey Fajita, Cackleberry Club Brown Sugar Meatloaf*, and *Pumpkin Pie*.

Doogie gave a low whistle. "That's a fine lineup today," he told her.

"Yes, it is," agreed Suzanne, dotting the *i* in pie. Doogie was a man who appreciated real home cooking, probably because he didn't get much anymore. He was a widower whose wife had died of breast cancer some five years ago. After her death, he'd resigned from the state patrol and run for sheriff. Opposed by a former garbage hauler, he'd been elected in a landslide. Over the years, a few women had made a run at Doogie, but none had caught his eye. Doogie remained polite but standoffish.

"Is that pie made fresh from real pumpkins?" asked Doogie. "'Cause if it is, I'll have me a piece."

"Of course, you will," said Suzanne. When did Doogie not get a free ride at the Cackleberry Club? "I was asking about the murder?" she prompted again.

Doogie sucked air in through his front teeth. "Thing's are goin' slow. I've been doin' this by the book, following procedure, conducting interviews, but . . ."

"No hot leads?" said Suzanne.

"I got dog poop," admitted Doogie. "Ozzie didn't seem to have any enemies."

"How about friends?" asked Suzanne. "Sometimes friends can become enemies. Anger, jealousy, disputes over money . . ."

"Funny thing about that, too," said Doogie. "Ozzie didn't have a lot of close friends. Maybe folks are hesitant to cozy up to an undertaker . . . I don't know."

"Maybe so," said Suzanne. Although Missy had. For a while, anyway.

Doogie leaned across the counter. "You heard anything, Suzanne?"

Her front teeth worried her bottom lip for a moment and

then she said, "Earl Stensrud was in for breakfast a little while ago, trying to stir up rumors about George Draper."

"What kind of rumors?" Doogie asked, as his hooded eyes roved across the back counter.

"Apparently Earl sold Driesden and Draper some key partner insurance and now George Draper is set to collect."

Doogie let out a sigh that sounded like a balloon deflating. "George already mentioned that to me."

"He did?" Suzanne was surprised. George Draper was either a completely forthright guy or else a master at setting up an excellent smokescreen.

"Anything else?" asked Doogie. Now he seemed fixated with the chocolate-covered doughnuts that sat plump and glistening, covered with pink and yellow sprinkles, in the pastry case. Before the sprinkles, Suzanne used to decorate with little silver balls. But when a customer busted a filling biting down on one, she switched to the more dental-friendly sprinkles.

"I have a theory," said Suzanne. "That I'd like you to hear."

When Doogie scrunched up his face in disapproval, Suzanne pulled a doughnut from the case, set it on a small plate, and shoved it across the counter toward Doogie. That seemed to soften him up.

"Okay, what's your theory?" asked Doogie, grabbing the doughnut and taking an enormous bite.

Doogie, the doughnut whisperer, Suzanne thought to herself. Then she shook her head to clear it and proceeded to lay out her meth lab theory. Basically postulating that crazy, whacked-out crackheads had swarmed out of the hills, on the hunt for supplies.

"Already thought of that," Doogie told her as he brushed

away some of the sprinkles that had cascaded haphazardly down the front of his shirt. "Or, I should say, George Draper mentioned it. He said it's not uncommon for meth lab freaks to break into funeral homes and veterinarians' offices, looking for chemicals to brew up their poison."

"So drugs were missing," said Suzanne.

Doogie nodded slowly. "Appears so."

"You think there's any merit to the meth lab idea? Are you going to look into it?"

Doogie turned a flat-eyed stare on her. "You mean am I going to cruise Logan County, rousting folks from every cottage, cabin, farmhouse, and outhouse?"

"Put out an APB?" Suzanne asked, weakly.

"Nope," said Doogie. "Although that's what most people think I should do if I want to win reelection."

"By most folks you mean Mayor Mobley and his toadies?"

"You got that right," said Doogie. Then his nose twitched spasmodically and his head swiveled as though set on ball bearings as he watched Toni slide past them, carrying two steaming platters of Cackleberry Club Meatloaf. "Now *that's* what I really need," exclaimed Doogie, "to perk up a shitty day."

CHAPTER 11

THE Silver Leaf Tea Club was an afternoon tea club you had to be over fifty to belong to. The tea club had been Petra's brainstorm and had proved to be more popular than reruns of *Friends*. Always held the first Tuesday of the month, the Silver Leaf Tea Club attracted a huge following of wonderful, older women. To top it off, they were funny, gregarious, and always dressed to the nines.

Besides attending church or going out to dinner at Kopell's over in Cornucopia, there weren't a lot of places around Kindred that gave a lady an opportunity to get all dolled up. But when they flocked to the Cackleberry Club for tea, the women of Kindred and the surrounding small towns pushed fashion to the max.

One contingent of women always seemed to opt for the classic British look. Tweedy skirts and jackets, cream-colored blouses with pussycat bows, sensible shoes, tams and berets perched rakishly on well-coifed heads. Your basic Miss Marple wannabes.

Another contingent went for the sophisticated Brooke Astor socialite look. Tailored suits, sheath dresses, strings of opera pearls, vintage crystal pins on their lapels, fifties-style felt hats, and antique mink stoles draped around their shoulders, the pelts clamped nose to tail with tiny mink paws dangling.

Suzanne and Toni had worked feverishly to transform the Cackleberry Club into a proper tearoom. White linen tablecloths were draped over battered wooden tables. Small candles flickered enticingly in glass teapot warmers. Sugar cubes were piled in silver bowls with matching tongs alongside. Place settings included hand-embroidered placemats, elegant Haviland china with plates and matching teacups in the Annette pattern, and polished flatware. In addition, pink tapers and crystal vases filled with pink tea roses adorned each table.

"What do you think?" asked Toni, lighting the final candle and stepping back to assess their artistry.

"Very posh," said Suzanne.

"That's the exact word I was thinking of," said Toni with a grin.

At ten to two, the Silver Leaf Tea Club ladies bunched excitedly outside the door. At two o'clock promptly, they entered the Cackleberry Club, oohing and aahing at the table settings that seemed so elegant and magical.

Then Suzanne and Toni were off and running yet again, taking orders for pots of tea. Today's offerings included Formosan oolong, Assam, Chinese Hao Ya black tea, and Egyptian chamomile. Of course, once a table had finished their pot of tea, they were free to select another variety.

As Toni raced out with pots of tea, Suzanne worked beside Petra in the kitchen. They were serving all the food at once today, using three-tiered curate stands. This not only made serving a breeze, but the three-tiered silver stands were show-stoppers when laden with goodies.

Scones graced the top tier, of course, which today consisted of Petra's special cinnamon date scones served with mounds of Devonshire cream. The middle tier, traditionally used for savories and tea sandwiches, was filled with crab salad sandwiches, goat cheese and cucumber sandwiches, and cheese and honey bruschetta. Strawberries dipped in chocolate, almond bars, and small squares of lemon cake lined the bottom tier.

Suzanne was finalizing the arrangement of the strawberries and almond bars when Toni came flying into the kitchen. "Everything ready?" she chirped. "Our dear ladies are sipping away and making polite inquiries regarding food." She glanced at the trays laden with food. "Oh, wow, don't those look special."

Petra gave an elfish grin as she added a few edible flowers to the arrangements. "And pretty, too."

"You're so right," exclaimed Toni. "Our guests are gonna jump out of their skins when they get a load of all this gorgeous food!"

"Shall we carry out the trays, ladies?" asked Suzanne. "And make our presentation?" With great care, each partner picked up two of the food-laden trays, then carefully eased through the doorway and into the café. And their guests did not jump out of their skins at all, but instead gave their hostesses an enthusiastic and well-deserved round of applause.

Halfway through the tea, Suzanne introduced herself (though they all knew who she was) and did a lighthearted presentation on tea etiquette.

First up was a quick lesson on scones.

"The proper way to eat a scone," Suzanne explained, "is to split it in half horizontally with your knife. Then spread a little butter on the scone's crumbly side, and top it with jam."

"What about adding Devonshire cream?" asked a lady in a plum-colored suit.

"Put a judicious dollop right on top of your jam," said

Suzanne. "Enough for a bite, then use your small spoon to keep adding more dollops if you want."

"What about lemon in tea?" asked a woman in tweeds.

"Personal preference," said Suzanne. "But the accepted method is to put a thin, almost translucent slice of lemon in your teacup, then add your tea." There was a soft murmur, then Suzanne added, "but never add lemon *and* milk to your tea. The citric acid in the lemon will surely make your milk curdle."

A woman way in back raised a hand tentatively.

"Yes?" said Suzanne.

"How long do you boil your water for tea?"

"Ah," said Suzanne. "You really don't. The trick is to pull your kettle off the stove just as it *begins* to boil."

"Interesting," said another woman. "Then how long should you allow your tea to steep?"

"The rule of thumb," said Suzanne, "is two to five minutes for green tea, four to seven minutes for black tea. But, of course, timing is always dependant on personal taste. And the variety of tea."

The woman in the plum suit raised her hand again. "How did you learn all this?"

Suzanne gave a slightly embarrassed shrug. "Trial and error. And some really good books."

WHILE Petra poured refills and chatted with friends on the café floor, Suzanne and Toni gobbled up the leftover tea sandwiches that had been sliced crookedly or, for some reason, weren't up to Petra's exacting standards.

"They still taste good," mumbled Toni.

"And this cucumber and goat cheese is to die for," said Suzanne. "Even if it's not everyone's taste."

"Cheese," said Toni. "I wanted to tell you, we're down to our last wheel of cheddar. I hope you were able to get Mike Mullen on the horn."

"I did and he says he's busier than a one-armed paperhanger," Suzanne told her. "So I'm gonna have to rattle on out there myself."

"I got an idea," said Toni. "Are you still going to Ozzie's visitation tonight?"

Suzanne nodded. "Sure. Though I can't honestly say I'm looking forward to it."

"What if I picked you up," said Toni, "and then, afterward, we drove out to Cloverdale Farm together?"

"Sounds like a plan," said Suzanne. "Is Petra coming, too?"

"No," said Toni, licking her fingers. "She's going to visit Donny. But she'll be at Ozzie's funeral tomorrow."

Petra came flying through the swinging door. "My ears are burning. Someone's been talking about me."

"Are you psychic?" asked Toni.

"No, just psychotic," Petra said with a laugh. "Suzanne, there are ladies drifting toward the Book Nook. You want to do the honors?"

As a lucky strike extra for the Cackleberry Club, book sales were suddenly as brisk as the tea. And Suzanne found herself riffling through cardboard boxes in her office, pulling out extra copies of books that prominently featured tea and baking.

"Remember me?" asked a short, pleasant-faced woman who hoisted a stack of books onto the counter.

Suzanne gazed at her, then snapped her fingers. "You live out Highway 22. The Miss Marple fan. Or, I should say, Agatha Christie fan."

"Lolly Herron," said the woman, offering her hand to

Suzanne. "I'm so glad I finally got it together and came to one of your marvelous teas. What great fun. And marvelous food!" She patted her tummy and rolled her eyes.

"Please do come again," Suzanne urged her, as she rang up the books, then gave her a ten percent discount.

"I will," Lolly promised.

"And don't forget," Suzanne told another group of ladies, "Tomorrow our own Carmen Copeland will be right here signing her newest book, *Ramona's Rhapsody*."

"We'll be back," promised Minerva Bishop, a tiny little octogenarian whom everyone simply addressed as Mrs. Min.

Once the ladies of the Silver Leaf Tea Club had taken their leave, once Joey Ewald, their slacker busboy, came in to clear tables and load up the dishwasher, Suzanne ducked into her office to make a few calls. She had a to-do list that was a mile long and most of it had to do with their Take the Cake Show.

Suzanne checked in with Sharon Roper at SugarBakers in Jessup to make sure she was still willing to serve as one of the judges for the cake-decorating contest, then called Claudia Dean over at Darlington College to make sure she was still on for the fondant and frosting demos.

Jotting notes, double-checking, and going over her final plans, Suzanne felt fairly confident they'd be able to pull off the event.

What she didn't feel confident about was helping Missy. She'd noodled the various suspects around in her mind—Earl Stensrud, Bo Becker, George Draper, and even Missy herself—and nothing seemed to add up. No one seemed to have held that much of a grudge against Ozzie Driesden.

Of course, you never knew what anger or despair a person could hold and hide, deep within their heart. But a significant piece of the puzzle still seemed to be missing. Even Sheriff Doogie had pretty much said the same thing, in his own inimitable shit-kicking way.

Wandering back into the kitchen, Suzanne was suddenly struck by a weird sensation. A memory thing—synapse or flashback—that felt very unsettling, though she couldn't quite put her finger on it.

"Honey, what's wrong?" asked Petra. "You look like you just saw a ghost!"

"It's . . . nothing," said Suzanne, trying to figure out what had made her so jumpy. But the memory or sensation or whatever it was, wouldn't dredge up. "You know how you sometimes get a weird déjà vu thing going in your head? You think you saw or heard or smelled something familiar, something kind of unsettling, but you can't quite figure it out?"

Petra continued frosting her almond cake, a special order for tonight's PTA meeting. "Uh-huh. I guess."

"That's what I . . . oh, never mind," said Suzanne. "It's probably just some crazy synapse thing."

"Or hormones," said Petra.

WHEN Suzanne jogged down her sidewalk that evening and climbed into the passenger seat of Toni's car, the first thing she said was, "You got a new car." Toni generally drove an old navy blue Honda, infamous for belching black clouds of oil until Junior hauled it into the garage and installed a new exhaust system. This car was a Ford Custom 500. Not so new, but not so dotted with rust, either.

"Naw," said Toni, "this is Junior's car. He wanted mine for his deliveries, so he traded with me. I guess my Honda has newer tires or something."

"But this one's got a bigger engine," said Suzanne, fastening her seat belt, as Toni rumbled away from the curb.

"It *does* have that touch of muscle car," said Toni, sounding pleased.

"And a CB radio." Suzanne pointed at a box with dials and a backlit digital tuner display that had been haphazardly bolted to the dashboard.

"Police scanner," corrected Toni.

Suzanne frowned. "Seriously?"

"Monitors police, fire, and EMS channels," said Toni.

"You're telling me that Junior monitors *police* channels?" said Suzanne. This seemed like a red flag to her. Another indication that Junior could be up to no good.

Toni spun into a left turn so fast, Suzanne had to clutch the dashboard to steady herself.

"You say stuff like that," said Toni, "you make me nervous."

"You know," said Suzanne, "I think you might have good reason to be nervous."

CHAPTER 12

To see Ozzie laid out in his own funeral home was bizarre beyond belief. For years he'd been the sober meeter and greeter for most of Kindred's deaths and burial services. Now, here he was, lying in a gunmetal gray casket, wearing his black three-piece funeral director's suit.

Or at least Suzanne hoped it was his funeral director's suit and not one of those awful, cheesy suits that were slit up the back.

"Creepy, isn't it?" murmured Toni, standing at Suzanne's elbow and peering at Ozzie.

"It's like watching a bad movie," said Suzanne. "Only this is really happening." She took a step backward, took in the arrangements of peace lilies, listened as Amy Grant's "Say Once More" played discreetly from the hidden sound system in this, the larger of the two visitation parlors. And wondered who had made all these decisions? Who had selected the casket, the flowers, the music? Ozzie's brother, she supposed. Although glancing around at the crowd, which was already quite sizeable, Suzanne didn't see anyone that particularly resembled an Ozzie-type relative.

"This is totally freaking me out," whispered Toni. "Maybe we should go out into the lobby and sign the guest book or something. Besides, it's freezing in here."

Shivering, Suzanne nodded. "Good idea. Sign the guest

book, take a good hard look at the guests. Because . . . well, you never know." They grabbed each other and scurried out into the entry hall.

"Sad, isn't it?" said a tall, white-haired man as Suzanne finished writing her name. "Ozzie was such a wonderful man."

Suzanne set the pen down and favored the white-haired man with a sympathetic smile. Then did a sort of double take. "Oh," she said, "you're . . ." She couldn't quite dredge up his name.

"Ted Foxworthy," said the man. "I used to own the funeral home over in Jessup. Foxworthy and Sons."

"Used to?" Suzanne asked. "Did you retire? Are your sons running the place now?" She'd been there a year or so ago for a visitation and funeral.

Foxworthy glanced at his feet for a moment, then said, "No, nothing like that."

"Business couldn't have been *that* bad," offered Toni.

Foxworthy gave a rueful smile. "The whole funeral industry has changed," he told them.

"In a bad way?" asked Suzanne. She figured now that the baby boomers were aging, business would be booming, so to speak.

"Changed in a big way," said Foxworthy. "Now the big conglomerates are taking over and running things."

"Isn't that always the case?" sighed Toni.

"So what exactly happened?" asked Suzanne, curious now.

"I did what most independents are doing today," said Foxworthy. "I sold out."

"To what company?" asked Suzanne.

"Roth Funeral Home Consortium," Foxworthy told her.

"The funeral home over in Cornucopia has been sold to them, too." He sighed. "I guess it's the way of the future."

Something didn't sound right to Suzanne. "Sounds like you didn't want to sell," she said to him.

Foxworthy kept a stoic look on his face.

"Did this Roth Consortium pressure you?" asked Suzanne.

Now Foxworthy scrunched up his face. "Not direct pressure. In fact, they were always extremely polite and businesslike with their propositions. But after we declined their offer a few times, our suppliers started demanding payment up front and a lot of the medical sales reps seemed less anxious to call on us."

"So there *was* pressure," said Suzanne.

"I suppose you could call it that," said Foxworthy, picking up a black pen and turning to sign the guest book. "Just nothing . . . illegal."

"But you made money," said Toni, trying to find some solace in the situation.

"Oh yes," said Foxworthy, but he didn't look happy.

As Suzanne stepped aside, she noticed a small camera hung overhead. It seemed to be focused directly on the front door. Probably installed up there so whoever was working in back could keep a watchful eye on whoever came in. Or at least that was the probable intent. Suzanne wondered if Doogie had checked out this camera and vowed to mention it to him.

"Oh no," Toni hissed. "Missy's here."

Suzanne turned toward the front door and saw that Missy, accompanied by Earl Stensrud, had just entered the funeral home. Dressed in a somber black suit, Missy looked tired, drawn, and sad. Earl just looked bored.

When Missy saw Suzanne and Toni huddled together, she sped over to greet them. "Thanks for coming," she said in a breathless voice, administering hugs and air kisses to each of them.

"How are you doing, honey?" asked Toni.

"Okay," said Missy, trying to keep a game face.

"A tremendously big turnout," said Suzanne.

"Probably tomorrow, for the funeral," said Missy, "the place will be even more jam-packed."

Interesting, thought Suzanne. Hadn't Doogie mentioned that Ozzie didn't seem to have a lot of friends? So this big turnout signified . . . what? Professional interest? Or just a macabre fascination with Ozzie's death? Probably so, since word had traveled like wildfire, just as Doogie had predicted, that Ozzie had, indeed, been murdered.

Missy put a hand on Suzanne's forearm. "I have a favor to ask of you," she said.

"Of course," said Suzanne. "Anything."

"I was wondering," said Missy, "if you'd be one of the models in our informal fashion show this Friday?"

"Oh no, I couldn't," said Suzanne.

"You just said you'd do anything," Toni pointed out, giving Suzanne a sharp poke in the ribs.

"Anything . . . um . . . reasonable," said Suzanne, feeling a little embarrassed.

"You'd be a wonderful model," said Missy. "You're . . . what? About a size ten?"

Suzanne nodded. "About." *On a good day. If I've sworn off carbs for two entire months.*

"And still great-looking for your age," said Missy.

"Thank you," said Suzanne. "I think."

"You should do it!" urged Toni. "You'd be great!"

"Plus you're well-liked around town as a business-woman," added Missy. "Which would certainly lend credibility to the new boutique."

"Suzanne's got street cred," chirped Toni.

After a few more encouraging words from both Toni and Missy, Suzanne finally relented. After all, Missy just looked so sad.

WHEN Suzanne finally spotted Sheriff Doogie's Smokey Bear hat bobbling above the crowd, she sidled back into the parlor to talk to him.

"Suzanne," he said, staring at her with eyes that were red-rimmed and tired, as though he'd stayed up late for too many nights.

"There's a camera out in the foyer," she told him. "I was wondering if you looked at the tape?"

"Yup," Doogie told her. "Nothing."

"So the killer came in the back door?" asked Suzanne, hypothesizing. "Maybe had a key?"

"Or Ozzie knew him and let him in," said Doogie.

"Knew him," said Suzanne, mulling over the idea. "If Ozzie knew him, that could be significant."

"Sheriff!" called a loud, aggressive voice.

Suzanne and Sheriff Doogie both turned at once. Saw Mayor Mobley signaling with one chubby hand in the air.

"A moment of your time?" called Mobley. It was more of a command than a question.

"I'll get back to you," said Doogie, turning away from Suzanne. "Soon's I talk to the grand poo-bah shithead over there."

And still the surprises kept coming.

"Suzanne!" called Carmen Copeland. "I was hoping to see you here tonight. She sped across the floor, elbowing people out of her way.

"Hello Carmen," said Suzanne, not exactly thrilled to be cornered by the obnoxious author.

"Hey, Carmen, what's up?" asked Toni as she joined them.

Carmen ignored Toni completely and instead launched into a litany of requests concerning tomorrow's book signing.

"I don't know how well my publicist briefed you," said Carmen, "but I'm going to need a comfortable swivel chair with a seat height of at least thirty-eight inches. I will also require bottled water—still, not effervescent—classical music playing in the background, and an assistant to open books to the correct front page."

Suzanne just stared at Carmen, while Toni giggled.

"Oh," said Carmen. "And I must have my back against a wall."

"Excuse me?" said Suzanne. Had she heard Carmen correctly?

"I detest people moving around behind me," said Carmen. "Makes me uneasy. Gives me the creeps, in fact."

"Carmen," said Suzanne, fighting now to keep a straight face, "I'd be delighted to back you into a corner."

"Good evening, ladies." They all three turned to find Dr. Sam Hazelet smiling at them.

"Sam," said Suzanne. "You know Toni. And this is Carmen Copeland."

Carmen thrust a gloved hand at Sam. "Delighted to meet you. These are sad circumstances, of course, but the pleasure is all mine." She batted her eyes at him and Suzanne wondered about the feasibility of simply reaching out and pulling off Carmen's false eyelashes. Too radical? Or not rad enough?

"I've just come from the most wonderful art dealer over in Cornucopia," Carmen said, moving in on Sam Hazelet. "He has a tiny little gallery, but access to the most amazing outsider artists." She paused. "That's what I'm collecting now. Outsider art."

No, thought Suzanne, *you're trying to collect compliments. And my date for Friday night.*

"I understand that type of art is a hot commodity right now," Sam Hazelet replied, his eyes dancing with mirth.

"But so much more speculative than the modern art being done in New York right now or some of the very contemporary British artists," said Carmen.

Sam stole a glance at Suzanne, smiled, then said, "I've got to speak with George Draper. If you'll excuse me . . ."

"Isn't he a cutie?" said Carmen, narrowing her eyes at the retreating Dr. Hazelet. "And divorced, I understand."

Suzanne edged away from Toni and Carmen. She really didn't need to hear Carmen's fawning remarks.

Carmen finally acknowledged Toni's presence with a knowing smile and said, "I wouldn't mind getting to know *him* better. Do you know any juicy tidbits about him? Or, better yet, do you think you could hook us up?"

Toni raised her eyebrows and pretended to look shocked. "*Excuse* me, do I look like Heidi Fleiss?"

SUZANNE caught up with Sheriff Roy Doogie just as he was storming out of the funeral home. "Sheriff," she called. "A word?"

Doogie didn't look happy, but stopped anyway to let Suzanne catch up to him.

"Trouble with the mayor?" she asked.

Doogie rubbed the back of his hand against his stubbly chin. "He's just putting pressure on me. Thinks I oughta be working harder to solve Ozzie's murder."

"Seems to me you're doing the best you can," said Suzanne. "It's only been, like, two days."

"These days, everyone wants instant gratification," sighed Doogie. "I got all my people workin' this case, but . . ." He spread his hands in a gesture of exasperation. "There's just so much we can do."

"Maybe you should call in the BCA," suggested Suzanne. The Bureau of Criminal Apprehension helped solve crimes state-wide.

"I'd rather give it another couple of days," said Doogie. He wasn't a man who readily asked for help.

"So your prime suspects are still Missy, Earl, and George Draper?" asked Suzanne.

Doogie pulled a piece of Juicy Fruit gum from his pocket, unwrapped it slowly, and folded it into his mouth. Suzanne didn't know if Doogie was upset by her question or stalling for time.

"They're on the list," Doogie said, finally. "As well as a homeless guy who's been spotted around town."

Suzanne thought back to that Sunday afternoon at Kindred Spirit Days. Hadn't Petra taken pity on some homeless guy and slipped him some cupcakes? Sure she had. Should she mention that to Doogie? Hmm. Maybe wait and see.

Doogie rattled on, unaware that Suzanne had actually seen his so-called homeless guy suspect. "Word is, he might be living in a cave. Probably one on the far side of the bluff. Me and Deputy Driscoll took a trip over there and crawled around some, but we didn't see signs of anybody living there."

Suzanne knew exactly what caves Doogie was referring to. She'd climbed around them and played inside them the whole time she was growing up here. In fact, that far hillside was fairly honeycombed with caves. Lots of secret little places for a guy to hide. But why on earth would some drifter or homeless guy have killed Ozzie? What possible motive could he have had?

"So you've also put this homeless person on your list," said Suzanne. "Four suspects now."

"Five," said Doogie.

"What?" said Suzanne. Who else had fallen under Doogie's shrewd gaze?

Doogie cocked an eye at her. "Bo Becker."

"Ozzie's assistant?"

"Former assistant," said Doogie, "since he's now officially missing."

"That's interesting," said Suzanne. "Considering I just saw Bo Becker last night."

Doogie registered surprise. "What?" he stuttered. "You did? Where?"

"Why . . . right outside here," Suzanne told him. "In the back alley. Becker was loading a big batch of flowers into his car."

"I wish you would have collared him," said Doogie, "'cause I can't find him anywhere."

"You think Becker skipped town?"

"I told him not to. But it sure looks like he might have hightailed it out of here."

"With a load of funeral flowers in his car?" said Suzanne. "Doesn't make a whole lot of sense."

"Nothin' makes sense," mumbled Doogie.

"Did you ask George Draper about the flowers?" asked Suzanne.

"Ayup," said Doogie. "Becker was supposed to take 'em up to Memorial Cemetery, but he never made it. Probably just dumped 'em somewhere."

"You checked all over town for Becker?"

"Not *all* over, but Becker's not at his apartment. Landlady says she hasn't seen him since early Monday."

"Seen who?" asked Toni, joining the twosome.

"Sheriff Doogie says Bo Becker skipped town," said Suzanne.

Toni let loose a low whistle. "That doesn't bode well."

Doogie nodded. "I already put out an APB for him."

Becker still didn't seem right to Suzanne and she said so: "But if Bo Becker killed Ozzie, what was his motivation? Seems to me Ozzie had been nothing but kind to him. Giving him a job when other folks wouldn't." She pondered the situation. If Becker had left town, what was he running from? Ozzie's murder or something else entirely? And with that distinctive red Mustang, you'd think he would have been spotted by now.

But Doogie seemed to have his mind made up. "He's the one," said Doogie, "I'm sure of it."

"So the case is closed," said Toni.

Doogie looked grim. "It will be once I find him."

CHAPTER 13

"Do you think Carmen Copeland's as fancy as she looks?" asked Toni. They were speeding along a dark county road, twisting through the hilly countryside, headed for Cloverdale Farm. Hot on their cheese run.

"I've been to Carmen's house over in Jessup a couple of times now and it's really something," said Suzanne. "Big palatial place decorated to the nines."

"So a mansion," said Toni.

"You could say that," allowed Suzanne. She was well aware that Toni worked her butt off and could only afford a one-bedroom apartment.

"What if Carmen really drinks wine from a box and eats Spam burgers?" asked Toni, giving a nasty giggle.

"Nothing would surprise me with that woman," said Suzanne. She gazed out the side window, saw trunks of trees and lights from farmhouses flicker by. "So pretty out here," she murmured.

"Better without lights," said Toni. Without warning, she flipped off her headlights. And, suddenly, they were hurtling through the darkness at sixty miles an hour!

"What are you doing?" Suzanne demanded, frightened out of her wits.

"It's like flying, isn't it?" said Toni, focusing intently on the straightaway ahead. "Like we're in some kind of rocket ship, piercing a black membrane."

"You're crazy, you know that?" replied Suzanne. Her eyes had adjusted to the darkness and now she was nervously but secretly enjoying this strange adventure. A stand of pine trees and a small pond slipped by, blue and black, like wispy images from an art film.

"Oh yeah," said Toni, happily. "I know I'm a little loco."

"Good thing you've got excellent night vision," said Suzanne.

Toni nodded as she flipped her headlights back on.

"Thank you," said Suzanne, her respiration and heartbeat slowly returning to normal.

"Oh, we coulda gone a lot farther," said Toni, "but we passed the marker for Deer County a little while back, so I think Mike's place is coming up."

"And there it is," said Suzanne. A sign advertising Cloverdale Farm—Farm Fresh Milk and Cheese flashed by, then Toni swerved into the driveway and bumped down the dusty drive that led to the farmhouse and barns.

Mike Mullen watched them arrive, silhouetted in the yellow light of a doorway. Tall and beefy, he was dressed in striped denim overalls and green rubber boots.

"How are the deliveries going?" asked Suzanne, peering past him into the dairy barn.

"A huge success," grinned Mike. "Two new calves."

"Can we see 'em?" asked Toni, ever the animal lover.

"Sure," said Mike, beckoning for them to follow. They trod down a narrow cement walkway between two rows of stanchions where dairy cows contentedly munched organic alfalfa. At the end of the barn was a row of box stalls. "In there," said Mike.

Suzanne and Toni peered through wooden slats into a dimly lit stall. A lovely brown Guernsey lay placidly with her hours-old calf nestled beside her.

"Ain't she a beauty?" asked Mike. He was acting like a proud papa.

"Adorable," purred Toni. "You said there's two?"

"Over here," said Mike, leading them to the next box stall. "This one was born just an hour ago."

"Oh my gosh," exclaimed Suzanne, gazing at the calf that was all legs and enormous, soft doe eyes. "What a beautiful baby."

WITH wheels of Gouda, cheddar, and Swiss cheese packed in cardboard boxes on their backseat, Suzanne and Toni headed back toward Kindred.

"Do you know Earl is in the million-dollar club?" asked Toni.

"You mean Missy's Earl?" said Suzanne.

Toni nodded. "She told me he's already sold a million dollars' worth of insurance."

"The thing is," said Suzanne, "if an average life insurance policy is, say, a hundred thousand dollars, then you really only need ten sales to hit that number."

"When you put it that way, the number's not so impressive," said Toni. "I guess a million dollars isn't what it used to be."

"Only if you have it, cash money, in the bank," replied Suzanne.

Toni reached over and flipped a dial on the scanner. "For a lark," she said. "Let's just listen in."

"Sure," said Suzanne, gazing out the window, pressing her forehead against the cool of the glass.

"Hmm," sniffed Toni. "Nothing but static." She batted at the dial, trying to give it another twirl.

"Want me to do that?" Between Toni's so-called flying and her fussing with the scanner dial, she wasn't exactly the most conscientious driver on the road.

"Have at it," replied Toni.

Suzanne bent forward and slowly turned the dial. It blipped and bleeped and a few crackly voices faded in and out. "Not much," she said.

"Keep trying," said Toni. "If you get, like, the highway patrol or something, it's really cool. They're always ten-fouring or ten-twentying about something."

Suzanne worked the dial some more, picking up some hollow-sounding chatter, but nothing all that discernible or even particularly interesting. "No luck," she told Toni.

"Wait," said Toni, "you just went by something."

Suzanne turned it back and the tuner burped a few words that sounded like "dispatch ambulance."

"Hear that?" said Toni. "I think you got the EMT guys. Maybe a car accident somewhere."

"Now it's faded," said Suzanne frowning. "I don't think it's the best . . ." she began, then hesitated as the scanner suddenly let loose a high-pitched beep and a man's voice, crackly but understandable, uttered the words "red Mustang."

"Say what?" said Toni, perking up.

Suzanne's nimble fingers were already working the tuner, trying to pull in a stronger signal.

". . . reported on County Road 47," came the gruff voice again. "Eastbound."

Toni cocked her head. "Sounds like that old coot, Sheriff Burney." Sheriff Bill Burney was the sheriff in Deer County.

". . . possible ten-twenty-nine," came Burney's voice again.

"What's he babbling about?" asked Toni.

"He said red Mustang, didn't he?" asked Suzanne, a little excited now. "I think that's what he said."

"And County Road 47," added Toni. She cast a sideways glance at Suzanne. "What?"

"I think he might have been putting out a call on Bo Becker's car," said Suzanne.

"I thought you told me Becker skipped town," said Toni.

"He did," said Suzanne. "Does this look like town?"

"Noooo," said Toni, slowing her car slightly. "In fact, if we backtracked a mile and cut over that twisty old sawmill road, we'd intersect with 47."

"I'm not sure I've ever been out that way," said Suzanne.

"That's 'cause it's like . . . the back end of the county."

"I'm sure all the local residents would be thrilled to hear you talk that way."

"Are you kidding? Hardly anybody lives out that way," said Toni. "There's just an abandoned church that's half falling down."

"Huh," said Suzanne, thinking.

"You want to check it out?" Toni asked. "Because we could . . . like . . . be over there in ten minutes."

"No way," said Suzanne. "We should stay out of this."

"Yeah," said Toni, speeding up again. "You're probably right."

"On the other hand," said Suzanne, "I did kind of promise Missy . . ."

"You sure did," said Toni, whipping her car into a quick u-turn before Suzanne could finish her sentence.

"But we gotta be careful," cautioned Suzanne. "If Bo Becker's driving around out here or, for some reason, parked his car out this way, we gotta make sure law enforcement moves in first. Then maybe we can cruise in, real casual like."

"How are we going to explain our showing up?" asked Toni.

"If anybody asks, we'll tell 'em the truth," said Suzanne. "That we were out this way and heard the broadcast on Junior's police scanner."

"Scanners aren't illegal, are they?" asked Toni.

"Not that I know of," said Suzanne. "I think you can pick one up at any Radio Shack."

"Okay then, that's our plan," said Toni, putting the pedal to the metal and barreling down the road full-bore. They found the turnoff for the sawmill road and turned onto it, a narrow blacktop road filled with twists and turns and dipsy-doodles.

"This is like a roller coaster," said Suzanne.

"But kind of fun," added Toni.

Suzanne peered out at scraggly pines and what looked like soggy fields and wetlands. "You're right, not a lot of homes out this way."

"Bad farmland, I guess," said Toni. She came up a narrow draw, then hit the brakes when her headlights caught the marker for County Road 47.

"Now what?" asked Suzanne, as Toni's car rumbled beneath them. "We went through so many twists and turns it's hard to tell which way's east."

"Hang on a minute," said Toni, "while I consult my onboard navigation system."

"Wow," said Suzanne, impressed, "where did you pick up one of those gizmos?"

Toni reached down into a pile of empty Lay's Potato Chips bags and Zagnut wrappers, and pulled out a tattered map.

"At the Sunoco station," said Toni with a laugh. She turned on the overhead light, wrinkled her brow as she studied the map, then said, "left."

THEY drove for the next three miles and didn't see a dog-gone thing. One desultory-looking farmhouse with a dim yard light, but nothing else. No red Mustang, no Bo Becker hunkered down with an accomplice, nothing.

"Disapointing," muttered Toni.

Suzanne leaned forward, concentrating on the road. "I think that might be the turnoff for that old church you mentioned. Just up ahead." There was a broken wooden cross on a hill of weeds.

"Take a look," said Toni, pumping the brakes and cranking the steering wheel. And then they were creeping down a road where patches of dead yellow grass far outnumbered the hunks of broken blacktop.

"What's that up ahead?" asked Suzanne. It was swampy out here and a faint ground mist permeated the atmosphere, making everything slightly dreamlike and out-of-focus.

"The old church," said Toni. "Guess when everybody moved to town the parishioners just let it go to rack and ruin. Or else they all died off." She crept ahead slowly, then rolled to a stop in the patchy weeds that flourished directly in front of the church. "Nobody here," she said. "Not even the sheriff or highway patrol." She sounded even more disappointed.

"Must have missed him," said Suzanne.

"Just a wild-goose chase," agreed Toni. "Well, it would

have been interesting." They sat in the dark for a few moments, each lost in her own thoughts. Finally Toni turned her gaze on Suzanne. "Maybe we should take a quick look-see?"

"You think?" said Suzanne.

In answer, Toni leaned over and popped open the glove box, pulled out a flashlight.

"Flashlight," said Suzanne. "Good."

"Ah," said Toni, grinning, "this isn't just an ordinary, garden-variety flashlight. It's a combination flashlight and stun gun."

"You're not serious," said Suzanne.

"Sure. Junior got it for me. He's nuts for any kind of crazy gadget."

"You know," said Suzanne, "maybe Junior really is delivering auto parts, after all. Except you better watch out which end of that thing you turn on."

"You got that right," Toni said with a laugh, as they both climbed from the car.

"We probably shouldn't be doing this," said Suzanne, glancing about nervously.

Toni nodded. "I know." She buttoned her jean jacket, turned on her flashlight, and bounced the beam around. The thin stream of light cut through the night. Toni shuddered. "Cold."

"And spooky," added Suzanne. For some reason, most of the nearby trees appeared half dead. Maybe they'd drowned from encroaching swamp water, or maybe they'd just succumbed to Dutch elm disease or some other tree malady. It also didn't help that a sharp wind had sprung up. Sweeping through bare, dead branches, it made them click and clack like rattling bones.

"Lookit the church," Toni pointed out. "Completely falling apart." They moved toward the dilapidated structure, saw that years of hard weather had stripped every speck of paint from the wood, giving the old building a sodden gray color.

"Roof's caved in, too," added Suzanne, noting that the few curved beams that had once formed the roof now looked decidedly like ribs. "Sad that an old church ends up abandoned and broken down like this."

"There's nothing going on here," said Toni. "If Bo Becker was seen out this way, this sure wasn't one of his stops."

"Maybe . . . check in back?" asked Suzanne.

They stumbled around the side of the church through the weeds, but there was nothing out back but an old cemetery.

"Now this is certifiably creepy," said Suzanne as they stepped tentatively between a row of gravestones.

"These graves are really old," said Toni, flashing her light on a row of stone tablets pitted with age. Canted in all different directions, they looked like broken teeth. "This one dates to the eighteen hundreds."

"I wonder if the descendants still come out here?" mused Suzanne. "To . . . you know . . . visit the graves?"

"Doubtful," said Toni. "This whole place looks abandoned. No perpetual care here. Or sign of any relative who's come to visit."

"The grass hasn't even been mowed," said Suzanne. "Kind of sad, really."

Toni flashed her light around again. "Nada," she said. "Time to go?"

"Wait a minute," said Suzanne. Either her eyes were playing tricks on her or she'd picked up a flash of something. "Shine your light over that way again." She pointed toward a distant outcropping of trees.

Toni ran her beam across a round-topped crypt that stood maybe six feet high, then across the statue of an angel whose head had long ago been lopped off. "Nope," she said. "Nothing here." She kicked at something with her toe, frowned, then aimed her light downward. "Weird," she muttered.

"Hm?" said Suzanne. She'd already turned to leave.

"It's like dead flowers," said Toni.

"Everything's dead out here," said Suzanne. She looked back. "Are you coming?"

"No," said Toni, "I mean, like, recently dead."

"What are you talking about?"

Toni took a step back and moved her light across the ground. There, scattered in an almost semicircle around her, were a dozen or so half-dead lilies.

"Oh crap!" exclaimed Suzanne.

"What?" asked Toni. "You think somebody's been here?"

Suzanne nodded.

Toni's teeth were chattering now. "Are these like . . . funeral flowers?"

"I think so," said Suzanne. She gestured with her hand. "Gimme your flashlight." Toni handed it over. Slowly, Suzanne moved the beam across a row of gravestones, past a cluster of wrought-iron crosses, over a waist-high tomb, toward the very back of the cemetery. A tiny sparkle of red seemed to taunt and glint. "Look there," cried Suzanne. "Over to the left." The vastness of the surrounding woods seemed to suck up the light, but Suzanne still thought she'd caught a faint illumination of red.

"What is that?" asked Toni. She'd seen it, too.

"Almost like a reflection from a taillight," said Suzanne.

"Holy smokes!" cried Toni. "There's a car over there?"

The two women stepped carefully through waist-high grasses, moving slowly and nervously. Finally, as they drew closer, they were able to see the dark outline of a car parked beneath a gnarled oak.

"Definitely a car," said Suzanne.

"What if it's Becker's car?" asked Toni. "What if he ditched it here and made a switch or something? Had an accomplice? Here, give me that light." Toni took the light and walked slowly toward the car. "It's red," she called back. "Mustang."

"Becker's," said Suzanne. She reached up, pushed her hair behind her ears, listening for footsteps. For danger. Out here in the darkness, she'd noticed that her eyes and ears seemed to play tricks on her, while the wind whipped by and touched her with chilly tendrils.

"We gotta call this in," said Toni. "This is big-time." She spun back toward Suzanne, her light tracing a circle.

"Dear Lord!" Suzanne gasped suddenly, her voice tight with fear. Toni's moving flashlight had picked up a dark shape that suddenly materialized right beside her.

"Huh?" said Toni abruptly. She frowned, glanced at her friend, and aimed her light at the thing that seemed to hold Suzanne in a grip of terror.

There, hanging from a tree limb, slowly twisting in the wind, was a dead body.

"OH my God!" Now Toni's voice rose in a pained, horrified wail. "You see those black motorcycle boots? I think it's . . . it's *Junior*! Oh no, somebody hanged Junior!" Her flashlight tumbled to the ground as Toni threw her hands over her face and let loose a high, keening howl.

"No, no," Suzanne cried, pulling herself together and scrambling for the flashlight. "It's not him! I'm sure it's not him!"

Toni's fingers spread apart gingerly and two dark, doubtful eyes peeked through. "Then who?" she asked in a jittery voice.

Suzanne steadied herself and directed the beam up the hanging body, moving it slowly, feet to head. Finally, she said, "It's Bo Becker."

"Get out!" said Toni, aghast. "Bo Becker hanged from a tree? Murdered?" Her words seemed to resonate within the both of them, and they backed up several paces. As if they feared that Becker's limp body might suddenly be injected with life, like Frankenstein's monster, to twist loose and come lurching after them.

"This is some crazy stuff," Suzanne muttered.

Toni's teeth chattered loudly, from cold and fear. "What if he hung himself?" she whispered. She quickly made the sign of the cross. "It's a sin, you know . . . the worst sin of all!"

Suzanne grimaced as she studied the limp, swaying body. "The rope was tossed over a branch maybe three feet above his head, then stretched across to a V in the trunk, then . . ."

The rest of her sentence was lost in the loud wail of a siren.

"Oh cripes!" screeched Toni, as they were suddenly caught in the spotlights and high beams of three different vehicles that roared along the edge of the cemetery, then converged directly upon them.

The driver's side door flew open on the lead vehicle and a tall, thin man jumped out, his gun pointed directly at them. Suzanne could have sworn it was a pearl-handled revolver. "Hands up!" he ordered.

"Lord love a duck," muttered Suzanne. "It's Sheriff Burney."

Sheriff Bill Burney, head law officer of Deer County, was joined by two other deputies who were just as stone-faced and serious as he was, and aiming even more fire-power at them. Suzanne wasn't sure if they had actually crossed official lines into his county, but Burney and his men had obviously responded to the call about the sighting of Becker's car. Only now it wasn't just the car that was the problem.

"Excuse me," said Suzanne, "this is not . . ."

"Quiet!" snapped Sheriff Burney. "I'll do the talking."

"How deep in doo-doo would you say we are?" whispered Toni, her hands extended up over her head.

Suzanne managed a quick glance around. "We got a dead body swinging from a tree and the two of us goofs standing right next to it," she whispered back. "I'd say we're in way over our heads."

And still the excitement continued as another siren wailed and a fourth vehicle, blue and red light bars puls-ing like mad, roared up to join their little circle of Dante's Hell.

But this time, Suzanne and Toni caught a small break. Because the new arrival was Sheriff Roy Doogie. He climbed from his cruiser, hitched at his pants, and scowled ferociously at them.

"We got a homicide here," Sheriff Burney called to Sheriff Doogie. Burney was a by-the-book kind of guy. Tall, rail thin, a former marine drill sergeant.

"Dang!" yelled Doogie. He snatched his hat from his head and threw it to the ground. "Dang!" he shouted again.

"What?" called Burney. *"What?"*

"They ain't your killers," cried Doogie. "They're just pain-in-the-butt pests!"

Suzanne and Toni were given a chance to explain themselves, of course. And then were given a lecture that fairly scalded their ears. They knew all the fiery words, of course; they weren't complete innocents. But they'd never heard them strung together in the context of such barbarous, blistering prose!

CHAPTER 14

WEDNESDAY morning dawned overcast and gray. Wind stripped yellow and gold leaves from trees and sent them swirling, in miniature tornadic clouds, down the blacktopped streets of Kindred. To add insult to injury, rain spat down in icy little pellets. It was the kind of weather that set the stage perfectly for Ozzie Driesden's funeral.

Suzanne, Toni, and Petra were huddled in the back of Hope Church, whispering among themselves. Obviously, Suzanne and Toni's big adventure last night was their topic du jour.

"I can't believe you actually found Bo Becker's body!" breathed Petra. She was stunned and a little taken aback by their crazy confession. "I mean . . . what were you two *doing* out there? What on earth were you *thinking*?"

"Jeez," said Toni, glancing at the conservatively attired mourners, then buttoning the top button of her black cowboy shirt, "we were just on a cheese run."

"That escalated into a harebrained plan," admitted Suzanne.

"And ended in a complete debacle," scolded Petra, gazing from one to the other.

"You know, it was really Junior's fault," said Toni, looking studiously innocent.

"How do you figure that?" asked Suzanne. They'd both been complicit in their urge to snoop, hadn't they?

"If Junior hadn't traded cars with me," said Toni, "we'd never have had access to that police scanner." She gave a sharp nod of her head and her frizzled, pinned-up hair bobbed in silent indignation.

"That's bordering on situational ethics," said Petra.

"No," said Suzanne, "what happened was . . . we were just plain stupid last night. And morbidly curious."

"Speaking of morbid, my friends," said Petra, dropping her voice. "We'd better go in and take our seats. Ozzie's funeral will be starting soon."

Glancing out the double doors of the church, Suzanne saw a long, black hearse glide to a stop. It bore a discreet Driesden and Draper crest-shaped logo etched on the side window. "Since our guest of honor has just arrived," she told them.

"Oh you," fluttered Petra. "Please be serious . . . for once."

SUZANNE decided that Ozzie's funeral ranked about a seven out of ten possible points as funerals go. There was a full house, of course, with a few curiosity seekers shuffling around in the back of the church. So all the mourners from last night and then some.

The flowers and decor were quite lovely. A large cross made out of white mums and red roses with a lemon leaf border stood behind Ozzie's gunmetal gray coffin. A casket spray of gladiolas and carnations sat on top. Black velvet bunting was draped across the front pews.

Eulogies were delivered by several of Kindred's more prominent citizens, including Mayor Mobley. Mobley, dressed in a black suit that wouldn't quite button, came across as upbeat mixed with his own brand of greasy charm. He spoke about Ozzie's many contributions to the community, then went on to talk about vigilant law enforcement and seeking final justice in what was certainly a wrongful death. Suzanne knew Sheriff Doogie was in the audience. Was he squirming at Mobley's pointed words? Had to be.

But the best eulogy of all was rendered by Reverend Strait. He spoke gently of Ozzie's kindness in shepherding so many people through their hour of grief. Of his dedication to the community. Then finished with, what Suzanne decided, was the perfect line pulled from Emily Dickinson: *Because I could not stop for death, he kindly stopped for me. The carriage held but just ourselves and immortality.*

These final words elicited great, gasping sobs from Missy, who was seated in the third row from the front. Her ex, Earl Stensrud, sat beside her, comforting her. But his comfort seemed to extend to a few genial pats on her shoulder.

Then George Draper and two assistants in somber black suits seesawed Ozzie's coffin and pointed it, feet first, down the center aisle. There was a subdued rumble as everyone rose to their feet, then the organist chimed in with a slightly off-key version of Eric Clapton's "Tears in Heaven."

Suzanne brushed tears from her eyes as Ozzie's coffin rolled past her on squeaky wheels. Then came a stolid-looking man who had to be Ozzie's brother, a small entourage of hastily summoned relatives, and Missy and Earl.

Glancing at Toni and Petra, Suzanne noticed that Petra was wiping her eyes with a white hanky while Toni picked a bit of lint from her shirt. Then again, Suzanne reminded herself, Toni had yet to experience the death of someone close to her. Hadn't felt that iron band of grief close around her heart in a way that felt like it would never loosen. Hadn't experienced the dreams that haunted and taunted.

Then Toni surprised her by sniffling loudly. "That was so sad," she said. The three of them sat there numbly, watching the rest of the mourners file past.

Petra nodded. "I feel just awful for Ozzie's brother. What must he think of our town? That something this horrible could happen to his only brother?"

"You can bet he's heard about last night, too," said Toni. She gave a quizzical look. "Don't you guys find it awfully strange that two people from the same funeral home were murdered?"

"I hadn't thought of it that way," said Petra. "But you're right. It is an odd coincidence."

"Maybe not a coincidence at all," said Suzanne.

ONCE everyone was milling about outside the church, Suzanne looked around for Sheriff Doogie. And saw him clumping toward his cruiser.

"I'll be right back," she told Toni and Petra, then scurried after him.

"Now what do you want?" asked Doogie when he caught sight of her. He had his hand on his car door, looking like he'd been hoping for a clean getaway.

"About last night . . ." began Suzanne.

"You and your friend are in serious trouble concerning that," came Doogie's stern warning. "Charges could be filed."

"We didn't do anything wrong," said Suzanne.

"Interfering with the law . . ."

"Stumbling across a dead body is hardly interfering," said Suzanne. "It's just . . . bad luck."

"Bad luck and trouble seem to follow you around," snarled Doogie.

Suzanne backed off then, hoping to deflect some of Doogie's anger and get to the point where she could ask him some serious questions. "I'm sorry about that," she said. "We really didn't mean to get in the way."

"You *should* be sorry," sniffed Doogie. He was still nursing hard feelings. Or maybe he'd just felt embarrassed in front of Sheriff Burney.

"What I wanted to ask you," said Suzanne, "since law enforcement packed us on our merry way rather hastily last night, was . . . did Bo Becker hang himself?"

"What?" said Doogie.

"Because if Becker *did* kill Ozzie, maybe he was overcome with remorse."

Doogie folded his arms across his broad chest and stared at Suzanne with flat eyes. "No remorse," he finally said.

"You don't think Becker murdered Ozzie, do you?" said Suzanne. "You've changed your mind, shifted your paradigm."

Sheriff Roy Doogie continued to stare at her. Sometimes no answer was an answer.

"And Becker didn't hang himself, either, did he?" said Suzanne, a little excited now.

"Let's just say we now have parallel investigations," said Doogie.

SUZANNE knew she shouldn't, knew it was probably in horrible taste, but she just had to talk to George Draper. She caught him just as he and his assistants slid the casket into the hearse and slammed the back hatch.

"George. Mr. Draper," she called.

George Draper stood by the side of his hearse, looking even more gaunt and haggard than usual. "Hello, Suzanne," he said.

Suzanne didn't waste any words. "I'm assuming you heard about Bo Becker?"

Draper's face sagged. "Of course. Sheriff Doogie phoned me last night. Roused me out of bed, in fact. I drove out there immediately, had to see for myself." He shook his head. "Shocking, absolutely shocking."

"So you think Becker was murdered, too," said Suzanne. "Not a suicide."

That seemed to stun Draper. "Well . . . I . . . yes, I suppose so," he finally stammered.

That was all Suzanne needed to hear. "Do you have any idea what Bo Becker might have been involved in? I mean, outside of the funeral home?"

"Not really," said Draper. "Of course, he was mostly Ozzie's assistant. I think Ozzie had been trying to get him into a program to be a morgue assistant."

"When was the last time you saw Becker?" asked Suzanne.

Draper scratched his head. "He helped with the Carr funeral Monday morning, then took off immediately afterward. I never saw him again. Must have . . . I don't know . . . run into some kind of trouble." He sighed. "*Obviously* he did."

"But Becker was loading flowers into his car Monday night," said Suzanne. "I saw him."

George looked stunned. "Where?"

"At the back door of your funeral home."

"Did you tell Sheriff Doogie about this?"

"Of course," said Suzanne. "What I'm trying to figure out is . . . why did Becker end up at that deserted cemetery?"

George Draper stared at her. "I don't know."

"Was he supposed to deliver flowers there?" asked Suzanne.

Draper blinked. "There were a few flowers in the back-seat of Becker's car. I saw them last night. They let me look inside his car."

"Whose flowers were they?"

"I'm guessing they might have been from the Carr funeral on Monday," said Draper.

"They didn't get left at Memorial Cemetery with the body?"

"Obviously not," said Draper. He had a look on his face as though someone had screwed up. "Must have come back in the hearse."

"So why would Bo have taken them to that particular cemetery?"

"I don't know," said Draper. "He doesn't . . . he didn't . . . always listen terribly well."

"What if someone called the funeral home and told him to take the flowers there?" postulated Suzanne. "Or left a message to that effect?"

"Then he might have done it," said Draper, jingling his keys nervously. "I mean . . . it's possible."

"And someone could have followed him," said Suzanne. "Or been waiting for him."

George made a motion to open the driver's side door. He was anxious to get going.

"And drugs were missing from the funeral home?" pressed Suzanne.

"Well . . . yes," said Draper, making a sour face. "We

don't make a big deal of it. The families prefer to think of their loved ones as looking quite natural. But to accomplish that kind of miracle we do employ a rather large arsenal of chemicals."

JUST as Suzanne was about to climb into her car, Doogie pulled up alongside her. Suzanne pocketed her keys and hurried over to Doogie's driver's side window.

"I had a feeling you weren't finished with your questions," said Doogie.

"You're right," Suzanne told him. "And I've got a whopper of a question for you."

"Shoot," said Doogie.

"Do you think maybe Bo's killer wasn't after Bo at all? That he was really after George Draper?"

"First Driesden, then Draper," mused Doogie. "The thought had crossed my mind."

"Missy's not looking much like a suspect anymore, is she?" said Suzanne.

"Nobody is," grumped Doogie.

"Maybe," said Suzanne, "we should be looking at George Draper. What he might be involved in, if he has any prior—"

"No," interrupted Doogie, "*I* need to do all that. *You* need to keep your flat little nose out of my investigation."

"What about that funeral home consortium?" began Suzanne. "What's their name again . . . ?"

"Roth Funeral Consortium," supplied Doogie.

"Could they be involved in something like this?"

"No idea."

"Could you contact other law enforcement agencies in the states Roth Consortium is in?"

"Why?" asked Doogie.

"See if there have been any similar murders of funeral home directors?"

"That ain't a bad idea," allowed Doogie.

ON her way back to the Cackleberry Club, Suzanne had another small brainstorm. *Who owns the deserted church and graveyard, anyway?*

If the property was in Deer County, she'd have to run all the way over to Cornucopia to dig through records. But if the church was situated in Logan County . . . well, then she might be able to pull up that information at the county courthouse.

Five minutes later, Suzanne parked in front of the red-brick building, sped up the sidewalk, then hurried down a linoleum-tiled hallway that smelled faintly of disinfectant.

At the battered wooden desk that stretched ten feet across, a barrier that separated the record keepers from the record seekers, Suzanne ran into Nadine Carr. Nadine seemed to be in the middle of filing papers related to her husband's death. Suzanne's heart went out to the poor woman. It wasn't so long ago that she'd had to deal with the same heartbreaking tasks.

"I'm so sorry about your husband," Suzanne told her. "My sincere condolences." Nadine's husband, Julian, had been a soft-spoken man who'd eaten at the Cackleberry Club a couple of times. Purchased books at the Book Nook, too. On World War II and the Korean War.

"Thank you, dear," said Nadine. "But Julian had been sick for a very long time. I was . . . we all were . . . *prepared*, as they say."

"Still," said Suzanne, "these things are never easy."

"I saw a poster down at Kuyper's Drug Store about the Knit-In at the Cackleberry Club," said Nadine. "I thought I might drop by. Give me something to focus on."

"You'd be more than welcome," said Suzanne, wishing now that she'd gone to Julian Carr's funeral the other morning. It probably would have really meant something to Nadine.

Now Nadine's lower lip trembled slightly, as if the harsh realization of her husband's death had struck her yet again.

Suzanne put her arms around Nadine and embraced the woman who was at least a head shorter than she was. "I know how you feel," she commiserated.

"I know you do, honey," said Nadine. "I know you had a tough time yourself a while back."

They held each other for a few more moments, sniffling, tears hot on their cheeks. Then Suzanne said, "I have kind of a strange question for you."

Wiping away tears, Nadine looked up at her. "Yes?"

"The flowers for your husband's funeral. Do you know . . . were they left at the cemetery or brought back to the funeral home?"

Nadine gazed at her. "That's a strange question."

"It has to do with Ozzie's murder," said Suzanne. "And . . . another strange development." She didn't know if Nadine had heard about Bo Becker yet.

Turns out she hadn't. So Suzanne hastily filled her in.

Nadine's eyes widened in horror as Suzanne's story unfolded. She put a chubby hand to her chest as if her heart could barely withstand this terrible news. "Awful, just awful," she murmured. "It sounds like someone's targeting people at the funeral home." Needless to say, Nadine was more than a little stunned.

Suzanne nodded. "It sounds strange, but that's what I was thinking, too."

"Why would someone do that?" asked Nadine.

"No idea," said Suzanne.

Nadine peered at Suzanne with a questioning, half-fearful look. "And you're involved in this . . . ?" Her voice trailed off. A reasonable question, for sure.

"Because I found Ozzie," said Suzanne. "And because my friend Missy Langston has come under suspicion."

Nadine's mouth opened and closed in surprise. "Ah," she finally said. "She dated Ozzie."

"That's right," replied Suzanne. "And I've been sort of . . . investigating a couple of different angles."

"Missy as a suspect?" said Nadine in a weary tone of voice. "I simply don't see it." Then her expression morphed from sadness to approval. "But aren't you a dear," she told Suzanne. "Standing up for one of your friends."

"So . . . about the flowers?" asked Suzanne.

Nadine shook her head. "There were so many details that . . . well, I have no idea where they ended up."

Once Nadine had finished her business, Suzanne filled out a request form for a title search.

The young woman at the counter, clad in black T-shirt and leggings, her eyebrow pierced with a skinny silver bolt, gazed at Suzanne's request and looked blank. "Oh," she said. "I don't know if we can do this."

"It's a fairly straight-ahead record search," Suzanne pointed out.

The young woman, who couldn't have been more than twenty, reached up and twirled a tendril of long dark hair.

"Yeah, but I'm not sure *how* to do this. See, I'm only temporary. The regular lady is on vacation, so it's gonna be a couple days."

"There's nothing you could do to expedite things?" asked Suzanne.

The young woman shook her head. "No, sorry."

CHAPTER 15

By the time Suzanne got back to the Cackleberry Club, every seat in the house was occupied and a few latecomers milled about on the front porch.

"We're getting slammed!" cried Petra. Hunched over the grill, she poked at strips of bacon and links of spicy sausage, while eggs, pancakes, and French toast sizzled off to the side. Oversized spatulas were clutched in both her hands.

"Slammed means making money," quipped Toni, as she arranged little garnishes of fresh mint and sliced strawberries.

"The more you chase money," said Petra, "the harder it is to catch it."

"Nicely put," replied Suzanne. "Now tell me what I can do to help."

"Spread out about a dozen big plates so I can dish up these orders," said Petra. She glanced over at Toni. "You let Suzanne arrange those garnishes, honey, and go back out and take orders."

"You sure?" asked Toni.

"Oh yeah," said Petra. "This is just a warm-up for our big day on Saturday."

For the next ten minutes, Suzanne sprinkled powdered sugar and arranged sliced strawberries on French toast, topped omelets with chopped chives and red onions, and scooped mounds of fresh sour cream onto plates of Jumpin' Jack Spuds. As each breakfast was painstakingly prepared and plated, Toni ferried it out to waiting customers. Finally, when all the orders had been filled, when all their customers were munching away contentedly, Suzanne grabbed a coffeepot and made the rounds. And collected more than a few appreciative comments on their cooking.

"I guess we did it, huh?" said Toni. She stood behind the counter, nervously sipping from a mug of coffee, keeping an eye on the front of the house.

Suzanne slid behind the counter to join her. "You okay?"

Toni shook her head. "Can't say's I am."

"Still upset about last night?" asked Suzanne. Of course she was, thought Suzanne. Because she herself had dreamt about Bo's dark, swollen face.

Toni took another sip of coffee and pursed her lips. "To tell you the truth, I'm scared to death about Junior."

"How so?" asked Suzanne.

"Maybe I'm just picking up your vibes," said Toni, "but I've got the worst feeling he might be involved in this mess." She seemed afraid to meet Suzanne's eyes. "You know . . . the drugs. Maybe even the murders. Not that he'd actually *kill* somebody, but he could be, you know . . . involved peripherally."

"And you're basing your fears and suspicions on . . . what?" asked Suzanne.

Toni made a face. "A bunch of things. First, Junior's a dope. Anybody with half a brain can turn his head with a little fast talk. Especially if you promise him money."

"Okay," said Suzanne. No contest there.

"And I know Junior's been hanging around Hoobly's

roadhouse a lot. Factor in all those deliveries he's been making . . ."

Suzanne decided not to pull any punches. She drew a deep breath and said, "Maybe Junior hasn't been making deliveries at all. Maybe he's just seeing another woman. Junior does have a wandering eye. I mean, any piece of fluff in low-slung jeans is bound to catch his eye."

"You got that right," snorted Toni. She took another sip of coffee, then turned worried eyes on Suzanne. "But this time Junior's up to something more. I mean, he really has been earning extra money."

Suzanne hated to ask, but did. "A lot of money?"

Toni shook her head in the affirmative. "More than he usually does."

"Oh," said Suzanne.

"What if Junior's involved with drugs?" asked Toni.

"You mean like drugs missing from the funeral home?"

"That," said Toni, "or any drugs."

Grimacing, Suzanne said, "Then I'd say he's in big trouble."

"Which means I've gotta pull his sorry butt out of the fire," said Toni. "Before he ends up like Bo Becker, swinging from some lonely, bare tree, with his boot heels dangling five inches above the ground."

"Dear Lord!" exclaimed Suzanne. Toni's imagery was just too much.

"I mean it, Suzanne!"

"You want to save Junior from himself?" asked Suzanne. "I'm not sure you can do that. I'm not sure anybody can do that."

"But I gotta try," said Toni. "He told me he's meeting somebody out at Hoobly's tonight. So here's the thing. Will you go out there with me? To sort of spy on him?"

"Um," said Suzanne. She really didn't want to.

Toni threw her a pleading look. "There's no book club tonight, so we're both free . . ."

How could Suzanne say no?

BECAUSE the Cackleberry Club opened two hours late today, lunch was slightly abbreviated. Chicken noodle soup, crab salad, ham au gratin, upside-down French toast for the breakfast-at-lunch-fans, and devil's food cake for dessert.

Just as Suzanne finished writing their luncheon offerings on the blackboard, their busboy Joey Ewald came charging in. He was a skateboarding freak who dressed the part and was perpetually being reprimanded for hitching rides on the back of cars. In fact, Suzanne had once towed Joey a couple of miles without even knowing he was hanging on behind her like a remora. Scared her to death.

"Hey, momma," was Joey's offbeat greeting today.

"I'm not your momma," said Suzanne. "And you're ten minutes late for work."

"Whatever," said Joey. He gave her a wink and a winsome smile and shrugged.

Kids, she thought, what can you do?

"You guys got busy," said Joey, grabbing a gray plastic tub, ready to go to work clearing tables.

"And we're gonna be a whole lot busier for lunch," Suzanne told him. "So kindly march yourself in back, wash your hands . . . with antibacterial soap, please . . . and slip on an apron."

"Do I get to wear a scarf, too?" asked Joey.

Ever since Suzanne had let him pinch-hit as a waitperson, Joey wanted to wear a head scarf fashioned as a do-rag. "There's a clean bandana of Baxter's you can use," Suzanne told him. "But be sure to leave it when you're finished. It's his favorite."

"Cool," said Joey. He ducked in back, then emerged a few minutes later with his apron and a bandana worn pirate-style. "See?" he said, arms extended, striking an exaggerated pose. "All duded up."

"Cool," echoed Suzanne.

"Is your back bothering you again?" asked Toni. Petra seemed like she was more hunched over her griddle than usual.

Petra placed her hand in the small of her back and rubbed. "Gotta call the chiropractor."

"Is your guy a back cracker?" asked Toni.

"Yes and no," replied Petra. "He uses modified chiropractic, a touch of osteopathy, creative visualization, and good old-fashioned prayer."

"Nothing wrong with prayer," said Toni.

"But not quite your AMA-sanctioned treatment," said Suzanne.

"Except it works!" exclaimed Petra.

"I need to run something by you guys," said Suzanne as she centered blue ceramic bowls on white plates.

"Uh-oh," said Petra. "Something to do with the murders?"

"No," said Suzanne, "nothing that colorful. It's about me being a model this Friday."

"What!" squealed Petra. This little bit of news made her straighten right up.

"Haven't you heard?" Toni giggled. "Our Suzanne has been asked to strut her stuff, such as it is, on the catwalk."

"More like a quick loop around a garment rack," said Suzanne, a little embarrassed. "It's the grand opening of Alchemy. Missy asked me last night. I think they want a middle-aged model so everyone else looks fresh and young."

"They do start 'em at an early age," allowed Toni. "Kate Moss was just fifteen when she started working the runways in Paris."

"Where'd you read that?" asked Petra.

"The *Inquisitor*," said Toni. "All the hot, hip people are profiled in there."

"Uh, yeah," said Petra. Then she peered at Suzanne. "Are you gonna do it? 'Cause I think you should."

"That's what I said, too," said Toni. "Suzanne's a natural."

"Sure," agreed Petra. "She's got a nice long stride."

"Especially when she's wearing her cowboy boots," said Toni. "She's like, 'Hey, I'm a lady gunslinger.'"

But Suzanne was still anxious. "I'm just afraid Carmen's only gonna stock the tiny sizes. Two, four, six."

"I'm a fourteen," volunteered Petra. "And that's on a *good* day."

"What constitutes a good day?" asked Toni.

Petra made a sour face. "Right after a bout of stomach flu when I'm totally dehydrated."

"Oh man," marveled Toni, "and I have trouble keeping weight on."

"That's so unfair," said Petra. "Since you eat like a truck driver."

"Nerves," explained Toni. "I'm extremely high-strung." She giggled. "Or maybe I'm just strung out."

"I don't think I should do it," said Suzanne. "Model, I mean."

"I think you'd be great," urged Petra. "With the right clothes and makeup you'll look just like a supermodel."

"Or she can strap on a pair of wings and look like those babes in the Victoria's Secret show," chortled Toni.

"I know what Victoria's Secret is," Petra told them in hushed tones.

"What?" asked Suzanne and Toni in unison.

Petra grinned. "Nobody over forty can fit in her lingerie!"

TRUE to Suzanne's prediction, lunch was crazy busy. She and Toni took orders, delivered them to Petra, and tried their best to cajole customers into settling for apple pie when they ran out of cake.

Just when things were at their busiest, Mayor Mobley walked in, accompanied by a dark-complected man wearing a well-tailored pinstripe suit. But the mayor wasn't there to eat; rather he ambled from table to table, glad-handing customers and passing out red, white, and blue campaign buttons with bouncing type that proclaimed "Reelect Mobley" above a photo of his chubby, smirking face.

"We're a little busy here, Mayor," Toni told him, balancing a tray on one hip and trying to edge by him.

Mobley, dressed in khaki pants and a red polo shirt, just grinned his imperious politician's grin and slapped one of his oversized campaign buttons into Toni's free hand.

"Well, look at this," Toni announced loudly, so everyone could hear. "A fancy-schmancy button with a picture on it. Too bad it's not your butt." She made a big show of turning the button around. "Oh wait, I had it upside down. It *is* your butt!"

The crowd roared as Mobley glared at her.

"You got a smart mouth for such a little gal," he told her.

Toni glowered back, assuming the attack pose of a rabid Doberman pinscher. Which was when Suzanne stepped in.

"Can I get you a table, Mayor?" Suzanne was polite but decidedly firm. When you came to the Cackleberry Club, you were here to eat, buy books, or learn how to knit. No way was this turning into a political rally.

"Just passing through," said Mobley. "Doing a little last-minute election work." He gave a self-important, throat-clearing harrumph, then added, "Not that I need to. Unlike some law officers I know."

Suzanne knew Mayor Mobley was making a heavy-handed dig at Doogie not being reelected.

"Got somebody you should meet," said the mayor, suddenly beaming at her. "This here's Ray Lynch. Ray represents the acquisitions department of the Roth Funeral Home Consortium."

Ray extended his hand to Suzanne.

"Suzanne is one of Kindred's new breed of female entrepreneurs," said the mayor, managing to sound slightly condescending.

"How do?" said Suzanne as she slowly shook Ray Lynch's hand. She stared at him as he fixed her with unblinking, steel gray eyes. A tough guy, she decided. With a bottom-line, bean-counter mentality.

Mobley slapped Ray Lynch on the back and said, "Ray is a real blue-chip business guy."

"And you think blue chip means buying up local businesses and replacing them with faceless, out-of-town corporate owners?" asked Suzanne.

Mobley's face turned red as a cooked lobster, his eyes became piggy little slits. "You sound like a doggone socialist, Suzanne. Next thing you know you'll be parading around town spouting the *Communist Manifesto*."

"It's a free country, Mayor," said Suzanne. "Get used to it."

As Suzanne delivered pumpkin bars and slices of apple crumb pie, she couldn't help but wonder about Ray Lynch. If Ozzie had turned down an offer from the consortium, could Ray Lynch have taken matters into his own hands? What if he wasn't just the acquisitions guy, but also the company muscle? Suzanne knew it was a stretch, a huge supposition on her part, but if Ray Lynch had killed Ozzie, could he have gone after Bo Becker, too?

Suzanne stepped behind the counter, rang up two checks, hit the keys on the old brass cash register, and returned a few dollars in change to a couple of customers.

Maybe, she thought, Ray Lynch had also gone after Bo Becker because he thought Bo viewed him as a suspect. As Ozzie's killer. Then Lynch would have just been tying up loose ends.

Suzanne stared across the café, her eyes landing on the high shelf that held their collection of ceramic chickens. A little white hen squatted next to a reddish brown rooster. A flock of yellow chicks was scattered nearby. She shook her head. No answers there.

So where am I going to find the answers?

Even though Missy was now a long shot as a suspect, Suzanne had to admit she was clearly fascinated with this case. Or cases, really. And Doogie didn't seem to be making much forward progress, even as the mayor seemed to relish Doogie's tenuous situation.

Could Mayor Mobley be in bed with the Roth Funeral Home Consortium?

It was possible, she supposed. Anything was possible.

Suzanne wove her way through the tables, letting random ideas rumble through her brain. Pushing open the door to the kitchen, she turned in the direction of their big industrial stove and yelled, "Petra, how much do you know about Mayor Mobley?"

But Petra wasn't in her usual position. Suzanne's gaze switched to the back door. Petra was just closing it, turning toward her with a smile, dusting her hands together, and asking, "What?"

"You should let Joey haul out the garbage," Suzanne suggested. "Since your back is bugging you."

"Oh," said Petra, looking slightly embarrassed. "I wasn't carrying out garbage. I was . . ." She colored slightly. "This fellow came to the back door and I . . ."

"One of our suppliers?" asked Suzanne. "Because you know I'm happy to handle that stuff."

"No," said Petra. "Actually, there was this raggedy-looking man asking for a handout." Her cheeks flared pink. "And I felt sorry for him—he looked so tattered and tired—that I gave him a couple of sandwiches."

"A homeless guy?" asked Suzanne. Could it be the same homeless man Sheriff Doogie had mentioned?

"You know," said Petra, thinking, "I think it might have even been the same guy we saw in the park Sunday. Kind of a strange coincidence, huh?"

Suzanne was out the back door in a flash, searching right, then left, wondering why Baxter, who was tied out here, hadn't sounded any kind of alarm.

But Baxter was reclining on the grass, looking like the canine grand duke of the universe, giving her a look of supreme curiosity.

And there wasn't a soul in sight.

CHAPTER 16

THINGS went from barely normal to strangely bizarre when Carmen Copeland came sweeping in for her book signing.

"Good Lord," muttered Toni, as Carmen posed in the front hallway, then strode forcefully toward them. "Batman just dropped in from Gotham City."

Carmen was, indeed, wearing some kind of black cape— Suzanne figured it had to be cashmere from the genteel way it fluttered—over a black form-fitting dress that featured a very plunging V-neckline. At least a dozen chains of twisted, intermeshed gold nestled in that deep V.

"Oh good," said Carmen, dropping a bright blue bag on the signing table and whipping off her cape in one carefully calculated motion. "You've stocked plenty of books." She waggled a finger at Suzanne and Toni who gazed placidly at her. "I have a tingly feeling about today. I think we're going to sell beaucoup books."

I sure hope so, thought Suzanne. *I hope having Carmen here is worth all the drama.*

"Dear," said Carmen, plopping down in the author's chair and addressing Toni, "I'd like a bottle of water. Still, not carbonated."

Toni rolled her eyes and sauntered off. Suzanne figured

Toni would probably just bring her a glass of tap water. Warm tap water at that. Filched from Baxter's dog dish.

Digging in her blue bag, Carmen pulled out a stack of bookmarks and arranged them on the table. "Always like to hand these out, too," she told Suzanne. "Since they feature my backlist."

Staring at Carmen's blue bag, Suzanne experienced a slight ping. She'd seen that bag before, only in a different color. "Your bag is . . ." began Suzanne.

Carmen reached a hand out and caressed her bag gently. "A Birkin bag," she said, with just a hint of a satisfied smile. "From Hermès."

"Like Samantha's bag on *Sex and the City*," said Suzanne. She really was a hard-core viewer.

"Yes, I believe they did feature a similar bag."

A bag that cost seven thousand dollars, thought Suzanne. *Holy cow, how many books does this lady sell in a year?*

Suzanne forced herself to stop thinking about Carmen, her money, and the intimidation factor that went along with it. Instead she said, "You might be interested to know that the Cackleberry Club is offering a special purchase with a purchase today."

"Oh?" said Carmen. Her dark eyes, lined top and bottom with black kohl, burned into Suzanne.

"Customers who buy your new hardcover book can also get a special tea plate for six ninety-five," Suzanne explained.

Carmen wasn't impressed. "And what exactly does a tea plate consist of?"

"A bottomless cup of jasmine tea and a plate with two tea sandwiches, small slice of quiche, brownie bite, and miniature scone."

"All that for six ninety-five?" asked Carmen. Suddenly, she did seem impressed.

"Only if you buy the book. Otherwise the price is nine ninety-five," Suzanne pointed out.

"I wouldn't mind having one of those tea plates myself," said Carmen. She batted her eyelashes. "Is it too early?"

"Not really," said Suzanne. "But your fans are starting to line up, so you might want to hold off." Two women had already sidled up to the table, wanting an autographed book, and Suzanne could see a couple more fans headed toward the Book Nook.

Carmen waved a manicured hand. "No problem. I'll just make it all work. I'm an expert at multitasking, you'll see."

"Okay," said Suzanne. "Sure."

TURNS out, having Carmen *was* worth the trouble. A long line snaked from the Book Nook out into the café. Dozens of romance fans showed up to meet Carmen in person, as well as other book lovers who were naturally curious and wanted the chance to rub shoulders with a top-selling, local author. Surprisingly, to Suzanne anyway, Carmen conducted herself like a total pro. She signed books, chatted with her fans, and even posed for pictures.

And, of course, there was a huge spillover into the café. Which kept everyone hopping.

When there was a slight break in the action, Carmen murmured to Suzanne, out of the corner of her mouth, "I understand you were first on the scene last night."

"How did you hear about that?" asked Suzanne. Carmen seemed to have a direct pipeline for current information.

It was as if she'd bugged Doogie's phone down at the law enforcement center.

Carmen crinkled her eyes, trying to look mysterious. "I have my ways," she purred.

"Thinking about getting into the mystery writing business?" asked Suzanne.

"You never know," was Carmen's cryptic reply. "I have quite a few irons in the fire right now."

Suzanne wondered if Carmen knew she was modeling at Alchemy this Friday. "You must be excited over the opening of your boutique," she said to Carmen.

"Absolutely," purred Carmen. "I'm all about high style, which, until now, has been sadly lacking in Kindred and the surrounding communities."

Suzanne smoothed her white blouse, which she knew wasn't remotely high style. "Missy seems to be handling opening plans nicely."

Carmen touched the end of her pen to the tip of her nose. "She's doing a passable job."

"Like I mentioned last night," said Suzanne, perturbed, "Missy's still pretty upset about Ozzie."

Carmen waved a hand in an imperious grand duchess gesture. "And like *I* said, she'll get over it soon enough."

"Carmen Copeland!" called an energetic male voice.

Suzanne and Carmen both looked up to find Gene Gandle of the *Bugle* loping toward them. Tall and gangly, his squarish head seemed to bob on his thin stalk of a neck.

Gene didn't wait for an introduction, just grabbed Carmen's hand in a gesture of sheer delight. "I'm so glad to finally meet you!" he simpered.

Carmen narrowed her eyes. "And you are . . . ?"

"Of course, introductions," murmured Gene. He flashed

her a large, hopeful smile. "I'm Gene Gandle from the *Bugle*."

"Charmed," said Carmen.

"Come to do a little write-up, if you don't mind, Miss Copeland," said Gene.

"Publicity," cooed Carmen. "Another one of the necessary evils of my profession."

"The oldest?" murmured Suzanne.

"I promise, Miss Copeland, this little interview will be a breeze," said Gene, as he pulled out pad and pencil and juggled his camera.

Suzanne could only watch in amusement. She'd never seen Gene simper over anyone quite so much.

In between signing books, nibbling scones, and sipping tea, Carmen managed to give Gene the semblance of an interview. She yapped on about herself, her writing style, her rule of thumb for plotting, and her meteoric rise to fame.

"According to the information on your Web site," said Gene, "you've inked yet another book contract with Pennington Publishing."

Carmen dimpled prettily. "A three-book contract."

"For six figures?" asked Gene, his pencil poised eagerly above his notepad.

"Seven," corrected Carmen.

Gene made a few quick scratches, then looked up and said, "A little bird told me you've got a few other projects going, as well."

"Whatever are you referring to?" asked Carmen.

"I hear you might be opening a fine dining establishment," said Gene.

At this Suzanne almost choked. A fine dining establishment? That was *her* dream! How could Carmen Copeland just waltz in and usurp her special dream!

"That's still in the early planning stage," said Carmen, trying to sound mysterious. "Very sketchy."

"My understanding," said Gene, "was that you made an offer to George Draper on his funeral home."

"What!" exclaimed Suzanne.

"At this point it's a competing offer," said Carmen. "Since Mr. Draper's already entertaining another possibility."

"Are you serious?" shrilled Suzanne. Information seemed to be flying at her left and right. "You mean from the Roth Funeral Home Consortium?"

Both Carmen and Gene glanced at her with curiosity.

"Yes," said Carmen, "I believe it was from that particular company."

Gene bent closer to Carmen. "You're a woman who deals in rather sensational story lines and plot twists. What do you make of all that's going on in Kindred right now?"

"Strange times," murmured Carmen.

"And you," said Gene, suddenly focusing on Suzanne for the first time. "Discovering a *second* murder victim." He seemed to relish his words. "How do you feel about that? Better yet, what quirk of fate made you the harbinger of all this bad news?"

Suzanne sighed heavily. Gene may as well have dubbed her the angel of death. "I take it you're writing a story on Bo Becker's murder?" she asked in a dry tone.

"How could the double murder of Ozzie Driesden and Bo Becker be anything but front-page news!" exclaimed Gene.

"It wasn't technically a double murder," Suzanne pointed out.

"Whatever," said Gene. "Two homicides in Kindred all within a matter of days? That constitutes high drama."

"And you're just the one to write the story, aren't you?"

said Suzanne. She was suddenly disliking Gene Gandle more and more.

As a late influx of fans suddenly pushed their way in to meet Carmen, Suzanne grabbed Gene's arm and pulled him away from Carmen's table.

"Do you have to put such a grisly perspective on things?" Suzanne asked. "Have a heart and consider the victims' families, will you?"

"You must know something," pushed Gene.

"Nada," said Suzanne.

"You know anything about this mysterious homeless guy?" he asked.

"No," said Suzanne. *And if I did, I wouldn't tell you.*

"Notice anything unusual last night when you found the body?"

"Nope," said Suzanne. That was her story and she was sticking to it.

"What about Toni?" asked Gene. "I know she was out there with you."

"We just took a wrong turn," said Suzanne. "Ended up in the thick of things by mistake."

Gandle smirked. "You're thick as thieves if you ask me."

"And what's this crap about Carmen opening a fine dining establishment?" asked Suzanne. She was more upset over that little tidbit of information than she was about Gene's probing questions on the murders.

"Carmen's a pistol," said Gene, glancing over at her with admiration. Then he gave Suzanne a sly look. "What's wrong? Afraid of a little not-so-friendly competition?"

"Absolutely not, Gene," said Suzanne. "It's a big free-market economy."

"In that case," said Gene, "how would you like to place a couple of ads in the *Bugle*?"

"You're selling ad space now, too?" asked Suzanne.

"It's commissionable, Suzanne. A guy's got to earn a living."

"I think I'll pass for the time being."

"You should support your local paper, Suzanne," glowered Gene.

"I will just as soon as you start supporting your local café," countered Suzanne.

CHAPTER 17

"YOU'VE got to be kidding," said Suzanne, when they pulled into Hoobly's parking lot at eight o'clock that night. "This dump is jumping."

The oversized Quonset hut out on County Road 18 had desultory strings of Christmas lights dangling from its rooftop, flashing yellow lights on the giant Hoobly's sign over the front door, and a parking lot jammed with pickup trucks, SUVs, and older-model cars. There were even a couple of eighteen-wheelers parked out back where the gravel edged up to a bean field.

"Are there this many sorry people in the world?" asked Suzanne. Hoobly's really did have a rotten reputation. Bikers, bookies, and even a few dope peddlers were known to populate its murky interior.

"Appears so," said Toni. "Place is jam-packed." She fluffed her hair, wriggled her shoulders, and pulled her snug-fitting jean jacket down over her hips.

"Their drinks are supposedly watered down," commented Suzanne. "And I'm sure the food is to die *from*. Literally."

They clomped up onto the front porch and Toni put a hand on the rough-hewn door handle. Sensing Suzanne's reluctance, she said, "You're not going to change your mind, are you?"

"No, we've come this far," said Suzanne, as faint strains of country and western music wafted out to greet them. "And I'm just curious enough about Junior."

"Okeydoke," said Toni.

But when they pulled open the door and walked in, it was another story altogether. Country and western music blared from the jukebox, a long bar filled with patrons stretched off to their left, a sea of pool tables and a pull tab booth was off on the right. A permanent blue cloud of cigarette smoke seemed to hover over everything.

"Didn't they ever hear of the Indoor Clean Air Act?" sniffed Suzanne.

"Not here," said Toni, pulling Suzanne through the crowd. "Not at Hoobly's."

A man in a black T-shirt and trucker's cap loomed in front of them. "Either you gals care to dance?" he asked.

"No, thanks," said Toni, propelling Suzanne toward an unoccupied booth in back. "Maybe later."

"Maybe never," said Suzanne, sliding across a cracked black plastic seat.

"You can't be too harsh on these men," said Toni. "These are the real people. The guys who drive the trucks, farm the land, and . . ."

"Hustle the chicks." Suzanne laughed.

"Yeah," said Toni, laughing with her. "That's about the score, I guess."

"But not with us tonight," said Suzanne.

Toni turned grim. "Not until we figure out what that moron, Junior, is up to."

"What if he doesn't show?" asked Suzanne.

"He'll be here," Toni assured her. "I talked to him earlier and casually asked if he was gonna drop by my place tonight. He specifically said he was meeting somebody here and that he'd come by late. Like not until eleven o'clock."

"So now we wait," said Suzanne, glancing around.

"Maybe have a drink?" asked Toni. A waitress in low-slung blue jeans and a pink belly-grazing T-shirt plopped down coasters in front of them.

"Why not?" said Suzanne. "Miller Lite. Bottle, if you have it."

"Same here," said Toni.

The waitress lifted an eyebrow. "You ladies see those two dudes sitting over there?"

All three of them peered up the line of booths at two guys in western shirts and hats.

"Uh-huh," said Toni. She sounded just this side of interested.

"They offered to buy you a drink," said the waitress.

"Tell 'em no thanks," said Suzanne. She gave a little wave toward the two cowboys. "Thanks anyway, guys."

One of them smiled and tipped his hat at her.

"Well, wasn't that nice and friendly?" said Toni.

"Toni," said Suzanne, "we're here to spy, not do a meet and greet with cowboy Bob and his sidekick."

"Still," said Toni, a little wistfully, "it's nice to get hustled once in a while. Helps build a girl's ego."

But Suzanne had turned her eyes on a tawdry red velvet curtain that was rigged across a postage stamp–sized stage. The music had suddenly changed from Kenny Chesney's "Down the Road" to Rod Stewart's "Do You Think I'm Sexy."

"Oh man," said Suzanne. "They have strippers!"

Their waitress, who'd just arrived with their beers, said, "Oh sure," as if it was the most natural thing on earth.

"You didn't mention strippers," Suzanne hissed at Toni.

"I thought you knew that," said Toni. "Heck, I thought everybody knew that."

The red velvet curtain suddenly parted to reveal a shiny brass pole.

"And not just regular strippers," said Toni. "Pole dancers." She sounded impressed.

"And now," came a deep, male voice over a crackly loudspeaker, "please welcome Lady Dubonnet!" There were hoots and whistles as Lady Dubonnet, clad in skimpy black push-up bra, fishnet stockings, and red thong, took the stage.

"Ai yi yi," Suzanne said with a laugh.

The scantily clad young woman crooked her leg around the pole and spun enticingly as the music pulsed and throbbed: *If you really need me, just reach out and touch me, come on, honey, tell me so.*

"Now that takes skill," said Toni. "Plus a certain amount of poise."

"Are you referring to parading in your undies in front of drooling men or just wriggling around in general?" asked Suzanne.

"In general." Toni giggled.

"I'd think all that spinning would make a person dizzy," Suzanne observed.

"Probably just part and parcel of the job," said Toni. "Occupational hazard."

"I'd probably get an imbalance in my inner ear," said Suzanne.

They sipped their beers and watched Lady Dubonnet perform her routine. When the song ended, she bowed to an energetic round of applause and picked up several dollar bills that had been carefully placed on the stage.

When Lady Dubonnet came hustling toward them, on

her way to the ladies' room, Suzanne did a slight double take and said, "I think I know her!"

"Who is she?" asked Toni.

"Kit Kaslik.

"Oh wow," said Toni.

"I'm going to talk to her," said Suzanne. And just as Kit went flying past their booth, Suzanne reached out and grabbed her arm.

"Watch it!" snarled Kit, jerking away fast, her dark eyes snapping with anger. "You can't treat a girl like . . ." Then she saw Suzanne and Toni and paused, midsentence. "Who're you two?" she asked, thrusting out a hip and placing a hand on it in a confrontational gesture. "The local Salvation Army do-gooders come to save my sorry soul?"

"It's me, Kit," said Suzanne. "Suzanne Dietz. You remember, I used to teach at your high school?"

"Oh . . . yeah." A faint smile flickered across Kit's face and she seemed to relax a bit.

"And this is Toni Garrett," said Suzanne.

"Hey," said Kit, nodding slightly.

"How do?" said Toni. "I really liked the way you wiggled your way through that song."

"She didn't really," said Suzanne, hastily. "Fact is, you shouldn't be working here at all."

"I guess it's not exactly a high-test career path," added Toni.

"Tips are good," said Kit. She projected a wry smile, but there was sadness in her eyes.

"Honey," said Suzanne, sliding over and pulling Kit into the booth with her. "You are so much better than this. *So* much better."

That was all it took. Kit shook her head and sighed deeply. "It's hard to find a really good job around here."

"It sure is," agreed Toni.

"Don't tell me you enjoy this," said Suzanne, in a soft voice.

"Not really," said Kit, sniffling now. "Frankie, the manager, is always pushing us to *fraternize* with the customers. That's what he calls it, fraternizing. But he really means hitting on them. Hard. Get the guys to offer to buy a drink, then order something fancy and expensive like a Pink Squirrel or a Golden Cadillac. Or a bottle of five-dollar champagne that Frankie marks up to thirty bucks."

"Whatever happened to a plain old brewski?" muttered Toni.

But Suzanne was focused on the bigger picture. "This is not a job with a good future," she told Kit. "From here it's a slippery slope to gosh knows what."

"Or a slippery pole," added Toni.

"Tell you what," continued Suzanne. "The Cackleberry Club . . . you've heard of the Cackleberry Club?"

Kit nodded.

"We're having a big event this Saturday," explained Suzanne. "A Take the Cake Show plus an evening gourmet dinner. And we could use a little extra help. Maybe . . . well, would you be interested?"

"You mean like waitressing?" Kit wasn't particularly thrilled.

"More like an assistant for the cake event," said Suzanne. "And, yes, a waitress in the evening. But I can pretty much guarantee you wouldn't have to wear fishnet stockings."

"Or take anything off," added Toni.

"That's a really nice offer," said Kit. "And you both seem very kind. But . . . can I think about it?"

"Seems like you already are." Suzanne smiled as Kit slipped out of the booth.

"Sweet girl," said Toni, once Kit had left.

"Too sweet for this place," said Suzanne. She was relieved there weren't any more pole dancers performing for the time being. Just a song playing on the jukebox with one of the longest titles in history: "How Could You Have Believed Me When I Told You that I Loved You, When You Know I've Been a Liar All My Life?"

"Listen," said Suzanne, "they're playing Junior's song.

"Where is that little creep, anyway?" wondered Toni, fidgeting nervously.

"Hey," said Suzanne, "did you know that Carmen Copeland may have made an offer on the Driesden and Draper Funeral Home?"

"What?" Toni swiveled her head back toward Suzanne. She obviously hadn't heard. "What are you talkin' about?"

"Gene Gandle mentioned it today. When he came in to do the interview with Carmen."

"Draper's gonna sell out?" asked Toni.

"Maybe," said Suzanne. "Although the whole thing sounds fishy to me."

"What's Carmen gonna do with an old funeral home?" asked Toni. "Fill it with bats and broomsticks and move in?"

"The words *fine dining* were mentioned."

"No way!" screeched Toni. She stared at Suzanne, her mouth agape. "That's what you've been talking about."

"Yes, it is," said Suzanne, a little glumly. "In fact, I already checked out a little house over on Arbor Street. An adorable bungalow-style place that has a dining room with French doors that would convert perfectly into a wine bar. And room for about seven or eight tables in the rest of the downstairs."

"Cackleberry Club West?" asked Toni.

"I was thinking more of Crepe Suzanne's."

A grin lit Toni's face. "Perfect! Oh, Suzanne, you're such a smarty. A real entrepreneur."

"Still," said Suzanne, "all that's a pipe dream. Gotta make the Cackleberry Club profitable first."

"I thought we were making a profit."

"Making a living," said Suzanne. "Big difference."

"See?" said Toni. "That's why you're CEO. You're plugged in to all this tricky business stuff."

"Unless Carmen aces me out."

"She's one mean malefactor," said Toni.

Twenty minutes later, they'd nursed their beers about as much as they could and fended off several unwanted advances.

"Where is Junior anyway?" worried Toni. She alternated between nervousness and full-blown hostility.

"Maybe he came and left," suggested Suzanne. She was ready to call it quits herself.

"No," said Toni. "I've kept an eye out. He'll show up. He has to."

Those seemed to be the magic words, for suddenly Junior Garrett swaggered in through the front door.

"There's the little runt now," Toni hissed, as she watched Junior walk halfway down the bar, then swing up easily onto a bar stool.

"Gonna have himself a drink?" mused Suzanne, sliding down in her seat, but still keeping an eye on him.

But Junior didn't seem to be placing any kind of drink order. Instead, he reached inside his leather jacket, pulled out an envelope, and slid it across the top of the bar. A youthful-looking bartender quickly put his hand on the envelope and made it magically disappear.

"Whoa," said Suzanne.

Junior lit a cigarette and looked around nonchalantly for a couple of minutes, seemingly studying the crowd of bikers and truckers that stood arguing by the pool tables. Then he stood up and casually sauntered back outside.

"Did you see that exchange with the bartender?" asked Toni, looking morose. "Junior *is* up to something."

"Hmm," was Suzanne's measured response. "I don't suppose those were auto parts."

"You ever see a crank shaft fit inside a business-size envelope?" Toni snapped.

"Can't say's I have," said Suzanne.

"So now we gotta follow him," said Toni. "See what the deal is. See if Junior's gonna run back to some lab that's pumping out crystal meth."

"You're talking about investigating," pointed out Suzanne. "We stuck our noses in somebody else's business last night and look where it got us."

"Suzanne . . . please!" There was real panic in Toni's eyes.

"Okay, okay." Suzanne couldn't bear to see Toni in such turmoil.

They tossed down a five-dollar tip, sped along the dingy hallway that led past the restrooms, then slipped out the back door. As they were climbing into Toni's car, Junior rumbled past them.

"There!" exclaimed Suzanne, pointing. "He's pulling out onto the road."

Toni gunned the engine and her tires spit gravel.

"Easy," warned Suzanne. "We don't want to tip him off."

"I'll hang back," promised Toni.

Suzanne glanced at her friend. Toni looked determined, but sad. As though Junior, who'd betrayed her time and again, had finally managed to drive a stake through her heart. On the other hand, Toni had resolved to save Junior from himself or whatever drug-dealing loonies he was involved with. So she must still have feelings for him. Suzanne shook her head. Toni was between a rock and a hard place without a cushion to sit on.

They spun down County Road 18, hanging back, but always keeping Junior's taillights in view.

When they came to a series of S-curves, Suzanne said, "Now drop back a little more. We don't want Junior to catch us in his rearview mirror."

"I will, I will," said Toni, following him through the turns. Then they were on the straightaway again.

"I wonder where he's going?" asked Suzanne. This part of the county was hilly and slightly woodsy, populated mostly by cattle ranches and dairy farms. Then again, most drug operations weren't set up in the heart of town, right next to the post office for ease of shipping.

"He's turning," said Toni, in a tight voice. She slowed way down and they both watched the sweep of headlights and flash of taillights as Junior hung a left turn.

"If we follow him through that turn," said Toni, he's gonna catch on sooner or later that he's being tailed. He's not *blind*."

"Then do your flying thing," prompted Suzanne.

"Are you serious?" asked Toni as they turned onto the gravel road behind him. Really?"

"Do it carefully," said Suzanne.

Toni punched out the lights. "Just pray we don't hit a deer or skid on a loose patch of gravel."

They didn't. In fact the road was fairly straight and Junior's taillights, a quarter mile ahead, served as a solid beacon to guide their way.

Then the road twisted through a grove of trees and dipped across a narrow, single-lane bridge, the boards echoing loosely as they crossed.

"Lost him," said Toni, wrinkling her nose.

"Where'd he go?" wondered Suzanne, peering into the night.

Toni suddenly hit her brakes, snapping their heads and causing Suzanne to flail out and grab hold of the dashboard. "There he is!" she whispered.

Suzanne followed Toni's gaze out the driver's side window. It took a few moments, but finally her eyes grew accustomed to the darkness and she could see a glint of something—Junior's car—half hidden behind a small, ramshackle building. To the left of Junior's car stood an old farmhouse where a few lights glowed. Behind it was a large, hip-roofed barn.

"Now what?" asked Suzanne.

"Now we sit and wait," said Toni. Slowly, quietly, she backed her car down a small incline and into a grove of poplars. Branches scratched against car doors and windows, sounding spookily like fingernails.

"What are we waiting for?" asked Suzanne. She was shivering slightly, now that Toni had turned the heater off.

"Junior," was Toni's single terse word.

They sat there for five minutes. Then their wait stretched into ten. When Suzanne was about to suggest the futility of this night watch, Junior surprised them by suddenly reappearing as a shadow. Hastily crossing the yard, Junior slithered into his car, fired up the engine, and rocketed away fast.

"Should we follow him?" asked Suzanne.

"No!" hissed Toni. "We gotta see if this place really is a meth lab!"

"How will we know that?" asked Suzanne, curious and leery at the same time.

"I dunno," said Toni. "Maybe we can peek in the windows or something."

"Do you actually know what a meth lab looks like?" Suzanne asked.

Toni thought for a moment. "Maybe like bubbling beakers full of green goop with steam rising up?"

"You know what?" said Suzanne. "You've been watching too many old Frankenstein movies on the late-night creature feature. You've developed a William Castle fixation."

"The only scary movie I watched lately was *Saw*," said Toni. "And it scared me to death."

They climbed from the car and tiptoed quietly across the road, easing their way toward the farm house. Halfway there, a dog, an aging black Labrador, padded up to greet them.

"Hey, baby," whispered Suzanne. "You're not going to bark, are you?"

The dog gave a desultory tail wag in response to her voice.

"Seems like a sweet old mutt," said Toni. "Thank goodness he's not exactly your crackerjack guard dog."

"If Baxter was here, he'd be barking his head off," said Suzanne. She dug into her handbag and pulled out a plastic bag filled with jerky treats.

"You keep dog treats in your purse?"

"At all times," said Suzanne. "It's the only bargaining chip I have with creatures of the canine persuasion. The only thing that stands between reason and chaos."

She handed the jerky to the dog, who accepted it with a certain gravity. Suzanne gave him another. She liked the dignified old fellow. "Now lie down and be cool," she told him.

They slid behind a clump of dried lilac bushes. Not much cover, but better than nothing. Then eased their way gently up to the back of the house where two windows glowed an eerie green.

"No way," said Toni in a low voice. Lights were obviously on inside, but their view was blocked by window shades pulled snuggly down.

Suzanne tried peeking in from the side, but no luck. Just a sliver of . . . nothing.

Toni made a forward motion with her hand. Got to get closer.

Suzanne inhaled sharply. This was not a promising scenario. Two women, out in the middle of nowhere, playing a dangerous game of Peeping Tom. What's wrong with this picture?

But Toni was moving forward aggressively. Along the length of the house, toward the front porch. She hesitated, then put one foot on the porch step, then another. Waved for Suzanne to follow.

Against her better judgment, Suzanne did. Climbed up three steps, crossed a broad porch badly in need of paint, and joined Toni at a window that was pushed up a few inches. A tattered window shade, the color of old parchment, fluttered in the breeze. Shadows moved back and forth behind that shade. Soft voices formed indistinct words.

Gripping the window ledge, Toni put her face flat against the house, and tried to peer in.

"Anything?" Suzanne whispered.

Toni put a hand up to silence her, twisted her body

slightly, moved her feet to get a slightly better angle, and . . . creak!

The offending board underfoot sounded like a rifle shot in the still of the night.

One of Toni's hands flew to her mouth, then she gazed at Suzanne with wild eyes. "Oh shiznit!" she cried. "They heard us!"

CHAPTER 18

"RUN!" Suzanne cried hoarsely, as she grabbed Toni's arm and gave a rough jerk.

They pounded down the three steps onto a brown lawn that was more hardpan than grass.

But they weren't fast enough.

One man came thundering out the front door, another man barreled out a side door they hadn't noticed before. Not only were they trapped like rats, but front-door guy carried a gun!

"Who are you?" demanded the guy with the gun. He was in his late twenties, wearing jeans and a dirty Pantera T-shirt.

Suzanne slid to a stop. Toni bumped hard against her. "Uh . . . is this where the party is?" asked Suzanne. She tried to still her wildly beating heart and sound upbeat and a little coy, too. Slightly flirtatious.

That stopped the two guys dead. "Party?" said the one in the dirty T-shirt. He lowered his gun slightly. "You know anything about that, Eel?"

Eel, who wasn't much of a prize in his rumpled blue shirt and grey sweatpants, leered at Toni. "Can't say's I do, Lenny."

"Sure," said Toni, grinning like a maniac, picking up on Suzanne's ruse immediately. "We were just tipping back a few beers at Hoobly's and heard a rumor about a party out here."

"No party," said Eel. He sounded a little wistful.

"Okay then," said Suzanne, backing away. "Wrong house. Sorry about this, guys. We sure didn't mean to barge in on you, uninvited."

"Maybe some other time," added Toni.

"Not so fast, snoopy lady," said Lenny. He waggled his gun, a gray, snub-nosed revolver, directly in Suzanne's face.

"Hey," said Suzanne, "do you guys know a fellow named Bo, by any chance?" She sounded far bolder than she felt. If she could put together a connection here . . .

Eel gaped at her. "Who?" There wasn't the slightest bit of recognition in his voice. "Don't know who you're talking about, lady."

"Man," said Toni, giving a goofy smile and smacking her palm against her forehead, "we really got our signals crossed. Crazy us, huh?" Again she and Suzanne tried to pull away.

Lenny moved to block them again. "No," he said, and this time he sounded decidedly thoughtful, "something's going on here."

Eel frowned. "You think they're . . . like . . . DEA?"

DEA, thought Suzanne, *that's Drug Enforcement Administration. These guys do have something to do with drugs.*

"Nothin' like that," Lenny said slowly, "but we gotta think this through. We can't just let 'em waltz out of here scot-free."

"What do you wanna do with 'em?" asked Eel, as Toni threw him a hopeful smile.

"Lock 'em in the barn for now," said Lenny. "Till I make a couple of phone calls and figure this out."

* * *

"I'm gonna kill Junior when I get my hands on him," snarled Suzanne. She was perched on a hay bale in the dusty, dimly lit barn. "I don't know what Junior's up to with those two assholes, but something illegal's going on!"

"Stand in line," said Toni, pacing back and forth. "Because I guarantee there won't be anything left of Junior except *scraps* when I get through with him!"

"Gonna run him through the meat grinder," growled Suzanne. "Then fry his skinny butt."

Toni let loose a deep sigh. "Look," she said. "I'm really sorry about this. Since *I* was the birdbrain who got us into this."

"Why did we leave our cell phones in the car?" seethed Suzanne.

"'Cause we didn't count on getting caught," said Toni. "That stupid Junior!" She scuffed at the dirt with the toe of her boot.

"If it wasn't for his crappy, shady dealings, we wouldn't have followed him out here," grumped Suzanne. "Wouldn't be locked inside this *stupid* barn!" She stood up, walked a few paces, then kicked the barn door for good measure. "Ouch!"

"The thing is," said Toni, as Suzanne hopped around on one foot, "what are we gonna do now?"

Suzanne limped back to her hay bale, plopped herself down, and studied their surroundings. "Well," she said finally, "it's a frigging barn, not a cement block prison with razor wire strung around it. There's a hayloft upstairs, so maybe we can climb that stupid ladder over there and jump out a window or something."

"And break a hip?" said Toni. "We're not getting any

younger. Bone loss starts as early as your forties, you know."

"Please," said Suzanne. "Don't remind me."

Toni plunked her bottom down on a hay bale as well, put her chin in her hand, thinking. Minutes passed. Then Toni said, "Was that guy's name really Eel? Did I hear that correctly?"

"Eel and Lenny," said Suzanne. "Some tag team, huh?"

"Yeah," muttered Toni. She turned up the collar on her jacket. "Cold in here."

"Gonna get colder," said Suzanne. "And more dangerous once those guys come back for us."

"Then we gotta figure a way out," said Toni. She stretched her legs out, staring morosely at her cowboy boots.

"You hear something?" Suzanne asked. She cocked her head, frowned.

"No."

"Because I'd swear there was a distinct rustling coming from that far corner."

"Maybe . . . mice?" proposed Toni.

"Pretty big mice," said Suzanne. She got to her feet, brushed off her bottom, then crept over to the corner of the barn. "Oh man!" she said.

Toni came over, curious now. "What?"

"Animals," said Suzanne, pointing at two stalls. "Two goats and a mule."

"Say now," said Toni, "we could always get some goat's milk if we're thirsty. That could help with our bone loss, too."

"As long as one of them is female," said Suzanne.

"Oh," said Toni, peering speculatively at the underside of one of the goats. "Good point."

"So how can we put these critters to good use?" wondered Suzanne.

"What if we got the goats to head butt the door?" asked Toni.

"It's a pretty big door," mused Suzanne. "And awfully small goats."

"Okay then," said Toni, determinedly, "what if we used the mule to kick down the door?"

"Interesting idea," said Suzanne. She didn't know much about mules except that they were half horse and half donkey. And even though she wasn't familiar with donkeys, she knew how hard a horse could kick. Had experienced it first hand a few times.

But getting a mule to kick down a barn door turned out to be a lot harder than it sounded.

"Backing up this mule is like trying to back up a dump truck," complained Toni. She was hanging on for dear life from the big mule's halter. "This guy is ginormous and I can't seem to find reverse."

"Just keep backing him up," urged Suzanne, patting the mule on the flanks, trying to urge him backward with gentle pats and kind words.

"What am I, the mule whisperer?" asked Toni. "Hey, this ain't working."

"If we get him close enough," Suzanne reasoned, "maybe he'll just do what comes naturally." She paused, then took a quick step backward. "Uh-oh."

"What?" asked Toni, peering around the mule.

"He just did what comes naturally."

"Huh?" asked Toni. Then she caught a whiff. "Oh man, did he just do what I think he did?"

"Afraid so," said Suzanne.

Which set them to giggling.

"If I had a plastic bag," said Toni, still trying to wrangle the mule, "I'd stuff some of his equine output inside and set it on fire."

"For what purpose?" asked Suzanne. "And, may I add, you are completely off the hook."

"Throw it at that farmhouse," said Toni. "Get back at 'em."

"A twisted idea," said Suzanne, "but appealing, none-theless, for what they're putting us through." She joined Toni at the front of the mule. "This isn't working."

"No kidding," muttered Toni.

"What we need is . . ." Suzanne glanced around the barn.

"A whip?" asked Toni.

Suzanne's eyes searched the pegs on the walls, skitter-ing over curry combs, leather leads, and more halters. Fi-nally, she found something that might work. "How about a harness?" she asked.

Once it was settled over the mule's shoulders and flanks, controlling the mule was a little easier. In fact, the mule seemed to pick right up on the notion of pulling and back-ing up. And it wasn't long before they had his backside rubbing directly up against the barn door.

"Now kick!" Toni implored the mule. "C'mon, gonzo guy, give it a real whack!"

"We gotta back him up even more," said Suzanne.

"His tail's already flat against the door," sputtered Toni. "But he's not *doing* anything."

"Then we have to frustrate him," said Suzanne. "Goad him into kicking."

"Gotcha," said Toni. She tugged at one side of the mule's harness. "Give it a try, boy, you can do it. Give that door a good, swift kick and there's a carrot in it for you."

The mule stared stolidly at Toni without blinking.

"Apple?" asked Toni.

Suzanne stepped in front of the mule and threw up both arms. "Hyah!" she yelled loudly. She made a loud, clicking sound. "Move it! Move it!"

The mule tossed his head back, the whites of his eyes suddenly showing, as if to say, *Say what?* And, wonder of wonders, let loose a thunderous kick against the barn door.

"Awright!" cried Toni. "Progress! You've developed an excellent rapport with this animal, Suzanne. Now do whatever you did again."

Suzanne waved her arms crazily and clicked and clucked until her tongue ached.

Bam! *Blam!* The barn door shuddered on its antique hinges.

"He's doing it!" yelled Toni. "All we need is one more good . . ."

Crash! The barn door suddenly split up the middle!

". . . kick!" finished Toni. "Atta boy!" She reached up and patted the mule's broad forehead.

Suzanne grabbed the mule's halter and eased him forward, out of their way. Then they both put shoulders to the door and shoved . . . hard!

"It's giving way!" yelled Toni. "I can feel it!"

But it wasn't the door that gave way. Instead, the old latch simply capitulated.

"All that kicking must have loosened it!" Suzanne cried excitedly, as they shoved open the door. Fresh air assaulted them and little bits of moonlight filtered down through the trees as they made a mad dash for Toni's car.

"What about the mule?" asked Toni, as they ducked

under an old wash line, then skittered around an old pump. "I promised him a carrot! Or maybe it was an apple!"

"I'm sure he'll be fine," Suzanne cried, as they pounded across the blacktopped road, slid down the grassy incline, and jumped into Toni's car.

Suddenly, a yard light flashed on and they heard faint yelling from inside the farmhouse!

"They know!" said Toni.

"Then we gotta get out of here!" responded Suzanne.

Toni cranked the ignition, floored it, and then they were fishtailing crazily up the incline and onto the road. Her wheels spun wildly for an instant, laying a thin carpet of rubber. And then they rocketed down the road, Toni handling her car like Danica Patrick at Indy.

"They'll never catch us now!" chortled Toni.

Suzanne put a hand to her chest to still her beating heart. "That was awful." She reached over and put a hand on Toni's shoulder. "Take it easy. Don't put us in a ditch."

"What a rush!" cried Toni, still reveling in her surge of adrenaline.

"It was a disaster," replied Suzanne, enjoying the gush of warmth from the car's heater. "We have to drive directly to the law enforcement center and tell Doogie or whoever's on duty what just happened!"

"Whadya mean?" cried Toni. She'd gone from crazy happy to flustered and upset.

"I'm talking kidnapping and probably drug dealing."

"No way!" screeched Toni. "If we tell the cops what happened, we implicate Junior!" She slowed the car down. "Please," she begged, "we can't tell anyone about that place until I talk to Junior. I gotta try to extricate him from this mess!"

"Then you'd better set him straight ASAP!" warned Suzanne.

"First thing tomorrow," pleaded Toni. "Okay?"

"But Junior's coming to your house tonight," said Suzanne.

"Good point," said Toni.

"So," said Suzanne, cooling down a little, trying to come up with a logical plan, "you'll stay over with me."

"Then we talk to Junior first thing tomorrow," said Toni. "Both of us together." Her eyes darted from the road to Suzanne, then back to the road again. "Right?"

"And then we'll call Doogie," said Suzanne. "And report those jerks."

"Of course, we will," said Toni. "Only . . . can't we do it anonymously?"

CHAPTER 19

THURSDAY morning at the Cackleberry Club was Foggy Morning Soufflé day, which Toni had taken to calling Soggy Morning Soufflé. In any case, it was a worthy concoction of whipped eggs, milk, and flour, combined with grated Swiss cheese, butter, and mustard, sizzled in a fry pan, then thrust into a hot oven to pouf said soufflé up to towering proportions.

Petra hummed in the kitchen, prepping her soufflés, while Junior Garrett slumped at the counter of the Cackleberry Club, looking all the world like a beaten-down prisoner of war. His black T-shirt hung loosely on his skinny frame, even his normally tight jeans seemed to sag.

Toni had called him in early on the pretext of car trouble and now Suzanne and Toni had been haranguing Junior for a solid ten minutes. Sometimes they took turns, sometimes they yelled in tandem. Once in a while, as she was whipping her eggs, Petra yelled out her two cents' worth as well. Obviously, they'd clued her in regarding last night's fiasco.

"Don't you ever go near Lenny and Eel again!" Toni warned.

Junior gave a pitiful shrug. "How can I? Since you guys probably ruined it for me."

"I don't want to hear that crap from you, Junior," said Toni. "You were dealing dope!"

"Which," said Suzanne, "last time I looked, was highly illegal!"

"Everybody smokes a little weed," Junior whined.

"No, they do not," said Toni, shaking a stern finger at him.

"Besides," said Junior, "I wasn't making the actual *deals* or delivering the actual *stuff*. I was just handling the financial end. You know, collecting money."

"You were the bag man," said Suzanne, disgustedly.

Junior brightened at her characterization. "Yeah, that's it, I was just the bag man. No big deal, huh?"

"Al Capone's bag man went to prison right alongside him," said Toni, winging it.

"Is that so?" said Junior.

"All the money men are going to prison these days," Suzanne told him. "Bernie Madoff, the Enron guys, sleazy hedge-fund managers, mortgage fraud guys, IRS cheats, even a few governors. And, unless you're careful, you could end up as their cell mate."

Junior gave her a wary stare. "What are you gonna do? Try and send me to the 'lectric chair?"

"Unfortunately," said Suzanne, "we don't have the luxury of capital punishment at our disposal. We are, however, going to send Sheriff Doogie out to that farmhouse. Hopefully to discover a serious amount of incriminating evidence and place your pals Lenny and Eel under arrest."

Toni gave Junior a menacing stare. "And just what exactly is Sheriff Doogie going to find out there?" she asked.

"Just a few measly plants and some grow lights in the back bedroom," mumbled Junior. "I told ya, it ain't *that* big a deal."

"Of course it is!" thundered Suzanne. "Which is why you have to lie exceedingly low. Fact is, we could have had

all of you busted last night! The only thing standing between you and a felony conviction is Toni's good grace!"

Junior grimaced.

The front door rattled and all three of them turned nervously to look. But it was Joey Ewald coming in for his
stint as busboy.

Joey grinned when he saw them clustered at the counter.
"Hey, ladies," he called to Suzanne and Toni. Then turned
his focus on Junior. "How ya doin', Junior?"

"Never better," said Junior, giving Joey a cocky grin and
a thumbs-up sign. At which point Toni grabbed a pot holder
and whacked him in the head.

"Ouch," whined Junior. "What'd I do to deserve that?"

"You know!" hissed Toni.

"You still skateboarding?" Junior called to Joey, trying
to muster his dignity.

"Oh yeah, man," said Joey. "Thinkin' about changing
my name to Joey Crash."

"Cool," said Junior, as Joey disappeared into the
kitchen.

Toni smacked him with the pot holder again. "What are
you . . . ten?" she asked. "Grow up."

"I *am* growed up," argued Junior. "Fact is, I could probably be a heckuva role model to that kid."

"Are you serious?" snorted Suzanne. "You barely
squirmed your way through vo-tech, you've been arrested
for drunk and disorderly conduct and forced to do community service, and your hobbies are gambling, fast cars,
and faster women." She glanced at Toni. "Well, they used
to be anyway."

"No," said Toni, "they *still* are."

"And now that we have your undivided attention," said
Suzanne, "I have a few *more* questions."

"Shoot," said Junior. "I'm an open book."

"A comic book," muttered Toni.

"Did you ever have dealings with Bo Becker?" asked Suzanne. "And I want an honest answer."

"No," said Junior, looking earnest for the first time that morning. "But I always considered Bo a stand-up guy. And a heck of a good driver, too. He used to whip that Mustang of his around the track pretty good when they had amateur night over at the speedway."

"Do you know anything about what happened to Becker?" asked Toni.

Junior shook his head and frowned. "Uh-uh. Just heard that he got killed. Hunged, I guess."

"Hanged," corrected Toni.

"Was he dealing drugs?" asked Suzanne.

"Not that I know of," said Junior. "Not with my guys anyway." He swallowed hard, then said, "At least I don't *think* he was."

"Junior," said Suzanne, "you have to promise you'll stay clean. Cross your heart and hope to die."

"Yeah, sure," said Junior. "Until lately, I pretty much have been clean." His earnestness was suddenly replaced by his old swagger. "Fact is, I've been a doggone entrepreneur."

"Do you even know the definition of an entrepreneur?" asked Toni.

"'Course, I do," said Junior.

Toni folded her arms in front of her, daring him. "What is it, Mr. Smart Guy?"

Junior scratched his head vigorously, then scowled, as though he was engaging in deep thought. "It's a guy who does business."

"Nice try," said Suzanne. "See if you end up a financial reporter for CNN."

A few minutes later they allowed Junior to make his escape. Giving him a final cautionary warning and a freshly baked corn muffin.

"I'm gonna call Doogie right now," said Toni. "Anonymously."

"Jeez," said Suzanne, thinking. "Won't he be able to trace the call right back to us?"

"I thought of that," said Toni, "so I'm gonna use a trick I learned." She pulled a phone card from her jeans pocket and waved it at Suzanne. "I'll use a phone card, which is virtually untraceable. I saw how the whole deal worked on an old episode of *The Sopranos*. This mob guy used a phone card so there was no way the cops could trace his call."

"Good to know," said Suzanne, spinning on her heels and heading into the kitchen. She really didn't want to know too much about Toni's phone call. She was way too involved already.

Petra was in the kitchen, humming to herself and whipping up a batch of pancake batter.

"How's your back?" asked Suzanne, draping an arm lightly around Petra's shoulders.

"I saw my chiropractor last night, who helped enormously," said Petra.

"Excellent," said Suzanne.

"But then he told me to go home and do bicycle crunches."

"Sounds athletic," said Suzanne.

"Oh, they are," said Petra. "They're nasty semi-sit-up things where you lie on the floor and touch your elbow to your opposite knee, alternating sides."

"Ouch," said Toni, pushing her way through the swinging door. "I heard that."

"But I have a confession to make," continued Petra. "All I did was curl up on the couch, watch old movies, and polish off a giant Toblerone candy bar."

"Ah," said Toni, grinning. "*Le chocolat thérapie.* Always a tried-and-true treatment."

"Swiss, I think," said Suzanne with a laugh.

BY ten o'clock Petra's knitters began arriving in droves. Some of them hustled into the Knitting Nest, where dozens of extra chairs had been installed. The overflow set up camp in the Book Nook. And a dozen or so knitters plopped down at tables in the café where they ordered up coffee, tea, muffins, scones, and slices of Foggy Morning Soufflé.

"So all the knitters have sponsors?" Suzanne asked Petra as she deftly plated breakfasts.

"Right," said Petra. "Kind of like the dog walk you participated in last spring," said Petra. "You took pledges for every mile you walked, right?"

"Sure," said Suzanne. Although, after three miles, Baxter had pretty much made it clear he was bored out of his skull.

"The Knit-In works almost the same way," explained Petra. "All my knitters have sponsors who'll pay so many cents for each row knitted."

"That's pretty cool," said Suzanne, as she pulled a tin of blueberry breakfast squares from the oven.

"And then, once the items are finished . . ."

"That's right," said Suzanne, "it's all coming back to me now. Whew, guess I had a senior moment."

"Happens to me all the time," said Petra.

"All done," said Toni, bursting into the kitchen. She made a big show of dusting her hands. "I made the call."

"I don't want to know," said Suzanne.

"Neither do I," said Petra.

"Then mum's the word," said Toni, putting her thumb and index finger to her mouth and making a little zipping motion.

JUST before lunch, amidst the low hum of conversation and gentle clacking of needles, Suzanne took a quick tour of the Knit-In. And was charmed by what she saw. One knitter, who was curled up in a cozy armchair in the Knitting Nest, was working away on a cranberry red cardigan with cable accents down the front. Delicious!

Another knitter was using an almost iridescent green and gold-flecked mohair yarn to knit a shawl-collar sweater.

In the Book Nook, Suzanne fell in love with an indigo blue sweater vest with a generous flounce of ruffles down the front. She wondered if she could ever learn that type of stitch, then quickly relegated it to that part of her brain where she secretly nursed a desire to *parlez-vous Français*, take classes in ballroom dancing, and learn how to snowshoe—none of which had come to pass yet. Petra *had* tried to teach her to knit, but she hadn't been the most gifted student.

"Hey, Suzanne," one knitter greeted her. "Grab a pair of needles and join us." Suzanne glanced over and recognized Toby Baines, who worked part time at the phone company and wrote a fun advice column for the *Bugle*. She was in her mid-fifties with smiling brown eyes and shoulder-length brown hair pulled back into a loose, low ponytail. Though she didn't wear a speck of makeup, her complexion was smooth, clear, and practically unlined.

"Hey, Toby," Suzanne said as she eased over to see what she was working on.

"Hasn't Petra taught you how to knit yet?" Toby asked, with a mischievous smile.

"She tried, but I'm a poor student," confessed Suzanne. "I tried a couple times, then flunked out."

"You didn't flunk knitting class, you just flunked attendance," Toby told her. "You didn't put in enough time. There *is* a bit of practice involved, you know."

"Probably right," agreed Suzanne.

"I heard about the other night," said Toby, lowering her voice.

"About . . . ?" said Suzanne.

"You finding that young man swinging from a tree. And, of course, helping out the sheriff and all."

"Who said I was helping Doogie?" asked Suzanne, her curiosity roused. Did everyone in Kindred know she was looking into things?

Toby gave a benign smile. "Oh, that's just the talk around town. You know how folks gossip."

Yes, she did.

"And such an awful thing about Ozzie," whispered Toby. "It's very strange . . . two murders . . . two people who worked together . . ." Her voice trailed off as she seemed to gather her thoughts as well as her stitches. "People are locking their doors at night, giving strangers an extra-wide berth."

"What else are people saying?" asked Suzanne.

"Lots of speculation," said Toby, as she continued to

work on what was taking shape as a beret. "Of course, there's always the chance the deaths aren't connected."

"Maybe not," said Suzanne, "though I'm still wondering why Bo Becker ended up at that abandoned church."

"You're a smart lady," said Toby. "I'll bet you figure it out."

CHAPTER 20

BECAUSE of the Knit-In, the luncheon menu at the Cackleberry Club was fairly simple. Cackling Chicken Salad, corn and red pepper pancakes, and green eggs and ham.

Nothing put a damper on customers, though. In addition to the twenty-five knitters who'd poured in earlier, the ladies of the Cackleberry Club also found themselves with a full seating by the time eleven thirty rolled around.

And wouldn't you know it? Ozzie's partner, George Draper, was one of them.

"George," said Suzanne, as she hastened to his table to take his order. She hadn't known him all that well, had always referred to him as Mr. Draper. But since their terse conversation following Ozzie's funeral, it just seemed easier to call him George.

"Suzanne," he said back to her. Obviously, they were on the same wavelength.

"I understand you're thinking about leaving the business," said Suzanne.

Draper hunched forward and puckered his lips. "Well . . . perhaps."

"What happened?" asked Suzanne. "What made you change your mind? Did Ray Lynch get to you? Were you threatened?"

"No, no," said Draper, frowning slightly. "I'm just re-thinking things. Getting my priorities straight."

"And one of those priorities might be to accept the Roth Funeral Home Consortium's offer?"

"Could be," Draper responded. He was trying to appear agreeable, but seemed unhappy deep down.

"Sounds like you're drinking the Kool-Aid, George." Suzanne smiled at him, but not all that warmly.

"Not at all," said Draper. "Fact is, I'm entertaining an-other offer, too." He managed a hoarse chuckle. "When it rains it pours."

"You're talking about Carmen Copeland?" asked Suzanne.

George looked slightly taken aback. "How would you know about that?"

"Everybody knows about Carmen's offer by now," said Suzanne. "She's probably Facebooking and Twittering her little head off." *And if someone hasn't heard, Carmen will make it a point to inform them personally.*

Draper nodded. "Carmen told me her offer was pretty spur-of-the-moment. That she was toying with the idea of opening some kind of bookstore or art gallery."

"Is that so?" said Suzanne. "I heard restaurant."

"Really," said Draper, sounding surprised.

"She's quite the busy little bee," said Suzanne. "Her clothing boutique, Alchemy, has its grand opening tomorrow."

"Maybe Carmen's trying to buy up the town," said Draper, letting loose a weak chuckle.

That was one angle Suzanne hadn't thought of. A rather unpleasant angle at that. Carmenville.

Draper squinted at the chalkboard. "Does that really say 'green eggs and ham'?"

"Yes, but only the eggshells are actually green," Suzanne told him. "A lovely mint color. Laid by Araucana hens."

"Mmm," said Draper. "I think I'll have the chicken salad."

"Good choice," said Suzanne, jotting the order down on her order pad. But she wasn't finished with George Draper yet. "Have you spoken with Sheriff Doogie today?" she asked.

George shook his head. He seemed to sense where Suzanne was going.

"I know he's been busy with the two murders . . ." began Suzanne.

Now George looked downright unhappy. "That's all folks want to talk about. The murders." His voice became a raspy whisper. "And both victims from Driesden and Draper . . ."

"Must make business rather difficult," offered Suzanne.

George threw her a sharp glance. "Business? There hasn't been any business, unless you count Ozzie." He curled his fingers around the side of the table as if to steady himself. "I don't know if I'm ever going to be able to conduct business in this town again."

"Unless you sell out," said Suzanne. "And isn't it amazing that the Roth Consortium is conveniently standing by?"

"I know what you're saying," said Draper, "but I still don't believe they'd resort to murder. They're a . . . well, the company has a solid reputation."

"Still," continued Suzanne, "they're suspects. Of course, not the only ones."

"No," allowed Draper.

"I understand Sheriff Doogie questioned Earl Stensrud at some length," said Suzanne.

"Because of his connection to Missy Langston," said Draper. "And Missy's former involvement with Ozzie."

"Mmm," said Suzanne.

"But Earl's involvement still feels like a long shot to me," said Draper. "In fact, the only thing I've heard about Earl is that he's contributing heavily to Mayor Mobley's reelection campaign."

Suzanne nodded, thinking that a hefty campaign donation might buy a guilty man a good deal of protection.

"The last thing I heard from Sheriff Doogie," said Draper, "was that he was looking for some homeless guy who was spotted in the park last Sunday."

"I heard that, too," said Suzanne, thinking about the guy Petra had given a handout to.

"So you see?" said Draper. "The wheels of justice turn slowly, but they do turn."

"Let's hope so," said Suzanne, flipping her order book closed and edging away from Draper.

Back in the kitchen, Suzanne called out, "Hey there," to Petra.

"Yes?" Petra, pepper shaker in hand, was liberally seasoning the chicken salad.

"You remember that homeless guy who stopped by here yesterday? The one you gave the sandwiches to?"

Petra set down the pepper and grabbed for the salt. "Uh-huh." She let fly a couple of quick sprinkles.

"Do you remember what he looked like?"

Petra wrinkled her nose. "Oh gosh, not really."

"Think hard," said Suzanne.

"Well," said Petra, wiping her hands on her blue-checked apron, "for one thing, he was sad and ragged-looking. And definitely seemed hungry."

"Okay," said Suzanne. "What else did you notice about him?"

Petra thought for a couple of moments, then gave a sad smile. "His skin looked awfully weathered and worn and he wore a faded green jacket, kind of like an army jacket." She paused. "Now that I think about it, I suppose that's why I felt so sorry for him. Because I thought he might be a veteran." A shadow crossed Petra's face. "Donny was a veteran, you know. Served two tours in Vietnam starting with the Tet Offensive. The doctors at the VA won't admit it, of course, but I think the chemicals, the so-called rainbow herbicides they used over there, are to blame for his Alzheimer's."

"I know you do, honey," said Suzanne. "And I don't think you're far from wrong." She paused. "Anything else come to mind about this guy you saw?"

Petra shook her head. "Nope." She slid her hand into an oven mitt, pulled open the oven door, grabbed a pan of oatmeal muffins.

"Okay," said Suzanne. "You've been a big help."

"Is that homeless guy a suspect in the murders?" Petra asked.

"I don't know," said Suzanne. "Maybe."

"Too bad," said Petra. "He seemed awfully despondent and . . . vulnerable." She tumbled the steaming muffins onto a bright orange Fiesta platter, righted them, then arranged them in a tight cluster.

"He could still be a killer," said Suzanne.

"I suppose," said Petra. She balanced the plate in one hand, then handed it to Suzanne. "You want to put these in the case out front?"

"Sure," said Suzanne. She grabbed the plate, turned, and bumped against the swinging door with her right hip.

"Oh," Petra called after her, "you know what? There is another thing."

Suzanne stopped short. "What's that?"

Petra touched a tentative hand to her blouse, as if that small act helped her to remember. "I think there was a name stenciled on his jacket."

"You remember what it was?"

"Maybe something like . . . Dilley or Dillon?"

THE Knit-In was still going strong. Leticia Sprague, who lived outside Jessup and raised her own sheep and alpacas, showed up with a basket full of her wonderful, lustrous yarns. A throwback to a simpler, more hands-on era, Leticia sheared her animals herself, spun her own yarn, then hand-dyed the fibers. When she announced that some of her precious yarns were for sale, a joyful hubbub ensued and they were gone in about half a minute.

With lunch almost finished, Petra finally stepped out of the kitchen to honcho the Knit-In, while Toni schmoozed, served desserts, and rang up customers at the checkout.

Feeling guilty, Suzanne ducked out the back door, heading for her fitting at Alchemy. As she dashed for her car, big fat raindrops splattered down, kicking up the dust like a spray of bullets. She prayed the bad weather would blow over for the weekend.

CHAPTER 21

JUST as Suzanne scrambled from her car, obsessing about how she was going to squeeze her bod into a tiny camisole or supertight miniskirt, Mayor Mobley waylaid her. He planted his stocky body on the pitted sidewalk outside Alchemy and grinned crookedly like some weird Easter Island statue.

"I hope I can count on your vote this election, Suzanne," he said in a flinty voice.

Suzanne fixed him with a cool smile. "Voting's a private matter, Mayor." *And none of your frickin' business.*

"I understand that," said Mobley, "but I also believe in asking people for their support."

"I can see that," said Suzanne.

"No harm in campaigning," said Mobley. Now his voice was raised in a false hearty bray.

"Mmm," responded Suzanne.

Mobley curled a lip and nattered on. "Doogie's up for reelection, too, you know. But I'm fairly certain that if he drops the ball on these two murder investigations, it'll be the end of him."

"I have faith in Sheriff Doogie," said Suzanne.

"You and about two other people in Kindred," came Mobley's hard laugh.

"The guy that's running against you . . ." said Suzanne. "Your opponent?"

Mobley nodded vigorously. "Yeah, yeah. You mean Charlie Peebler?"

"I think I'm going to vote for him."

"SUZANNE!" Missy threw her arms into the air and came running to greet her. Suzanne returned Missy's ebullient hug, even as she gazed about the brand-spanking-new boutique. And let out a low whistle of approval.

Alchemy was, to put it mildly, utterly breathtaking.

The walls were a rich plum hue, plush silver gray carpeting spread out underfoot like velvet fog, and an enormous crystal chandelier dangled overhead, casting a jewellike glow on everything.

And the clothes and handbags and jewelry! Oh my!

There were denim jackets trimmed with velvet and jeweled buttons.

J Brand jeans and Love Quotes scarves. Black-lacquered mannequins modeled long, filmy skirts paired with black leather motorcycle jackets as well as black cocktail dresses—some with only one shoulder. And there were cheetah-print T-shirts, colorful Lucite bangles, leather slacks, silk blouses, multicolored graphic hoodies, strands of pearls, giant statement rings, reptile handbags, and cashmere scarves.

Everything was arranged impeccably on circular racks and pedestals, or tucked enticingly in glass towers and shiny white cubes that hung on a side wall.

"You like?" asked Missy. She looked exhausted, but pleased.

"This place is like fantasyland for fashionistas," exclaimed Suzanne, who was already eyeing a burnished green leather belt. She also decided this beautifully edited boutique was a far cry from Hawley's Dry Goods down the street, where you could buy serviceable checkered blouses and generic blue jeans. "We're not in Kansas anymore, Toto," she added with a chuckle.

"I'm so glad you're here," said Missy, pulling her toward the back of the shop. "We've already picked out a couple of outfits for you to model. So, obviously, I'm dying to see how they work."

Suzanne let herself be pulled along by Missy, past two stylishly dressed women who were artfully arranging more clothing and accessories. "Your assistants?" she asked.

"I wish," said Missy, rolling her eyes. "No, they work for a couple of the vendors Carmen buys from. Here to make sure everything's styled properly. That I don't screw it up," she added in a low whisper.

"If you're responsible for even half the displays," Suzanne told her, "then you're amazingly talented."

"I've done my share all right," said Missy, shepherding Suzanne into an all-white dressing room ablaze with lights. "I just wish Carmen would acknowledge some of my accomplishments."

"Don't wait for Carmen's approval," warned Suzanne, "because it will probably never come. But if . . . when . . . you draw an appreciative crowd tomorrow afternoon, you'll know in your heart that all your hard work was worth it."

"Thank you," said Missy. "I needed to hear that. Now . . ." She smiled expectantly. "Let me show you the outfits." She grabbed at a rack and held up clothing in both hands. "We pulled two outfits. A skirt with matching tunic . . . and jeans paired with a leather bomber jacket."

"Wow," said Suzanne, gazing at the clothing. It was a lot more sophisticated than her normal slacks and T-shirts. "Carmen put these together?"

Missy nodded. "Great stuff, huh?"

Suzanne fingered the filmy skirt. "It's awfully see-through."

"That's the look," said Missy.

"The look," repeated Suzanne. "Yes, I do believe I'd get looks if I wore this."

"Okay," said Missy, "then how about the jeans and leather jacket?"

"Awfully small sizes," said Suzanne.

"Carmen assured me the sizes are correct," Missy told her. "It's called the shrunken look."

"Last time I wore the shrunken look, it stemmed from a mistake," said Suzanne. "I threw my crop pants into the dryer with a load of towels and twenty minutes later they came out as Bermudas."

"This is a slightly different concept," said Missy.

"I realize that," said Suzanne. "Still . . ." But when Missy suddenly looked defeated, she said, "Tell you what, why don't I slip into these things and see how they work?"

"Thank you!" breathed Missy.

Alone in the dressing room, Suzanne slipped out of her khaki slacks and pulled on the jeans. Or at least tried to pull them on. Turns out, they weren't just shrunken, they were skintight. *How can eating a one-pound box of chocolate truffles add up to an extra five pounds around my hips?* she wondered. *It isn't mathematically possible. Or maybe it all has to do with quantum physics or some sort of black hole theory. I mean, the calories have to go somewhere!*

"How are we doing in there?" called Missy.

"We're having a little trouble with our thighs," Suzanne called back. "And our hips."

"Keep tugging," said Missy. "I told you they were tight."

Suzanne wiggled and squirmed and wormed the jeans up. Then she slipped into the leather jacket. It was black leather, smooth and buttery soft. Lambskin, with a shiny brass diagonal zipper.

"Oh wow!" said Missy, when Suzanne stepped out of the dressing room.

"Sexy!" called one of the stylists.

"I don't know . . ." hedged Suzanne.

"I do," said Missy. "It's perfect." She spun Suzanne around and aimed her at the three-way mirror.

"A little tough-looking, don't you think?" asked Suzanne. She decided she looked like a motorcycle thug from *The Wild Bunch*. Or maybe . . . the Fonz?

"The outfit's edgy," said Missy, touching both shoulders. "Just like you."

"In my dreams," said Suzanne.

"Oh, did I tell you?" cooed Missy. "Brett and Greg from Root 66 will be here tomorrow doing hair and makeup."

"Oh dear." One of Suzanne's hands flew up to her hair. She was slightly overdue for a cut and touch-up on her roots.

"Not to worry," chuckled Missy. "They're not going to get radical or anything. No purple extensions or wacked-out Amy Winehouse streaky eye makeup."

"Thank goodness," said Suzanne, wondering which one Amy Winehouse was. The singer with the smeared lipstick and ripped fishnets? Or was that Courtney Love?

"But all the models will definitely be made up," said Missy. "Carmen was very specific about that." She reached forward and pulled up the collar of Suzanne's jacket. "There. Even better."

"Missy," said Suzanne.

Missy smiled. "Hmm?"

"Has Sheriff Doogie been asking you about Earl?"

Missy took a step backward. "What are you talking about?"

Suzanne tried to phrase her next words delicately. "I get the feeling Doogie still considers Earl a suspect."

Missy shook her head. "From the way Doogie treats me, I think *I'm* still his number one suspect." Her eyes clouded over slightly. "You don't think I had anything to do with Ozzie's death, do you, Suzanne?"

Suzanne shook her head. "No, I don't." *At least I hope not.*

"And you don't think Earl's a killer, do you?"

Suzanne managed another small shake. *I don't know what to think.*

Missy surprised her with a quick hug. "You're a dear to model this outfit," she told Suzanne. "And an absolute angel for looking into things. I know you've been trying to deflect Doogie's scrutiny off me and for that I'm eternally grateful."

"Not a problem," said Suzanne. Although it really kind of was.

When Suzanne emerged from the dressing room, happily back in civilian clothes, she saw that a white satin curtain had been draped across the entire back of the store. Groups of white folding chairs were being arranged out front.

"Wow," said Suzanne. "There's going to be a runway?"

"Of sorts," said Missy. "We'll lay down white vinyl runners and weave them through the shop. That way everyone will be able to get a good look at the clothing."

"Gulp," said Suzanne. Then she and Missy both turned as a little bell tinkled and the front door swung open.

It was Earl Stensrud. "Hiya, sweetheart," he called to

Missy, a big smile on his face. "You paste up that program I'm supposed to take to Copy Shop?"

"I'll grab it," said Missy, hustling toward the back counter.

Earl finally noticed Suzanne. "Hey there," he said to her. "You thought any more about that extra insurance?"

"Not really," said Suzanne. "I'm not anticipating any earthquakes, floods, or fires of biblical proportion."

"Okay," said Earl. "Suit yourself." He bounced from foot to foot, waiting for Missy, looking pleased.

"Earl," said Suzanne, "you look like the cat who swallowed the canary."

"That sounds awfully accusatory, Suzanne," said Earl. His smile had suddenly vanished.

"Chipper, then," Suzanne amended. "I'd say you're looking exceedingly chipper."

"Now that Missy's available again," said Earl, brushing past Suzanne and homing in on Missy, "I feel like a million bucks."

BACK at the Cackleberry Club, the Knit-In was still chugging along. A few finished pieces were already up for sale and the café had drawn a large crowd of women for afternoon tea.

Petra had gone back into the kitchen to whip up crab salad and ham and Swiss cheese tea sandwiches and bake a few pans of blueberry scones. Toni had just finished brewing pots of lemon verbena and orchid tea, so those lovely aromas wafted languidly across the café, turning the Cackleberry Club into an aromatherapy bazaar.

"I have to have that ruffled shawl," Suzanne said, as Petra positioned the second tier on a newly baked cake.

"Then you better hustle into the Knitting Nest and claim it," Petra advised. "Everything's flying out of here like crazy."

"So a big success," said Suzanne.

"Totally," agreed Petra. "In fact, some of us gals who are also quilters have been so inspired, we're going to do a quilt trail next month."

"Never heard of that," said Suzanne.

"Oh," said Petra, "it'll be really neat. We're going to display large wooden quilt squares as well as some actual quilts on the sides of historic barns, churches, and homes. Then there'll be an accompanying quilt trail map that will lead tourists along the most scenic back roads and also indicate fun stops like antique shops, farmer's markets, restaurants, and orchards."

"Wow," said Suzanne. "Talk about weaving history into the mix and helping boost business! I bet you can even partner with the county historical society and get lots of sponsors, too."

"I think so." Petra smiled.

"In fact, I'll do anything I can to help," said Suzanne. She nodded toward a couple of cakes that were cooling on the window ledge. "What's the deal with those cakes? For us?"

Petra shook her head. "Nope. Special order for Carmen Copeland. Gonna make her a cake in the shape of a handbag."

"You're kidding," said Suzanne. "Really?"

Petra nodded. "Carmen ordered it when she was here yesterday. Even gave me a magazine photo to work from. See?" Petra reached in her apron pocket and pulled out a *Vogue* ad that featured a fancy pastel blue quilted leather bag with a chain strap. "For her grand opening tomorrow."

"Gadz," said Suzanne. Carmen really was going over-board to woo the local ladies.

"Hey, take a plate of scones into the Knitting Nest, will you? Those ladies have been holed up in there all day."

"Gotcha," said Suzanne.

But just as she grabbed the scones from the display case, just as she was about to swerve into the Knitting Nest, Suzanne spotted Sheriff Doogie edging his way through the front door. So she changed direction and headed him off.

"Suzanne," said Doogie, sweeping his hat from his head, running a hand through his thinning gray hair, all in one motion. "What's going on?" He seemed surprised and curious to see so many women sitting around with knitting needles clacking and balls of yarn unrolling.

"A Knit-In," she told him. "It's a kind of charity event."

"Hah," was his response.

"I don't mean to criticize, Sheriff, but you're looking a little discombobulated."

"Heck of a thing," said Doogie. "We got an anonymous tip this morning on a couple of guys who were growing marijuana."

"No kidding." Suzanne let her uneasiness come across as surprise. "Wow."

"And then we got a call about those wild boar are run-ning around the county, tromping through yards and dig-ging up gardens."

"Hard to catch," said Suzanne.

Doogie glanced toward the counter where his eyes wandered to the pastry case. The action was not lost on Suzanne.

"You got time for a cup of coffee?" Suzanne offered. "And maybe a scone?"

"Don't mind if I do," said Doogie.

Suzanne delivered her scones, then scampered back and poured coffee into an oversized white ceramic mug for Doogie. She placed a scone on a plate, tapped on a dollop of Devonshire cream, then slid the whole shebang across the counter to him. While Doogie munched and slurped, she quizzed him gently.

"So what's the deal with the marijuana guys?" Suzanne asked. "You think they were running a meth lab, too?"

"Not that I could see." Doogie took another bite, half closed his eyes, and chewed appreciatively. "Dang, these are good."

"Petra whips up a tasty scone," agreed Suzanne. She waited a couple more beats. "Do you suppose those guys are somehow connected to the murders?" Doogie stopped chewing for a moment and stared at her. "Why would you say that?"

"Oh, I don't know. Maybe because people will chitchat and try to draw a connection?"

"The nice thing about living in a small town," muttered Doogie, "is that when you don't know what you're doing, somebody else does."

"Good one," said Suzanne.

Doogie finished his scone, then turned an eye on the pastry case once again.

"Another one?" she asked. "To keep up your strength?"

Doogie nodded. "I need to stay at the top of my game."

"Because you're up for reelection, too," said Suzanne.

"Ayup, and I intend to get it," said Doogie, though his eyes suddenly seemed troubled.

"You know Mayor Mobley will bad-mouth you like crazy if you don't solve these murders," Suzanne told him.

"The old fart already is. Plus he's standing squarely behind Bob Senander. So much for loyalty."

"Does Senander have any real experience?"

"He's been highway patrol for eleven years."

"So . . . a serious contender," said Suzanne.

"Yup," was Doogie's tight reply.

A few minutes later, Doogie slid off his stool, hitched at his belt, and said, "Gotta get back out to that farm. Walk the scene again."

"Sounds exciting," said Suzanne.

"It ain't," Doogie assured her. "Law enforcement ain't nearly as glamorous as they make it look on TV."

"Nothing really is, is it?"

"To top things off," said Doogie, "we found a darn mule wandering around. Now we're gonna have to find a home for *him*."

"I could take him," offered Suzanne.

Doogie planted himself squarely and squinted at her. "What on earth for?"

"Keep my horse company. You know, like a stable mate."

"Cost you fifty bucks. The Deer County Humane Society's gonna have to trailer him over."

"Bill me."

As Doogie slid out the door, Toni magically appeared at Suzanne's elbow, like some sort of friendly ghost. "You think he suspects it was our tip?" she whispered.

Suzanne grimaced. "I sincerely hope not."

CHAPTER 22

HUMMING Billy Joel's "Uptown Girl," Suzanne puttered around in her kitchen. It was almost seven by the time she got home, but since she'd snarfed a few tea sandwiches earlier, she wasn't all that hungry. So, after feeding Baxter, praising him to high heaven for eating, and giving him a Milk-Bone for good measure, Suzanne bent down and searched her refrigerator.

Locating a thawed chicken breast, she decided on a quick version of chicken Normandy. Butter, little bit of flour, touch of brown sugar, then a dash of cream, a few apple slices, and the chicken. She whipped it up fast in an eight-inch sauté pan, dreaming about the restaurant she'd always wanted to open, planning the pluperfect menu in her head.

Locally produced trout, of course, from Asbury Trout Farm over by Jackson. The tender pink meat grilled over apple wood and drizzled with a light sauce of white wine, butter, lemon, and capers.

Got to have roast pork on the menu, too, she decided. Accompanied by a squash puree, baked figs, and maybe a medley of root vegetables.

And a nice duck breast. Maybe served with cranberry compote, potato gratin, and grilled chanterelle mushrooms.

Unless, of course, Carmen Copeland bought the Driesden and Draper Funeral Home, converted it to a fine dining establishment, and hired herself a big name chef. Pulled the rug right out from under her. And wouldn't that be a dandy kettle of fish!

Or would it?

Would people choose to wine and dine in a former funeral home? Would Carmen convert the embalming room, with all its stainless-steel cabinets and sinks, into a kitchen?

That notion made Suzanne shudder. And if it affected her that way, then wouldn't others be just as squeamish? Yeah, maybe. Hopefully.

Suzanne plated her chicken Normandy, poured a half glass of Chardonnay, placed everything onto a tray, and carried it into the living room. Settled onto the couch and snapped on the TV.

She nibbled a few bites, watching an action film about Vietnam. The soundtrack featuring songs by the Doors, Creedence Clearwater Revival, and the Rolling Stones.

'Nam, she thought. Love the music, hate the subject.

Grabbing the remote control, Suzanne spun through the cable channels. Found sports, a reality show where people were frantically stuffing raw squid into their mouths, some kind of fake sports show with a big rubber obstacle course, another reality show, reruns of an old sitcom about a girl's school where everybody was smart and rich, and news. She watched a few minutes of CNN, decided her mutual funds were *still* taking it in the shorts, then turned the TV off. Suzanne wondered if this might be the evening she'd start reading *People of the Book*. And let her gaze wander to her bookshelf.

Actually, there were quite a few books stacked in her

to-be-read pile. Three mysteries, four cookbooks, and a tome on Napoleon that, for some reason, had seemed exceedingly appealing when she'd stumbled across it in the catalogs the publishing houses sent her.

Something else caught her eye, too. A kind of scrapbook Walter had put together after he'd served as an army doctor in Kuwait during the Gulf War. She smiled, thinking of the stories he'd told her. And as those memories flooded back to her, she wandered over to the bookshelf and picked it up.

Suzanne turned the stiff pages, gazing at the black and white photos, her interest tempered by sadness. Walter had been proud of his service in the Gulf War, and he'd toted his little Nikon along to chronicle his experiences. Which, all in all, had turned out to be pretty amazing.

There was the helicopter flight into Iraq to airlift out some severely wounded marines. In the process, they'd picked up a wounded Iraqi boy whose leg had been partially crushed. They weren't supposed to fly the boy back to Kuwait, of course; it was against regulations. But Walter had done it anyway, saving lives and limbs in the process.

Turning another page, Suzanne smiled proudly. Here was a grainy black-and-white photo of Walter and three other doctors posing in front of a dusty Humvee. The desert docs they'd called themselves. Proud, tough, compassionate.

She'd met Walter after his service, but had been fascinated by his stories. And his courage.

Suzanne continued to turn pages, wondering what these people were doing today, some twenty years later? Soldiers cast back as civilians. Had their memories long since dimmed? What were their feelings about the more recent Iraq War?

She smiled as she scanned the rest of the photos. "All good men," she murmured to herself.

The final photo showed Walter and another man standing in front of a large tent.

Walter and another doc?

Suzanne studied the picture. No, this fellow was a combat soldier. Dressed in telltale desert camo gear, he had an M16 slung carelessly across his body. The two were facing each other, all sunburned faces and crinkled eyes.

Suzanne was about to close the album when she glanced at the photo again. There was something about it. She squinted carefully, studying the photo. And noticed that the soldier's camo jacket carried the name tag Dillworth.

Her brain pinged with sudden recognition.

Good heavens! Could this be the same guy she'd seen in the park last Sunday? The one Petra had given a handout to this morning? Whose jacket Petra thought bore the name Dilley or Dillon?

Suzanne carried the book over to the leather sofa and sat down hard.

Could this be the same fellow who was also a suspect in two murders? Suzanne shifted uncomfortably and the cushions let loose a low whoosh.

The same guy Walter had reminisced about, had referred to as Dil?

Oh jeez! It couldn't be, could it?

She thought it could.

But what was this guy doing in Kindred? And how was he involved? *Was* he involved?

Had he come here to find Walter? Or was something more sinister afoot?

Suzanne knew she had to find out. Had to get some answers. She tapped her foot against the glass table, setting off a vibration that made the silverware on her tray jangle.

Could this homeless guy still be holed up in the caves,

like Doogie had thought? And if she went looking for him, to ask a few questions, would she be at risk?

Suzanne pondered that notion for a few moments. Wondered about the wisdom of taking things into her own hands.

Bad idea. Really bad idea.

She settled back on the sofa, glancing over at Baxter, who was stretched out on the carpet, and said softly, "Hey Bax."

His tail twitched once.

She hesitated, then said, "Want to go for a ride?"

DRIVING through the dark streets, Suzanne's brain whirred like a cyclotron.

Tuesday night, Sheriff Doogie had definitely been on the lookout for a homeless guy who'd been seen wandering through town. Doogie had postulated that the man was hunkered down in one of the caves that honeycombed the hills and bluffs just outside Kindred.

And Petra's homeless guy with the faded camo jacket . . .

Same guy? Could be. Had to be.

The rational part of Suzanne's brain told her she shouldn't go looking for this guy by her lonesome. She should get on the horn to Doogie, tell him what she knew, and hope that he'd round up a proper search team.

On the other hand, Doogie and his deputies might go cowboying in and launch a SWAT team–type assault. Scare the bejeebers out of the guy. Roust him, drag him down to the law enforcement center, shout questions all night.

Better if she and Baxter go alone?

No, probably not.

But, for now, that was how it was going to be.

"EASY, Bax," Suzanne told her dog as she clipped a long leash on him, then stood aside as he jumped from the car. It was pitch-black in the empty parking lot just below Bluff Creek Park. Low-hanging clouds had driven the temperature into the low forties, a crisp, nagging wind carried the promise of rain, and Suzanne was pretty sure there was another storm hanging out over the Dakotas, ready to steamroll its way in.

Baxter stretched languidly, lifted his leg on a nearby post, then turned to stare at Suzanne.

"Just do your thing," she told him in a low whisper. "Sniff around, see if you come up with anything."

That seemed to suit Baxter just fine and he was soon leading Suzanne along a narrow path, pulling her deep into the dark, dense woods even as the path he chose rose in a steady grade. Bare branches tugged at Suzanne's hair as they scrunched through overgrown passages of buckthorn. Clusters of burrs snagged on her denim jacket.

Twenty minutes of hard climbing led them to a small outcropping of rocks where the Parks Committee had constructed a small wooden bench on a sort of ledge. Feeling slightly winded, Suzanne plopped down to rest. Baxter took a cue from her and sat back on his haunches. From up here, Suzanne could peer down a steep gorge and, through the haze, catch a few twinkles of light from town. The oaks and poplars had already lost most of their leaves. The rest would soon be stripped off if more wind and rain moved in. A chill Midwestern autumn, winter lurking like a hungry lion.

Still, Suzanne thought the view peaceful from her perch.

And pretty in a kind of Norman Rockwell old-timey way. You'd never guess two murders had taken place in this innocuous little town within the span of a couple days. Never guess it in a million years.

Baxter stood up and stared fixedly into the woods.

"What's wrong, Bax?" Suzanne asked. "Something out there?" But she knew a whole host of nocturnal critters were probably scrabbling about, in their element and practically undetected. Raccoons, opossums, foxes, coyotes, and cougars. Even the troop of wild boar Doogie had mentioned.

And a murderer?

Yeah, maybe. Maybe so.

Suzanne stood up and reeled in Baxter's leash. From here on the going was much more rugged. Lots of twisting paths that jagged around sandstone outcroppings that sheltered small caves.

Lots of caves.

She'd crawled through a few of these caves when she was a kid, but had always been jittery about exploring the deeper ones. The caves whose walls narrowed sharply, forcing you to scramble on hands and knees or worm your way along on your belly as passages drilled sinuously into the hillside.

Keeping Baxter at her side in a "heel" position, Suzanne picked her way carefully up the hillside. Loose rock and sand made the climb arduous. So did not knowing what lay beyond every twist and turn.

Dark mouths of caves yawned at her like black holes. But none looked inhabited.

"Nothing here," she whispered to Baxter. She'd covered half of one side of the bluff and hadn't seen hide nor hair of anything. Human or animal.

Maybe the homeless guy wasn't up here at all, she decided. Maybe he'd been scared off by Sheriff Doogie's initial probe. Maybe he'd just boogied on out of town.

Or maybe not. Maybe a guy who'd been army trained, who'd learned how to dig himself into a hostile desert environment, wouldn't go for the most obvious hidey-hole.

So where?

Suzanne lifted her eyes and scoured the peak above her. Could she even get up there?

Only one way to find out.

Hands clawing for a stable rock, feet probing for foot holds, Suzanne slowly climbed the smooth rock face. Baxter stood below, leash clipped to a tree, watching her progress, seemingly happy to remain behind and hold down the fort.

Upper-body strength was not Suzanne's forte and her shoulder muscles trembled from the exertion. This rock face was far steeper, the elevation much higher than she'd initially thought. Her fingers burned from clutching minimal handholds. There was no way she could keep this up.

Best thing—the smartest thing—to do was ease her way back down to where Baxter was waiting, pray she'd find the same rocks and nubbins to grab onto for her descent.

Standing practically spread-eagled against the cliff face, her face beaded with sweat, Suzanne cranked her head sideways to wipe her forehead on her jacket sleeve.

And there, off to her left, she caught the faint orange glow of a campfire.

Easing herself across the cliff, grasping for foot- and fingerholds, Suzanne moved with renewed energy. Boldly, yet quietly. She strained to keep her breathing under control, though her curiosity was revved to warp speed.

Just one quick look, she promised herself. *I'll see what I can see and then I'm outta here!*

Her left foot searched for a solid perch, finally found it. She shifted her weight onto the rock, testing for stability. It felt good. Suzanne paused, trying to gather her energy and her wits, then tilted her head back, ever so slightly.

He stood, silhouetted in the mouth of the cave, a foot or so above her. With the glow of the fire behind him, he looked like a dark, almost primordial figure. Close enough to casually lift a boot and step on her fingers if he felt like it. Crush them like a pack of saltines.

CHAPTER 23

BUT he didn't. Instead, the man reached down and extended a hand.

And Suzanne made a split-second decision she hoped she wouldn't regret for the rest of her life. She reached up and grabbed his hand.

Like a dream sequence that unfolded in slow motion, Suzanne felt herself being hoisted higher and higher. Dangling precipitously, her legs paddling in thin air, Suzanne scrambled for purchase until, finally, finally, she connected with solid rock and found herself standing on a narrow ledge.

Heart hammering in her chest, Suzanne said, "Who are you?"

The man turned his back on her and retreated into a shallow cave. Crouching down, he stuck another branch into the fire. It crackled, popped, and released a burst of sparks that reminded Suzanne of fireflies.

"Excuse me?" she said, taking a step forward.

The man bowed his head and seemed to fold in on himself, pulling himself into a cross-legged position, his back against the wall of the cave.

"Doesn't matter," he said in a low, papery voice.

"Do I know you?" she asked.

He shook his head. No.

"But I think I know who you are," Suzanne told him.

Again, a shake of his head.

"You knew Walter," said Suzanne.

There was no response.

"Is that why you came here?" she asked. "To see Walter?"

Silence for a few moments, then the man said, "What?

"You knew Walter Dietz?" asked Suzanne.

The man seemed to fade away for a while, then said, in a low voice, "Walter died."

"How do you know that?" Suzanne asked, edging closer.

More silence, then, "Went to the hospital. They told me."

"Is your name Dillworth?" asked Suzanne. "Did you serve in the army with Walter?"

Time spun out again, then the man said, "Doesn't matter now. It's all in the dim."

"The dim," said Suzanne. "You mean the past?"

The man stared into the fire.

"What's your name?" asked Suzanne.

Dark eyes stared at her. "Anson."

"Anson Dillworth?" she asked.

A slight nod. "Just Dil."

"What are you doing here?" Suzanne asked.

He fed a few more sticks into the fire, then said, "Nothing. Just . . . passing through."

"You can't stay here," Suzanne pointed out. "It's going to turn cold pretty soon. And eventually snow. This isn't a very good place to hole up."

"No place is," Dil replied.

"Where did you come from?" asked Suzanne. "Where were you living before?"

"Home."

"Your home?" asked Suzanne. Maybe Dil had a family who was frantic with worry. Maybe he'd wandered off because of drugs or alcohol or . . .

"A home," said the man.

"Oh man," said Suzanne. She put a hand to her head, scrubbed at her hair. This was a guy who needed serious help. She wanted to give it to him but . . . how? And, she had questions to ask.

Suzanne edged closer to the fire. "Did you know Ozzie?" she asked him.

Dil shook his head.

"How about Bo?"

Again a shake of the head.

"But you knew about the Cackleberry Club," prompted Suzanne. "You went there the other day. Yesterday."

A ghost of a smile played at Dil's lips. "Sandwiches. Good ones."

"Dil . . . can I call you Dil?"

The man nodded.

"How did you know about the Cackleberry Club?"

He lifted his head and stared at her then. "They told me . . ."

"Who told you?"

"Lady at the hospital."

"What did she tell you?"

"Said Walter's wife ran it."

"That's right," said Suzanne. "I'm Walter's wife."

Dil stared at her, licked his lips, stared some more. Finally said, in an incredulous tone, "You're Walter's wife?"

"Yes. I'm Suzanne. Suzanne Dietz."

The man slowly reached out his hand. "Nice to meet you."

Suzanne accepted his hand. "Nice to meet you, Dil."

Dil picked up a long stick and poked at the fire, while Suzanne tried to figure out what to ask next. She didn't want to go there, but she knew she had to at least broach the subject.

"You were in the park last Sunday," she said.

"Park," he repeated.

"During the fair," Suzanne pushed. "You remember, the face painting and the food and stuff."

"Okay," said Dil.

"Did you see something?"

Dil pulled his knees up and lowered his head. "No."

"Did you *do* something?"

Dark eyes stared up at her. "What?"

Suzanne swallowed hard. "In that big house over on Front Street?"

"I walked by it," he said. "That's all."

"Did you see anything?" asked Suzanne. "Anything at all?"

Dil's eyes were glassy. "I don't know," he whispered. "I don't think so."

"But you came up here," said Suzanne. "You were hanging around downtown, then you came up here." She paused. "To hide?"

"People were looking for me."

"Do you know who?" she asked.

He shook his head again. No.

"But they scared you."

"They scared me," Dil echoed. He gave a little shiver. "Sometimes it's hard to remember things."

"I understand," said Suzanne.

She sat with him by the fire for a while. Talked to him softly, trying to pry a little more information from him. Pretty much convinced that he couldn't have had anything to do with Ozzie's murder. And certainly not Bo Becker's.

As Suzanne carefully cajoled Dil, he finally let loose with a jumbled, rambling explanation. She learned that he'd seen combat in the Gulf War, returned home and gotten divorced, then fallen on tough times. He'd been treated for depression, held down menial jobs off and on, and then landed in a halfway house for veterans somewhere in St. Louis. One day—Suzanne wasn't clear if it was two years ago or six years ago—Dil had finally walked away from his halfway house and embarked on an aimless journey that had led him from one town to another.

Dil had seemingly crisscrossed the country, occasionally circling back to the Midwest where he'd originally had roots. Last week, when he'd randomly hit Kindred, some spark of memory had ignited within his brain and he'd remembered Walter. His long-ago buddy from the Gulf War.

But, of course, Walter wasn't here anymore.

IT took a world of convincing to get Dil to come down the bluff with her. And then some more fast talking to put him at ease with Baxter. But in the end, Dil relented. Drawn, finally, by the promise of a cheeseburger and French fries. And a motel room at the local Super 8.

"Wait here," Suzanne told Dil, pulling up in front of Schmitt's Bar on Main Street and taking the car keys with her, just in case. "I'll be five minutes at most." She held up a finger to Baxter. "You. Be good." Then she hopped from the car and scampered into the bar.

Schmitt's was dim, semi-crowded, reeked of stale beer, and easily cooked up the best burgers in town. Greasy beef patties sizzled on a hot grill alongside piles of stringy, crunchy onions. Big, fat sesame seed buns steamed atop the burgers. While she waited for her order, Suzanne chatted with the bartender, an amiable coot who wore old-fashioned, round John Lennon glasses and sported a braided goatee. Freddy.

"I understand there was quite an argument here last Friday night."

Freddy eyed her warily. "Says who?"

"Says Sheriff Doogie," said Suzanne. "He said Ozzie Driesden and Earl Stensrud really got into it."

"And then Ozzie got his self killed," mused Freddy. He peered quizzically at Suzanne. "The sheriff thinkin' Earl done it?"

"I think it crossed his mind," said Suzanne.

"Nah," said Freddy. "That was just bar talk. You know how men are after a few drinks. Puffin' up their chests and trying to outbrag each other."

"Yeah, I know," said Suzanne. Her eyes fixed on a sign that hung behind the bar, next to a big taxidermied muskie. It said: Beauty is in the eye of the beer holder.

"Say," said Freddy, leaning forward. "You want a drink or something? I make a pretty wicked gin fizz. You ladies always seem to appreciate a nice gin fizz."

"No, thanks," said Suzanne. "Maybe some other time."

Ten minutes later, Suzanne dropped Dil off at the Super 8. She registered as Suzanne Marley, her maiden name, and paid cash. That way she could hopefully keep Dil hush-hush until she figured out what to do with him.

Standing outside room twelve, Dil clutched a backpack and his white paper bag leaking grease and thanked her. "This is really nice of you, missus."

"No problem," she told him. "Listen, I'm gonna stop by tomorrow afternoon and we're gonna figure out what to do with you, okay?"

Dil gave a faint smile and nodded.

"Good," said Suzanne. "So you just stay put."

"Okay."

"You promise?"

"Sure."

By the time she finally rolled into her own driveway, dragged herself into the shower, and let the hot water cascade down her body and ease the tension in her shoulders, Suzanne was pretty much convinced that Anson Dillworth wasn't a viable suspect. Although Sheriff Doogie might disagree, Suzanne thought it was too far-fetched to view him as a wandering serial killer or even a spree killer. He was just too timid, too psychically wounded.

The question was, what to do with him?

"What do you think, Bax?" Suzanne asked, pulling on an oversized T-shirt and climbing into bed.

Baxter, who was already tucked into his expensive L.L. Bean dog bed, sighed deeply, essentially ignoring her.

So much for an outside opinion.

Settling back on her eiderdown pillow, Suzanne pulled the covers up to her chin and closed her eyes. But sleep was slow in coming tonight, so she forced herself to make her mind go blank, and slowly chanted a sleepy time mantra that she'd adopted as her very own. *Cham-o-mile. Cham-o-mile.*

And it worked. For a few hours.

Three o'clock brought Suzanne wide awake from a fragmented dream. She sat straight up in bed with a sharp gasp, not knowing why, then thinking in her still sleep-fogged brain that she'd *heard* something. Had she? She shook her head as if to clear her thoughts. And listened.

For some bizarre reason, the word *ghost* popped into her brain.

What? The ghost of Ozzie Driesden come to call on me? Or the equally unhappy ghost of Bo Becker? No. No way, silly girl.

Suzanne woke up a little more, remembering there weren't such things as ghosts roaming about. Just . . . dangerous people.

Climbing out of bed, Suzanne tiptoed to the window, the Chinese carpet feeling warm and smooth underfoot. She pressed her face to the cool glass and looked down into the backyard.

Nothing.

She sighed, turned, and eyed the bed. Overwhelmed by fatigue, she desperately wanted to slide back under that mound of feathery covers.

But . . . she'd heard *something*.

Padding silently downstairs, Suzanne paused on the landing to try to get a sense of things, to figure out what person or thing had disrupted her sleep, had pierced the membrane of calm in her house. The antique clock in the hallway ticked steadfastly away. The faint, mechanical hum of the refrigerator reassured her.

Still . . .

Suzanne came all the way downstairs, turned, wandered through the living room. A faint blue light from a button on the TV cast an eerie glow as harmless shadows loomed up at her.

When she got to the kitchen, Suzanne paused and looked around. Nobody in the house. But, like an animal whose guard hairs have been riffled, she had the sensation that *something* had gone on. Moving to the back door, she peered out into the backyard again. Dark, quiet, nary a thing moving.

Maybe she'd heard a raccoon tippy-tapping at a garbage can lid? One of the neighborhood's masked bandits on a nighttime errand?

Suzanne gave a low snort, was about to turn, when, out of the corner of her eye, she caught a flutter of something. *What?*

Her hand crept up to the super-duty Schlage lock she'd installed on the back door, hesitated for just a moment, then turned the latch. Pulling open the door, Suzanne stared at a piece of paper that had been taped to the outside storm door.

She drew a quick breath, opened that door, snatched the paper, slammed both doors, and clicked the lock. All in the space of about two seconds.

Carrying the piece of paper with both hands, Suzanne walked over to the stove, punched on the night light, laid the paper down, smoothed it out.

It was a typed note. Probably composed on an old-fashioned typewriter. All it said was *Back Off.*

CHAPTER 24

"WHO do you think left the note?" asked Toni. It was Flapjack Friday at the Cackleberry Club and they were all in the kitchen, shredding potatoes, pulling tins of muffins from the oven, stirring pancake batter, pondering Suzanne's rather amazing account of her encounter with the mysterious Dil last night and her subsequent discovery of the note taped to her door.

"I've no clue about the note," Suzanne told them. She'd moved on from shredding potatoes to frosting cinnamon rolls. "Could have been anybody. Between George Draper, Earl Stensrud, Ray Lynch, and those two drug dealers, seems like we've got a whole cast of suspects."

"Don't forget Missy," said Petra.

"Missy . . ." said Suzanne.

"I thought the drug guys were in custody," said Toni.

"They probably still are," said Suzanne, licking a bit of frosting from her thumb. "So, okay, that narrows the list somewhat."

"Well," said Petra, looking nervous as she added golden raisins and chopped walnuts to her pancake batter, "the note was obviously from someone who knows you've been investigating."

"Which is pretty much everybody in Kindred," added Toni. She draped an apron over her hot pink T-shirt and blue jeans, piled her hair on top of her head, and popped on a pink scrunchie. "You haven't been all that subtle," she told Suzanne as she washed her hands at the sink. "Asking questions and all."

"I thought I was the height of discretion," said Suzanne, rolling her eyes.

"What I want to know," said Petra, "is what you plan to do with Anson Dillworth?"

"Talk to him, for one thing," said Suzanne. "I get the feeling that he saw something or knows more than he's letting on."

"Maybe you should turn him over to Doogie," said Petra.

"In this particular case," said Suzanne, "I'm not sure I trust Doogie's interviewing skills."

"More like interrogating skills," said Toni. "If you turn him in and . . . say . . . nothing comes of it, Doogie might still lock your guy up as a vagrant."

"Now that I think about it," said Petra, "there's another scenario. A bad one."

"What?" asked Toni.

Petra wiped her hands on her apron. "If Doogie's desperate to find a fall guy, he could browbeat this Dil fellow into confessing to Ozzie's and Bo's murders."

"I wouldn't put it past Doogie," said Toni, "since the entire town is breathing down his neck, hoping for a break in the two cases."

"I just don't believe Dil was involved," said Suzanne. "And there's no evidence, even circumstantial, that would link him."

"Hah!" said Toni. "When did Doogie ever need evidence?"

"Toni's right," said Petra. "You need a plan."

"An escape plan," said Toni. "Get your poor soldier boy out of town fast."

"What I'd like to do," said Suzanne, "is hook him up with some sort of veterans' group." She glanced at Petra. "You know any groups that might lend a hand?"

"Not personally," said Petra, "but Donny's case worker at the VA might be able to put us in touch with one. I could give her a call."

"Would you?" asked Suzanne. "I'd really appreciate it."

"What a crazy week," lamented Petra. "Murders, book signings, the Knit-In, and now we've got Take the Cake happening tomorrow."

"Along with our gourmet dinner," Toni pointed out. "And Suzanne's gotta go strut her stuff this afternoon!"

"Wish I didn't," muttered Suzanne. There was way too much going on in her head as well as her life.

"We're never going to get all this done!" exclaimed Petra, suddenly looking frustrated.

"You know what they say," joked Toni. "If life hands you lemons, get a receipt!"

"One good thing," said Suzanne, pulling back a chintz curtain and gazing out the window, "is that the sun is starting to come out. And, oh . . . hey, here's the truck with the tents and chairs, I think."

"Excellent!" said Toni. "I'll run out and show them where to set up."

"Hang on a minute!" exclaimed Petra. "Group hug and a prayer, okay? I think we could all use it."

The three of them linked hands and bowed their heads.

"Dear Lord," began Petra, "be with us today and bestow upon us Your gifts of peace, serenity, and wisdom."

"And dear Lord," added Toni, "please, especially, give me patience. And if I could *GET IT RIGHT NOW*, it sure would help!"

"Amen," said Petra, shaking her head, as Toni dashed out the door.

SUZANNE was busy then, as customers began piling into the Cackleberry Club. She took orders, hustled them back to Petra, delivered breakfasts, and poured refills on coffee and tea.

When things finally settled down, Suzanne brewed herself a quick cup of Earl Grey tea and hovered in the kitchen near Petra, who was pouring batter into various-sized cake pans, getting ready for a marathon bake.

"How much money did you raise yesterday?" Suzanne asked her. "From the Knit-In?"

"Almost two thousand dollars," said Petra, pouring batter into three five-inch-round pans.

"Whatcha going to use the money for?"

"We all voted to donate it to the Baby Lamb Club," said Petra.

"Lovely," whispered Suzanne. The Baby Lamb Club was a small band of dedicated women who knitted tiny hats, booties, and blankets for premature babies as well as critically ill infants. These tiny knitted treasures were distributed in the neonatal and PICU units at nearby hospitals.

Once in a while, the Baby Lamb Club was even asked by one of the nurses to knit a small burial gown, since the last thing on the minds of bereaved parents was finding suitable clothing for their infant.

"The club will use it to buy the very best yarns," said Petra. "Alpaca, angora, cashmere, lamb's wool . . ."

"You and your Baby Lamb Club friends are so kind and unselfish," said Suzanne. A tear oozed from the corner of her eye as she put an arm around her friend and gave a quick squeeze.

Petra smiled back, looking both sad and hopeful. "I can't stand the thought of a sick or dying infant not having one item that's been crafted with love."

"YE gadz!" exclaimed Toni, as she banged through the swinging door into the kitchen. "The tent's up and billowing and the tables and chairs are being unloaded."

"How's it all look?" asked Suzanne.

"Like the Ringling Brothers Barnum and Bailey Circus just lurched into town," said Toni with a laugh.

"That's because it *is* a circus here," added Petra. "All we need is a dancing bear." She barked a sharp laugh. "Maybe we could get Doogie to step in."

"I prefer to take the high road and think of our situation as organized chaos," said Toni. "But, please, will you two stop worrying? After lunch I'm going to check in with all our volunteers and cake-decorating people to make sure they're locked and loaded for tomorrow."

"Maybe I should stay and help?" said Suzanne, hopefully.

"Not on your life!" shouted Toni. "No way you're chickening out of modeling today. And you better believe we're going to demand a full report on your runway activities!"

"Toni's right," said Petra. "The opening of Alchemy is a milestone for Kindred. It's a big deal."

"Our Take the Cake Show is a big deal, too," said Suzanne.

"I know," said Petra, "but the boutique is *different*. Kind of a watershed moment for our little town to be suddenly thrust into the mainstream of fashion."

"We'll see about that," said Suzanne, wondering if liquid leggings and Ed Hardy T-shirts really were that big a deal.

SUZANNE was still worrying about Anson Dillworth as well as her modeling gig when she printed the luncheon offerings on the board. Lentil soup, coconut shrimp, lemon dill egg salad, chicken croquettes, and chocolate flapjacks.

Two farmers in plaid shirts, sitting at the marble counter, watched carefully.

"Is that croquet?" asked the first one. "Like with mallets and balls?"

"Couldn't be," the second sniggered.

"Croquettes," said Suzanne. "Like with chopped chicken and onions made into little patties and fried to a toasty brown."

Suzanne moved about the Cackleberry Club, taking orders, keeping a watchful eye on the clock. She wanted to get to the Super 8 before one o'clock, checkout time.

"I talked to Margie Gregory with the VA," Petra told Suzanne, when she ducked back into the kitchen. "She says there's a halfway house for veterans in Jessup. Place called Honor House. It's transitional, not permanent, but if you can get your guy over there, they'll do what they can to help."

"That's wonderful news," breathed Suzanne. "I'll drive Dil there today." She glanced around. "Now, if you think you can make do without me . . ."

"Go right ahead," murmured Toni, who was standing at the grill, humming and gently turning chicken croquettes. "Man, I've got a bad case of stuck song syndrome. You know . . . when you get a song whirling around in your brain and it just keeps playing over and over?"

"I hate when that happens," said Petra. "Once I had the *Gilligan's Island* theme song in my head for two days. I thought I'd have to get electroshock therapy just to get rid of it."

"Delete the old hard drive," said Suzanne with a laugh.

"Remember how simple TV was back in the sixties?" Petra asked. "Every show had an opening song that basically told the gist of the story."

"Oh my gosh, you're right," said Suzanne. "Like . . . 'Here's a story of a lovely lady who was bringing up three very lovely girls.' And 'Just sit right back and you'll hear a tale . . .'"

"Don't!" shrieked Petra, covering both ears.

"Look at you," Toni said to Suzanne. "Not nervous about modeling anymore."

"Oh, I'm nervous," said Suzanne. "You don't see it, but I'm schvitzing like crazy."

"Hey," said Toni. "You know who else is modeling?"

Suzanne shook her head. "Who?"

"Barbara Welch from the feed store." Toni flashed a slightly wicked grin.

"Seriously?" Suzanne recalled Barbara as being rather short and beamy.

"See?" said Toni, "you don't have a thing to worry about. You'll look like Heidi Klum next to her!"

"No," said Suzanne, "I'm just afraid I'll look like Heidi Clodhopper!"

TWENTY minutes later Suzanne pulled her car into a parking spot outside room twelve at the Super 8 Motel. She knocked on the door, got no answer, knocked again. After ten minutes of banging, she went to the office and asked the young girl at the front desk if she knew what was up with the guest in room twelve.

"Oh, he checked out," said the girl. She sat on a high stool, her knees tucked up, chewing gum and watching a grainy black-and-white TV.

"Checked out," repeated Suzanne.

The girl nodded. "Guy walked in, laid the key on the counter, and walked out again."

"Just like that," said Suzanne. She could see the key for room twelve hanging on the board in back of the girl.

The girl snapped her gum viciously and nodded. "Yup."

"When did this happen?"

The girl switched her gaze from the TV to a large black-and-white clock that was protected by a silver grate. "Maybe . . . oh . . . forty-five minutes ago."

"You know where he went?"

"Nope."

"Okay . . . thanks," said Suzanne.

She walked out of the office, stood in the gravel parking lot, and looked around speculatively. Out on the road, a thin stream of cars crawled by, but she could see no one walking away from the Super 8.

Rats.

CHAPTER 25

CARMEN Copeland's fashion show was Suzanne's worst nightmare realized in the flesh. First there was the scene in the changing room. At least two dozen waifs, in various stages of undress, wiggled and giggled and squirmed their youthful bodies into cute little outfits, the operative word being *little*. Suzanne decided that Carmen hadn't heard the news—heralded on CNN and FOX, and even trumpeted by Oprah—that the average U.S. woman now wore a size fourteen.

No, she decided, stealing glances at all the skinny, midget, waif girls, Carmen didn't have a semblance of a clue.

Who were all these little women? Suzanne wondered. What planet did they come from? Did they disembark from a space ship or the death star Anorexia?

"Suzanne!" squealed Missy, "you're *finally* here!" Dressed in a long, black, skinny dress, her hair pulled back in a severe bun, Missy was barely recognizable to Suzanne. Her peaches-and-cream complexion had been replaced with streaks of wine-colored blusher, sooty eye shadow circled her eyes, and a gash of dark lipstick delineated her mouth. Her lush figure seemed to be reined in by a torturous body shaper.

"You hired *real* models?" sputtered Suzanne. The subtext being, *What am I, the silly little hometown ringer?*

Missy administered air kisses to Suzanne, a la Carmen Copeland, and said, "Carmen hired them. From the Fashion Merchandising program over at Darlington College. Don't they look fabulous?"

"Uh . . . no," said Suzanne. "They look like models. So . . . where's Barbara Welch from the feed store?"

"Carmen dismissed her," said Missy. She shook her head and her long, dangly earrings lashed about her cheeks and neck.

"Then why do you need me?" asked Suzanne, hoping she might also be dismissed, as ignominious as that word sounded.

"Because you're my friend," said Missy, grasping Suzanne's hand. "And you're here to help us keep it real."

Carmen Copeland's tight, hard face suddenly loomed in front of them like a mask that had been flung across the store. "This one hasn't been to hair and makeup yet!" she rasped, pointing a finger at Suzanne.

"I just got here," explained Suzanne. "I was *working*."

Carmen dug her manicured talons into Suzanne's shoulder and propelled her toward the back of the store. Shoving her down into a plastic-covered chair, Carmen shrieked, "Gregg!" at the top of her lungs.

Gregg Montag, one of the owners of Root 66, suddenly appeared. He was gay, tall, blond, a trifle ethereal.

"You've got your work cut out for you," snarled Carmen. Then, as if Suzanne were a waxworks figure, incapable of seeing or hearing, Carmen rattled on about her deficits. "Eyebrows," said Carmen, studying Suzanne's face and looking unhappy. "For God's sake, try to give her some kind of arch." Carmen's eyes narrowed. "Smoky eyeliner and eye shadow as well, then highlighter for a semblance of cheekbone. As far as her lips are concerned . . . well, it's a good thing she's still got an upper lip at her age."

"Thanks a million, Carmen," said Suzanne, getting up. "And lotsa luck with your fashion show, because I have to . . ."

Gregg grabbed Suzanne's shoulder as Carmen flew off to accost her next victim.

". . . leave," finished Suzanne, as Gregg's grip intensified.

"Relax," soothed Gregg. "Carmen's been like that all day. Acting like the Wicked Witch of the West to everyone who comes near her."

"I don't really want to do this," said Suzanne, protesting, as Gregg eased her back down in the chair and pinned a short, black plastic cape around her shoulders.

"I'll just do a light touch-up," promised Gregg. "Sort of strengthen some of your best features."

"According to Carmen, I don't have any," said Suzanne. "My arches have collapsed and I've got the lips of a turtle . . ."

"Honey, you're gorgeous," Gregg assured her. "A real woman. Beautiful and with true character in your face. Not like all of these . . ." He waved an arm, theatrically. ". . . teenage waifs."

So Suzanne calmed down and put her trust in Gregg, telling herself that if she didn't like what she saw, she could *still* stomp out. After ten minutes of brushing and blushing and lining and spackling, Gregg held up a hand mirror so Suzanne could judge for herself.

"What do you think?" Gregg asked.

Suzanne studied herself in the mirror. Her brows were arched and slightly filled in. Her eyes were suddenly lush pools of exotica. And her nose . . . well, Gregg had worked some form of magic with three different shades of foundation that made her nose appear far straighter and narrower than the one she'd actually inherited from her forebears. Apologies to Aunt Lucille, of course.

Suzanne was literally taken aback. "I think I . . . I like it," she told him.

"Excellent," said Gregg, whipping off her plastic cape. "Now let's get you over to Brett's chair so he can work on your hair."

That proved far less traumatic.

Ten judiciously placed hot rollers, then a quick blow out, were followed by some fussing, teasing, and hair spraying. Suzanne's hair fell to her shoulders in a lush, smooth bob that was more elegant than she could have ever imagined.

"This, I love," she told Brett. "You've worked wonders."

"The look may be a trifle more socialite than fashion model," confided Brett with a wink, "but it becomes you."

Suzanne tossed her head back and studied herself in the mirror as she struggled into her clothes. What unsettled her most was that suddenly *looking* different made her *feel* different. Was that a good thing? she asked herself. Yeah, maybe . . . for a while. For a "let's pretend" moment. But her own natural skin and looser-fitting clothes were still awfully comfortable.

"Fabulous!" declared Missy, when Suzanne presented herself, fully dressed. "You're an absolute vision!"

But Carmen was not quite so approving.

"Oops," said Carmen, pointing a finger at Suzanne's backside. "She's got VPL."

"Huh?" said Suzanne, whirling around, not sure what she was going to find. Had somebody planted a Kick Me sign on her backside?

"Visible panty line," said Carmen, grimacing. "Suzanne, you'll have to wear a thong under your jeans."

Missy grabbed a small box and pulled out the teeniest of undergarments. "This should work." She handed it to Suzanne.

"Pull 'em down," commanded Carmen.

Suzanne was slightly aghast. "No way I'm giving up my underpants," she told them. Her hand crept down to the waistline where her Hanes three-for-nine-dollar undies lurked underneath.

"The jeans will look terrible," Carmen moaned. "The entire effect will be ruined!"

"You're asking me to wear what amounts to a piece of dental floss!" sputtered Suzanne.

"A thong isn't as uncomfortable as you might think," said Carmen.

"No," said Suzanne, "I imagine it's worse."

"Suit yourself," sniffed Carmen.

"Carmen," said Suzanne, "what's this I hear about you opening a fine dining restaurant?"

"What are you talking about?" asked Carmen, slightly startled.

"Don't play coy," said Suzanne. "Gene Gandle brought it up the other day and rumors are running rampant."

"I don't know *what* you've heard," huffed Carmen, "but whatever it is, I'm sure it doesn't involve me!" She tottered off on super high Manolo Blahnik heels, her tight black satin dress rustling loudly.

"What a crank," Suzanne muttered to Missy.

Missy nodded her head in agreement.

"If Carmen's always this caustic and nasty," said Suzanne, "how can you stand working for her?"

Missy gave her a hangdog look. "It isn't easy."

"People!" Carmen hissed in a loud stage whisper. "Places! The show is about to start!"

"Oops," said Suzanne, starting to develop serious butterflies. "Where do I go?"

"You're tenth in line," said Missy. "Right after the girl in the purple cashmere hoodie."

"Excellent," said Suzanne, positioning herself next to the purple hoodie girl and telling herself this was all in fun. A jest. Nothing to worry about. A quick strut around the showroom floor and then it would be over. Her fifteen seconds of fame.

But when the music rose in volume, when "Under My Thumb" by the Rolling Stones blasted from the loudspeakers, Suzanne's knees began to shake. The pulsing, pounding rhythm seemed to synch with her rapidly beating heart. *The change has come* . . . thump, thump . . . *she's under my thumb* . . . thump, thump.

But there was something else going on out there, too. Applause. And cheers that greeted the models who were already out there walking the runway.

Gotta try to have fun. Not look like I'm doing the chicken dance out there.

And then, way too soon, Suzanne was at the head of the line. Missy put a hand on her shoulder and urged, "Smile!"

Suzanne gritted her teeth and smiled.

"You look like you're bracing for a root canal," Missy hissed.

Suzanne tried again.

"Better," said Missy. She put her hand in the small of Suzanne's back, gave a slight push. "Now . . . go!"

Suzanne stepped out from behind the curtain to face a low bank of stupendously bright lights as well as a sea of familiar faces. She smiled, cocked her head, stuck her hands into the pockets of her oh-so-stylish leather jacket, and strode down the white Mylar runway. Six steps in, she felt the excitement and the beat grab hold. The high-heeled boots she'd been given lent her walk a little swagger. Gaining confidence now, she kicked up her heels a bit and moved her shoulders in a slight exaggeration, appropriating the walk of the supermodels she'd seen parading around in teddies and glittery angel wings on the Victoria's Secret TV fashion show.

Suzanne high-stepped down the runway, chin up, smile for real. She was headed for the sweet spot Missy had pointed out. The point where you were supposed to pause, pose, then turn around.

I can do this! she told herself. *I'm feeling it!*

She swished past purple hoodie girl, who was returning from her pause and pose moment and heading for the second half of the runway. And that's when it all fell apart.

The front door of the shop crashed open loudly and a large shadow suddenly loomed in the doorway! Then the figure surged forward and the sound of stomping boots contrasted crazily with the thumping soundtrack.

Heads turned, models suddenly faltered in their tracks, and from the back of the shop, Carmen yelled a shrill, "What the Sam Hill?"

Sheriff Roy Doogie, dressed head-to-toe in unfashionable khaki, his chapeau a modified Smokey Bear style, had blundered in and brought the entire fashion show to a screeching halt!

Caught like a deer in the klieg lights, Doogie lurched to a stop and let his beady eyes roam the crowd. Finally they landed on Suzanne. His face turned the color of a ripe persimmon and seemed to swell up. His mouth and jaw worked frantically.

Uh-oh, thought Suzanne. *Here it comes.*

"Suzanne!" Doogie shouted at the top of his lungs.

Doggone, she thought to herself. *He picked up Dil!*

Turns out, she was way wrong.

"*You* were the one who called in that anonymous tip!" Doogie thundered in front of everyone. His brow furrowed angrily as he shifted from one clodhopper to the other while a sea of startled faces stared at him. But—and here, Suzanne had to give Doogie full credit—he didn't back down.

Like a crazed wraith, Carmen Copeland suddenly flew out from behind the white curtain and hurled her fashionable self in Doogie's direction. Which woke Suzanne from her semi-stupor and sent her catapulting toward Doogie as well.

"Are you insane?" Carmen shrilled at Doogie. "What do you think you're *do*ing? Who do you think you *are*!" Her hands, clutched like claws, were poised to inflict bodily harm on the sheriff.

"Carmen," pleaded Suzanne, as she threw herself between them like a human sacrifice, "let me take care of this!" Grabbing Doogie's arm, Suzanne tried to pull Doogie away from the spotlight and toward the still-open front door.

"I . . . excuse me," Doogie muttered to Carmen. But he still wouldn't budge as he cast furious glances at Suzanne.

"Pleeease," Suzanne begged, tugging Doogie again. But it was like trying to move a locomotive. "Let me explain."

"You'd better," snarled Doogie.

"Please," Suzanne repeated. "Outside?"

Doogie finally relented and allowed Suzanne to lead him by the arm. "You better explain," he seethed, as they trod past shocked and sniggering onlookers. "You'd just better have a doggone *brilliant* explanation!"

"I do," said Suzanne, when they were finally outside, away from prying eyes, away from the fashion show itself.

"Because you and Toni were at that farm the other night!" screeched Doogie. "How do I know?" he continued angrily. "Because those two potheads finally broke down and spilled their guts. They told me you two girls were out there Wednesday night—snooping around!"

"Okay," said Suzanne, deciding the best thing to do was let Doogie carry on with his rant. Sooner or later he'd wear out and wind down. Wouldn't he? Then maybe she could talk some sense into him. Or at least explain.

"And I *know* for sure it was you two," Doogie rasped, "because those bad boys *described* you and Toni to a T!"

"Those guys pulled a gun on us!" said Suzanne, trying to muster a serious amount of rage and indignation. "And locked us in a barn!"

Doogie was unimpressed. "I don't care if they locked you in the storm cellar, filled it full of water, and threw away the key! You gotta tell me about this stuff when it *happens.* The minute it goes down!"

"I know that," said Suzanne, sounding slightly contrite. "And I'm sorry."

"You *should* be sorry," grumbled Doogie. He was beginning to lose his head of steam. "In case you haven't noticed, I've got my hands full right now!"

"Those dope guys didn't have anything to do with Ozzie and Bo's murder," said Suzanne. "You know that, don't you?"

Doogie pulled off his hat, reached in his baggy trousers for a hanky, and mopped his forehead as well as the top of his head. "I been figuring that out." More mopping. "S'not the point."

"Okay," said Suzanne. She sincerely wished the people driving by would stop staring at them. Or maybe they were staring at her tight jeans and leather jacket. Or maybe they were utterly horrified by her visible panty line. Who knew? Who cared?

"Just what in blue blazes were you two *doing* out there anyway?" demanded Doogie.

Suzanne decided she'd better fess up. "Toni was all hot and bothered about Junior," she told Doogie. "She was afraid Junior was involved in some sort of meth lab deal."

"Those two yahoos I got sitting in the can over at the law enforcement center say Junior *was* involved," said Doogie.

"No," said Suzanne. "We found out he wasn't. Trust me." She cast a glance toward the sky, praying a bolt of lightning wouldn't descend from the low-hanging clouds and strike her dead. *Please, Lord, just forgive me this one little white lie, okay? I promise I'll make amends. I'll help out at the senior citizens' home. And with the next pancake supper at church. I'll even knit scarves for orphans, just as soon as I learn how to knit.*

"Junior wasn't involved?" said Doogie. He looked more than a little skeptical.

"That's right," said Suzanne. "We thought he was, but he wasn't. We were just . . ." She took a gulp. ". . . we were completely overreacting."

"Huh," said Doogie, half buying her story. "I wonder what else those potheads are lying about?"

"I don't know," said Suzanne. "Probably a great many things. But I do know this—Toni is working extra hard to keep Junior Garrett on the straight and narrow."

"That so?" asked Doogie.

"Absolutely," said Suzanne, holding up two fingers, changing it to three. "Scout's honor."

"You could have been hurt, you know," said Doogie, starting to edge toward his cruiser.

"But we weren't," said Suzanne. "We used our wits to get away."

"Sheesh," snorted Doogie. "No wonder you wanted that stupid old mule."

"YOU owe me big time," Suzanne told Toni when she stopped by the Cackleberry Club around four o'clock.

Toni looked up from where she was sweeping the floor. Little bits of dust mingled with bread crumbs and a hunk of doughnut. "Huh?"

"Remember our good pals Eel and Lenny?" said Suzanne. "Turns out they ratted us out."

Toni's broom clattered to the floor. "Those dirtballs ratted us out? Aw, man! You mean they told Doogie we were out at their farm?"

"You got it, sister," said Suzanne.

"Did they rat out Junior, too?" Concern suddenly clouded Toni's eyes.

"They tried to," said Suzanne, "but BFF that I am, I lied like a rug about it. Swore up and down to Doogie that Junior wasn't involved. Told him we *thought* he was, but then we found out he was pure as the driven snow."

"Now you're making me feel bad," said Toni. "I mean, I'm happy you pulled Junior's fat from the fire and all, but sorry you had to lie."

"Yeah . . . well, let's just say it's not the first time I blew past the ninth commandment," replied Suzanne.

"It's the other commandments that are the real biggies," said Toni. "Although . . ." She frowned, thinking. "Maybe it's best we don't go there."

"Let's not," agreed Suzanne.

"And you're sure Junior's safe?"

"As long as his phony baloney story jibes with ours," said Suzanne

Toni clapped a hand to her heart. "As long as Junior fibs, too," she murmured.

"For now," said Suzanne, "let's just think of it as moral relativism."

Toni blew out a glut of air. "Okaaay." She stared down at her broom and dustpan for a couple of moments, then knelt and gathered everything up. "So. How was the fashion show? I see you got to keep the clothes. And may I just say your makeup looks fantastic! Did Gregg do your eyes? Because your look kind of reminds me of Kathleen Turner, back in her gorgeous, pre-pudgy days."

"I'll take that as a left-handed compliment," said Suzanne, as they walked into the kitchen together.

"Was it really fun?" Toni asked, almost wistfully.

"The fashion show," said Suzanne. *Where to start?* "First of all, there was a phenomenal turnout. It looked like one of those paparazzi scrums you see at the Academy Awards or something."

"Wow," exclaimed Toni. "I guess I should have come after all."

"Oh, I don't think so," sighed Suzanne. "The program did get slightly derailed."

"Carmen did something stupid?"

"That's a given," said Suzanne. "But Sheriff Doogie was a big hit on the runway, too."

Toni stared. "*That's* where Doogie accosted you about Eel and Lenny?"

"Oh, yeah," said Suzanne. "Right in the middle of Carmen's precious fashion show! It made for quite the dramatic moment."

Toni suddenly grinned like a maniac. "I can just see it!" she chortled. "And now the latest in wrinkled khaki, with a tarnished gold badge worn as a single, bold statement piece."

"That's about the size of it," said Suzanne.

"Extra large if it was Doogie," said Toni with a giggle. She paused. "But you had fun."

"Only if you consider removing my clothes in front of younger, skinnier women, and having Doogie scream at me in front of everyone as the height of hilarity."

"But not a total loss," said Toni. "You got your makeup and hair done professionally."

Suzanne stabbed an index finger at Toni. "Lady, you just found a ray of sunshine in the middle of a shit storm."

"Ever the optimist," said Toni.

Suzanne, glancing into the cracked mirror that hung by the back door, said, "You don't think the eye makeup's too garish, do you?" She poked a finger at her newly en-hanced eyelashes, testing them. They felt rubbery and a little spidery.

"You look gorgeous," Toni assured her. "Perfect for your big date tonight."

"I just hope Sam doesn't think it's too over-the-top," said Suzanne.

"Honey," said Toni, "take it from me. He's gonna *love* what he sees." She paused. "You gonna wear the clothes, too?"

"The jacket, yes," said Suzanne. "The jeans, no."

CHAPTER 26

TONI wasn't far off with her prediction. In fact, the date was going swimmingly well. Sam Hazelet had arrived promptly at seven o'clock. Parked his BMW right in front of Suzanne's house and ran up the walk to meet her at the door. Very proper and courteous, unlike Junior who tooted his horn outside Toni's apartment, then scowled and drummed his fingers impatiently while he waited for her to dash out.

Then they'd driven over to Kopell's Restaurant and B and B, in nearby Cornucopia. Sam had popped a Rihanna CD into the player and they'd chatted easily as they enjoyed the music. Once they'd arrived at Kopell's, they were shown to a cozy table for two near the fireplace. Sam perused the wine list, asked a couple of questions, then ordered a bottle of Rombauer Cabernet Sauvignon. Once the cork was popped and they'd gone through the swirling-sniffing-tasting ritual, the Cabernet turned out to be quite spectacular.

"You know wine," Suzanne said, sounding pleased.

"Just enough to be dangerous," Sam told her, pouring a little more into her wineglass. "You like this Cab?"

"Love it," Suzanne told him. Actually, she was loving the evening out. It had been well over a year since she'd sat across a candlelit table from a man. Feeling relaxed, enjoying each other's company.

"May you live in interesting times," said Sam, raising his glass.

"Cheers," said Suzanne, gently clinking her glass to his, then taking another sip.

"So," said Sam, leaning forward slightly. "How was your day?"

"You wouldn't believe it if I told you," said Suzanne.

"Then you have to tell me," said Sam.

"I let someone twist my arm and convince me to be in a fashion show."

"Huh. The one at Alchemy?"

"How would you know about *that*?" asked Suzanne. Men didn't really pay attention to fashion and clothing trends, did they?

"Are you serious?" said Sam, rolling his eyes. "That's all the women at the clinic have been talking about. They're all charged up because now they can buy K Brand jeans in Kindred instead of driving all the way to Minneapolis or Sioux Falls."

"J Brand," corrected Suzanne.

"And something called Spanx," said Sam, looking puzzled. "I assume Spanx are also some kind of fashion item?"

"Uh . . . yeah," said Suzanne, deciding this might not be the ideal time to elaborate.

"That Carmen Copeland's quite a go-getter," remarked Sam. "Though I'm not convinced she can wave her magic wand and turn all the women of Kindred into fashion plates overnight."

"She's convinced she can," said Suzanne.

Sam leaned back in his chair. "I also heard something about Carmen making an offer on the Driesden and Draper Funeral Home."

"That's the rumor around town."

Sam looked interested. "I got the feeling it's more than just a rumor."

"Not sure," said Suzanne. "Carmen's pretty sly about getting a buzz going—over *anything*. But if she wants the property bad enough, I imagine she figures now's the time to take advantage of the situation."

"The murders," said Sam.

Suzanne nodded. "Sure. With George Draper still being a suspect."

"And I heard Earl Stensrud, too," said Sam. "And . . . well, I probably shouldn't say anything, because she's a friend of yours . . ."

"Missy Langston," said Suzanne. "Who now works for Carmen at Alchemy."

"Does this whole murder conundrum strike you as being slightly incestuous?" asked Sam

Suzanne thought for a moment, then said, "A little. But that's pretty much the small-town way." She peered at him. "You didn't grow up in a small town, did you?"

Sam shook his head. "Not really. Lynn. Outside Boston."

"In a small town everyone is always slightly involved with everyone else," said Suzanne. "Or at least they think they have a pretty good bead on them."

"One big happy family," said Sam.

"Oh, there are always a few enemies tossed in for good measure," added Suzanne. "Although, for the life of me, I'm not sure who had it in for Ozzie Driesden. He always seemed like a pretty decent guy. Got along with everyone."

"You're talking about motive," said Sam.

"Sure."

"What about the kid who worked for him? The kid they found hanged?"

"Bo Becker," filled in Suzanne.

"Did he hate Ozzie? Or have his own enemies?"

"No clue," said Suzanne.

Sam stared at her. "That's what you've been looking for, isn't it? Clues."

"Excuse me?"

"The rumor mill's been churning overtime about you, too," said Sam with a laugh. "I understand you're the odds-on favorite to solve the two murders."

"Oh, I don't think so," said Suzanne. She grabbed the linen napkin from her lap and blotted her lips.

"But you've done it before," said Sam. "Solved a murder, I mean."

Suzanne let a hand flutter, as if to say, *not really.*

"Come on," he urged her.

"Stumbled on an answer is more like it," she finally admitted.

"But you've been nosing around," said Sam.

Suzanne's shoulders lifted half an inch. "Some."

"More than *some*," said Sam. "You were the one who found Becker's body. So . . . ?" He waggled his fingers in a friendly "gimme" gesture.

"I'm not any closer to solving those two cases than Sheriff Doogie is," said Suzanne.

"But you must have a theory . . ."

Suzanne picked up the menus and handed one to Sam. "The Muscovy duck is excellent," she told him. "So is the standing rib roast. But watch out for the hanger steak; it can be a little on the tough side."

"I'm just going to keep asking you," Sam told her. "And maybe if I ply you with enough wine . . ." He grinned at her.

"Maybe," she replied, her mouth twitching at the corners.

While Sam perused his menu, Suzanne glanced about the dining room. The wood-paneled walls with brass sconces lent a warm, cozy feeling. A fire crackled in the large stone fireplace that practically dominated an entire wall. Deer antlers and a shelf of antique ceramic beer steins contributed to a German *schloss*-like atmosphere.

She and Walter had enjoyed their share of dinners here, of course. And had once spent a night upstairs at the B and B. There'd been an antique sleigh bed with billowing feather-beds, as well as a small gas fireplace in the corner of their room. Suzanne let loose a small sigh. Just one of a thousand *good times*, relegated now to that quadrant of her brain reserved for special, cherished memories. Memories she could pull out and peruse at will. Of Walter. Her parents, long gone now. A few uncles and aunts. A dear friend, Gayle, who had succumbed to breast cancer.

"Suzanne?" A large man wearing a chef's jacket and towering white hat suddenly hovered at her elbow.

She looked up, blinked once. "Bernie? Hi!" she exclaimed. "How are you?"

Bernie Affolter, the head chef at Kopell's, leaned down and brushed his stubbly cheek against her smooth one. "Great to see you here. It's been . . . ages." He grinned again, this time in Sam's direction. "Hello."

Suzanne made hasty introductions. "Sam Hazelet, this is Bernie Affolter, head chef."

"Pleased to meet you," said Sam, extending a hand. "We were just going over your menu. Everything looks terrific."

"Mind a few suggestions?" he asked.

"That'd be great," said Sam. "Direct from the man who knows."

"The Copper River salmon is fresh, never frozen," said Bernie. "And the Muscovy duck is our specialty."

"I'll keep that in mind," said Sam.

"And tonight we're doing grilled rib eye with caramelized onions and roast carrots," added Bernie. "So, Suzanne," he continued, "when are you going to open your own restaurant?"

"I already did," said Suzanne with a laugh.

"I mean a fine dining place," said Bernie. "That's always been her dream," he confided to Sam.

Sam looked interested. "Is that so?"

"More of a pipe dream, I think," said Suzanne. "Still going to be a couple years before the Cackleberry Club is humming along on its own."

"Hey," said Bernie, "that recipe for crab chowder you gave me?"

Suzanne nodded.

"When I put it on the menu last month," said Bernie, "we sold out every night."

"Wow," said Sam.

"I'm thinking now," said Bernie, "that I might substitute lobster for the crab and add a little sherry."

"No reason why you couldn't," said Suzanne, thrilled her recipe had been so popular.

When Bernie returned to the kitchen, Sam gave Suzanne a mischievous smile. "I didn't know you were a foodie."

"I'm not," said Suzanne. "Not really."

"Do you own a food processor?" asked Sam.

"Of course," Suzanne replied, reaching for a slice of molasses bread, the house specialty.

"How about a wire whisk and mandolin for slicing paper-thin potatoes and veggies?"

"Yes," she said, spreading a thin layer of unsalted butter on her bread.

"Subscription to *Food and Wine*?"

Suzanne nodded. "Guilty as charged."

"Then there's no denying you're a foodie," said Sam. "Maybe you're not a pilgrimage-to-Le Bernadin, quaff-the-Beaujolais-nouveau-foodie, but you're right up there."

"Could we please change the subject?" asked Suzanne.

"No," said Sam. "I enjoy talking about food. It's one of my passions, too. Of course, what I really prefer is *eating* it. Really good food, that is."

Suzanne toyed with her salad fork, thinking about their gourmet dinner tomorrow night. Should she invite Sam? Would it be too soon to see him again? Would she appear too eager?

Bag those thoughts, she told herself. Do whatever the heck you feel like doing.

"You know," she said to Sam, "the Cackleberry Club is hosting a gourmet winners dinner tomorrow night."

"Winners," said Sam.

"That's right," said Suzanne. "The winners of our cake-decorating contest will be there along with a few other folks who bought tickets." She hesitated. "I don't know if you already have plans, but I'd sure like it if you came."

Sam dropped his chin into his hand and stared at her across the table. "Mmm, really? Tell me the menu."

"Oh, now you're being selective!"

"I'm curious," he told her.

"Let's see," said Suzanne, feeling slightly flustered. "Well, our starter course is going to be salmon medallions with mustard sauce and dilled cucumber. Then Boston bib lettuce with walnut dressing and Maytag blue cheese. Squash soup with fennel and onion garnish. And fillet of beef with potato gratin."

"That's it?" said Sam.

"Dessert will be honey-poached pears with gingerbread and fresh-brewed espresso."

Sam's dark eyes stared intently at her.

Uh-oh, she thought. "So . . . what do you think?"

"Are you kidding?" he exclaimed. "I wouldn't miss a dinner like that for anything! Thank you!"

That seemed to really break the ice, or what small chip was left of it. Sam had the grilled rib eye while Suzanne ordered the Muscovy duck. They ate, chatted, ate some more, drank wine, gabbed, and laughed. By the time dessert arrived, a cheese sampler accented with thin slices of Granny Smith green apples and a balsamic vinegar reduction, the candle in the center of their table had burned low, and the wine bottle was pretty much empty.

Sam pushed what was left of the Camembert toward Suzanne, drew a breath, then said, "I know that your husband passed away . . . what? . . . maybe six or seven months ago?"

Suzanne nodded. She figured the subject would rear its head sooner or later. How could it not?

"You seem very . . . pulled together," said Sam. "Like you're really charging ahead with your life."

"You think so?" she asked.

He nodded. "Absolutely. Otherwise you wouldn't be sitting here with me."

"You're probably right," said Suzanne. "No, you *are* right. But I want to tell you something, okay? A little story."

Sam nodded. "Sure."

"One rainy Tuesday night," Suzanne began, "I was going through Walter's top dresser drawer when I came across a lovely white shirt." She gazed at Sam. "The shirt had never been worn. In fact, it was still carefully swaddled in tissue paper. Then I remembered that Walter had bought that shirt a couple of years earlier at a fancy shop on Michigan Avenue, when we'd driven up to see the Matisse show at the Chicago Art Institute. I'd ribbed him mercilessly about the price of the shirt and he'd taken it to heart. He was, obviously, saving the shirt for a special occasion."

Sam continued to gaze at her, brows arched, not quite certain where she was going with this.

"So," continued Suzanne, "I took the shirt from the dresser drawer and laid it next to the suit I was planning to take to the funeral home the next morning."

Silence hung between them.

"Now I don't wait for anything," said Suzanne, in a quiet voice. "No more waiting for planets to align, the economy to rebound, or someone to hand me a blank check. And I particularly try not to worry about what others think. To be perfectly honest, I don't much care what they're thinking. Now I just try to push ahead and do my best to be optimistic, hopeful, and fearless."

"Does it work?" asked Sam, reaching for her hand.

Suzanne smiled back at him. "Sometimes."

CHAPTER 27

BY ten o'clock Saturday morning, it really did look as though the circus had arrived, pitched camp, and was operating in full force. Like mainsails from gigantic, oceangoing schooners, two shimmering white tents billowed heroically in the front parking lot of the Cackleberry Club. Riding the soft breeze were the mingled aromas of Jamaican Blue Mountain coffee, fresh-baked orange muffins, brown sugar scones, melted chocolate, fresh marzipan, and powdery confectioners' sugar.

In the largest of the two tents, cake-decorating demonstrations had just gotten under way. Cece Bishop from the Culinary Arts Program at Darlington College and Jenny Probst from the Kindred Bakery had teamed up to demonstrate fondants and frostings. Cece had arrived with a three-tiered cake that was covered in vanilla icing and just waiting to be turned into a majestic art deco–inspired work of art.

Suzanne presided over the second tent. Jammed with tables she'd positioned in a large U-shape arrangement, gorgeous cake entries had been pouring in all morning. After wrestling with her choice of categories, Petra had finally settled upon four different cake-decorating divisions: wedding cakes, tiered cakes, sheet cakes, and sugar arts. This last division being the most popular and encompassing all sorts of imaginative designs from floral romps, to swans and swags, to pulled and blown sugar sculptures.

Much to Toni's dismay, Petra had jettisoned her idea for a weird cake recipe contest. So no deep-fried tempura cakes, chocolate chili cakes, or potato pecan cakes. At least not this year.

Suzanne sat at the registration table, checking in cake entries and handing out name tags and programs. About fifteen cakes had come in so far, and she expected another thirty or so to arrive by their 2:00 P.M. cutoff time. She suspected that more than a few hopeful bakers were still struggling to perfect their fondant frills!

"So how was the big date?" Toni asked, sidling up next to her.

"Really nice," said Suzanne, jotting a note to herself.

"Nice?" said Toni, looking slightly askance. "Nice is when somebody knits you a pair of argyle socks for your birthday."

"Okay," said Suzanne. "If you must know, I had a pretty terrific evening. It was fun, challenging, and even a teensy bit romantic." She peered sideways at Toni. "There. I've spilled my guts. Happy?"

Toni clasped her hands together in a grand theatrical gesture. "Ah, sweet romance. I so adore hearing the details. Hugs, kisses . . ."

"And that's *all* I'm going to reveal for now," cut in Suzanne. "This dating thing is brand-new territory for me."

"Sounds like code for *you're planning to take it slow*."

"Absolutely I am," said Suzanne. "Think snail speed. Or better yet . . . classier, yet . . . escargot speed."

"No, no, no," said Toni, dancing about and twirling a finger at her. "Bad idea. Romance is all about being wildly impetuous and crazy!"

"And spontaneous?" asked Suzanne, raising a single, quivering eyebrow. "Like *you* were with bad-boy Junior? Running off to the Cupid's Kiss Wedding Chapel in Las Vegas and getting married by an Elvis impersonator?"

Toni wrinkled her nose and made a face. "We did have 'Blue Hawaii' playing in the background, but . . . I see your point." She sounded deflated. "And thanks so much for dropping me back to terra firma with such a resounding thud."

"Truth hurts." Suzanne laughed.

"Hey," said Toni, perking up again. "Some of the cakes that have come in so far are really fantastic!" She pointed toward the table that held the sugar art cakes. "Did you see the one with the Fabergé egg? And the one that looks like King Arthur's castle?" She eyed the castle cake thoughtfully, like she wanted to take a nibble. "What would you say that was? A toffee drawbridge with peanut brittle parapets?"

"Looks like," said Suzanne, shifting her gaze to a smiling woman who'd just placed a pink-and-white five-tiered wedding cake in front of her, replete with fondant hearts and flying doves.

"Yum," joked Toni. "I'd like to storm that castle."

Suzanne left Toni to handle cake entries, while she hurried into the other tent to check on demos. Jenny was hand painting a fondant orchid, while Cece was piping silver icing. Excellent. So . . . now to check on Petra.

"Sharon just called and cancelled," said Petra, when Suzanne walked into the kitchen.

"Oh no," said Suzanne. Sharon was one of their judges. "Now we'll have to tap somebody else."

"Well, think about it sooner than later," said Petra. " 'Cause I'm going berserk here with everything else."

"Okay, okay," said Suzanne, thinking she'd better get back outside.

Petra poured olive oil into a mixing bowl that already held egg yolks and powdered mustard. "Any word on your buddy, Dil?" she asked. When she'd found out Dil had wandered away yesterday, she'd been particularly saddened.

Suzanne shook her head. "No, and I don't expect there's going to be any. Dil's gone. Slipped down a couple of alleys and hightailed it out of town."

"You never know," said Petra. "He could turn up again."

"I don't think so," said Suzanne. "I have the feeling he's gone for good."

"Pity," said Petra. "Maybe we could have helped him."

"And I have this niggling feeling," said Suzanne, "that just maybe he saw something last Sunday that could have shed some light on two very gruesome murders." A wave of guilt surged through her. Should she have driven Dil directly to the law enforcement center and let Doogie question him? Or would her actions simply have pushed Dil over the edge?

"Now we'll never know," said Petra. She wiped her hands on a towel, then paused for a few moments to consider her next words. "Unless, of course, you talk to Doogie and ask him to put out some sort of police bulletin. That way law enforcement could . . . I don't know . . . pick him up in the next county or something?"

"I hear you," Suzanne said, glumly. "And I've been thinking that exact same thing."

"What you have to balance," said Petra, "is whether finding your guy might help solve two murders or just screw him up even more."

"I don't have the answer to that," said Suzanne. "Nobody does."

"Just noodle the whole thing around," urged Petra. "You'll figure out what's right. You always do."

"Then you have more faith in my judgment than I do," said Suzanne.

"Look at it this way," said Petra, "everything we grew up trusting—banks, our government, the financial market, big corporations—have let us down in recent months. So . . . do I believe, in my heart of hearts, that the three of us will always try to do what's right? You bet I do!"

"Thank you for reminding me to keep the faith," said Suzanne. She picked up two coffeepots, ready to bump through the swinging door into the café, when a sharp rap sounded at the back door. She turned and saw a wavering shadow looming on the other side of the screen door.

"Holy Toledo," muttered Petra. "That's probably Bill Crowley with a couple crates of eggs." She shook her head and frowned at the crates of lettuce, boxes of tomatoes, and various and sundry ingredients that were already strewn everywhere. All stuff for tonight's gourmet dinner. "It's a mess back here. And the cooler's jammed. What are we gonna do with the darn things?"

Suzanne dropped her coffeepots onto the wooden counter and said, "I'll take care of this." She scurried to the back door, said, "Bill, is there any way you can . . . ?" Then stopped. Because it wasn't Bill who was hovering on the other side of the door.

"Hey," said Kit, squinting at Suzanne with a tentative smile. "Remember me?" She added a brief wave.

"I do," said Suzanne.

"Bet you didn't think I'd show up," said Kit. She stared through the screen, taking in Suzanne's startled expression and added, "No, you *really* didn't think I'd accept your offer."

Suzanne recovered quickly, smiling warmly as she pushed open the door. "But here you are, so come on in." She was pleased Kit had elected to spend her Saturday at their Take the Cake Show instead of jiggling at Hoobly's roadhouse.

"Petra," said Suzanne, taking Kit's hand and gently pulling her toward the stove, where Petra was deeply involved in caramelizing large rings of Vidalia onions. "We have reinforcements. This is Kit."

Petra glanced at the girl in the white T-shirt and denim skirt. "Kit?" She studied her for a moment, then said, "I remember you."

Kit seemed to pull back slightly.

"You worked at the Dairy Bar a couple of summers back," said Petra. "Scooping ice cream and making milkshakes." She shot a glance at Suzanne, who'd clued her in yesterday about Kit.

"That's right," said Kit.

"Haven't seen you there lately," said Petra.

"Been trying out some other stuff," said Kit, a little nervous now.

"Well, plop one of those aprons around your neck, darlin'," said Petra. "And, say, how are you at frosting cake? We're serving mocha cakes for our cake and ice cream social this afternoon, which means each individual piece has to be frosted with coffee cream icing, then rolled in chopped walnuts." She paused. "Can you do that?"

"I can do that," said Kit. "In fact, it sounds like fun."

"Then you're heaven-sent," replied Petra.

"Well . . . not quite." Kit giggled as Suzanne gave her a reassuring pat on the shoulder.

Ten seconds later, Toni came crashing through the swinging door. "It's crazy busy out there!" she exclaimed.

"Folks are pouring in from all over the county. And not just women. There's a fair share of guys, too. You wouldn't think fondant fairies and flowers would be that popular with the fellas, would you?"

"Calm down, Toni," instructed Petra. "Take a deep breath."

"I would," responded Toni, "except Joey's out there ladling lemonade like a one-armed paperhanger, and I'm pretty sure we're gonna run dry in about two minutes flat." She glanced around the kitchen, finally noticed Kit. A big smile creased Toni's face. "Hey, it's Lady Dubbonet! How ya doing, girlfriend? Did you bring your dancing shoes?"

Suzanne held an index finger to her lips. *Shhh* was the mantra, discretion the watchword.

"Oh ho," said Toni, "no stage names today, huh? Okay, no problem."

Petra rolled her eyes. "You're incorrigible, Toni."

Toni gave a wicked grin. "Incorrigible. That's good, huh? That's a good thing, right?"

JUST as the pulled sugar demonstration was about to begin, Suzanne took a little break. Stepped around back to give Baxter a Milk-Bone. She'd brought him along today, since chances were good she'd be at the Cackleberry Club until well past ten tonight. And here he could be close to her and still enjoy the out-of-doors with minimum supervision.

"Bax," she said, holding out the treat.

Baxter's plumed tale thumped dry dirt as he pulled himself to his feet.

"Got a goodie for you."

"Rwrrr?" *Really?*

"You deserve it because you're such a good guy," Suzanne told him. "Staying here, putting up with our silly cake party. All those cars rolling in and people out front."

Baxter took the treat and gave it a good crunch. One half fell from his mouth, while he happily tossed back the other half and chewed with relish.

"Suzanne?" A low voice called to her from the back line of trees.

"What?" Suzanne replied, startled, spinning around. But she didn't see anything. Had she really heard a voice? Or just a shout from out front? Narrowing her eyes, Suzanne took a single step and peered at the cedar trees and underbrush that stood in a jagged line behind her back shed. "Who's there?" she called. Baxter picked up the other half of his bone and held it in his mouth while he gazed silently.

There was a flutter of green and, for a moment, Suzanne thought it was just remnants of leaves or cedar branches moving in the breeze. Then a figure, dressed in camouflage colors of olive green and drab, seemed to unfold and rise up from the underbrush. It was Dil.

"Good Lord!" exclaimed Suzanne. "I've been wondering where you disappeared to!"

Dil extended both arms out to his side in a gesture that seemed to say, *I'm here now.*

"Where have you been?" Suzanne asked, rushing toward him. "Where did you run off to?"

"Back to the cave," said Dil. His voice was low and hesitant, like he was still getting used to conversing with people. "Safer there."

"You went back to . . ." Suzanne stopped, stared at him, then grabbed the lapels of his tattered jacket with her fingertips. "Never mind, we've got to get you out of here."

Dil glanced around, as though he was suddenly fearful of being discovered.

"There are a hundred people out front," began Suzanne, "any number of whom would like to see you questioned about a couple of murders."

Dil's eyes grew large. "I didn't do no murders. I *wouldn't*."

"I believe you," said Suzanne. "The thing is, what am I going to do with you?"

"I could stay by your dog," Dil volunteered.

Suzanne stared at him. "What do you . . . ?"

He made a casual gesture. "Over in that shed."

"The *tool* shed," said Suzanne, suddenly catching on. "Gotcha. Great idea. Brilliant idea." She knew she had to get Dil out of sight now!

Grabbing one arm, she half pulled, half dragged Dil into the shed where her old Toro lawn mower was stashed.

"Now you stay here," she told him, quietly. "Until I figure things out."

Slamming the door, Suzanne dusted her hands together. *Okay, now what?*

She turned, a little unnerved . . . and found herself staring directly into the steely gray eyes of Sheriff Roy Doogie!

CHAPTER 28

"Doogie!" Suzanne screamed. "Whoa!"

Doogie took a step backward and held his arms out toward her, palms facing up. "Easy, easy, Suzanne," he murmured. "I didn't mean to scare you."

Suzanne clamped a hand to her chest, trying to still her timpani drum-beating heart. "Well . . . you did," she told him, fear and a little anger creeping into her voice. She drew a deep breath, hoping against hope that Doogie wouldn't notice how discombobulated she suddenly was.

"Toni said you were out here," said Doogie. His eyes slid past Suzanne toward the old shed. "Said you were just . . . putting stuff away?"

"Right," said Suzanne, adding a touch of brightness to her voice. "Packing stuff away . . . um . . . hoses and things. Probably don't need them anymore. Sure don't need them today." Still panicked, she glanced up at the sky where storm clouds seemed to be bunching in the west, ready to crowd out the gradually thinning sunshine. "It's probably going to rain later on."

"Could be," said Doogie, who turned his languid focus back upon Suzanne.

Suzanne smiled. "How you doing, Sheriff? How's the investigation going?" She was terrified Dil would suddenly come lumbering out from the shed and announce his presence. Get himself arrested, plunge her back into hot water.

"I'm still pretty ticked at you," said Doogie, arranging his face in a stern, stoic gaze. "Going out to that farm and all."

"Sorry," said Suzanne, trying to lead him toward the back door, praying Baxter wouldn't give anything away. "It was all a big oops. A complete blunder."

"No kidding," said Doogie. He stood with his feet spread wide apart, listing ever so slightly.

"You didn't find anything else out there, did you?" Suzanne asked. "Chemicals or anything?"

"Nope," Doogie told her. "If they'd had some of the same chemicals that were stolen from Driesden and Draper, then I'd be on to something. But for now . . ." He blew out air, making a slight whistling sound between his front teeth. "I'm perplexed." And, with his bushy brows knit together, Doogie really did appear perplexed.

"So you're back to square one?" Suzanne asked.

"It ain't *that* bad," said Doogie, backpedaling now, trying to save face. At the same time, he certainly wasn't bubbling over with hot, new leads.

"My money's still on Earl," Suzanne told him. "There's something hinky about him. Especially his . . . what would you call it? Whirlwind second courtship with Missy?"

"Some people are just naturally hinky," said Doogie. "They look suspicious and act suspicious, but they don't really have anything particularly sinister going on."

Suzanne nodded. She understood what Doogie was talking about.

"Although," continued Doogie, "that hale-hearty type of personality can sometimes be an outward manifestation of someone who's actually quite secretive."

"Seriously?" said Suzanne. "Did you read that in a book or did you postulate your own theory?"

Doogie glowered at her and struck a slightly defensive pose. "For your information, I once took a class on psychological profiling. Given by an ex-FBI agent fella. And that was the basic gist of one of his hypotheses." Doogie shook his big head and his jowls sloshed. "Jeez, Suzanne, sometimes you make me feel like I'm some poor dufus who can't find his way out of a corn maze."

Suzanne patted his arm. "Sorry, Sheriff, I didn't mean to insult you. Truly. Last thing on my mind." *And the number one thing on my mind is to get you as far away from here as possible.* "I think you're running a heck of an investigation."

Doogie cast his eyes downward and did everything but dig his toe in the dirt.

"Also," said Suzanne, "I'm delighted you dropped by. I have a favor to ask."

"What arc you talkin' about?" asked Doogie.

"I was wondering if you could lend your expertise and be a guest judge."

"Guest judge?" said Doogie, looking faintly surprised. "For what?"

"You saw all the tents and people and cakes?"

"Yeah," said Doogie, "I ain't blind."

"Well, I was hoping maybe you could help Petra judge the cake-decorating contest. One of our judges cancelled at the last minute."

That simple request seemed to throw Doogie for a loop. "Really? Cakes, huh?" He looped a finger through his belt. "Do I get to taste them?"

It took all the fortitude Suzanne could muster not to smile. "No, but there's going to be a cake social later on.

That's a cake tasting of sorts. We'll be serving up little slivers of five or six different kinds of cake along with dabs of ice cream and sorbet."

Doogie straightened up. "That sounds mighty good," he said, then glanced over toward Baxter. "What's your dog sniffing at?"

"Coyotes," Suzanne said, quickly. "Doggone things are all over the place. Running wild."

"Little pests," agreed Doogie.

"So let's go get you a piece of cake," Suzanne cajoled. "And then you can help with the judging. You'll be a duly elected official serving in the Cackleberry Club's official capacity."

"Yeah," Doogie said, playing a little hard to get. "I *suppose* I could help out. But I gotta be out of here by three. I'm on my way to check some county records, then do a patrol."

"This won't take long," Suzanne assured Doogie as she led him around to the front of the Cackleberry Club and into the large tent where Petra was hovering at the back, watching a silver-and-Tiffany-blue wedding cake take shape. "Look who I found," Suzanne told Petra. "And it's our good luck that Sheriff Doogie's graciously agreed to help with the cake judging."

"Wonderful," trilled Petra. "Pleased you can lend your opinion, Sheriff. We have four dozen cakes already and there are more trickling in." She fluttered her hands nervously at Suzanne. "Suzanne? Could you . . . ? In the other tent?"

"Of course," said Suzanne. Together, she and Doogie strolled into the other tent, where five of the six tables were laden with cakes waiting to be judged.

"All these cakes need to be judged?" asked Doogie. He

seemed surprised and a little overwhelmed at the number of entries.

"Well, there are only four basic categories," said Suzanne. "So it's not as tricky as it looks."

Doogie gazed across the sea of cakes toward the parking lot, where a silver SUV was just pulling up. It rocked to a stop, then Missy climbed out the passenger side, followed by Earl from the driver's side. "Huh," was all Doogie said.

Suzanne watched Missy and Earl as they headed for the demonstration tent. "Couldn't you just sort of *talk* to Earl again?" she asked Doogie. "Question him?"

"What I'd really rather do is find that homeless guy who's probably still squatting up in those caves," replied Doogie.

"Why?" asked Suzanne.

"Because he was near the park last Sunday," said Doogie, still following Earl and Missy with his eyes. "And he's been spotted around town."

"I don't think he's your guy," said Suzanne.

Doogie gave her a studious look. "Now why would you say that?"

Suzanne shrugged. "Call it a hunch? An instinct I have about this whole thing?"

Doogie planted his feet wide. "You're not keeping something from me, are you, Suzanne? Like when you scouted that farmhouse of dopers?"

She smiled at him, hoping her smile conveyed sweet innocence. "Nope."

Doogie studied her for a moment. "Good. Because I'd sure hate to arrest you for obstructing justice."

"I only want justice," said Suzanne.

"What people *want* and what people *do* are often two separate matters," said Doogie.

"I couldn't agree more," said Suzanne.

"Sheriff?" said Petra, coming up behind Doogie. "Are you ready to feast your eyes on a few cakes?"

"Ready as I'll ever be, I guess," said Doogie, as Petra took him by the arm and led him toward the table filled with decorated sheet cakes.

Whew, was Suzanne's only thought. She plopped down onto a folding chair, picked up a stack of entry forms, and tamped them briskly on the table, straightening them.

"Oh, Suzanne," came a sugary voice.

Suzanne stared up into the hard, bright eyes of Carmen Copeland. *What's she doing here?* was her first thought. And then she spotted the cake Carmen was carrying. A compact, four-layer cake, frosted in luscious orchid-colored frosting. It was covered with delicate green swirls and twined with miniature Dendrobium orchids.

"I've come to enter your cake-decorating contest," Carmen said in a smooth voice. "See?" She placed her cake in front of Suzanne, looking infinitely pleased with herself. "It just so happens I know a bit about baking and cake decorating myself."

Suzanne stared at Carmen, a vision of sophistication in her sleek, black shift and matching emerald earrings, and then at her cake. Just like Carmen, the cake was sleek and gorgeous. A total knockout. In fact, it looked like something a Park Avenue patisserie had created for a New York high-society party. And Suzanne was pretty sure . . . no, she was almost positive . . . that Carmen Copeland had not slaved in her kitchen all morning long, sifting flour, beating eggs, baking and frosting her cake, then piping on swirls and arranging live orchids with her own French-manicured pinkies.

No, Suzanne figured Carmen had probably placed a

discreet phone call, instructed some commercial baker to whip up this amazing creation, then nonchalantly charged it to her gold American Express card.

What if she wins? was Suzanne's next troubling thought. *It won't be fair and we won't know how to reward her.*

"Oh," said Carmen, touching a delicate forefinger to the hollow at her neck. "Looks like the judging's already started."

"Actually, you just squeaked in," said Suzanne, pushing an entry form across the table to Carmen. "Fill this out and we'll get you registered."

Carmen pulled a Montblanc pen from her crocodile bag and, in big swooping letters, completed her form.

"Great," said Suzanne, without much enthusiasm, wondering if Carmen was going to scold and rebuke her about the fashion show yesterday. Or demand she bring the clothes back. "That should do it."

"Dear," said Carmen in a simpering, nattering tone. "Are tickets still available for the gourmet dinner this evening?"

"Ah . . . you'd have to check with Toni," said Suzanne. She tilted her head. "Inside."

Carmen slipped away with a whisper of Gucci-shod feet.

Rats, thought Suzanne. *Carmen Copeland is the absolute last person I want at our winner's dinner tonight.*

CHAPTER 29

But it turned out Carmen wasn't the only late entry. Just as Suzanne was arranging registration forms in four neat piles, Nadine Carr rushed in, balancing her cake.

"Did I make it?" Nadine asked, a little breathless. "Can I still enter my cake?" She placed it carefully on the table in front of Suzanne with a worried, anxious look. "Sorry I'm so . . . late."

Suzanne glanced at her Timex. It was five minutes past the deadline they'd set, but Nadine looked so eager and hopeful. And, of course, she'd just lost her husband a week earlier, so Suzanne felt more than a little compassion for her. "Of course we can squeak you in," she told her. "No problem. Let's see what we have here . . ." While Nadine filled out her entry form, Suzanne studied her cake. It was a small, round, three-layer cake covered with vanilla crackle glaze and artfully decorated with chocolate swirls. On top, enormous pieces of shaved chocolate formed a glistening poufy bow. It was beautifully done. A cake that might even give Carmen Copeland a run for her money . . .

Nadine pushed her completed entry form across the table as she uncrumpled a blue flyer. One of the flyers Toni and Petra had passed out all over town advertising the cake-decorating contest. "Are Sharon and Petra still doing the judging?" she asked.

Suzanne shook her head. "Slight change in plans. Now Sheriff Doogie will help do the honors. Along with Petra, of course." She indicated the two of them, who had their heads together, whispering, down at the other end of the tent.

"Oh," said Nadine. "Doogie."

Suzanne reached out and patted Nadine's arm. "Don't worry, I know what you're thinking. What does Sheriff Doogie know about cakes anyway? Am I right?"

Nadine's head moved slightly.

Suzanne continued. "But Doogie actually has a rather discerning palate." She laughed. "At the very least, he can tell a cinnamon scone from a cake doughnut."

"Well, that's *something*," agreed Nadine, with a good-natured grin.

Iτ took Petra and Sheriff Doogie some forty minutes to study all the cakes, jot a few notes, then decide the winners in each of the four cake-decorating categories, as well as first runner-ups. In fact, they were still marking their judging sheets when Ray Lynch poked his head into the tent.

"Sorry," Suzanne told him, waving her hands and hurrying over to bar him from entering. "This tent's closed for judging." She gazed at him, wondering why Ray Lynch, of the Roth Funeral Home Consortium, had chosen to show up here and now.

Lynch seemed to spot the question mark in Suzanne's eyes, so he said, "I was just driving by and noticed all the commotion."

"It's our Take the Cake Show," Suzanne explained.

Lynch regarded her with a slightly curious look.

Suzanne let loose a deep sigh. "If you'd like, there's a

cake social starting in about ten minutes. You can go into the other tent and take a seat."

"That sounds lovely," said Lynch.

Lovely? thought Suzanne. *This from a guy who buys distressed funeral homes for a living?*

Petra was suddenly standing at Suzanne's elbow. "We've got a problem," she said in a terse voice.

"Hmm?" said Suzanne, whirling about.

"We simply don't believe Carmen Copeland decorated her own cake," said Petra. She cast a conspiratorial glance at Doogie. "Do we?"

He shrugged. "If you say so. It's awful nice and fancy, though."

"It's gorgeous!" agreed Petra. "But since she already asked me to create that handbag cake, do you really think Little Miss Romance Writer knows how to feather frosting or do garrett frills?"

Suzanne's mouth twitched. "Maybe she took a class?"

"And maybe she's out-classed," replied Petra in a huff. "A lot of hard work and love went into baking and decorating all these other cake entries. They're the ones who are the most *deserving*."

"So what are you gonna do?" asked Suzanne. More and more, she was becoming a bottom-line gal. Define the problem. Figure out a solution. Don't agonize or burst a blood vessel in the process.

Petra made an unhappy face. "Since I can't *prove* Carmen didn't decorate her own cake, we're probably going to have to award her a ribbon. Her cake is *clearly* the best in the sugar arts category."

"What about the other categories?" asked Suzanne.

Petra squinted at her judging sheet. "Nadine is the hands-down winner in tiered cakes, Lynda Jenner in sheet cakes, and Kathy Cromley in wedding cakes. And, of course, we also have our first runner-ups."

"Okay," said Suzanne. "So seven out of eight's not that bad. The contest's not a total disaster."

Petra was still unsure. "But don't you think everyone will *guess* that Carmen didn't decorate her own cake?"

Suzanne raised an eyebrow and flashed a snarky, knowing grin. "Yes, I think that might well happen. So . . . it's not a total capitulation on our part, is it?"

Petra stared at her, then a gradual smile stole across her broad face. "Yes," she said, clearly warming up to the idea. "I see what you mean."

THE cake social proved to be an even bigger hit than when the Kindred Sluggers faced off against the Jordan Brewers in the state finals.

Toni and Kit brought out all the cakes Petra had baked and set them up as a veritable cake buffet. Thin slices of coconut cake arranged on a sterling silver tray. Devil's food on a three-tiered curette. Chocolate cake decorated with fresh strawberries on a tall crystal cake pedestal. Marble cake on a marble slab balanced atop two silver columns. Petit fours on a fancy lacquer tray. And scattered among the cake display were flickering candles and elegant floral bouquets.

"Oh my goodness," Laura Benchley marveled to Suzanne. "Forget Old Country Buffet or the potluck at St. Sebastian's. This is what *every* buffet should look like!" As editor of the *Bugle* turned eager reporter, Laura was snapping photos and jotting notes like crazy.

"Sugar, gobs of frosting, and fruit glazes," agreed Suzanne. "I think I could live on this stuff." *And sometimes I have,* she thought, feeling a small pang of nutritional guilt.

"What kind of ice cream are they serving?" asked Laura. She pointed toward the far end of the table where Toni and Kit were doing the honors, scooping ice cream and sorbet.

"Vanilla bean and peach mango," said Suzanne. "Along with Petra's homemade strawberry sorbet."

"Dear Lord," murmured Laura. "Petra *makes* her own sorbet?"

"She's just an old-fashioned gal," laughed Suzanne.

"Deep down, don't we wish we all were," replied Laura.

Suzanne worked her way down the cake buffet line and stepped behind Toni and Kit, who were scooping like mad. "How's it going?" she asked.

"Great," said Toni, "except for the fact we've got frostbite up to our elbows." Toni shook her right hand to warm it up. "This is even worse than going ice fishing!"

"You never . . ." said Suzanne with a laugh, then did a double take. "Ice fishing? Really?"

"I'll have you know Junior dragged me out onto Lake Elmo last winter," said Toni. "Or, rather, *I* dragged the ice auger, spincast reels, and night crawlers, while Junior dragged two six-packs of Budweiser."

"You see," murmured Suzanne, "that's one of the reasons your relationship doesn't work."

"Incompatibility?" asked Toni.

"Inequality," said Suzanne.

SOME fifteen minutes later, Petra and Sheriff Doogie stood in front of the group with fluttering purple and blue ribbons in hand. Somewhere during the judging process, Doogie had picked up a chef's hat that matched Petra's. So now they looked like a pair of giant white mushrooms performing a song and dance act in front of the crowd. Toni, who had relinquished ice cream duties to Kit, perched at one of the tables, clinking her fork against her glass.

"Attention, please!" called Doogie, obviously relishing his role as judge and jury. "Petra and I are about to announce the division winners in the cake-decorating contest!"

A burst of applause followed and chairs were scooted around so everyone could face front. Laura Benchley crept toward them down the center aisle and snapped another quick photo.

Petra took a step forward and began. "After careful consideration and delicious deliberation Sheriff Doogie and I have determined grand prize winners as well as first runner-ups in the Cackleberry Club's first annual Take the Cake cake-decorating contest."

More bursts of applause echoed through the tent as Suzanne slipped into a seat beside Toni and grinned. Somehow, they'd managed to pull it off! Now if they could only get through tonight!

"Take the Cake's a hit!" said Toni, clapping and adding a few high-pitched whistles for punctuation.

"Thank goodness," murmured Suzanne.

"We'll have to make it a permanent event," said Toni.

Suzanne nodded as she glanced around the tent, where good fellowship and a definite sugar high seemed to prevail. In fact, two tables down, Carmen Copeland leaned over to whisper in the ear of Ray Lynch. And not just a discreet, casual whisper, either. Carmen had a distinctly flirty, conspiratorial look about her, while her body language projected something akin to *Look at me, I'm still a little hottie.*

Suzanne nudged Toni with her elbow. "Carmen."

Toni stole a quick glance, then rolled her eyes in disdain. "She's something else. Little Miss Muffet on her tuffet."

"She does have a way of putting it all out there," admitted Suzanne.

"Maybe Carmen should be shaking her moneymaker at Hoobly's," whispered Toni.

"Did she ask you about tickets for tonight?" said Suzanne.

"Oh yeah," snorted Toni. "Afraid so. And since we had a cancellation, Carmen bought two tickets."

"Say it ain't so," said Suzanne.

"From the looks of things," said Toni, "I'd say Carmen probably invited Ray Lynch."

"Shhhh," said Suzanne, "Petra's going to hand out ribbons now."

With a big grin on her face, Petra held up one of the purple ribbons for all to see. "In the sheet cake division, I'm pleased to award the grand prize to Lynda Jenner."

More thunderous applause.

"In the tiered cake division," said Doogie, "grand prize goes to Nadine Carr." He looked around. "Nadine, come on up here, girl."

Nadine, shy little lady that she was, shuffled forward reluctantly to accept her purple ribbon.

"In the wedding cake division, our grand prize winner is Kathy Cromley," said Petra.

"And last, but not least," said Doogie, "grand prize in the sugar arts division goes to Carmen Copeland!"

Carmen clasped a hand to her chest and dropped her jaw in mock surprise. *Me?* she mouthed, even as she leapt from her seat and ran to collect her purple ribbon.

When Carmen finally settled down, Petra announced

the four runner-ups and Doogie proudly handed them ribbons.

"And so," said Petra, wrapping up the awards ceremony, "all of our grand prize winners are cordially invited to our gourmet dinner this evening."

"The winners' dinner!" shouted Carmen. She searched for the camera, smiled prettily, then waved her purple ribbon like a crazed cheerleader shaking her pompoms. "Hoo*raaay*!"

Toni sighed deeply. "Don't her batteries ever wear down?"

CHAPTER 30

"Where's the pepper mill?" shrieked Petra. She spun fast with a saucepan full of melted butter in her hand, bumped the table, and watched helplessly as butter spattered everywhere. "Oh great!"

Suzanne grabbed a rag and knelt down swiftly to wipe up the glistening mess. "Don't worry about it," she told Petra. "Calm down, take it easy."

Suzanne, Petra, and Toni were all jammed in the kitchen, trying to pull together their gourmet dinner. Suzanne had just trimmed out the salmon medallions, Toni had set out stacks of plates for the various courses and had just finished rinsing and drying the Boston bib lettuce. It didn't help that it was pouring like crazy outside, rain drumming on the roof of the Cackleberry Club and gurgling loudly in the downspouts. And, of course, just steps away in the café sat a full complement of dinner guests—cake-decorating winners, runner-ups, and another dozen or so assorted diners.

"Everything simpatico out front?" asked Petra.

"Quaffing their aperitifs," said Toni, who'd poured out judicious servings of Lillet into small crystal glasses.

"Sipping," said Petra, still a little stressed. "They should be sipping."

"They are," said Suzanne, snicking open the door to the pass-through and peering out. "And, believe me when I say this: everyone has been highly complimentary so far. We've even gotten compliments on the table arrangements."

"See?" said Toni. "Who says you can't take dried milkweed, judiciously coat it with a little gold spray paint, arrange it in white country crocks, and then light the room with a million white candles?"

"There *are* a lot of candles," allowed Suzanne. Toni had gone slightly overboard in that department.

Petra allowed herself a smile. "It looked like midnight Mass last time I peeked out."

"The café is simply gorgeous," Toni said with pride. They had set the tables with crisp, white linen tablecloths, laid out the good silver, and rented crystal stemware from Fancy Nancy's Party Rental over in Jessup.

Petra turned her attention toward the mustard sauce cooling on the counter. "There's so much going on, I feel like I'm in an old Marx Brothers movie. *A Day at the Races* or *A Night at the Opera*."

"Which Marx Brother am I?" asked Toni, playing along.

"You're Groucho," said Petra. "Always making with the cryptic comments."

"No, no." Toni laughed. "You're thinking of Suzanne."

"Not me," said Suzanne. "You take the honors on that front." She glanced around quickly. "What now?"

"I'm going to lightly grill our salmon medallions," said Petra. "Then we'll arrange them on individual appetizer plates, drizzle on mustard sauce, and add our dilled cucumber garnish."

Joey Ewald creaked open the swinging door and peeked in. "Got any more of that fancy wine?" he asked. "Some guy is asking for a refill."

"Earl Stensrud," said Kit, shuffling in behind Joey.

"The answer's no," said Toni. "Honestly, we only had three bottles to begin with. Doesn't he know Lillet is an aperitif? Doesn't he know there'll be more wine with dinner?"

"Oh, he *knows*," said Kit.

"He was just being rude to me," said Joey. "'Cause I'm a kid."

"Earl was being rude," said Suzanne, "because he's a rude person. It's not about you, it's about *him*." *Or maybe it's about the Lillet,* thought Suzanne. *The wine's sweet notes of candied orange and mint are awfully intoxicating. Appealing, even, to a lout like Earl.*

Joey flashed a lopsided grin at Suzanne. "Will you adopt me, Boss? Can I be Baxter's half brother?"

"Sorry, cutie," Suzanne told him. "No can do."

"I'll take ya," said Toni, linking an arm around Joey's neck.

"You're too permissive," said Petra, gently slipping her medallions onto the grill. "Witness the way you deal with Junior. No," she continued, "Joey needs someone who'll ride herd on him. Help unleash the gentleman hidden within, and maybe channel his aspirations into something besides skateboarding."

"Skateboarding's cool," said Joey.

"But you can't make a living at it," argued Petra.

"Some guys do," said Joey. "In California."

"Unless the town fathers truck in a load of sand and re-name this place Redondo Beach," said Suzanne, "I'd say you're out of luck."

"Why is Earl Stensrud here, anyway?" asked Toni, pulling four bottles of Pinot Gris from the cooler. Suzanne had selected it to complement the salmon appetizer. The wine's acidic flavor to balance the oily richness of the fish.

"Missy purchased tickets a couple of days ago," murmured Petra. "If you ask me, the girl's in love."

"A poor choice," murmured Kit.

"On the rebound from Ozzie," said Toni, knowingly.

"If you ask me," said Suzanne, "I think Missy's completely heartbroken over Ozzie and that she's just sublimating."

"Earl's her pacifier?" asked Kit.

"So she might . . . what . . . dump him?" asked Toni. "Once everything settles down?"

"We can only hope," said Suzanne.

THE salmon medallions, when served to their dinner guests, were an instant hit. Ditto the Boston bib lettuce with walnut dressing and Maytag blue cheese. Suzanne, Toni, and Kit did the honors serving while Joey cleared dishes. Sam Hazelet, who was seated across the table from Carmen Copeland and Ray Lynch, fairly beamed at Suzanne every time she brushed past him. At one point he grabbed her hand and declared, "Your food is fantastic!"

"You ain't seen nothin' yet," she whispered back.

When Kit removed Earl's empty salad plate, she purred, "Hello, Earl, long time no see."

Earl's face suddenly puckered in recognition and turned tomato red. "Huh?" he grunted.

"You used to be a real regular at Hoobly's, but I haven't seen you for a while," said Kit.

There were giggles all around the table. They all knew about Hoobly's. It was no big secret.

"I wouldn't say *regular*," said Earl, looking defensive. He shifted nervously in his chair, then tipped it back onto two legs, looking as if he'd been caught with his hand in the proverbial cookie jar. "I had a *meeting* out there once. This one client . . ." But the rest of Earl's words were suddenly lost as his chair skidded out from under him and banged hard against the café wall, causing a tremor in the wooden shelf directly above his head. That tremor seemed to send seismographic waves down the length of the shelf causing Suzanne's prized collection of ceramic chickens to tremble and rattle.

"Oh jeez!" shouted Toni as a yellow chicken with red tail feathers tottered dangerously, then, like a reluctant dive bomber, tumbled from the shelf!

"Watch . . . !" began Carmen, who was sitting across from Earl.

"Incoming!" yelled Toni, as the chicken struck Earl on the back of his head. Thwack!

"Owwwww!" Earl let loose a howl that sounded like a scalded banshee. He jumped up, stomping about like he'd been stung by killer bees, while his chair continued its unfortunate trajectory and crashed over backward.

"What an idiot," muttered Toni, and the people close to her chuckled.

Earl continued hopping up and down like a madman, pointing an accusing finger at the smashed chicken. "That . . . that *thing* attacked me!" he screeched.

Toni hurried over to gather up pieces. "Take a chill pill, Earl," she told him. "It's just a fricking chicken." She smirked and held up the chicken's jagged head. "Not much left," she said. "A head, a tail, a few paltry fragments."

"Doggone thing smacked me!" complained Earl, rubbing his hand against the back of his head. "Gonna have a goose egg."

"Some kind of egg," murmured Suzanne.

"What's going *on* out there?" asked Petra, sticking her head through the pass-through.

"Ceramic chicken," Sam called to her. "Fell off your shelf. Smacked Earl."

Petra gave a wry smile. "The chicken has spoken."

SQUASH soup with fennel and onion garnish was the next course on the menu.

"How're you doing?" Suzanne asked Petra as she hurriedly braised the last bits of fennel.

"Good," replied Petra. "Fennel's nice and tender with a lovely caramelization."

"Let me rephrase that," said Suzanne. "How are *you*?"

Petra turned with a grin. "I am woman. I am invincible. I am pooped."

"Of course, you are," said Toni, flying through the door. "We've been at this all day. And by the way, Suzanne, Carmen Copeland is flirting shamelessly with your boyfriend."

"He's not my boyfriend," said Suzanne.

"Yet," said Toni.

"Besides," added Suzanne, "Carmen flirts with anyone and everyone in pants, long or short. You should know that by now."

"Good point," said Toni, "since Carmen's also making goo-goo eyes at Ray Lynch."

"Maybe you could con Carmen into taking Junior off your hands," suggested Suzanne.

"You'd have to pretend you were super jealous," said

Petra, going along with Suzanne's suggestion. "So Carmen would take up the challenge."

"You mean bait her?" asked Toni. "Like she's some kind of crazed, feral animal? I could do that. In fact, it sounds like fun."

CHAPTER 31

THUNDER pounded and lightning flashed overhead, but the rain had let up for the time being. One cell passing through, another one chugging its way toward them.

Suzanne glanced out the window as another brilliant flare lit the backyard, leaching color from the grass, trees, and far farm fields, giving everything the curious appearance of a black-and-white negative. Earlier, she'd run out and stashed Baxter in the shed with Dil. Now she fervently hoped they were okay together. In fact, as soon as she got a chance, she was going to sneak out and check on them again.

"I hope the power stays on," worried Petra. Their guests were enjoying the soup course and now she was in the process of broiling the fillets. "If not, we're going to be slogging away in the dark."

"Not to worry," said Toni. "We've got enough candle power out front to keep things cheery. And my handy dandy flashlight's sitting on the back shelf."

"We might need it," said Petra. "If the main transformer out by the highway decides to go on the blink. Literally."

"How's the potato gratin?" asked Suzanne, tactfully changing the subject. No sense courting disaster.

"Looking good," said Petra, pulling open the oven door. "Bubbling away and turning golden brown."

Joey struggled in with a gray plastic bin piled high with dishes, followed by an embarrassed-looking Nadine Carr. "Hey," Joey said, "I accidentally spilled soup on this lady and she was nice enough not to yell at me. Do you guys got some soda water or something?"

"Nadine?" said Suzanne. "Come over here and let me take a look."

Nadine waved a hand. "It's nothing, really."

"Suzanne," said Petra, "try soda water first. Need a rag?"

"Got one," said Suzanne. She was already scrubbing at Nadine's blouse and making a difference.

"What's the next course?" asked Joey.

"Fillet of beef with potato gratin," said Suzanne, as she continued to work on Nadine. "That's the main entrée. As soon as Petra and I start plating, I want the rest of you guys to start serving. Don't wait for us to finish. Just keep moving the entrées out."

"We're going to be short on servers," said Toni. "Kit has to leave in a couple of minutes."

"What?" said Suzanne, surprised, straightening up, Nadine's blouse forgotten for the moment. She'd assumed Kit was going to stay all evening.

"I promised Frankie I'd do a set tonight," Kit explained sheepishly as she slid behind Joey.

Suzanne sighed. "I thought you weren't going to dance out there anymore. I *hoped* you weren't."

"I know," said Kit, "but I haven't exactly given my two weeks' notice yet. You want me to be a conscientious employee, don't you?"

"Why don't you consider yourself an independent contractor?" suggested Suzanne. "And declare your independence?"

"I see why everyone says you're such a smart business woman," said Kit. "You have a real knack for this stuff."

"Suzanne's got great knackers," said Toni with a laugh.

"Toni!" said Petra.

"I could help serve," offered Nadine.

"Oh no," said Suzanne. "That wouldn't be right."

"It's the least I can do," said Nadine. "After all, you guys awarded me a big purple ribbon today."

Petra, juggling at the stove, glanced at Suzanne. "Suzanne? If it's okay with you . . . ?" she said.

Suzanne took a final swipe at Nadine's blouse. "In that case, Nadine, you're hired!"

THE main course was the biggest hit yet and garnered not just praise but a round of applause.

"You hear that?" said Petra, gazing at Suzanne. They'd just sent the last fillet out the door and were taking a well-deserved breather. "They like it." She put her hands on her hips, looking both pleased and relieved.

"It's a rousing success, honey," said Suzanne. "You did it."

"*We* did it," said Petra. "Now we just have to finish with a great big bang."

"You've already got your pears poaching," said Suzanne. "So we're on the home stretch."

"Your doctor seems awfully nice," said Petra, fussing at the stove.

Suzanne nodded as she set out dessert plates.

"You really like him, huh?" asked Petra.

"I think so," said Suzanne.

"There's a *but* there," said Petra.

"It's still awfully soon," said Suzanne. Her unspoken words were, *It's awfully soon after Walter's death.*

"I know that, dear," said Petra. "But you'll know when it's right. And you'll know *what's* right."

"You think so?" asked Suzanne.

"The Lord knows the ways of the heart," said Petra. "And helps guide us."

"Hey," said Toni, as she and Nadine ducked back into the kitchen. "Our guests are absolutely gaga over their fillets and potato gratin."

"We heard the applause," said Suzanne.

"You two should go out there and feel the love," urged Toni. "Everyone's dying to talk to you."

"Once we get dessert served," said Petra, "I'll be able to relax. Then I'll go out and do a little chitchat."

"Just remember," chuckled Toni, "stressed spelled backward is desserts!"

WHILE Petra ladled pears from their steaming bath of Riesling wine, cinnamon, and cloves, Toni sliced the gingerbread and placed small pieces on each dessert plate that was laid out. "Are we gonna get to enjoy some of this, too?" she asked.

"I think it's high time we enjoyed a sugary nosh," said Petra. "After all our hard work."

"Uh-oh," said Toni, counting plates. "We're a couple pieces short. Of gingerbread."

"What?" exclaimed Petra, whirling around. "We can't be. I had two whole pans of it."

"I only saw one," said Toni.

"Other one's not in the cooler?" asked Suzanne.

"Nope," said Toni, as she continued slicing.

"Crap," said Petra. "It probably got carted out and served during the cake social."

"Yeah . . . maybe," said Toni, in a vague sort of way. "Sorry about that. So . . . what do you want to do?"

Petra frowned. "Maybe . . ."

Nadine, who'd been a little mouse in the kitchen corner, raised a hand tentatively. "Excuse me, but if you need a couple more servings for dessert, I have an almond cake in my car. Unfrosted. I was going to drop it by my sister's house, but I can always bake another one tomorrow." She smiled sadly. "With Julian gone, I've got nothing but time on my hands."

Petra took two giant steps toward Nadine and swept her into her arms, pressing Nadine against her ample chest. "You're such a dear!" she said, hugging her. "It's no surprise you're a wonder at baking cakes—you're so sweet!"

"I'll just slip out the back door and get it," said Nadine.

"You know what?" declared Toni. "This has been a charmed day. Pretty much everything has gone right for us."

"It has, hasn't it," agreed Suzanne.

WHEN the poached pears were finally being served, and Petra and Toni had stepped into the café to pour glasses of Moscato dessert wine and answer the myriad of questions posed about the various food courses and ingredients, Suzanne hastily put together a plate of food and carried it out to Dil.

As she crossed the thirty feet of grass and mud, heading for the little shed, big, fat droplets began to plop down. Within seconds, the heavens had burst open once again.

"Dil!" she cried, banging on the door. "I brought you . . ."

The door was suddenly flung open and Dil's crazed, red-rimmed eyes stared into hers. "I got to leave!" were his startling words.

"What?" Suzanne put a hand on his chest and pushed him back, trying to step inside the shed and escape the downpour.

He bent down to grab his tattered backpack and cowered nervously.

"What's wrong?"

"Like I said, I gotta get out of here!"

"What happened?" asked Suzanne, stunned. "What's going on?"

"I just gotta go," said Dil. He looked past her, his bleary eyes rolling back and forth with fear. "It isn't safe," he told her in a hoarse whisper.

"You're not making sense," said Suzanne. And wasn't that an understatement?

"Can't stay," muttered Dil, struggling into his army jacket. "Scared," he added.

"Scared of what?" asked Suzanne. She was getting a strange feeling in the pit of her stomach. Like she'd eaten something that didn't agree with her.

"I saw the woman," Dil hissed. "She's a bad woman."

Suzanne stood stock-still and stared at him. "What?" she whispered in disbelief. She glanced back at the Cackleberry Club. What was Dil talking about? Had he seen Missy or Carmen enter the Cackleberry Club? Had he had a previous encounter with either one of them? Or maybe with Kit? Was something going on with Kit that she didn't know about? Suzanne glanced back toward the Cackleberry Club and frowned. Or . . . and it could be as simple as this . . . was Dil the gingerbread thief and Toni had scolded him about it earlier?

As if that notion seemed to hold a little credence, a shadow wavered inside the Cackleberry Club, behind the screen door.

"Wait a minute," Suzanne murmured. "Hold everything." She was trying to make sense of Dil's paranoia, to pull it all together into one nice, neat package. But her thoughts hadn't quite gelled yet.

"You stay here," Suzanne told Dil, "while I go check on something, okay?"

"No," said Dil, pushing past her. "Got to go!"

"No. Please!" cried Suzanne. She dashed out into the rain after him, reaching for him, but the tips of her fingers only caught the rough cotton of his army jacket. And then he was gone. Ducking around the side of the Cackleberry Club and virtually melting into the darkness.

"Please?" she called after him in a small voice. She stared into the night, rain slashing down at her, drenching her in a cold spray. Then she turned and noticed Baxter, who had followed her out into the rain. "You poor thing," she told him, "you're absolutely drenched. Get back inside, okay? I'll get a towel and dry you off. Doggone it," she muttered, as the door creaked open behind her.

Suzanne whirled around, expecting Petra to be standing there, peeking out the back door, gesturing for her to come inside. Or maybe even holding out a towel for her.

Instead, the cold, hard face of Nadine Carr stared at her.

"What?" said Suzanne, momentarily startled. "What's . . . ?"

That's when Suzanne noticed the gun. A Smith & Wesson pistol pointed directly at her heart.

CHAPTER 32

"WHERE is he?" demanded Nadine.

"Who?" said Suzanne.

"You know who I'm talking about," snarled Nadine. "That ragtag ex-soldier you were just talking to."

"Gone," said Suzanne. "And why are you . . . ?"

"Shut up," snarled Nadine. "Don't say a word. From now on you do *exactly* what I say."

"Okay," said Suzanne, staring at the small round hole that was so carelessly pointed at her rapidly thudding heart. "Sure. Whatever."

Nadine held out a hand. "Give me your car keys."

Suzanne stood still as a statue, her wet hair plastered against her head, her teeth beginning to chatter. "What?" she said, feeling stupid. *Is that what this is about? No, it can't be. She's after Dil.* "What's wrong with your car?"

"There are cars parked all around me," Nadine snarled. "So you're going to give me yours."

Suzanne patted the pockets of her khaki slacks and came up empty. "In my jacket," she told Nadine. "Inside." Cold water trickled down the back of Suzanne's neck. An even colder feeling had settled in the pit of her stomach.

"Where?" demanded Nadine.

Suzanne made a slightly futile gesture. "In the kitchen, hanging on the back hook."

"Get over here," ordered Nadine. "And don't you dare cry out. Don't utter a single word."

"Just the keys," murmured Suzanne. "I'll hand over the keys and then you'll leave?"

"Nothing's that easy!" barked Nadine. "You, Miss Snoop, are coming with me."

"No way," said Suzanne, finally putting some force in her voice. *Go with this crazy lady? I don't think so.*

The pistol in Nadine's hand waggled back and forth. "I have ways of making you do exactly what I want," said Nadine with a giggle. Her voice was a low mix of craziness and excitement.

What happened to the Nadine I thought I knew? Suzanne wondered. *What happened to Nadine Carr? Has some hellish doppelganger suddenly invaded her body?*

Could this possibly be the same woman who'd come to the Knit-In? Who'd just been awarded a bright purple ribbon at the cake-decorating contest? What was going on? Had the world gone completely mad and suddenly lurched off its axis?

Then it all hit Suzanne in a rush. Like a freight train steaming recklessly toward her, like a terrible cyclone churning its way across fields and city blocks, wreaking destruction. "You killed Ozzie Driesden!" Suzanne said, in a pained voice. "And Bo?"

Nadine's aged face pulled itself into an evil, knowing smile. "Aren't you the clever one."

"But why?" asked Suzanne. *Why on earth?*

"Not remotely your business," said Nadine. "Even though you took it upon yourself to *make* it your business. Always trying to stay one step ahead of our illustrious Sheriff Doogie. Well, we'll just see what happens when *you* disappear. See how fast it takes him to find *your* dead, decaying body."

Suzanne stared at her. "You're insane."

"No," said Nadine, her voice dripping with venom, "I'm just tying up loose ends. Because you, Suzanne Dietz, have been *way* too interested in my personal business." Nadine pulled her lips into a tight rictus of anger. "Now . . . move!"

"Not gonna happen," declared Suzanne. "No way, no how." She knew she had to make a stand. Here was as good a place as any.

Nadine swung her arm around and pointed the gun directly at Baxter's head. He was standing in the rain, some ten feet from Suzanne, watching the two of them as though he were a spectator at a tennis match, wondering in his little doggy brain what part he should play. As Nadine aimed directly at him, worry seemed to flicker in Baxter's brown eyes as lightning blazed in the sky above.

"No!" screamed Suzanne.

"Then *move*!" ordered Nadine.

Suzanne clumped woodenly toward the back door. Would Dil come running back to tackle Nadine? Or would Baxter come charging after them like Rin Tin Tin on a rescue mission? Grab Nadine from behind and shake her like a rag doll until the pistol flew from her hand?

None of that happened. Even though the night sky crashed and boomed above them, no deus ex machina descended from heaven to serve as Suzanne's ultimate salvation.

All Suzanne could do was grab the spindly little door handle and yank the back door open. And hope. Fervently hope that someone would come to her rescue without anyone getting shot!

There was another loud crack of thunder, a flicker of lights, and then a strange sulfurous, electrical smell seemed to permeate the air.

And just as Suzanne stepped across the threshold into the steamy, warm kitchen of the Cackleberry Club, every light in the place winked out!

NADINE jabbed the hardness of the pistol into the small of Suzanne's back. "Don't get any funny ideas, Suzanne. I'm right behind you and I know how to use this pistol. My husband showed me how, a long time ago. I can't imagine you'd want a bullet fired directly into the base of your spine, would you?"

"Not really," babbled a nervous Suzanne. "I'll do whatever you say, okay?"

"Just get the keys," Nadine told her in a cold voice. "And hurry up!"

Suzanne batted helplessly at the couple jackets that hung on the back pegs. "Can't see," she told Nadine. She was feeling disjointed and spacey, struggling to make her hands coordinate with the impulses in her brain. "Got to grab a flashlight."

"Then *do* it," snarled Nadine, jabbing the gun harder against Suzanne's backbone.

How can I signal Sam? Suzanne wondered. *Or even Toni? She's skinny, but she's feisty. Maybe the two of us together could take Nadine down.*

Feeling like an unwilling participant in a slow-motion dream sequence, Suzanne was acutely aware of Petra making an impromptu speech out in the café. This was followed by a round of applause. Would someone come tromping through the door into the kitchen? She held her breath. No, now Petra was talking again.

Suzanne's fingernails skittered across the back shelf, touching upon the hard rubber of Toni's flashlight. But she was shaking and shivering so badly that when she grabbed for it, the flashlight slipped through her hand. Tumbling wildly, end over end, it hit the floor with a loud clunk.

"Clumsy idiot," snapped Nadine. She shoved Suzanne roughly aside, then reached down and grabbed the end of the flashlight.

And that's when the gods finally smiled down and played their cool little trick.

Because the instant Nadine's fingers touched the flashlight, her body jerked and spasmed like it had been struck by a million volts of electricity! Her back arched sharply, her jaw snapped shut, her eyes bulged, and even her hair seemed to stand on end. "Waaaaah!" came a strangled moan from deep within Nadine's throat. "Hwaaaah!"

"Dear Lord," muttered Suzanne, "she's grabbed the Taser end of Toni's flashlight!"

"Waaaah!" screamed Nadine. Now she sounded like a wild animal caught in a leg trap. "Rwaaaah!"

The voices out in the café seemed to falter. There were hurried footsteps and the door swung open. Petra and Toni peered into the kitchen, each holding a candle aloft and looking scared. Joey was right behind them.

"What's going on?" asked Petra, her voice squeaky-scared.

"We heard weird noises," Toni said in a rush. "Horrible noises. Is somebody sick?"

"Or at death's door?" asked Petra.

Suzanne did a quick side step and kicked the pistol as well as Toni's tricky flashlight away from Nadine. Then she leaned down and carefully grabbed the right end of the flashlight and shone it on Nadine's crumpled body.

"Holy crap!" exclaimed Toni. "It's Nadine!"

"What did you *do* to her?" gasped Petra, as Nadine continued to gag and twitch.

Joey let out a low whistle as he peered over Toni and Petra's shoulders. "Get a load of her!" he exclaimed. "She's thrashing around like she needs an exorcist! Cool!"

Suzanne shook her head and backed away, as if Nadine were some nasty, poisonous reptile. "I didn't do anything to her," gasped Suzanne. "She did it herself. Grabbed the Taser end of Toni's flashlight." Suzanne kept the flashlight's wavering beam focused on Nadine, who was still jerking and quivering on the kitchen floor. "She murdered Ozzie," Suzanne said, shakily. "And probably Bo Becker!"

Petra let out a sharp scream, then her mouth opened and closed like a gasping fish.

"Yowza," breathed Toni.

Suzanne was trembling as she went on to explain. "Nadine held a gun on me. And when I wouldn't cooperate, she threatened to shoot Baxter!" Suzanne stumbled backward and sat down heavily in a cane chair that was parked there, while Nadine continued to writhe slowly.

Petra took a step closer. "She's in a very bad way, like she's having a fit!"

"She kind of is," said Suzanne, drawing a shaky breath. "And thank goodness for it." She glanced at Petra. "Can you go back into the café and tell everyone that I dropped the ice cream or something? Or banged my thumb? Tell them there's nothing to worry about?"

Unsure, Petra shifted from one Croc-shod foot to the other. Her nature, of course, was to help, to nurture. Finally she said, "Okay. I guess I can do that."

"Toni," said Suzanne, fighting hard to jump start her brain, "get on the horn and see if you can rouse Doogie, okay? Then we'll tie this monster up."

"No, ma'am," said a voice from the doorway. "I'll tie her up."

"Who're you?" asked a startled Joey. He jumped back as a dark figure loomed toward him.

"Wha . . . ?" said Petra. They all turned to find Dil silhouetted in the back doorway of the kitchen.

"Dil!" said Suzanne. "You came back!"

"I . . . I couldn't leave you with her," said Dil. "I couldn't do that."

"Why not, Dil?" asked Suzanne. She had to get to the bottom of this mystery once and for all!

Dil extended a trembling hand and pointed at Nadine. "I saw her coming out the back door of that funeral home," he said in a hoarse voice. "I was hiding back behind the Dumpster where she couldn't see me."

"And then what happened?" asked Suzanne. "What did you see?"

"I saw the cops and ambulance come," said Dil. He looked terrified. "I knew the man inside was dead."

"What man?" asked Petra, fascinated by Dil's strange narration.

"The owner," said Dil. "Ozzie. He gave me money a couple times." Dil looked like he was ready to cry. "He was nice."

"Yes, he was nice," said Petra. Now she sounded hoarse, like *she* was ready to cry.

Toni grabbed the flashlight from Suzanne's hand and shone it directly into Dil's face. "Your name is Dil?" she asked.

He nodded his grizzled head slowly.

"Howdy," said Toni. "Glad you showed up."

"Nice to finally meet you," Petra murmured, wiping her eyes.

"Dil," said Suzanne, "go out to the shed and see if you can find some rope so we can tie Nadine up, will you? And make sure Baxter's okay?"

"Sure," said Dil.

Petra shifted her gaze back to Nadine. "I can't imagine what got into her." She sounded deeply sad and utterly shocked. "You think you know a person . . ."

"But I guess you never really know their deep, dark secrets," filled in Toni.

Petra continued staring at Nadine. "You think she'll recover? Nadine sure looks wonky."

"Four hundred thousand watts ripping through your system will do that," said Toni, sounding almost philosophical. "She's just lucky she didn't wet her pants."

"Toni!" said Petra.

"I'm just saying," said Toni. She grabbed a length of twine off the shelf, knelt down, and looped it around Nadine's wrists. "You ask me, I think we oughta truss her up like a holiday hog." Toni yanked the twine tight around Nadine's wrists, then gave an extra hard tug.

PETRA did better than just explain the so-called mishap in the kitchen. She went back out into the café, jollied everyone up, thanked them for coming, then bid them all good night. Happy and sated from good food and drink, from companionship and laughter, their guests trooped out the front door of the Cackleberry Club and into the night, commending Petra for a job well done, a dinner elegantly prepared.

All except Sam Hazelet, of course.

"What's going on?" he asked as the last guest departed. Worry seemed to have etched some lines into his handsome face.

Petra raised her eyebrows and crooked an index finger. "Follow me."

"What?" he asked.

"You're not gonna believe this," she told him.

"Holy buckets!" Sam exclaimed when he saw Nadine curled up on the floor, her hands tied. "What happened to her?" He hurried to Nadine's side and knelt down, his practiced fingers searching for a pulse. "What did you *do* to her?"

"Not to worry," said Suzanne, her voice surprisingly calm now. "She's still alive and breathing."

"But not kicking," said Toni. "She's what you'd call stunned." She brandished her combo flashlight and stun gun and waggled it in front of Sam's face. "A slight mishap with a Taser."

"Who did this?" asked Sam, gingerly taking the stun gun from Toni's hands and handling it like he was carrying a vial of the Ebola virus. He stared at Toni, who shrugged and nodded at Suzanne. Sam shifted his surprised gaze to Suzanne. "You did?" He sounded shocked. "Why on earth?"

"Long, strange story," said Suzanne.

Toni pointed to the pistol that still lay in the corner where Suzanne had kicked it. Gray and dangerous, it looked like a nasty mechanized rat. "Nadine threatened to shoot Suzanne," she explained.

"What the . . . ?" asked Sam, still puzzling over the bizarre scene.

"You don't get it, do you?" said Suzanne. Her eyes sparkled for a few seconds, then tears coursed down her cheeks. "Nadine killed Ozzie. She killed Bo."

Sam leapt up and was across the floor in a heartbeat. Sweeping Suzanne into his arms, he pressed her against his chest while she sobbed softly. "Shhh," he murmured, gently stroking her head. "It's okay, you did good. You're safe now."

He held Suzanne, whispering softly to her, until Dil came clumping in with a coil of rope. Sam seemed surprised to see this strange, hulking man, but held his questions for the time being. Together, the two of them hoisted a rag doll Nadine onto the cane chair, then carefully bound her arms and legs. As Sam was tying the final knot, Nadine's head lolled drunkenly and her eyes peeped open.

"She's coming around!" said Joey, who'd remained pretty quiet until now.

"Wah?" said Nadine. A thin string of drool dripped from the corner of her mouth.

"Don't try to talk," Sam told her. "Just take a few deep breaths."

"Let her talk," said Suzanne. There was bitterness in her voice. "Let her confess."

"DEPUTY Wilbur Halpern's on his way," Petra told them. "Running fast, lights and sirens all the way. And Doogie's apparently five minutes out. He was blabbing on his cell phone, cruising for home, when the law enforcement center radioed his emergency frequency and told him to head for the Cackleberry Club."

"Thank goodness," said an exhausted Suzanne. Dil's presence had been hastily explained to Sam. Nadine had been tied up.

"Maybe we should . . . move out into the café?" suggested Sam. The lights had come back on, but they were all jammed, eyeballs to elbows, in the little kitchen, surrounded by the detritus of the evening's gourmet dinner.

Toni jabbed a thumb at Nadine, who was glaring at

them with hooded, angry eyes. "What are we going to do with her?"

Sam looked at Dil and shrugged. "Move her out, too?" he suggested.

The two men picked up Nadine, chair and all, and carried her out into the café. Toni and Joey hastily cleared one of the large tables so they could all sit down.

Suzanne settled into the chair farthest away from where they'd put Nadine. "What a day," she said, stroking her forehead lightly with her fingertips.

"What were we saying before?" asked Petra. "About this being a perfect day?"

"Not," said Toni, sounding exhausted.

Sam, who was seated beside Suzanne, looking more than a little worried, reached over and held his palm against Suzanne's forehead. "You feel hot," he told her. "And you're awfully pale. Shaking a little, too."

"Haven't eaten," she told him. The evening's events were starting to catch up with her and manifest themselves physically.

"Suzanne's always had a slight problem with low blood sugar," offered Petra.

"Then she should eat something," said Sam. "Right away." He peered anxiously at Suzanne. "Could you eat something?"

Suzanne nodded her head. "I think so." She was feeling slightly dazed and anxious. "Can somebody feed Baxter, too?" she asked.

Dil jumped up. "I'll do that."

Sam was still more than a little concerned about Suzanne. "Let's try to get her blood sugar level up. A few sips of orange juice, something sweet . . ." He started for the kitchen.

"Some cake," said Toni.

"And some protein?" asked Petra. She jumped up and followed Sam.

"Want me to help?" called Toni, but Sam shook his head. "You stay with Suzanne. Holler if there's a problem."

"I'm okay," Suzanne said, glancing across at Nadine. Nadine, who seemed to have recovered some of her angry defiance and contempt, stared viciously at Suzanne while a nasty smile played at the corners of her mouth.

"Don't pay any attention to Nadine," Toni told Suzanne. "That lady's ka-pow crazy out of her mind." She twirled an index finger near her head.

Thirty seconds later Sam was back with napkin, silverware, and a small slice of cake on one of Petra's floral china plates. "Petra's grilling a steak for you. But have a few bites of this first."

Suzanne, who really hadn't eaten much of anything all day, picked up her fork and stabbed a small piece of cake. She smiled a wan thank-you at Sam, put the fork to her mouth, and nibbled gently.

That was when a tremendous pounding, like a herd of stampeding cattle, suddenly rocked the front porch of the Cackleberry Club. The door crashed open and there stood Sheriff Roy Doogie, looking wild-eyed and tremulous, his thin, gray hair almost standing on end.

"Dear Lord," said Toni, stumbling to her feet.

Sheriff Roy Doogie gazed crazily about until his eyes fell upon Suzanne. He took one look at the fork in Suzanne's hand and the cake with the missing bite and suddenly launched himself across the floor of the Cackleberry Club. Landing in front of Suzanne, he smacked hard at her arm, then grabbed her around the waist.

Suzanne let out a terrified gasp as her fork and dish clattered noisily to the floor. Everyone else looked on in shock! Had Doogie suddenly lost his mind?

Sam was the first to intercede. "Sheriff!" he screamed at the top of his lungs. "Be careful! What on earth . . . !"

But Doogie was a man on a mission. Spinning Suzanne around, he flipped her forward and thumped a big paw hard against her back, causing her bite of cake to come flying from her mouth, almost as if she'd been burped!

"Poison!" Doogie wheezed. "That cake's poison!" He cradled Suzanne in his arms. "Help her, Doc! Help her!"

CHAPTER 33

SUZANNE, shaking and shivering, couldn't rinse her mouth enough. Over and over, she coughed, rinsed, spit, then repeated the process. Finally, she grabbed a saltshaker, spilled salt into a giant glass of warm water, rinsed thoroughly, then gargled.

Petra stood behind Suzanne, tears streaming down her face. She'd thrown an Indian-patterned blanket around Suzanne's shoulders and was gently patting her back. Doogie and Sam stood discreetly behind her, Sam giving a quick account of Dil's role to a still-startled Doogie.

Toni stalked from the kitchen out into the café, pounding her right fist into a cupped left hand, looking like she wanted to smack Nadine in the mouth. "Miserable piece of filth," she muttered as she passed by Nadine. Kicking the back of Nadine's chair, she threatened, "I oughta clock you a good one!" Then she scurried back into the kitchen.

"What . . . ?" said Suzanne, still leaning over the sink. "What kind of poison was in the cake?" She took a sip of salt water, rinsed, and spit again. Finally she straightened up and turned to face Doogie and Sam.

Doogie put his hands on his bulky hips and said, "Remember the ashes that were in that sink?"

Suzanne just stared at him.

"At Driesden and Draper?" prompted Doogie. "The day we found Ozzie?"

Suzanne nodded and frowned. She *did* remember the little bit of charred ashes smeared in the bottom of the sink in Ozzie's embalming room. But with Ozzie lying there dead, she hadn't given them much more than a cursory inspection.

"I just got a call from the state crime lab," said Doogie. "And I mean—*literally*—I just took their call! When I pulled in here!" Doogie looked shaken and wobbly, like his ticker might not be faring so well. "The crime lab determined that the ashes contained small bits of hair and fingernails."

"Oh . . . ick," said Toni, making a face.

"No wait," said Doogie, holding up a hand. "The thing is, they belonged to Nadine's husband."

"Dear Lord," said Suzanne, suddenly catching on. "She was poisoning him?"

Doogie gave a miserable nod. "Arsenic. That's what killed poor Julian. Poison. Nadine had been slipping it into his food, slowly, over time, until she finally killed him."

"Killing him slowly," murmured Suzanne.

"She murdered her husband?" said Petra. "Dear Lord."

"It's not unheard of," said Doogie. He wiped a hand against his cheek. "When Ozzie was prepping Julian's body, he must have noticed something funny. Had a suspicion about Nadine. That's why he collected evidence—hair and fingernail samples to send to the lab."

"But Nadine got nervous," said Suzanne. "Or maybe Ozzie even said something to her. So she killed Ozzie and then tried to destroy the samples."

Doogie nodded. "Until *you* came along and she slapped that chloroformed rag over your mouth."

"So . . . wait a minute," said Petra. "Nadine killed Bo Becker, too?"

"Holy cow," said Toni. "The lady's a regular black widow spider!"

Doogie scratched his head. "This all came at me pretty fast, but that's what it looks like. Probably because Bo worked so closely with Ozzie."

"And Bo might have been suspicious of Nadine," said Suzanne. "He might have been watching her during her husband's funeral or something tripped in his brain that she wasn't the sweet little old lady she pretended to be."

"Nadine was smart as a cobra," said Doogie. "She's the one who probably sent Bo to that deserted cemetery. Then got the drop on him and strung him up."

"Almonds," said Dr. Sam Hazelet, almost as if it were a non sequitur. "That's the smell of arsenic."

"And quite lethal over time," said Doogie.

"Exactly," said Sam.

Doogie stared at Suzanne with compassion in his rheumy eyes. "And then she tried to poison you. When I burst in and saw the cagey look on her face—watching you eat—I figured she'd somehow slipped poison to you, too."

"With her almond cake," said Suzanne in a hoarse voice. Suzanne held a clean terry-cloth towel to her mouth and blotted slowly. "I want to talk to her."

"Leave her alone," said Petra. "Let the law deal with Nadine." She put a hand on Suzanne's shoulder. "And a higher power." She paused. "There's really nothing you can say to her."

"Oh yes, there is!" said Suzanne. Not only was she feeling decidedly stronger, her anger was building into a terrific head of steam.

"Atta girl," encouraged Toni. "Go out there and knock Nadine's block off!"

"No violence," barked Doogie, spreading his arms wide. "Nobody's gonna touch a hair on that murderous woman's head. Nobody takes the law into their own hands in my county!"

But like an avenging angel, Suzanne swept past Doogie and burst through the door into the café. "Nadine!" she shouted. Definitely had her energy back and her hackles up.

Doogie was hot on Suzanne's heels, with everybody else piling in right behind him.

"I have a bone to pick with you!" cried Suzanne. Her blue eyes were frosted ice, her voice resonated with anger. She circled around Nadine, footsteps echoing sharply off the wooden floor of the Cackleberry Club.

"Easy now!" called out Sam.

"Be *careful*!" yelled a timorous Dil.

Suzanne came to a halt in front of Nadine, who was still tied to the cane chair, her coat draped over her shoulders, her purple ribbon pinned to one lapel.

"You are hereby *disqualified* from the Cackleberry Club cake-decorating contest," said Suzanne, as Nadine stared mutely at her.

A spatter of applause broke out behind her.

"It was a lousy cake anyway!" yelled Toni.

But Suzanne wasn't finished. Like lightning, her hand suddenly shot out toward Nadine.

"Dear Lord!" gasped Petra. "She's going to smack her!"

Instead, Suzanne grasped Nadine's purple ribbon and ripped it from her coat. "Your grand prize ribbon is hereby revoked!"

"You go, girl," chortled Toni.

Suzanne rolled up the ribbon, slowly twining it around an index finger. Turning her back on the sullen Nadine, she walked across the Cackleberry Club and into Sam Hazelet's open arms.

"You okay?" he asked her.

Suzanne nodded. "I think so."

"So," he said. "That optimistic, fearless thing you mentioned the other night. How's that workin' for you?"

This time Suzanne managed a crooked grin. "I think . . . pretty well." She tilted her head back, hesitated for the briefest of moments, then kissed him full on the lips.

"Now that," exclaimed Toni, "really takes the cake!"

Favorite Recipes
from the Cackleberry Club

Eggs Benedict Arnold

4 strips thick-cut bacon
2 eggs, poached
English muffin, toasted
English cheddar, ¼ cup shredded
Hollandaise sauce (jar or made from scratch)
Parsley, chopped

Using an oven-safe plate or shallow bowl, place strips of fried, crispy bacon on top of open-face toasted English muffin. Add 2 poached eggs and top with Hollandaise sauce. Sprinkle on English cheddar cheese and toast under broiler for about 45 seconds. Top with fresh, chopped parsley for garnish. Note: To make your Eggs Benedict Arnold even more British, substitute bangers (British sausages) for the bacon.

Frozen Lemonade Pie

1 can sweetened, condensed milk (14 oz.)
1 can frozen lemonade concentrate (6 oz.) slightly thawed
1 container frozen whipped topping (8 oz.) thawed
1 ready-made graham cracker piecrust

Whisk together condensed milk and lemonade concentrate. Fold in whipped topping. Pour mixture into crust and freeze for 4 to 6 hours. Garnish with candied lemon peel or ultrathin slices of lemon.

Carrot-Pecan Tea Sandwiches

8 slices cinnamon raisin bread
8 oz. cream cheese, softened
1 cup grated carrot
¼ cup pecans, chopped

Trim crusts from bread. Mix together cream cheese, carrots, and pecans. Spread mixture on 4 slices of bread. Top each one with another slice of bread. Cut sandwiches into long fingers or triangles. Keep cool and covered until ready to serve.

Cheddar Cheese Biscuits

2 cups flour
½ tsp. salt
2 tsp. baking powder
½ cup butter
1 cup cheddar cheese (shredded)
⅔ cup milk

Combine flour, salt, and baking powder. Cut in butter until mixture is crumbly. Add cheese and milk and mix with a fork until dough forms a ball. Place dough on floured surface and knead gently. Roll out dough to 1″ thickness and cut out with biscuit cutter. Place on greased baking sheet and bake at 425 degrees for 12 to 15 minutes or until golden brown. Serve with soup or stew or with sausage at breakfast.

Cackleberry Club Brown Sugar Meatloaf

1½ lbs. ground beef
1 medium onion, chopped
1 egg
6 slices white bread, cubed
½ cup milk
Salt and pepper to taste
3 tbsp. mustard (divided)
½ cup ketchup (divided)
4 tbsp. brown sugar

Mix together ground beef, onion, and egg. Mix in bread, milk, salt and pepper, 2 tbsp. mustard, and ¼ cup ketchup. Gently press meat mixture into a 9″ x 5″ loaf pan. In separate bowl, mix remaining mustard and ketchup with brown sugar. Pour on top of meatloaf and bake at 350 degrees for 2 hours.

Petra's Cinnamon Date Scones

2 cups flour
4 tbsp. sugar
2½ tsp. baking powder
¼ tsp. cinnamon
½ tsp. salt

²/₃ cups dates, chopped
6 tbsp. butter
2 eggs, lightly beaten
¹/₃ cup milk

In large bowl, combine flour, sugar, baking powder, cinnamon, and salt. Stir in dates, then cut in butter until mixture is crumbly. Combine eggs and milk and stir into mixture until it is blended and soft. Place dough on floured surface and knead gently, about 10 times. Gently pat dough into a 6″ x 9″ rectangle. Cut into 3″ squares, then cut each square diagonally. Place scones on greased baking sheet and sprinkle a little extra sugar on top.

Bake at 400 degrees for 12 to 15 minutes or until lightly brown. Serve warm with butter and jam or Devonshire cream.

Cheese and Honey Bruschetta

French baguette, 16 slices each ½″ thick
¼ cup extra-virgin olive oil
4 oz. Gorgonzola, sliced
2 tbsp. honey

Arrange bread on baking sheet and brush with olive oil. Bake at 400 degrees for about 8 minutes. Place cheese on the toasts and bake until melted, about 3 minutes. Drizzle with honey and serve immediately. This bruschetta is a nice savory teatime treat that can serve as a counterpoint to your sweet treats. Note: If Gorgonzola is too strong for your palette, try blue cheese, Gruyère, or even baby Swiss.

Upside-Down French Toast

4 tbsp. butter
¼ cup brown sugar
½ tsp. cinnamon
6 canned pineapple rings
6 thick slices of French bread or brioche
2 eggs
½ cup milk
½ tsp. vanilla extract

Melt butter in small pan, then stir in sugar and cinnamon. Spread cinnamon mixture evenly in 9″ x 13″ buttered baking dish. Arrange pineapple rings on top of brown sugar mixture, then place one slice of bread atop each ring. Whisk together eggs, milk, and vanilla, then pour over bread. Bake at 400 degrees for 30 to 35 minutes. To serve, gently slice with spatula and place on plates so pineapple rings are up.

Blueberry Breakfast Squares

1¾ cup sugar
1 cup butter
3 eggs
1 tsp. vanilla
3 cups flour
1½ tsp. baking powder
1 can blueberry pie filling (21 oz.)

Cream sugar and butter in blender. Add eggs and vanilla and beat. Add flour and baking powder and stir until well mixed. Spread half of mixture in a lightly greased 9″ x 13″ pan. Spread pie filling over mixture, then gently drop small pieces of remaining mixture on top. Bake at 350 degrees for 45 minutes or until golden brown and bubbly. Cut into squares and top with a dab of vanilla yogurt. (This also makes a great dessert!)

Chocolate Flapjacks

¾ cup butter
¾ cup unsweetened cocoa
4 eggs
1½ cups sugar
½ tsp. salt
2 tsp. vanilla extract
2 cups flour

Melt butter and stir in cocoa. In large bowl, beat eggs, then add in sugar, salt, and vanilla, beating well. Add flour and continue to beat, then add in melted butter mixture. Drop batter onto well-oiled griddle and cook pancakes about 2 minutes on one side, a half minute on the other. Serve pancakes with traditional syrup or with dollops of whipped cream and sliced strawberries.

Chicken Croquettes

2 cups chicken, cooked and chopped
1 cup bread crumbs
2 eggs, lightly beaten

½ cup onion, chopped
¼ cup cheddar or Parmesan cheese, shredded
2 tbsp. mayonnaise
Salt and pepper to taste

Combine chicken, bread crumbs, eggs, onion, cheese, and mayonnaise in a large bowl and mix well. Add salt and pepper, then form into slightly rounded patties. Heat oil in a skillet and fry until golden brown, taking care when turning them. Serve with a side salad or cole slaw.

Turn the page for a preview of the next
Tea Shop Mystery by Laura Childs . . .

The Teaberry Strangler

Coming March 2010 in hardcover
from Berkley Prime Crime!

A back alley crawl had certainly *sounded* like a tantalizing idea to Theodosia when she'd first conceived it.

A blue-black Charleston evening in early March. Candles flickering up and down the narrow cobblestone alleys that snaked behind Church Street's charming shops. And shopkeepers in historic costumes throwing open their back doors to invite visitors in for tea, Charleston cookies, steaming bowls of crab chowder, and special prices on antiques, oil paintings, giftware, sweetgrass baskets, and leather bound books.

And, as far as Theodosia Browning was concerned, entrepreneur and historic district booster that she was, the event had been a rousing success.

Hordes of folks, locals as well as tourists, had thronged the back alley, dashing from shop to charming shop. And a whole lot of them had dropped into her tea shop, too. She'd doled out more steaming cups of Darjeeling, tea sandwiches, and miniature quiches than she could remember serving in a long time.

But now, as the back door of the Indigo Tea Shop snicked shut, Theodosia peered down the length of the alley and suddenly had second thoughts about venturing out alone.

For one thing, the hour was late. Almost ten o'clock. And where visitors had swarmed up and down her alley some forty-five minutes ago, now there didn't seem to be any foot traffic at all.

Spooky, Theodosia thought to herself, as palm trees thrashed in the cool wind and dim, yellow gaslights glowed faintly in the mist. She wondered, just for an instant, if she shouldn't run upstairs and snap a leash on Earl Grey. Let her frisky guard dog Dalbrador prance along beside her. Or perhaps she should pop her head back into the warm, fragrant tea shop and ask Drayton, her master brewer and right hand man, to accompany her.

Silly, Theodosia reasoned. *I'm only going a few doors down.*

Pulling an old-fashioned cloak around her shoulders, the cloak that had served as her costume this evening, Theodosia gathered up her basket of tea and scones and set off down the alley. She was headed for the Antiquarian Map Shop, just down Church Street. The owner, Daria Shand, was a dear friend and probably in need of a little sustenance by now.

Theodosia felt the first drops of rain hit her shoulders and immediately thought, *Frizzies*. With masses of curly auburn hair to contend with, Theodosia sometimes projected the aura of a Renaissance woman captured in portrait by Raphael or even Botticelli. Smooth peaches-and-cream complexion, intense blue eyes, and the calm, often slightly bemused look of a self-sufficient woman in her mid-thirties. A woman who possessed a fair amount of life experience, but still looked forward to a wide-open future.

Flipping her hood up, resigning herself to the steady rain, Theodosia picked her way carefully along wet cobblestones. The squall that had been threatening for days had finally blown in from the Atlantic. Thank goodness it had held off this long.

She was passing the Cabbage Patch gift shop when a gust of wind flipped her cape up and threatened to send her airborne like the flying nun.

Theodosia fought the elements for a few moments, feeling like an umbrella turned inside out, then finally got her cape and basket righted. Glancing up as rain spat harder, she suddenly stared down the dim alley and beheld a bizarre scenario.

Theodosia's first, fleeting impression was of two people locked in a lover's embrace. Three seconds later she realized a nasty struggle was taking place.

A struggle? Really? Or were her eyes playing tricks on her?

With rain streaming in her eyes, the two figures appeared more like ethereal blue-black shadows, dancing and twisting in some grotesque embrace. But as their dance turned even more macabre, one figure grasped the other by the neck, forcing the other to drop to its knees.

Oh no!

A sharp burst of lightning lent bizarre special effects, leaching color from the landscape and giving the floundering figures the appearance of a slow-moving film negative.

"Stop!" Theodosia yelled. "Don't . . ."

Her plaintive cry was drowned out by a sharp crack of thunder that rattled nearby windows then continued to grumble ominously.

One of the figures was completely down on the ground now, unmoving, while the other bent over it, flailing like mad. Then, as if suddenly cognizant of a witness, the figure straightened up and gazed down the alley at Theodosia.

Theodosia's heart played a timpani beat in her chest as she sensed rage, and feared this person might turn on her. Instead, the person spun and darted off into the pounding rain.

Dropping her basket, Theodosia sprinted for the downed figure.

Panic triggered by recognition shot through her like another bolt of lightning. It was her friend, Daria Shand! But not the tall, reddish-blond beauty she knew and loved. This Daria's face was a grotesque mask of purple, her eyes half open and pupils staring into nowhere. And seemingly not breathing!

What to do? Call 911 or chase after the assailant?

911 won out, of course. And as Theodosia knelt in the alley, pummeled by wind and rain, clutching her cell phone, pounding frantically on Daria's chest, trying to recall her long-ago CPR training, a wave of helplessness washed over her.

Was there nothing she could do? But Daria still hadn't drawn a single, strangled gasp and the words *crime scene* were swirling sickly in Theodosia's brain.

Minutes later, two shrieking squad cars, red and blue light bars pulsing, rocked to a stop in the alley. They were followed by a boxy orange and white ambulance.

"Help her!" Theodosia screamed, though she feared Daria was beyond help. Probably, she was in her Creator's hands now.

Theodosia was caught in a swirl of activity then. EMTs working over Daria, more police officers arriving to cordon off the area, an officer firing questions at her, taking notes, trying to get a first-hand account.

At hearing all the commotion, Drayton and Haley came running down the alley from the Indigo Tea Shop, fear and concern etched on their faces.

And a familiar burgundy Crown Victoria slid to a stop in the alley.

"Tidwell," Theodosia murmured, when she caught sight of the car.

Detective Burt Tidwell, overweight, articulate, and perpetually suspicious, headed the Robbery-Homicide Division of the Charleston PD. He was prickly rather than gracious and routinely brusque with everyone who got in his way. Though his suit coats rarely buttoned over a stomach that sometimes resembled an errant weather balloon and he could sometimes look the buffoon, Tidwell was as predatory as they came. Smart, canny, a dogged investigator.

Pulling himself from his car, Tidwell donned an enormous black rain slicker and lumbered toward the victim, who still lay in the exact spot she'd fallen. At that same moment, the back door of the Antiquarian Map Shop burst open and a bearded man in a blue and white checkered shirt suddenly cried, "Daria! Is that Daria? What happened?"

"Who are you?" Tidwell asked in his big cat growl.

"Her boyfriend . . . let me through. Let me see her!"

Tidwell raised a hand and two uniformed officers immediately barred the way.

"Later," Tidwell told him. "Questions first."

"That's not right," Theodosia said, speaking up. "He's her boyfriend. He has a right . . ." She stared at Tidwell, anger and grief written across her face, thinking he looked all the world like a bloated vampire in his dark, shiny rain slicker.

"And you are here, why?" Tidwell asked her in a clipped voice.

"She discovered the victim," one of the officers told Tidwell.

"And only doors down from your little teashop," said Tidwell, turning his unblinking gaze upon Theodosia. "How very convenient."

"Be serious!" snapped Theodosia. "She was my friend. A good friend!"

"My sincere apology," said Tidwell, though he didn't sound one bit sincere. Or apologetic.

Theodosia shook off Tidwell's insensitivity and took a step closer to where Daria still lay. "It just doesn't make sense," she mourned. "Why would someone want to kill Daria?"

Tidwell leaned in and peered at the lifeless body that lay sprawled like a rag doll cast aside. And in a flat, almost impersonal tone, murmured, "Maybe they thought it was you."

Don't miss the next Cackleberry Club Mystery

Bedeviled Eggs

When a dead body turns up on a Quilt Trail, Suzanne searches for clues as she contends with rescued dogs, a prison break, dirty politics, and a spookier than usual Halloween.

**Watch for the next Tea Shop Mystery
also from Laura Childs and Berkley Prime Crime**

The Teaberry Strangler

A Charlestown Back Alley Tour goes horribly wrong and tea shop owner Theodosia Browning finds herself searching for a maniacal stalker, even as this Jack the Ripper-type phantom seems to be stalking her!

And the next Scrapbooking Mystery

Fiber & Brimstone

As Carmela designs a monster puppet for the French Quarter's Halloween parade, a Ponzi-scheme partner is gored by the razor-sharp horns of a giant Minotaur head. Now Carmela must contend with new enemies, old photos, a Ballet Dracula, and the mysterious Mr. Bones.

NEW IN HARDCOVER FROM

Laura Childs

TRAGIC MAGIC

A Scrapbooking Mystery

Carmela, owner of Memory Mine scrapbooking shop, and her best friend have a big project—converting an old mansion into an unforgettable haunted house. But when the owner's flaming body comes crashing through a tower window and "welcomes" them to the mansion, Carmela must crop out a killer from the throngs of people flocking to New Orleans.

M486T0509

ALSO AVAILABLE
FROM THE AUTHOR OF *DEATH SWATCH*

Laura Childs

FRILL KILL

For Carmela Bertrand, a New Orleans shop owner, this Halloween will feature more than the usual scares. On her way home from a ghoulish gathering, Carmela finds the dead body of a model—and is then attacked herself. As the witching hour draws closer, Carmela must find what's lurking in the shadows—or get the fright of her life.

"Delightful . . . Fascinating."
—*Midwest Book Review*

penguin.com

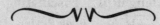

The Tea Shop Mysteries by
Laura Childs

DEATH BY DARJEELING

GUNPOWDER GREEN

SHADES OF EARL GREY

THE ENGLISH BREAKFAST MURDER

THE JASMINE MOON MURDER

CHAMOMILE MOURNING

BLOOD ORANGE BREWING

DRAGONWELL DEAD

THE SILVER NEEDLE MURDER

OOLONG DEAD

"A delightful series."
—*The Mystery Reader*

"Murder suits Laura Childs to a Tea."
—*St. Paul Pioneer Press*

penguin.com